Books in This Series

The Kate Morgan Series

Simon Says… Hide, Book 1

Simon Says… Jump, Book 2

Simon Says… Ride, Book 3

Simon Says… Scream, Book 4

Simon Says… Run, Book 5

Simon Says… Walk, Book 6

Simon Says… Forgive, Book 7

Simon Says… Swim, Book 8

Simon Says… Die, Book 9

Simon Says… Think, Book 10

Simon Says… Fight, Book 11

Simon Says… Believe, Book 12

Simon Says… Sink, Book 13

USA TODAY BESTSELLING AUTHOR

Dale Mayer

SIMON SAYS...
BELIEVE

A KATE MORGAN NOVEL

SIMON SAYS… BELIEVE (KATE MORGAN, BOOK 12)
Beverly Dale Mayer
Valley Publishing Ltd.

Copyright © 2026

All rights reserved. Except for use in any review, the reproduction or utilization of this work in whole or in part by any electronic, mechanical, or other means, now known or hereafter invented, including xerography, photocopying and recording, or in any information storage or retrieval system, is forbidden without the written permission of the publisher.

This is a work of fiction. Names, characters, places, brands, media, and incidents either are the product of the author's imagination or are used fictitiously. Any resemblance to actual events, locales, or persons, living or dead, is entirely coincidental.

ISBN-13: 978-1-834083-66-7
Print Edition

About This Book

Detective Kate Morgan wishes all holidays were filled with celebration and joy, but her latest crime scene tells a different story. The leftover festive spirits of Christmas and the new year are overshadowed by the grim reality of another murder. No amount of ribbon wrapped around the body or notations on a greeting card to *Believe* can change that.

As she delves into the first murder of this year, Kate unexpectedly uncovers a second case—another victim and another instance of holiday cheer turned sour. Are these cases linked, or is Vancouver experiencing an unusually grim extended holiday season?

Simon stands by Kate, offering his unwavering support in her investigations, just as she stands by him and his architectural rehab projects and his peculiar psychic visions. However, when these visions and unsettling rumors begin to threaten his real estate business, Simon realizes more is at play…

But what exactly is happening, and is Kate involved in all this?

CHAPTER 1

Last Week of January

FOUR DAYS LATER Kate was drowning in paperwork. She heard a noise and looked up to see Rodney come in. His face was still puffy and bruised from the fight in the ring, but he was smiling, cracked lips and all. She got up, walked over, and gave him a gentle hug.

He just held her and whispered, "Thank you."

She nodded. "So, was that thanks for saving your sorry ass or thanks for saving you from hospital food?"

He laughed. "Both. I don't know where in hell Simon got that breakfast, but, man, it was something else."

"It was, wasn't it?" she agreed.

"Is that how you eat all the time?" he asked, rolling his eyes. "I could really get used to that."

"If you order from the same places he does, you could have it whenever you want," she pointed out.

"I don't know that I could afford even a fraction of it."

She stopped to consider that, frowning. "I don't even think about it anymore. I have no idea what any of it costs. He orders it, and I eat it," she said, with a shrug. "It's a deal that seems to work for me."

He burst out laughing. "Of course it does," he muttered, shaking his head. "It would work for anybody. It's a damn-good thing you've got him to keep you on the straight and narrow. But then again, you also saved his sorry ass."

"In all fairness," she pointed out, "it was my turn."

"How about no more turns?" he grumbled.

"Yeah, I did mention that to him, and he was down for stopping whatever this score-keeping was," she admitted, with a smile.

"And I understand that things have been calm these past days."

"Yeah," she replied, "as calm as it ever is. Couple shootings, couple dead bodies on the streets. We're waiting for autopsies, but it seems to be drug overdoses. You know, … the usual."

"Right, … the usual," he repeated. "And it's still the season to be jolly—if the middle of January and beyond counts."

"It does in my book," she stated agreeably, "if anything jolly is to be had."

He looked at her and shrugged. "I don't know, maybe."

Just then Reese walked in, and the frown on her face said everything.

"*Uh-oh,*" Kate muttered, frowning back at her. "What's up?"

"We've got"—she hesitated and then relented—"I don't want to say it's a church killing or that it's a religious killing, as the holidays are well and truly over. … Or maybe we're gearing up already for Valentine's Day with this guy. … I don't know. What we do have seems to be a holiday season murder."

Kate frowned. "We all know that murders are the worst at holiday time. What have you got?"

"I've got a man, found in his apartment, no idea what's going on. He's dead, cause unknown."

"So, why is this one any different?"

She looked over at Kate. "Because he's been wrapped in a red bow, around his … manhood," she added delicately.

"What?" Kate asked, staring at her.

Reese held out the crime-scene photos. "Yeah, it'll be another strange one." She handed out files for each of the team—Kate, Rodney, Lilliana—being reduced in number at this time.

Rodney looked over her shoulder at the photo and whistled. "Good God. What is this about? Did someone not like their Christmas gift or something?"

Lilliana frowned as she opened her file copy.

"He was killed in bed?" Kate walked slowly over to her desk, carrying the new file, staring at that image in her folder. "His lips are already turning blue. Yet the crime scene photos show no drugs, prescription or otherwise. Not even a box of rat poison. This looks pretty deliberate."

"It does," Reese agreed.

"Please tell me there are no others."

"Nope, no others," Reese noted, "just the one victim, so hopefully it's an isolated incident."

Kate looked at the next photo and pointed. "What's with this note here?"

"The guy lives alone, but a poinsettia was in his bedroom, with a card. On the card was the word *Believe*."

"And?" Kate asked, turning to Reese.

"One of the techs declared that it'll be another one of those woo-woo cases, so he named it the *Believe It or Not* case."

"That makes no sense," Kate muttered.

"No, it probably doesn't, but all I can tell you is that's what he put it down as."

Kate didn't like it. She frowned. "Generally we identify the cases by the name of the deceased."

"Yeah, generally we do," Reese agreed, with a smirk.

Just then Simon texted her. **How about spending next weekend on the *Running Mate*?**

She sent back a quick reply. **I'm doubting it at this point.**

No, none of that. You have to BELIEVE.

She stared at his text, stared down at her case folder, and whispered, "Crap. Maybe that's what this one will be called after all." She held up her phone to show the text message that Simon had just sent.

Lilliana looked at it, turned to Reese, then back to Kate, and shook her head. "No. ... Hell no. Not another woo-woo case already. We're still buried in paperwork from the last one."

"Yeah, you're not kidding," Kate confirmed, as she stared at her phone.

Simon called and asked, "Is there a reason why I just used the word *believe*?"

"You tell me," she muttered, with a sigh. "I just got a case where the victim is wrapped up in a red bow, near a card in a poinsettia plant with just the word *Believe* on it."

"Crap. ... I picked up new blankets and cushions for the boat. Plus it's restocked with supplies and wine. So I thought maybe we could grab next weekend to belatedly set the right tone for the New Year."

"Let's just put it this way," she noted. "If I get free, that would be the real miracle."

"In that case, I'll end on the same note I started with. Just *believe*."

And, with that, he disconnected.

CHAPTER 2

KATE WALKED INTO the decedent's apartment building and stopped. Even for a Saturday morning, a number of people moved in and out at a hurried but steady pace. Some were from her team, and others appeared to be from other apartment buildings, looking to either get away or to see what was going on here.

It wasn't chaotic but still way too many people for her liking. She sent several uniformed officers to cordon off the area and to redirect any of the actual residents living in this building to use other entrances and exits. Then she stomped her way up the stairs to the second-floor apartment of the recently deceased man.

She had no trouble finding the exact apartment because so many forensics personnel came back-and-forth. As she stepped inside, she saw a familiar face, talking to another team member dressed all in white. The coroner glanced over at her. Immediately the frown on his face increased in wattage—to the point that the associate he was speaking with stepped back hurriedly.

Kate just smiled at the coroner.

"This is hardly a smiling matter," Dr. Smidge snapped.

"Nope, sure isn't," she stated agreeably. "And at the holidays too—or between them at least."

Immediately Smidge's shoulders slumped, and he nodded. "It's always worse at the holidays," he muttered. "I don't understand why people do the absolute godawful worst things at a point in time when we're supposed to celebrate life."

"Some people are just wired that way," Kate noted, shrugging.

He turned to face her. "You and I both know that has nothing to do with the holidays. That's just people being people." He snorted and turned his back to her. "This was not a suicide."

"I wasn't thinking it was," she noted, her tone sarcastic.

"Are you being cute with me?"

"No, I'm not. And, from what I've seen and read, suicide doesn't seem possible."

"No, absolutely not possible." Then he motioned with his arms and added, "Now that you're finally here, we can get started."

She laughed. "I came as soon as I could."

"Yeah," he replied, his tone hard, "so did I." He led her to the bedroom, where the nude victim was in a very suggestive position, with his legs out, arms spread wide. He must have been a gym rat if his sculpted body revealed anything. A big red ribbon had been tied around his … manhood, as Reese had put it.

Kate shook her head. "Definitely an attempt at cheer."

"As is the card," Smidge muttered, pointing at the greeting within the big poinsettia on the small table in the bedroom.

She shook her head. "Why would you have a poinsettia in the bedroom?"

"I don't know," he replied, frowning at her. "That's a good question. It's not exactly a place where you would normally have it, is it?"

"I wouldn't think so. There's a coffee table and room for it in the living room. Poinsettias are big, and this one's particularly huge," she noted, staring at it admiringly. "It also needs better light than what this room offers."

"You like them?" Smidge asked her.

"Not really," she shared. "They always remind me of death." Startled, he eyed her, and she shrugged. "Again, it's a seasonal thing, isn't it?" She frowned at the huge flower.

He studied her curiously. "Why so much interest in it?"

"It just looks very … fresh." She reached out to check the soil. Sure enough, it was still damp.

He frowned at Kate and then touched the soil himself. "I hadn't considered that. So, what then? Did our killer bring in this plant?"

"They can last for months, even longer with some extra care. Did our buff guy water this one? Or is it completely disconnected from the scenario we have here?" she asked, with a motion toward the victim, still lying on the bed. "And does the card match up with what's going on here?"

"It doesn't," Smidge stated, with a wry look. "At least I don't understand the connection. As long as this case is isolated, I'm okay," he added. "Yet the minute there's a second connected case, you know how I'll feel."

"You know how I'll feel too," she replied, glaring at the victim as if the poor hapless man were responsible for everything potentially to come.

Smidge snorted. "Yeah, I hear you. Anyway, I'm taking this guy away. I'll give you a cause of death soon enough."

"Nothing is obvious, other than the slightly blue lips," she pointed out, looking back at the body. "We're not talking about any major trauma. So, if not a natural death, and you've ruled out suicide, then we need a tox screen."

"Forensics found no pill bottles and no obvious indication of any way that he could have done it to himself."

Kate frowned and suggested, "Unless he took the drugs while he was still alive and moving around."

"But we've checked the garbage," Smidge stated, "inside and outside. So, unless he deliberately hid a bag of drugs somewhere else, that won't cut it."

She pondered that. "So, we're looking at some drug then?"

"I'm assuming so," he began, "but you and I both know …"

"Yep, I'll wait for your autopsy report."

He laughed. "If only I could believe that. You'll be on my ass within days."

"Hours," she corrected. "This one's hot. We need to get at it while we still have a chance to put it to bed."

"Yeah, well, … you take care of your shit, and I'll take care of mine." Smidge ordered his men to remove the body. She watched, hoping to see if anything else showed up during that process, but she found nothing new. As Smidge stood nearby, filling out a form, she asked, "Do you have a name, age, anything?"

"I do." Smidge handed her a piece of paper. "Name's here."

"You have an address for him?"

"Is this not his place?" he asked, glancing around.

"Maybe, but what if it's not?"

"Good thing we have you to figure that out. As of now, this is the address that goes down in my report, until you tell me differently," he declared cheerfully. "Happy to have you take care of everything else." And, with that, he turned and walked out.

She read the name on the greeting card. It was as unassuming as could be. *John Smith.*

She shook her head. "John Smith, if this apartment is leased to you, that would answer some questions."

But not all of them. And then the question she needed to answer was, *Why the red bow?* If she hadn't been a detective for so long, she would have immediately ID'd the killer as female, red bow and all. However, Kate knew better than to make that assumption too soon.

She needed something else to help her sort out who might have been John's latest visitor and what actions brought this on.

Smith appeared to be in his mid-thirties and was extremely physically fit. That *physically fit* part made her think *drugs* because how else did you take down this mountain of a man, without any bruises or defensive wounds, with no obvious signs of trauma anywhere on his body to suggest how and what he died of?

She found no needle marks on his arms. No needles were on the floor. She had searched his night table—as had the coroner, Dr. Smidge—and saw no sign of any drug paraphernalia. She slowly and methodically went through the bathroom. There were condoms, so this was probably his apartment. Also a shaving kit but nothing to suggest that he lived here full time with a woman.

In fact, nothing here suggested a woman had been around recently at all—or another man for that matter. She pondered that as Rodney raced inside the victim's bedroom. She turned to him, and he was flushed, out of breath.

"Hey, sorry I'm late," he muttered. "I had ... car troubles."

She didn't say anything because she didn't want to get

into *that*. "You just missed the victim."

"*Yay*," he muttered.

She knew the sentiment wasn't celebratory, just that he wasn't at all upset about it. Rodney found that part of the job more troublesome than interesting, so it made perfect sense. She smiled and shared, "Roughly thirty-six-year-old male, John Smith, no obvious sign of trauma."

"Of course the red bow was just icing."

"Yeah, the red bow was one indicator. And a huge—I mean, *huge*—poinsettia plant."

At that comment, Rodney looked around, checking over the man's bedroom.

"Forensics took it with them." Kate added, "I've gone through the bedroom."

"I'll take a quick look, just in case—"

"I missed anything?" she teased, with a smile.

Rodney shrugged.

Kate pointed. "I'm heading to the living room and the kitchen. Forensics was in there taking photographs, lifting fingerprints, and packing up a whole lot of other items that may or may not help solve this case." She was about to run out of time because those same forensics people would kick her out soon enough.

As she stopped at the coffee table in the living room, she noted a faint stain, outlining a potted plant, as if it had been watered, and some had leaked. Yet another poinsettia plant was nearby. As she stood in the doorway of the bedroom, she compared the size of the living room poinsettia plant and the size of its pot sitting on the coffee table to what had been in the bedroom—but seized by forensics. Kate nodded. The only difference between the two plants was a big cheerful metallic wrapping around the outside of the living room pot.

So, if any water leaked there, it didn't come from the pot in that metallic wrapping. Maybe it came from the bedroom plant, with no protective foil around its pot. She frowned in that direction.

"Problems?" Rodney asked, as he came up beside her.

She sighed. "I just noticed the big stain on the coffee table. Seems a plant had been moved."

"Except not that plant nearby because of the metallic wrap," he pointed out.

"Yeah, exactly."

But it wouldn't leave her alone. She stared at it for a long moment, shook her head, made a note of it, and then, unable to help herself, took a quick photo of the stain before walking back out into the main hallway. A number of neighbors stood around, talking in whispers. She turned to Rodney and stated, "I'll take the first group. You take the second one." They split up, and, as soon as she walked toward her target group, several of the neighbors tried to disappear. Kate held up her hands, calming them down. "I wouldn't do that if I were you."

Several of them froze, looked back at her, while a few scrambled. "I have a few questions I need to ask. Either we do it now, or I'll come back later—and later again until I talk to each and every one in this building. If needed, I can haul you all downtown."

One of them, an older lady, stared at Kate with a bright, inquisitive look. "Did you really think we were running away?"

"Yes," she declared. "From my experience, one group of people who hang around crime scenes want to be involved in these things. However, then another group just wants to watch from a distance. As soon as a cop approaches, they run."

The lady flushed. "I wasn't trying to run, but obviously you were about to do some police business, and I didn't want to be in your way."

Kate smiled at her, but it was a grim smile. "A man has been murdered." At that remark came gasps of horror, and she nodded. "That seems to surprise you."

"Of course. John's always been super friendly and kind to all of us," the older woman shared. "What a waste. It's a shock."

Kate came closer. "I'm Detective Morgan."

"Lisa Hanson."

"Lisa, … how well did you know John?"

"I didn't really know him well, but he's lived here a couple years. So, as any good neighbor does, we have some knowledge of each other and what's going on."

"And did he live alone?"

"Now he did, yes. He had an ex. They broke up about maybe six months or so ago."

As Kate glanced at the crowd, she singled out one of the other ladies beside her. "And your name?"

"Nancy."

Kate asked, "What do you think, Nancy?"

Nancy nodded. "I would say it was about that," she began. "He wasn't the kind to bring home strange women every night, but he certainly wasn't celibate. If you ask me if I know any of them, then no. I wouldn't know any of them except for the ex-girlfriend who lived here for about a year."

Kate made a note on the names and the time frame and asked the group, "And do you know any of his other friends that we could contact?"

Nancy replied, "Hopefully that'll all be in his phone."

Lisa nodded.

Kate replied, "That could be a source of information, but anything you guys can corroborate is helpful too."

Lisa shrugged, looked back at her friends, and added, "John was the guy you could call on if you needed help moving a piece of furniture or if you needed somebody to watch your place because you were going away for a few weeks or so."

"In my case, I had new appliances delivered," one of the women shared simply, "and he let the installers into my apartment for me."

"And you are?"

"Maureen."

"And you had absolutely no compunction about giving him the keys to your place?" Kate asked her directly.

Maureen, who was approximately fifty years old, flushed ever-so-slightly, then shook her head. "No, of course not. And it wasn't like that." Her voice went an octane higher as she continued. "That's an awful thing to say." She was an attractive woman in her fifties, and that stood out.

Kate's eyebrows shot up as she studied her. "I didn't say anything other than the fact that you let some neighbor have a key to your apartment. John wasn't a family member, I presume. So, your relationship to John is now, however, of interest."

"We were friends," she snapped. "That's all, nothing more, nothing less."

Kate didn't say anything. Her gaze slid over to the two women who had been quiet up until now. She quickly got the names and addresses for all of them. They all lived on this floor, including Jill and Lora. And, of course, nobody had heard or seen anything. "So, none of you have any idea who might have been with John for the last few days? You haven't seen him at all?"

"No, I haven't," Jill confirmed.

"We haven't seen him." Lora shook her head.

"I haven't seen him either," Maureen stated stiffly, still biting from the insinuation earlier.

Kate certainly wouldn't take responsibility for that as Maureen had brought that on herself. She was still a good-looking woman though. And John was a good-looking man. So, anything along that line would have been a reasonable suspicion. As her final questions, she turned to the women and asked, "Do you know why John and his current girlfriend broke up? And what was her name, by the way?"

"Norma," one of the women offered. "It's such an old-fashioned name."

Kate wrote it down and agreed. "That's not as common in the young people these days, is it?"

"Nope, sure isn't," she noted. "It's also my middle name, so it was pretty easy to remember." She smiled over at Maureen and asked, "Do you know why they broke up?"

"He mentioned something about they didn't have the same ideologies anymore."

"As in religion?" Kate asked.

"No, I don't think religion had anything to do with it. Yet I guess it could have," Maureen noted, "because I remember her heading off to church one morning, and she was in tears because John wouldn't join her."

Kate wrote that down and didn't say anything for a moment as she studied her notes. Then she asked, "And I guess you don't have any idea how to get a hold of her, do you?"

"Only that she went to the local church around the corner from here, but now that she's not living here, I don't know. You'll have to track her down yourself."

"And she was living here with him?"

"I don't know that either," she declared, her tone snappish. "She was just here a lot. They were in a relationship, so it made sense."

"Of course." Kate nodded. Keeping the thoughts bubbling up in her head to herself, she thanked the women, then turned and headed toward Rodney, who was just finishing off a conversation with the other group of men and women. Both crowds now dispersed.

As they compared notes, she asked Rodney, "Anybody in your group know anything about the girlfriend, Norma?"

He shook his head. "No, they didn't really have anything to do with him. What about the ladies back there?"

"Apparently he was one of those really nice guys you could give your apartment key to and have deliveries made inside. Plus, if they were going away for a while, he would look after the apartment. That kind of a guy," she shared, with a knowing look.

Rodney nodded. "I guess that makes sense. He had a girlfriend. Yet, according to my group, they split up about six months ago."

"Yeah, that correlates with the information I got. And did anybody have any reason for the breakup?"

He shook his head. "Nobody seems to know anything about him, other than he was just a nice guy."

"*Right.* So your normal, average, nice guy suddenly ups and gets murdered for no particular reason?" She snorted. "Somehow I don't think so."

"Oh, I don't think so either," he replied, "but finding out the whys and the wherefores will be a whole different story."

"As always," she muttered. "Anyway, let's keep canvassing, and I'll go talk to the manager." The manager, thankfully, was deep into all the noise and commotion with the police, now finding out one of his tenants had been murdered. It was a great conversation opener.

The officer stood back, and he didn't need to point out who she should talk to. "The super's name is Hank."

Hank just kept shaking his head, repeating, "He's just not the kind to get murdered."

She wanted to ask what kind of person got murdered because, in her eyes and with her experience, it really could be anybody. She didn't want to bring up that question, except that she needed to know in what way *John just wasn't that kind of a guy.*

"He's nice. He never got into drugs or anything."

"So, you knew him really well."

"No, but … I'm a good judge of character," he explained, almost as a last-ditch effort to justify his position. Then he frowned. "Surely you're not blaming him for anything, are you?"

She frowned at him. "I don't generally blame the victims for getting themselves killed."

He flushed and shifted nervously.

She couldn't tell whether his nervousness was due to something he knew and didn't want to share or he was just uncomfortable talking to the police. She asked, "So what about the girlfriend living with him?"

Hank shook his head. "He did approach me at one point, asking if there would be a problem if he had somebody move in full time. I told him that the lease itself wasn't affected, but that we would need to know for insurance's sake."

"Good point," she stated, and he seemed to brighten at that. "And did he come back and tell you?"

"He did not. I did see her every once in a while, and I didn't ask her outright if she was living there," he admitted ruefully. "Maybe I should have. It never even occurred to me. The lease is in his name, so I do business directly with him."

"And you didn't ask John about it either?"

"No." He shook his head. "And it seemed they broke up fairly quickly afterward," he added, with an eye roll. "I'm assuming they did. I didn't see her around anymore."

"And maybe he was just playing the field."

"I don't know," he said, his sadness evident in his expression. "The last thing I want to do is keep track of every single guy's romantic adventures in this place."

It was *this place* that made her stop and ask, "Why this place?"

He stared at her for a moment, as if he'd said the wrong thing. "Because most people here aren't married," he finally shared. "It's not exactly a building full of families, is it?"

She pondered that as she waved for Rodney to join her, and they both walked outside to their vehicles. Not that it *wasn't* a family location but definitely some homeless issues were seen not too far from here. Still, she wouldn't have considered this apartment building to be in an especially bad area. She asked Rodney about it as they met at her vehicle. "Do you consider this a good area of town or a bad area?"

Surprised, he glanced around and shrugged. "I wouldn't have said *bad*. I mean, he obviously was here because he could afford it. The rent was average. I would say it was just fairly typical of what we come across in this area."

Getting into her car, she added, "The landlord seemed

to think that it wasn't a great location. He made a comment about not wanting to have to police the residents' living arrangements, sex lives, or dating relationships among tenants, particularly in *this area*."

Rodney frowned as he thought about it. "If you want to go in that direction, an adult entertainment store is around the corner. And a strip club is not far away."

"There are?" she asked, startled.

"Yeah. We're a couple blocks from the adult entertainment store, but it's certainly within walking distance."

"I hadn't realized." She glanced around.

"That's the thing. ... It's just far enough out that you think it'll all be like this, but it's not. This is a residential area. A school is not far from here either, which would make it more family-oriented."

"But that adult element does give rise to the question as to just what this local demographic looks like. Plus where did John work? Nobody mentioned where he worked, only that he mostly worked from home."

"So, his phone and computer will be our most reliable information banks."

"We've got his phone and his computer too. Forensics has both."

"So, we should get that information fairly quickly, right?" Rodney asked.

She nodded. "And then the question is, *Who were his friends?* Damn, I forgot to ask the manager about security in this building."

"The forensics team used a buzzer to be let in."

"So, in theory, with a buzzer, our killer would have gained entry either via some resident or on their own," she noted, "particularly if they had lived here for a while."

He turned to her and asked, "Are you thinking the girl-friend killed him?"

"No, I'm not thinking anything for certain yet," she clarified. "However, a girlfriend doing the killing suggests a crime of passion, but this murder? … It seems cold, calculated."

"But there is a buzzer, so that might be useful."

"Which you and I both know you can get around by planning the timing just right. With somebody coming out, you slip right in."

He agreed, "It's an easy-enough thing to do."

"Unfortunately it is, isn't it?" She nodded. "Let's see what else we can come up with."

"Where do you want to go from here?"

"I want to drive around the neighborhood," she shared.

"I'll see you back at the office then." He got into his vehicle and took off.

Kate took a much more pragmatic approach and slowly drove around the neighborhood, pondering what the manager had said about *this place*. Was it a personal thing, or was it something else?

It was just one of those little questions that niggled at the back of her mind. Everybody she had spoken to and those whom Rodney had spoken to didn't appear to be the family-oriented types, which she also found interesting. If they weren't, then this was very much more of a singles' location, as suggested by the super, and that could have something to do with the *amenities* around this building.

Not to mention the price, because anybody with families needed larger units and would need schools nearby, which according to Rodney there were.

She drove around looking for the school, only to find it

was an alternative school, not a public school. That just added credence to the idea that this area was not a good location for a family. Main arterial roads connected everybody within a few blocks. So, from a commuting point of view, it also made sense. However, a great public transit system wasn't in this general area, which also could make it difficult for families.

Pondering all that, Kate decided to head back to her office. Just as she was about to pull back out onto the traffic, her phone rang. She popped back onto a side street and answered. It was Simon.

"Hey," he greeted her. "I understand you've caught another case. I was just checking in to see if you're okay."

She smiled. "You know, most people would not question a detective as to whether they're okay or not when they catch another case." She didn't know if she should be cross or happy that he obviously cared but ultimately decided that she would be in the middle somewhere. "On the other hand, you and I both know that sometimes these cases can get a little difficult and weird—and definitely odd when you are concerned."

"Am I concerned in this one?" he asked.

"I don't think so." She tried evading the question because he obviously was involved based on the text message he'd sent earlier. However, maybe not just that had happened. Had something else weird come up in his world already?

"I mean, except for the word *believe*, and I don't know that it's got anything to do with your case, does it?" he asked. When she didn't say anything, he went on. "I can't imagine how it would even relate."

"No, I can't imagine it either," she acknowledged, "but

that doesn't mean that it doesn't."

"Good point," he muttered. "Anyway, I'm heading off downtown, been doing paperwork all morning here. Did you ever hear from the insurance company on repairing your apartment's front door?"

"Not this morning," she grumbled, "and not yesterday either." Her insurance company was still stalling because, as Simon mentioned so aptly, she was a *bad bag*. "Nothing new. Why? Are you trying to get me out of there already?" The insurance company was trying to get out of paying her.

"Nope," he stated cheerfully. "I just thought it might be something I could help you with. I am a builder after all, and I know how these insurance companies work. If you are fine with it, I can take that off your shoulders while you're working on the case."

"Ah," she noted. "I'm sure the insurance company is not impressed that a cop lives there, and they'll raise my premiums through the roof just to confirm they don't end up in this position again."

Simon concurred. "I wouldn't be at all surprised if they did that, but let's not jump to conclusions. And, if they can't help you out with insurance at a reasonable rate, we'll talk to some of my brokers."

She almost heard the smile in his voice as he spoke. "Sure, you can do both," she agreed. "Anyway, I'm heading back to the office now. Everything's okay." She had no quarrel with his words but still heard that odd note in his tone. She frowned into the phone. "What are you not telling me?"

"Nothing. I don't have any insights. I don't have anything. I just ..." He sighed and added, "I wanted to hear your voice and to confirm you're okay."

She smiled. "I … am flattered. And since you're talking to me right now, you can tell I'm okay, and I'm doing just fine."

"Good enough," he said. "Sorry, I know I'm turning into a lovesick puppy. I'll talk to you later." And, with that admission, he ended the call.

She burst out laughing because the last thing in the world that she would ever expect him to say was *that*. Simon was a lot of things but *a lovesick puppy* wasn't one of them. And, with that, she headed her vehicle back to the office with the case on her mind.

She looked forward to whatever the forensics revealed, knowing without a doubt that Smidge would have plenty to say about it.

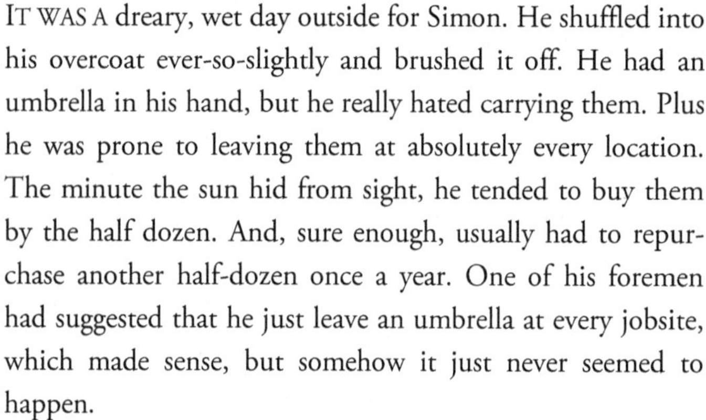

IT WAS A dreary, wet day outside for Simon. He shuffled into his overcoat ever-so-slightly and brushed it off. He had an umbrella in his hand, but he really hated carrying them. Plus he was prone to leaving them at absolutely every location. The minute the sun hid from sight, he tended to buy them by the half dozen. And, sure enough, usually had to repurchase another half-dozen once a year. One of his foremen had suggested that he just leave an umbrella at every jobsite, which made sense, but somehow it just never seemed to happen.

When his foreman Joe called him not too long afterward, he sounded disgruntled. "I've got some issues here. So, if you wanted to come by, today would be good."

Simon frowned at that. Joe never was one for theatrics. "Right now?" Simon waited a moment.

"Yeah, I need you to see this."

"Why? What's going on there?"

There was a grunt, and Joe replied, "Let's just say that we'll have to redo some of the structures on this one beam here. I don't like the look of it. I should have been watching him closer. He was the new guy from a couple months ago, who I had to fire. He told me he was some expert welder. No way in hell. He was a poser."

"Then you already know what the answer is. Fix it."

"It'll cost though."

"It always costs," Simon declared. "Just do it. I can certainly trust you to determine what'll need to be redone. After all, how many times have I come over there when you've said something similar, only to have me agree with you?"

"Almost always," he noted, with a snort.

"Then go ahead and just do it."

"We'll fix it, but we may think twice before we use this guy again."

"If he's doing shit work, no need to think at all."

"But we're short-handed."

"I don't care," Simon snapped. "Shit work is shit work, and I don't want to redo things because somebody can't handle the job."

"Oh, I hear you. Come take a look when you're nearby." And, with that, his foreman yelled at somebody close by.

Simon laughed because that was part of the job too. It seemed as if no matter what you did, some people were inconsistent, and you had to go back over their work and sort it out to see if they even understood what the hell they were doing. It drove Simon and his various foremen wacky, particularly from the perspective of somebody who had been in the industry as long as they all had been. It seemed completely ridiculous that this was still a thing, and yet it was.

As Simon made his way to the first job in question, it was one finally nearing completion. He stopped in to see his foreman here, Kevin, talking to somebody. As soon as his foreman saw him, he walked over, smiled, and noted, "Hey, I wasn't expecting you today."

"I needed to get out of the office," Simon shared. "Too much paperwork is not good for anybody."

"Any paperwork period is not good for anybody," Kevin clarified, with a laugh. "You and I both know that."

They'd worked together for a lot of years already. And both knew each other pretty well at this point in time. Even better, they trusted each other to do the job that they each needed to do.

As long as Simon kept coming up with new jobs, Kevin had no intention of leaving. And that was huge because consistency in staffing and in dealing with some of these projects helped Simon to create bigger and better deals for everybody.

His foreman faced him and asked, "How's Kate doing?"

"She got another murder case this morning."

Kevin shuddered, adding, "God, I don't know how she can do that job. She must see the absolute worst of humanity."

"She does," Simon confirmed.

Kevin shrugged and shook his head. "And yet somehow she can still smile through it all, which is freaking unbelievable," he muttered. "I don't know how anybody can do that."

"She is doing it, and I'm grateful for that. Now, have we got any problems here?"

"No, and we're getting to the countdown," he noted. "What about some of those new projects you've picked up?"

"Yeah, I've grabbed up quite a few of them, haven't I?"

"You have," he stated, turning to him.

Simon asked, "Is that okay? Or have we got problems?"

"No, we don't have any problems with it," Kevin declared. "I just need to sort out what we're doing and which jobs you want me working on, although we're still looking at approximately six months before we have a changeover here."

"Yeah, we should be well and truly done with this one by then, if not in half that time."

"That's probably being overly optimistic," Kevin suggested, as he studied the work going on around him.

Simon shrugged. "I would say we can probably call this one done in maybe four months."

Kevin shook his head. "Even that's pretty optimistic."

"I know, but I'm an optimistic guy." Simon smirked.

"So," Kevin began, "which of the buildings will we do next? I gather the last one that you picked up with all those bodies inside will have to be dropped."

"It'll certainly need to be gutted, if for no other reason than to confirm more bodies aren't hidden in the basement somewhere."

Kevin winced at that. "I think you should take her back to the studs. If the studs are no good, take those out too."

Simon sighed. "I was eager to work on that one, but the police aren't sure that they're ready to hand it back over to me, which is pretty wild considering what they already know. The owner has now passed away, so it's not as if anybody will be charged for any of the murders."

"What about the husband?"

"He didn't know very much about it apparently, and I'm not sure that I have any reason to doubt him on that. He's already been through quite a bit, once he understood the implications of what had happened."

"It's pretty shocking when you think about it."

Simon nodded. "Right, but her father was very much the, … if not the actual instigator of it all, he was certainly involved to the point that she felt she had to keep all the murders secret for a very long time."

"Keeping those kinds of secrets though," Kevin noted, "can just poison your soul."

"She died of a rare cancer. So, I would say that she's already suffered quite a bit for it. Now the police have their hands full, identifying bodies and contacting families," Simon shared in a bitter tone. "Thankfully that's not Kate's department."

"No, and that's a good thing, especially since she keeps catching new murders." Kevin grimaced.

"I know. Not everybody can do her job," Simon said, turning to look at the present building that was coming along so nicely.

Kevin added, "That's what's special about Kate in its own way. As long as she can keep doing what she's doing, she's a happy camper. The minute anybody makes any suggestion otherwise, you can bet she'll tear a strip off them."

"Some people don't have the calling for it, but she absolutely does, and we need her on our team. Who else will help the victims?"

"Exactly," Kevin concurred.

"Now," Simon began, "shall we get back to our problems? Kate's got more than enough of her own to handle." He gave a snort, and, with that, the conversation changed. "I've got three buildings that we'll be working on. I need to know which one you prefer. I have a preference for one of them for you to oversee, but it would be good if it lined up with your preference as well."

"I really want to be part of the old renovation down-town," he shared hopefully.

"Yeah, I was pretty sure you wanted to be part of that one." Simon grinned. "We're not ready for her though. I've got to get engineers in to see just how much we can save, and then we'll need architects in order to help rebuild her to her newly refurbished glory, whatever that'll look like."

"And that'll be dependent on a structural analysis."

"Yeah, so, I've got your name down for that one, but it's not next."

"You've wanted that one for a very long time," Kevin noted. "Presumably now though, you're not looking to buy any more."

"No, though I do still have a few on my wish list, and I have to watch for that. As soon as anybody knows—and with the face of Vancouver changing as rapidly as it is—a number of people could decide to sell, and I need them to not sell right now." He laughed and added, "I haven't overextended myself, so don't you worry. Still, I need to get some of this started so I have an idea of where the money will have to go."

"Yeah, I'll say," Kevin muttered, shaking his head. "I couldn't believe it when you bought the last one. I under-stand the land is good, and lots of potential is there but still …"

"I know, but I wasn't about to leave that one either, es-pecially not at that price."

"As long as you can fund it at the end of the day, you'll do fine," Kevin stated. "In the meantime, you're keeping me employed, so it's all good. You have one going on Georgia Street, right?"

"I do," Simon confirmed, with a nod. "That'll be a complete rehab, top to bottom. Do you like the look of that one?"

"Yeah," Kevin stated, with a huge grin. "I've always had some special connection to that one, so, if you're good with that, I'll take that one on."

"Perfect," Simon replied.

"And then you'll get, what … Joe to take on the other one?"

"He's working on one right now that will still be ongoing for quite a while," he pointed out, "but, yes, the other new project will probably end up being Joe's."

As Simon pivoted to walk away, Kevin called back to him. "Just checking but you're doing okay yourself, right?"

He turned to him and smiled. "Yeah, I'm doing okay."

"Because, you know, some of that *sight* stuff," Kevin muttered, with a visible shudder, "that's enough to keep me up at night."

"No, I'm doing fine with it," he shared. "Obviously it's not something I expected at this stage of my life, but I guess my grandmother was right."

"Yeah, well, when you got a grandma with the second sight," he noted, "you don't really have a whole lot of choice, do you?"

He smiled. "No, no, I sure didn't. I tried hard to fight it, but that's what happens. You fight it, and it doesn't do any good."

"You really did try though, didn't you?" Kevin asked, staring at him again.

"Yep, I was pretty adamant that I didn't want anything to do with it," he admitted. "Shit happens anyway."

"See? That part's really what I would struggle with," Kevin admitted. "I would want some semblance of control over it all."

Simon snorted. "Yeah, you don't get that," he stated,

with a knowing smile in his foreman's direction. "And I get that people would want control, including myself, but it doesn't do any good."

Kevin shook his head. "Look after yourself, and look after her. She's a good one. … Knowing what you know now, would you have changed anything?"

Simon's smile brightened as he thought about that first case, where he met Kate. "Nope. Honest to God, I wouldn't change a thing."

CHAPTER 3

B ACK IN THE office, Kate called forensics. Adam, one of the techs, picked up on the other end.

He greeted her with, "We just got back with all the stuff from the crime scene."

"Right," she agreed. "His phone, … I need that first."

"Then come on down here and work on it," he replied in exasperation. "You and I both know that there's no time or energy or budget money for most of this stuff."

"Good, I'll be there in a few minutes."

After a moment of silence, he snapped, "Fine, have at it." Then ended the call.

She laughed, looked over at Lilliana, and shared, "Heading down to forensics. I should have just brought the phone back with us, but they wanted to go over it first."

"It's fairly common," she noted, then glanced at her. "If they clear it, we can work on it up here maybe."

"That's what I thought, except he wants me to work on it down there."

She rolled her eyes at that. "I'm not surprised, but let's start with that cell number, check his phone records, all that good stuff," she suggested, with a nod toward Rodney, who was already on his phone, asking for just that.

"Good idea," Kate muttered. "Let me go get it." She stood, grabbed her phone, ready to exit her department.

Colby walked in and took one look at her. "Where are you heading?"

She gave him an evil smile and replied, "To light a torch under forensics." He gave her a worried look, and she held up a hand. "I'll just grab the phone. They can clear it first for whatever they want, but Rodney's getting John's cell number so we can see a list of John's calls. We have to start on that."

"Fine," Colby muttered, a frown creasing his forehead, "but don't push forensics. There's been some … unrest down there."

"That's fine," she said. "I get it. Unrest is part of working with a scant budget, but we also need to get on this case."

As she walked past Colby, he stopped her. "Hang on a minute. Do you think something else is here, other than a single murder?"

"I have no idea," she conceded, turning to him. "All I can tell you is that I need to get at it."

Colby seemed concerned that there was more to this.

Kate had tried to keep her voice calm, but she knew that look on Colby's face. She added, "If you're asking about Simon or anything else along that line, no. I don't have anything from him. I don't have any reason to believe this case is anything other than an isolated incident."

"Thank heavens for that," Colby muttered. "The last thing we need is another serial killer and a string of bodies attached to him."

"I understand. Thankfully not a lot of serial killers are out there," she noted, "but they are all deadly, either way."

"Get a move on it then."

And, with that, she walked out, leaving him staring behind her. As she headed to forensics and pushed open the door, Adam looked up at her, and his eyebrows met.

"You really don't give us much time, do you?" he grumbled.

She shrugged. "You and I both know that, as the body is getting cold, the trail's getting colder."

"And we don't have any time to spare either," he pointed out. "It's not me, per se. It's the case itself hasn't got any allowance, and we have a budget issue."

"We all have a budget issue, but I can't let it blow up in my face."

Adam didn't say anything at first but eventually nodded. "I guess your job is just as stressful as ours, isn't it?"

"It is," she confirmed, "and sometimes it's worse. Although I'm not interested in getting in a pissing contest with you, we're the ones who have to deal with the families, and it's damn hard to tell them, *Hey, everything's just sitting in forensics, while we wait for answers.*"

He shuddered. "I could not deal with the families. … That sounds godawful."

She smiled. "Give me what you got, and I'll get out of your hair."

"It doesn't matter if you get out of my hair now because you'll be back again in no time, looking for more."

She burst out laughing and coaxed a reluctant grin from him.

"Rodney forewarned me. So, as soon as I knew you were coming down," Adam shared, "I worked on the phone. We've taken any fingerprints from it, and I've pulled a history of his calls and text messages. So, if you want to dig around some more," he shared, pointing to a printed file, "we've already copied over the SIM card. Have at it. It's all in an email to you." He handed her the phone, still in its protective baggie.

"Perfect," she said. "Now I don't even have to bug you, see?"

He rolled his eyes and shook his head. "You'll bug me anyway."

"But not intentionally," she clarified. "We are on the same team, you know?"

"Sometimes it doesn't seem that way." And then he glanced around and added, "Things are rough here, with more budget cuts happening."

"I'm sorry about that," she replied, "because you and I both know you need a bigger slice of the pie to run this place."

"Yeah, we do. But it's not always as clean-cut as we want it to be. And, right about now, definitely some people are not as happy with our department as we want them to be."

She wasn't sure what to say to that. "What about Smidge? Does he have any say in this?"

Adam shrugged. "Who the hell knows." he stated. "He definitely walks to a different beat." Then he glanced at her and frowned. "You seem to be one of the few people who can keep up with him."

She laughed. "I don't know about keeping up with him because, when he moves, he moves. Yet … I get along with him just fine. So I understand that already makes me a novelty."

"Yeah, you're not kidding," he muttered. "People here want to see if the budget cuts include him."

She winced. "I don't want to see that." He gave her the side eye. "He's good, and we need good," she declared.

"He's good, but he's also impossible to work with."

She didn't say anything to that because she was pretty damn sure a lot of people might say the same thing about her. She didn't want to get into that right now. "Hopefully everything will work out." With a smile, she walked out with the phone that she needed so badly.

As soon as she got back to her office, she held it up so Lilliana could take a look.

"Perfect." Lilliana grinned.

Kate continued to her desk. "Adam's emailed some of the back history we could get off of it—text messages and the like. But I want to go through the phone myself." As she settled into her desk, she pulled up the email and ran a finger down her screen.

Rodney grabbed a chair, walked over to her, and flipped it around so he could join her, asking, "Anything interesting?"

"This number," she muttered, as she wrote it down. "John's been sending texts back-and-forth with that number multiple times, with the end of it saying, *No, and that's final.*" She frowned. "I wonder if that *final* ..."

He glanced at her and nodded. "Led to John's death?"

"Yeah, that will be one of the questions we have to answer," she muttered. "Still, it gives us something."

Rodney suggested, "Copy me on that email with the list of numbers and texts, and I'll start calling them. Maybe we can identify who they are."

"You call, and I'll keep reading through these texts." She sent him the email, pointing out the one number in particular. "From the gist of this, I'm thinking it's probably the ex-girlfriend, Norma."

"And how recently?"

She grimaced, shaking her head. "Up to the day he croaked, so yesterday. So, the very day he died," she noted.

"So, she's the last person to have contact with him."

"That we know of," Kate added.

He stared at her, as realization dawned. "Right, and that could change, depending on whether we can get anything from the apartment building cameras."

She sighed. "The cameras won't tell us much. None are in that hallway," she pointed out. "I checked."

"Of course not. It always seems as if cams aren't anywhere they are truly needed."

"And maybe that's what the super, the manager, was talking about. Run him too, will you?" she asked, turning to Rodney. "That comment of his made me question what he meant."

"And I wasn't with you at the time."

She nodded. "He made a backhanded comment. I'll have to find out more now because it won't leave me alone."

"What's that?"

"His comment about that building or that area not being for families," she stated.

Rodney eyed her. "Yeah. That's an oddity. I remember you mentioned that."

"And I don't like oddities," she declared, with a frown in his direction.

"Okay, that's not a problem. I'll run him anyway just because he's associated. What about the women who lived on John's floor?"

"Nobody was suspicious in the group I was talking to," she shared. "They were all older than him, like twenty years older. Yet all seemed to be half in love with him."

"Yeah, so we don't know whether he was poisoned or was drugged, which kind of is a female murder mode. Yet it doesn't seem the ladies on his floor would have been involved enough with John to do that."

"Agreed," Kate replied. "I'm not putting them on my suspect list for the moment at least. How about the men on your side?"

"Why the men?"

"Because John might very well be having an affair with other women in the building. Maybe he's not too particular as to whether they're married or not."

Rodney snorted. "Good point. Let me follow up with them and see what's going on."

"And you asked if anyone had seen John last night, right?"

"Yes, I did ask them," he confirmed, with a wave of his hand. "Nobody saw or heard anything. Nobody could say when they had last seen him, outside of possibly a couple days ago, when he was taking out the garbage. According to one of the men, John was whistling and seemed … happy, in a great mood. When the guy mentioned that to John, he answered, *Yeah, finally cleaning out the trash that needed to be gone for a while. Complete mind shift.*"

"Any idea what he was carrying?"

"No idea," Rodney said. "Just black trash bags so he couldn't tell what it was. He figured John had done some spring cleaning and was happy to get it out of the apartment, happy with the way it made him feel."

"I guess that's what we all would feel," she acknowledged, as she wrote down a note on that.

Rodney stared at her and added, "Aren't you reading too much into that? It could just be … cleaning."

"What if he cleared out the last belongings of his ex-girlfriend's?"

Rodney zeroed in on her and nodded. "Yeah, or maybe *somebody else.*"

She winced and then groaned. "God, Rodney, don't even say that. I'm still reeling from the last one. Let's not have another murder in that same apartment."

"That would be something, wouldn't it?" he asked. "Maybe this John guy offed somebody, only to turn around and get offed himself."

Kate sighed. "Let's stick to facts before we start delving into fiction," she muttered.

He laughed. "Are you kidding? You guys, you and Simon, you guys live in fiction."

With Rodney now working on checking up on some phone calls, Kate went through the rest of the text messages, finally found a work-issues message, and had a phone number. She picked up her phone and called it.

She reached the person whom John had been texting, then identified herself and asked him to identify himself and his company. When he hesitated, she asked, "Unless you have a problem with that?"

"No, of course not. I'm Bill Simmons, a coworker of John's, and we're an insurance company. What's going on with John? He hasn't returned any of my recent texts."

"When did you last text him?"

"Just a sec." Bill came back a moment later and replied, "A couple times this morning."

She confirmed that quickly because John's records sat in front of her.

"Last night I had a couple questions about work, so I sent him a text then too. Yet I told him it could wait until this morning because, well, it was obviously already after-hours."

"Did you often text him about work over the weekend?"

"If I had a problem, yes. John's a mentor to me as well as

a coworker," he acknowledged. "So I try not to bother him after hours, but sometimes I have to."

"Of course," she noted. "Same as my job."

He gave a grunt and asked, "Has something happened to John? That would be pretty rough if it did."

"Pretty rough in what way?"

He explained, "No matter how I say it, it'll sound wrong, but we had a couple big jobs due this morning, proposals for an underwriter, and John was supposed to get the work done, and he hasn't sent it yet."

"All I can tell you at the moment is that he won't be sending anything."

"Is he hurt?" he asked. "Oh no. Did you say you were with the homicide division?"

"I am, yes."

"Oh, no. No, no, no. Please don't tell me something happened to John," he cried out in almost a frantic tone. "He's my coworker, but also my friend," he shared. "We go to the gym all the time and hang out. Please, ... I need to know."

She sighed. "He was murdered. We don't necessarily have a specific time of death yet, but somewhere between 6:00 a.m. and 10:00 p.m. yesterday," she noted.

"Oh my God, oh my God."

Obviously she had completely rattled him. "So, when did you last speak with him?"

"Is this because of work? Oh, work, Jesus, my God, work."

"What about the work that was due to you? Did he email it to you?"

"I don't know," Bill wailed, still frantic.

Kate heard him clicking away on a keyboard.

Then he groaned and whispered, "Thank God, yes, the work is here, but I don't know how complete it is. Normally he does about 80 percent of it, and then together we figure out how to get that nicely locked in," he shared. "But, yeah, I've got the work. And I'm not an asshole." He kept ranting on and on. "I'm not just thinking about the work here. I know it sounds that way, but it's pretty devastating for us, if we lose this work, on top of losing him."

"Were there any issues with him at work?"

"No, not with those of us who worked with him. John was a good employee. The higher-ups weren't terribly impressed about his persistence to keep working from home, but it was part of his contract. The rest of us on staff all wanted him back in the office because it's so much easier to deal with people face-to-face," he explained. "Yet he didn't want to do that."

"Why was that?"

"Who knows? He was fighting his bosses on it," Bill stated, "but he wouldn't lose his job over this. From what he told me, he wasn't ready to come back to the office. Yet he never really gave a reason why."

"And did he have any other people he worked with consistently?"

"Sure, a whole team of us work with John. Oh, God, I'll have to notify them."

"Are they all in the office right now?"

"Yes. It may be a Saturday, but it's still a workday for us. We're all here. Only John worked from home."

"Interesting," she noted.

Bill jumped on that. "Interesting why? … What's interesting about it? God, I still can't believe it."

"I don't want you to say anything to anybody," she began and was met with only silence on the other end. "Do you hear me?"

More silence came.

She repeated again that she didn't want anyone told.

"But I've already got people here, waiting for me to get off the phone so I can fill them in on the details."

"Well then, you don't fill in any details, and you just say that the police are on their way. Do you hear me?" she asked. "I will be there soon." She glanced at her watch and added, "In about ten minutes, depending on traffic."

"I didn't even give you an address."

She quickly ran off the name of the company.

"Yes, yes, that's us."

And she gave the address that she'd already looked up.

"Yes, that's our office. ... God, okay."

"I'll be there in a few minutes," she told him. "And I'm being very direct here. *Do not tell anybody.* You leave that to me." And, with that, she ended the call, hopped to her feet, and snatched up her keys. "I'm going up to John's office to talk to them."

"Something suspicious?" Rodney asked, turning to her as he put down his phone.

"Not so much suspicious but apparently this coworker was also one of his best friends, and I need to check in on a few things there. You coming?"

"Yeah, I'm coming," Rodney confirmed, standing up. "Are you driving?"

"Yeah, unless you want to."

"Oh, I'm tempted, but it's all yours."

She rolled her eyes at that. "Why?"

He noted, "I just figured you're not paying for your gas either."

"We get per diem for it, remember?" she replied.

"Yeah, I know, but you're probably not paying for your own gas. I bet Simon's filling up your tank all the time."

She glanced at him and rolled her eyes. "You've got a real money thing going on right now. What's up with that?"

"No," he argued, "that's the problem. I have *no* money going on, and I'm feeling more than broke at the moment. So tagging along with you and not burning my own gas seems to be a nice option."

She snorted. "What are you spending it on?" When he flushed, she asked, "Dates, by any chance?"

"No. Why would I do that?"

"*Uh-huh.*" She didn't want to delve into that and didn't really want to keep hassling him either. It wasn't any of her business to begin with. Too bad her team didn't butt out of Kate's personal life. God knows they all had more than enough to say about her relationship with Simon.

As they made their way to the insurance company, she quickly pulled into the back parking lot and grabbed a spot. While walking around to the front of the building, she said, "Let me do the talking on this one."

"I don't have a problem with that. Any reason why?"

"Yeah, I've already got this Bill guy off kilter, and I gave him very specific instructions to not let anybody know. So, if he's broken that rule, I want to know why."

"It could just be that he's very rattled to hear his friend and coworker was murdered, and he's not used to talking to the police. Plus, if you were on his case, he might be scared."

"Yeah, and why would he be scared?" she asked, shooting Rodney a glance. "Unless he knew more or heard more or did more than he's letting on to me."

Rodney didn't have an answer for that.

As soon as she walked into the office, she noted all the crying and the silent stares. So Bill hadn't followed through with her instructions. She immediately asked to speak with Bill Simmons.

Bill came out of one of the offices. His eyes were red-rimmed, as if he'd been crying. He took one look at her and started blubbering. "I couldn't *not* tell them," he cried out. "I couldn't *not.*"

"*Right,*" she snapped. "So, you disobeyed a direct order."

He blinked at her, glanced around at the rest of the staff, and muttered, "It's not as if it was an *order*-order."

Kate raised her voice to address Bill. "It was very clearly an order that I repeated four times to you. You have absolutely no room for any miscommunication here. So, please explain yourself right now."

He started to blubber again.

A man came out of another office, glancing at her, and said, "Surely it isn't necessary to yell at him over this."

"I gave him an explicit order to not tell anybody here about what happened. And apparently he completely ignored my order."

The boss blushed. "Cut him some slack, please. He was good friends with John," he pointed out.

"Obviously he's overwrought, yes. But is he overwrought for a reason?" she asked, glaring at Bill. And the hapless kid blubbered more and more. He was supposedly about the same age as John, only with a baby face. His age was hard to pinpoint, and she did really want to know why he had completely ignored her instructions. She turned and looked at the man in charge. "Is this your company?"

"Yes, it is. We're associated with the parent company. So, I own this portion of it," he replied. "It's a franchise of sorts."

She nodded. "Then I must speak with you *privately*," she declared, sending a glare to Bill, "since privacy and following instructions aren't a priority around here."

At that, Bill started bawling louder.

Several of the women rushed over to talk to him.

"Every person here," she told the man in charge, before walking into his office, "will speak with me before I leave. In the meantime, all of you can gather in one room, and my associate will talk to you." She turned to Rodney. "Don't let anybody leave."

He nodded and motioned for all of them to sit down in the empty conference room, so that he could talk with them.

She heard them all clamoring to get the additional scoop as soon as they got inside. They didn't understand that Rodney would be asking the questions. Regardless, she was more focused on the boss.

"I can't see that Bill had anything to do with what happened to John," he noted. "Isn't this a little harsh?"

"If we find out that you were shielding a criminal who killed John in a moment of a completely irrational and emotional outburst, and his family wants to sue you, how would you feel about it then?"

He paled as that liability set in. "Right, it's not always about us, is it?"

"It's not about you at all," she snapped. "It is literally about John and his death. Everything I do from here on out is about getting justice for John."

The boss man's shoulders straightened.

"So, let's start at the beginning." She studied him closely. "What should I call you?"

"Killian Parker."

"How long has John worked for you?"

He brought up John's file on his computer and answered her every question.

She heard absolutely no red flags, which pissed her off even more. "What about his relationship with everybody in the company?"

"It's been good," Killian said. "We haven't had any problems."

"And what about his desire to continue working from home versus coming into the office to work?"

He frowned at her. "Wow, I didn't think you'd even picked up on that one."

She pointed out, "Whether you think they will or not, everybody talks. Case in point? *Bill Simmons*."

Killian shook his head. "I don't have anything to hide and had nothing to do with John's death. This is a horrible loss for all of us, but I am also grateful that he sent in the work we needed for our meeting this morning." He glanced down at the paperwork on his desk and winced. "Oh, damn, you won't let us have that meeting, will you?"

"If you can reschedule the meeting, it would be better. Otherwise, we'll take everybody one at a time into another room for our interviews."

"Do you really suspect somebody here?" he asked, staring at her.

"I don't suspect anybody. Therefore, I have to suspect everybody," she shared. "Nobody is off the hook. I can tell you that a man is dead, and we have yet to find his family to formally contact them. That is why Bill Simmons was told to not tell anyone, yet defied that order anyway."

"Right. The notifications to John's family should be done first." He glanced around the outer office. "Okay, I get that. I will pull out the people who I need for the meeting right now, and you can talk to the rest in the boardroom, which is where they're all assembled."

And, with that, he got up, led her to the boardroom, announcing, "Everybody will speak to the detectives and will answer every question." Then Killian took a look around and pointed. "Miranda and Simmons, both of you come with me for the meeting. Afterward you guys can speak with the detectives."

They both jumped up a little too quickly for Kate's taste. She took note of both of their expressions. "And I will speak with you in a little bit," she promised. They nodded and left. She glanced over at Rodney, who hid a smile. "Who have you spoken with so far?"

He pointed to the one gentleman, sitting off to the side. "I just spoke with him, and a couple people have corroborated his version of events."

"Did you get names and contact information for everyone here?"

He held up his sheet. "I've got everybody here and a handful who aren't in today."

"And why are they not here?" she asked, turning to look at the staff.

"One only works four days a week," explained the one gentleman who appeared to be calmer than the others. "She comes in to help with the clerical stuff, and today is her day off."

She turned to Rodney, and he nodded. "Yeah, I've got her information as well."

Another gentleman added, "A staff member called in sick too. Plus one is on holiday, and the other one comes in about an hour." He glanced down at the folder in his hand. "I understand the one on holiday is off in Greece."

"I'll check on that," Rodney told Kate, "and we will put a call into the one who's sick."

One of the men stared at the detectives, then asked, "Are we really, *really* suspected of having something to do with this? … Bill was really good friends with John, and I can't imagine him or anybody else having done anything."

She didn't respond to that. Bill Simmons had gone into the meeting with his boss, so he wasn't even here right now. That gave her a chance to cool off about his telling everybody of John's death, even after she had specifically and repeatedly told him not to. She quickly sent a message off to Reese, to confirm notifications had been done. Otherwise she would tear a bigger strip off Bill's hide. Then she asked the man who last spoke, "So, what was the relationship like between Bill and John?"

"They seemed to be great friends," he replied. "They went to the gym together, and they hung out every once in a while. They were just friends."

"It wasn't even so much friends," one of the women stated in exasperation, her tone hard. "Bill really admired John. He was doing everything that Bill liked to do and wanted to do. So, Bill looked up to John more than anything."

The man frowned at her, then shrugged. "If that's the case, then I don't know very much about their relationship at all. Yet maybe I agree on the admiration part. That's something you'll have to talk to Bill about."

"Oh, I will," Kate vowed. "Don't you worry."

He gave her a small smile and shrugged. "He's just a kid." She tried to shut him down, but he held up a hand. "He should be a full-grown adult, but definitely some immaturity is in there," he conceded. "So, when he found out, he just couldn't keep the news to himself."

She nodded. "And if John's own family didn't even know yet?" she asked. "How would that make you feel?"

He had the grace to look a bit ashamed. "Yeah, that's not cool," he stated. "I lost my sister in a car accident years ago. We also weren't informed first, and the neighbor came running over because she had been at the scene and told us all first. It was a god-awful mess." He took a moment to breathe. "So it's very understandable why you're so upset with Bill. Not to mention, he doesn't always follow orders very well."

"He follows orders," one of the other women argued. "It's just he's still"—she shrugged—"I guess *young* is a good word for it." She turned to the older man. "It really is a maturity thing, isn't it?"

He nodded. "It shouldn't be, but it feels like it. So, it would be nice if it weren't such an issue at work, but it seems we always have one in the room who is not quite there yet. As to Bill's age, don't get me started. … He's old enough to be mature, but he lived at home far longer than most people and never really had to deal with the actual fundamentals of living alone. I think, for that reason, John took him under his wing a little bit and gave him a hand getting adjusted."

The same woman noted, "Even with a supposed adjustment on Bill's part, John became more of a mentor than anything to Bill. I'm not sure even workwise that it changed. John was very independent, very capable."

"And Bill is not?" Kate supplied.

The man sighed. "He's just … green. He doesn't have the same get-up-and-go that John did, so, that will be a big loss for the company."

"And how was your relationship with John?" Kate asked the man.

He raised his eyebrows, then shrugged. "It was fine. I think all of us felt it was fine. We worked with him. There weren't any issues. But again, maybe I'm not necessarily the one to talk to about that." He turned and looked over at the woman who had spoken up earlier. "How would you put it, Madrid?"

She smiled. "We all had a decent working relationship with John," she replied. "He wasn't necessarily anybody we got close to because his working from home kept him more distant, more isolated. He changed when he had a girlfriend. Since they broke up, he's been friendlier again, talking about coming into the office a little more. He came in for meetings, but he had been avoiding a lot of the social gatherings. We often do barbecues and team-building events. Because he was never here and wouldn't come in for those social invites either, it kept John more distant."

Kate wrote notes as she listened, trying to get an idea of who John was. "And what about the girlfriend?" she asked Madrid.

"Don't know a whole lot about her, but I will say John changed," she noted. "And, when I say *changed*, when they broke up, he changed for the better."

"And how long ago was that?"

"Oh, I don't know. Maybe"—she turned to the others—"maybe six months or so. I mean, none of us—well, I don't know about Bill—but none of us were close enough to really get those kinds of details, I don't think. But I could be wrong," she added, with a shrug. "Sometimes you never really know who knows who."

Kate continued to ask questions of various people until finally the door opened, and Bill came back in.

He looked over at the older man and said, "The boss

wants you."

At that, he got up, looked over at Kate, and asked, "Need anything else from me?"

"No, I don't think so," she replied. "If so, I can contact you privately."

"Perfect," he replied, giving her a nod.

"We may not have had all that much to do with John because of the *work from home* thing," Madrid added, "but we were with him day in and day out on calls and meetings."

The older man heading for the door then added, "And we didn't have any personal issues within the group over it. At least I'm not aware of any. I'm just hoping you can get to the bottom of this quickly." And, with that, he walked out.

Kate let everyone else leave, except Bill. She and Rodney and Bill were all alone now.

Bill got nervous, shifting from one foot to the other.

She motioned for him to sit down, more because he was starting to piss her off with his shuffling back-and-forth.

He grabbed a chair and sat down way too quickly. "I don't know why you're so mad at me."

"Because you were given specific instructions to not say anything to anybody," she snapped, still trying to tone down her anger. "John's family hasn't been informed yet, so I could hardly have you telling all his coworkers." He didn't really seem to understand how important that could be. Kate huffed out a large sigh. "Anybody here could have potentially picked up the phone, just to offer condolences, and contacted the family before they were officially notified."

"Oh," he said, frowning, "I didn't think of that."

"No, you didn't," she snapped at him yet again. "All you could think about was passing gossip."

He turned beet red at that. "I wasn't trying to pass gossip. He was my friend. I was shocked and upset at everything going on. I wasn't trying to cause trouble."

"I'm *so* glad to hear that," she quipped, "because it certainly seemed as if that's *exactly* what you were trying to do."

"No, no, no, no." He shook his head. "I really wasn't."

She stared at him for a long moment. "If I find out differently …" She let her words hang in the air, but no way was he off the hook. "Now, I need to ask you a few other questions. What did you know about the girlfriend?"

He shrugged. "She hasn't been on his radar for quite a while. Maybe six months or so now," he said. "So, I wouldn't think she had anything to do with this."

"I didn't ask you if she had anything to do with it," she snapped, her tone hard. "I asked you about the girlfriend."

"Right," he muttered, trying to back up a little in his chair. Then he sobbed ever-so-slightly. "Look. This is really hard for me. He was my friend." He sobbed some more. "And now I feel as if somehow I'm being accused of something."

Her eyebrows shot up, and she asked, "You mean, other than not listening and not doing what you were told?"

He flushed bright red and muttered, "Yeah, other than that."

"That remains to be seen," she declared. "Let's get through these questions so I can move on." By the time she finished drilling him with more questions, he looked exhausted.

When she dismissed him, he got up slowly and conceded, "I don't really know that much about him, do I?"

She glanced at her notes. "Everything that you gave me was pretty generic. So, I would say, you don't know him that well, considering you called him a friend."

He nodded. "I only just now realized how much I really didn't know about him," he shared. "And that's a pretty disconcerting thought."

"Why is that?" she asked.

"I thought he was my best friend," he told her. "But if I didn't even know how to answer most of the questions you just asked, what kind of a friend was I?"

"Or maybe," she replied, "you should ask yourself, *What kind of a friend was he?*"

AS SIMON WALKED into the lobby of his apartment building, Edgar, the on-duty doorman, looked over at him.

The usual big smile on his face quickly turned to concern. "That bad of a day?"

Simon shrugged. "I didn't think so. Yet I got to tell you, I am pretty thrashed right now."

"And you look it," he confirmed bluntly, with the comfort of an old friend and somebody who had been around Simon in both good and bad times. "You're looking as if life was a little bit too much today."

"And yet," Simon replied, with a wry smile in Edgar's direction, "it seems as if it was a good day. So, I'm not sure when it all went south. Right now, I just want to go home, have a shower, and crash."

"And what about Kate?" Edgar asked him. "Is the detective coming tonight?"

He pondered that and noted, "I imagine she is. The repairs to her apartment are still being disputed, in terms of what the insurance will and will not cover."

Edgar snorted. "It got shot up by somebody trying to kill her, so they need to cover the cost of those repairs. Isn't that what insurance is supposed to be for? Of course they have to cover it," he declared, scandalized at the thought.

Simon chortled. "That's the thing about insurance companies. If they can get out of paying, they will find a way."

"But how is that her fault?"

"Something to do with the fact that she's a cop."

"And yet how many other cops in the city have had their apartments shot up?"

He laughed. "Those are very good arguments, and I wish I had an answer for you. However, as it stands right now, it's all still up in the air. So, I had a talk with one of our adjusters today to see if I could take a look at it and provide an opinion. He told me that he would contact somebody about it, but I haven't heard back." He yawned, gave a hearty headshake, and added, "I am heading up."

"Do you want me to let you know when she comes in?"

"No, I'll know as soon as she gets to the top anyway," Simon noted. "I don't think she'll be in all that early either, since she's got another case."

Edgar whistled. "I would like to say, *Oh, good,* because she's always the best at what she does. But then I think, *Oh, crap, that means somebody just died.*"

"Exactly," Simon replied, with a tired look in his direction.

He made it upstairs. As soon as he got into his apartment, he took off his jacket, pulled off his tie, tossing it right on top of his jacket, and kicked off his shoes.

He had no idea what was going on, but he knew he was about to drop. He just tried to get up here as fast as he could without raising any alarm bells. Edgar had been working here for a long time, and, if he thought something was wrong with Simon, Edgar would have offered to get him upstairs.

Simon was trying to hide his psychic side and what came with it, but definitely he had to consider it in terms of how much he would let people in on his *gift*. Edgar knew the bulk of it, but that didn't mean Simon wanted his doorman to scrutinize him with wary eyes every time he entered the building, checking if *something else* was coming on.

Most of the time, Simon himself didn't even know if something else was heading his way. He wanted to make it to his bed, but the couch was looking a whole lot closer, and he already felt the room starting to spin as everything disappeared from his sight. He had just managed to drop down flat on his face onto the couch when the room itself completely vanished.

He was suddenly standing in this strange room. ... It was so dark that he couldn't even describe it. Maybe a basement. Why here? He wasn't sure who was here or what was even happening.

He was completely under the spell of this vision and had absolutely no way to control it. So he listened. He heard a woman praying, fervently almost. He was trying *not* to come up with an answer because that was a guaranteed way to get bad ones.

He ended up second-guessing everything that he did after that because he questioned whether these were his thoughts or the other person's thoughts. But here Simon was, listening to her, seemingly praying for something. He heard caterwauling. He heard wailing.

It was all very emotional, whatever it was.

And then came heavy footsteps, as if somebody were coming downstairs, and her prayers got frantic, either afraid she would be caught or the person coming terrified her. Simon winced, knowing that it could be any number of things, and the bulk of them wouldn't be good.

Almost immediately the light went on, but the vision was still hazy, the room down here still dark.

A man spoke, his tone soft. "I understand your grief. Yet you must not drown in it. Perhaps you can stop now and return to the living?" the man asked.

He was calm. He was collected. His tone held no hint of violence, just seemed … *disciplined.*

The woman replied, barely in a whisper, "Yes, yes."

"Good. Now let's get back upstairs."

She got up slowly.

Even with a light on, Simon couldn't see anything around her. Yet she seemed to be familiar with this location, well enough that she could walk it in the dark, which she appeared to be doing right now.

Confused, Simon was not sure what he was even looking at or why he was here. Even when they went upstairs, they seemed to enter a storage room. It was dark and hazy here too. Simon did not recognize this place.

The man spoke to the woman, "Surely you can see it clearly now."

"Yes, of course," she muttered. "I just needed a little more time."

"You're always welcome as long as you know where you belong. I understand a crisis of faith."

"I know," she replied, her voice now calm, peaceful, so different from earlier. "It's God's will."

"Exactly. It's God's will that you be … as God intended you." After a pause, he added, "You just have to believe."

With that final word, the entire image just faded away. And someone shook Simon, hard.

CHAPTER 4

KATE SPIED SIMON, crashed on the couch, then walked over to see that he was breathing—because one of the things she absolutely loved doing in life was making sure he was still alive. When he didn't move, she gave him a shake, then a harder one.

He opened his eyes and stared up at her, his eyes glassy. Yet a lazy smile crossed his face as soon as his gaze cleared.

His ability to go from … wherever he had been … to this never ceased to amaze her. He came back to almost normal. Almost untouched, except when she really studied his eyes and realized just how deep and how dark they'd gone. She couldn't imagine the nightmares he had come back with. She sat down on the chair across from him, holding two glasses of wine.

He smiled at her and finally spoke. "Definitely something to be said about waking up to a beautiful woman holding a glass of wine after a very hard day."

She smiled. "Edgar told me that you were pretty well at the end of your rope today."

"Of course he did," Simon muttered, then yawned. "Even if I told him *not* to tell you anything, I suspect that he would take one look at you and blurt out absolutely everything he could possibly imagine saying. All because of that *look*, saying, *Don't you dare lie to me.*" Simon had to chuckle.

Kate snorted. "I don't even have to give him *the look*. He's always been extremely generous with information," she shared, "particularly when it involves those he cares about."

Simon opened his eyes wider, taking in the expression on her face, and then nodded. "That is very true. … I am fine, you know?"

"I'm glad to hear that." But her steady gaze on him wouldn't let up.

He sat up, stretched, and said, "I'll take that glass of wine as soon as I get back from the bathroom." When he returned, true to his word, he picked up the glass of wine, shifted on the couch, and patted the spot beside him. "You could sit here now."

"That depends on whether you'll crash out on me again."

He frowned at her and asked, "You weren't home when I did that, were you?"

"Nope," she replied cheerfully. "Yet now at least I know that's what you did."

He attempted to glare at her, but his lips twitched. "You're really good at stopping anybody from hiding crap. People just automatically open up and tell you everything, whether they want to or not. Probably because of that pissed-off look on your face." He sighed. "I made it home, and I made it horizontal before I crashed," he admitted, "so that's the good part."

She nodded, waiting.

"How was your day?" he asked her.

"Awful," she declared. "Nothing is good about finding a dead man wrapped up with a bow in his apartment, then everybody talking about what a great guy he was."

"Such a great guy yet somebody decided to kill him?"

Simon quipped.

"Yeah, and the bow was tied around his penis."

Simon's eyebrows raised at that.

"Then, on top of that, this very strange giant poinsettia plant was in his apartment and came with a card, a one-word note on it. *Believe*."

Simon just considered her and swirled the wine around in his glass.

She kept her gaze on him, trying to glean something from his pensive expression. "You wouldn't happen to know anything about that, would you?" she asked, her tone gentle but firm.

He stared at her, still swirling the red liquid. "That may have something to do with why I crashed. I didn't know it until I was deep … in a trance. And even now I'm not exactly sure what I heard."

"Good enough," she replied. "So, what did you hear?"

"Again, I'm not sure." He described the little bit he saw. "She seemed to be praying. I really don't know what that was, … whether really acting or praying to be released from something, but she asked to be saved."

"Or," Kate suggested, an odd note in her tone, "to become pregnant?"

"Ah," Simon nodded. "That is also an option, isn't it?"

"Some women desperately want to have children," she noted, with a shrug. "It's a big challenge for them if they can't get pregnant."

"I imagine it is," he agreed.

"I haven't ever had the urge to reproduce," she stated. "So, it's not something I can necessarily relate to. Yet I do understand that, for some women, it's a very high priority. And particularly when, in some cases, the men put a very high *value* on it too," she noted, for want of another word.

"Right. So, in other words, the men are telling their wives, *You're not a woman if you can't procreate?*"

"Something like that," she said. He gave her a smirk, and she added, "No."

"What do you mean, no?" he protested.

She shook her head. "Not going there right now. Definitely not. Now … back to what you saw."

"You are incredibly focused," he muttered, taking a sip of his wine. "Maybe I just want to enjoy my drink first, before getting intimate with the details of that dark vision."

"That's fine," she replied. "However, you and I both know that, once you have that little bit of wine, some of what you have just seen will likely be lost and forgotten."

"I'm surprised you don't have a recorder out."

She held up her phone, and, sure enough, the red light confirmed it was recording.

He slumped back and stared at her. "You know, for a cop who doesn't trust anything I say …"

Her lips twitched. "For a cop who doesn't know which way to think," she corrected. "How can I explain to my team what you saw when I cannot possibly recount all of it exactly? This is the easiest and simplest way to ensure nobody jumps to conclusions that it might have been *such and such,*" she explained. "You and I both know a great deal of delightful reactions are had at the station when you come up with this stuff. I won't however play it for anyone else, it is only for my own clarity."

He winced. "But not from you."

She shrugged. "I definitely love parts about this. Yet, when I can't see things, can't hear things, can't prove things, it makes my job even more difficult. I'm trying to be as open as I can, and that isn't always easy."

"I know," he noted. "Which is why I really appreciate the fact that you give me a chance to explain before tearing apart what I just shared."

She smirked. "I'm not trying to tear it apart, but, if I can dispute the notion that it's incredibly useful, it makes it a bit easier to fight off everybody at work."

"Do they really think I have something to offer?"

"Of course they do," she muttered, "and you know it. You've been involved in enough of my cases to prove that."

"Which you hate, by the way."

She sighed. "If I suddenly decided to go into real estate or construction work, coming along with you to work, completely out of the blue, telling you how to do your job, how would you feel?"

He stared at her for a long moment, and then he burst out laughing. "That thought boggles the mind."

"Exactly," she agreed. "I mean, I can get things done with a hammer, but I am certainly not in a position to tell you how to do the things that you need to do for your rehabs."

"Nope, you sure aren't," he acknowledged. His amusement was obvious as he kept chuckling to himself.

She asked him, "So, can you understand where I'm coming from?"

He waved his hand. "I understand totally. That is not an issue."

"I'm glad to hear that," she replied.

"And no," he said, "I don't really have anything else to offer. When I came home, I had an *I need to go crash* moment."

He yawned again, and she frowned. "It really takes a lot

out of you, doesn't it?"

"Sometimes," he admitted. "I know you want to stop that from happening to me, but I don't think even you can control that."

She glared at him and pointed out, "Somebody should be able to."

"I would think that, if somebody *should be able to*, that somebody would be me," he stated, laughing again. "And God knows that I haven't exactly put too much dedicated time and effort into controlling *this*."

"I don't know about that," she argued. "Seems to me that you have done as much as you could, as fast as you could. And I do thank you for all the assistance you have given us so far." She hated that such a formal note filled her tone, but she meant it.

He narrowed his gaze at her. "Thanking me is one thing, but making me feel as if that's all there is between us will just totally piss me off."

She snorted. "I was just thinking that too—about how that would make you feel. And it's not how I intended it, but it's hard to thank you and have it not connected to my job," she explained. "A lot of people in this world are doing much better now because of you."

"And because of you," he added. "Never forget that. You're the one who never gives yourself any slack in the work that you do."

"It's hard," she stated. "I always feel as if I should do more, could do more, would do more if …"

"And there will always be more of that," he stated. "You and I both know that."

She gave an irritable nod and then glanced over at the kitchen.

He sighed. "Sorry, I haven't put two thoughts into food."

"Okay," she said, as she got up and walked over to see if there were any leftovers—or anything to possibly cook, like eggs. As she opened the fridge, she found it bare.

He chuckled. "Even if we wanted to cook," he told her, "we don't really have much in the way of choices. The contents of the kitchen leave much to be desired."

"Yet, if we kept it full," she suggested, "we could cook certain things on nights like this."

"And, when you come home, tired and worn out, what is it that you would cook?" A hint of amusement filled his tone.

She glanced back at him and shrugged. "I don't know. I guess, a couple fried eggs on a piece of toast," she replied, as she opened up a drawer to see if he had any bread.

"And that's not suitable for you to work on. You go through more calories in a day than a lot of people I know who have very heavy physical jobs."

"It's my brain," she muttered. "Did you know chess players need about fifteen thousand calories a game because of the brainpower they're burning through?"

"Why do you know that statistic? Did you have a case with a chess player or do research for a book or something?"

"No, but that's not a bad idea. If I ever decided to change my job, I should probably write books." He stared at her in shock, and she laughed. "I'm kidding."

"Just the thought of you even changing jobs boggles the mind, and I know it won't happen."

"It won't ever happen because that's not who I am. What I'm doing is what I need to be doing."

"And, if you ever needed to change that," he shared, "I

would completely and fully support whatever decision you made."

She smiled at him. "And that's the real reason we're together." She flopped back down on the couch beside him, shifting to look at him sideways, one knee up on the couch as she reached for her wineglass.

"And what's that?" he asked.

She looked over at him and, with a shrug, she said, "Acceptance."

SIMON NODDED SLOWLY. Trust Kate to put it in a very succinct, no-nonsense way. He chuckled. "I can't say I considered it in that way, but you're right. That would be us."

She smiled. "Now we need food. Are you ordering it, or am I?"

He burst out laughing and asked, "What do you want to eat?"

"I don't know," she muttered, "but, if it doesn't come soon, I'll just go to bed without dinner."

At the ringing sound, Simon reached for his phone. It was Edgar downstairs.

"Are you doing okay up there, sir?"

"I'm doing fine, but the cupboards are bare, and we're hungry."

Edgar burst out laughing. "Good because a great big delivery is coming up to you," he announced. "I took the liberty."

Simon took a moment before answering.

"If you don't want it, I can take it home to the family, but you appeared to be pretty done. And you haven't had

Greek in a few weeks—or a few days at least."

"Where did you get it from?"

"Delaney's." Then Edgar added, "I know it's your money, but I also gave them a decent tip."

Simon smiled. "And we thank you for that. Is it here?"

"On its way up to you right now because I'm in the elevator with it."

At that, Simon got up and walked to the elevator door, the special penthouse-only elevator, Kate on his heels.

She asked him, "Did he really just order that on his own?"

The penthouse elevator doors opened, revealing Edgar, holding out a big bag. He looked over at Kate and nodded. "You looked as if you could use some food too." And, with that, he smiled at the two of them and left via the same elevator.

She frowned over at Simon. "Does the whole world think we don't eat?"

"I don't know," Simon admitted, "but I think the world may be afraid that, if we don't eat, we don't work."

She snorted. "That is quite possible." She carried the bag into the kitchen and quickly served up some food. "You know, there was a time when all I did was eat because I needed energy. You've spoiled me."

He looked as if he were about to burst into laughter.

She added, "Every time I eat now, it's a new food experience. Something I've never really had before."

"That's good because food should always be an experience you enjoy, something you absolutely love."

"Easier said than done," she noted.

"I understand, but that's part of our relationship too, togetherness and food," he stated. They sat down at the table, and she had barely finished eating when he looked over at her and asked, "What did you find out on the case?"

"Nothing really," she grumbled. "At least nothing that's putting any answers in my head." She quickly filled him in on the little bits she'd learned. "Oh, and he worked from home, and they didn't see him very often. He was a holdover from the COVID era and pretty much stuck to his *work from home* routine."

"How did the company feel about that?"

"Apparently they've been trying to get him to return to the office with everybody else, but he was very resistant to the idea."

Simon nodded. "A lot of people made some pretty physical moves in order to work from home and to get out of the crazy city rat race. The COVID era got everybody to reevaluate their priorities."

"And yet still the *back to work* movement continues, as more and more companies insist on that," she noted, slowly rotating her neck, wishing she had stopped by the dojo after work because she now needed to head over there tomorrow.

"Your neck sore?" he asked.

She smiled. "Not so much sore as stiff. I should have stopped for my workout today because now I'll have to do it tomorrow. And you know how I hate *have-tos*. It changes the whole vibe for me."

He smiled. "Like the rest of us, it becomes work. And, when it's work, it's a chore. And, when it's a chore, we don't want to do it," he noted, with a smile. "You should work out here," he suggested, and she rolled her eyes at that. "I mean, a gym is right downstairs."

"I know, but not exactly the place I think of."

"You want something more private?"

"Yeah, I probably do," she admitted, "but I don't have it, so that's all good. And I'm too tired tonight anyway." She yawned at that. She got up from the table, helped Simon to clean up and to put away the food. "Are you likely to dream about this tonight?"

He turned to her. "I can't tell you when my visions come. They just do."

She nodded.

"Does that mean you don't want to stay here tonight?" he asked.

Surprised, she turned to him and frowned. "It never stopped me before, so I don't know why it would now." He hesitated, but she waved her hand. "I'm fine, Simon. I guess I was just wondering if you felt that most-recent vision meant something personal to you. Or was it—sounds ridiculous but—was it just electrons floating around in the universe that didn't have a major connection to you?"

He stared at her, and his lips twitched.

She glared at him irritably. "I know. It sounded stupid to me too, but I couldn't figure out how to put it together. I'm just tired."

"And I get that," he shared, still smirking at her. "As for an answer to your question, I have no idea. It's not exactly what I was expecting in any way." He shrugged. "If it happens again, let's hope I get more than just her praying."

"And does that vision, with its mention of the word *believe*, have anything to do with my case?" she asked, as she walked back to the couch before turning to him. "That's the real question."

"Of course," he replied. "And the answer is, … I have no idea."

CHAPTER 5

KATE WALKED INTO her department the next morning, frowned over at Reese, who was here waiting for her in the bullpen. Reese frowned right back. Kate declared, "If you have bad news, I don't want to hear it."

Reese smirked and replied, "You're about the only person I can give this bad news to though."

"Oh, *great*," Kate muttered. "What does that mean?"

Reese paused, then blurted out, "There might be another one."

"No, no, no," Kate ranted. "Oh, hell no. You don't understand how this works, Reese. This is an oddball one-off between-holidays killing. We do *not* have another one."

Reese gave her a sad smile and handed over a file. "I found it over in the Coquitlam files."

"And?"

"It's from about two years ago. I know how you like paper copies, so I made you one. And you know where you can find the online file."

"Okay." Kate frowned as she accepted the folder and asked, "Why the devil would a case that happened two years ago have anything to do with my current case? Why now?"

"I don't know," Reese replied. "I can't tell you that, but what I can tell you is that it may or may not be connected, but I wouldn't let it pass by."

"No, of course you wouldn't." She thanked her as Reese walked away. Then Kate headed to her desk, took off her coat and threw it around the back of her chair. She then pulled out her keys and a little card pocket she carried, dropping them into the top drawer, along with her phone, and headed for the coffeepot.

She'd had one cup this morning at Simon's, but the traffic had been just hectic enough that she was craving a second cup to shake off the traffic blues. By the time she managed to get a cup and returned to her desk, Rodney was there, talking with somebody passing through the bullpen.

He looked up as she walked by. "Hey," he greeted her, then frowned. "What's with the face?" And he froze for a moment. "Unless … we caught another case."

"I don't know whether we caught another case or people just like me to catch cases that might be connected."

His eyebrows shot up, and he asked, "How could anything be connected to the *Believe* case?"

"That's what I don't know," she admitted. "So, we have to find out."

He shook his head. "It was just a between-holidays one-off. People have a hard time over the holidays."

"You're telling me," she muttered, glaring at him. "All I can say is that Reese handed it to me when I walked in. I haven't had time to check it out yet."

He frowned at that and asked, "Why not me?"

"I don't know. Did she see you? She's not favoring me, if that's what you're worried about," Kate pointed out. "But she saw me as I walked in and brought it over. So, I rather imagine I just got *lucky*."

He smiled, obviously relieved that she wasn't being favored.

She asked him, "Have you ever thought that was a problem around here?"

"No," he declared forcefully. "It's not that. I just had that split-second moment where I wondered if she deliberately didn't contact me."

"I don't think so," Kate replied. "I've never known Reese to play favorites. Have you?"

"No, and this game isn't for favorites anyway."

"Exactly," she agreed. "You and I both know that. Unfortunately Reese unearthed something and had to hand it off to anybody who had a moment to handle it."

"Yeah, that's true enough," Rodney admitted. "Sorry. I was just having a moment."

She nodded and didn't say anything. Yet, in the back of her mind, she wondered how many of these moments he was having. If it was an issue, the last thing she wanted was to cause trouble with any of the team, especially coming in the way she had, as an unwanted replacement for a really great guy they loved working with, but he died. Yet what could she do about that?

Although, with the increased success rate they had enjoyed since she'd been here, it might be considered perfectly normal for some to have hard feelings, but she hoped not. She just didn't want to be in the middle of office politics and just wanted to focus on what was important—getting the job done. As she sat down, she pulled up the online Coquitlam case file.

She quickly scanned through the details, as Rodney pulled up a chair beside her. "What does it say?"

"Reese is right in the sense that it's definitely something we need to check out. Both cases share two major similarities," Kate noted, "and they make my skin crawl."

Rodney frowned and took a look at what was on her monitor. "How can they both say *Believe* in a card?"

"Yeah, that's the thing that got to me. Also did you see this?" Kate pointed to the handwritten addition.

As Rodney read it, he frowned. "And a red ribbon? Jesus."

"Yeah, and a red ribbon," she confirmed.

"Okay," Rodney began, "we need to contact the family and find out who all knew anything about what was going on in this guy's life at the time he was killed."

Kate sighed. "You know that won't go over well."

"That's quite true. It's been, what?" He looked at the report and glanced through it. "A year and something?"

"Almost two, I think. Yeah, closer to two years."

"That definitely won't go over well with the family."

"Yeah, but on the other hand," she pointed out, "maybe they'll open up because it looks as if we're trying again."

"If people only knew how much trying we do and how little time we have before the next case comes along," he grumbled, as he returned to his desk and was on the phone within minutes. When he ended his call, he turned to Kate and called out, "They're willing to talk, but she was pretty upset."

"What was her relationship to the victim?"

"Sibling. The victim was her brother."

"Okay, let's make a trip." She glanced at her watch. "Nobody else is in yet."

"Nope, and Lilliana felt she was coming down with something yesterday. Hopefully it's not that really bad flu. I'm not sure whether she's coming in or not."

"*Right*," she scoffed. "Par for the course since we're constantly shorthanded these days."

He nodded but didn't say anything. They got up just as Colby walked out of his office, muttering to himself. She waited until he looked up.

He frowned as he saw the two of them preparing to go out. "Now what?" he asked.

She told him about the second case that Reese had brought her, and his eyebrows shot up. "Seriously?"

"Yeah," she confirmed, her tone somber. "So, we want to talk to the victim's sister and take a look at the crime scene. Although it is now a rented apartment. So, we probably can't get in, but I want some idea if we've got the same setup."

He just stared at her for a few moments, his jaw twitching, and he finally relented. "Good God. I thought for sure this would be a one-off."

"Yeah, you and me both," she agreed.

"A one-off hopefully and a one-and-done." Colby groaned. "Lilliana called in sick. She's picked up whatever bloody flu has been going around the place. So, odds are, she's probably out for a good two days or more."

"So, we are truly shorthanded, down to just the two of us?" Kate asked. "And don't say *budget cuts*. After so long, we no longer hold out any hope for a replacement for Andy. And what is going on with Owen? An *extended Christmas holiday*, my ass."

Colby sighed. "Lean on Reese and the department's two assistants whenever you can."

She snorted at that. "We'll be gone for most of the day, back-and-forth with this second case. And I want to go to whatever church is close by."

Colby turned very, very slowly. "And why is that?"

She frowned, not sure how much to tell him, not sure

she had grounds to get him worried. Yet it might be a shock if later something did come from Simon's words. "So, none of this is for real, for sure, nothing like that. But Simon …" She let his name hang there for a moment, and Colby closed his eyes.

"Simon what?" he muttered.

She smirked. "Yeah, now you know how I feel. I got hit with this shit when I got home last night. I walked in to find he had crashed and was just coming out of a vision."

"What did he see?" Colby asked, facing her.

"I was staring at him, the one pulling him back out," she shared, trying to keep her tone neutral. "So, anything you want to say, I've already said myself."

Now Colby snorted. "Fine, go on. What exactly did Simon find out?"

She began, "As usual, it's not that he found out anything, but he tapped into something."

"Spit it out. Stop procrastinating."

She rolled her eyes. "That's a big word for you." Colby just glared at her. She smiled and added, "I don't know if it means anything, but …" Then she told him about Simon's vision and the mention of *that word* again.

"Seriously? The man in his vision actually said, *Believe?*"

Beside her, Rodney chimed in. "Not just that, but he also texted her, right about the time that we got the first case, and he wrote something about *believe* even then."

"Yeah," she confirmed, "he did."

"So, you're thinking a church?" Colby asked.

"Not necessarily," she hedged, keeping her voice low. "With a woman praying, possibly about getting pregnant, it could be someone waiting for … Is any fertility clinic around the corner from a church?"

Colby frowned at her. "We're in a big city that has virtually everything." He waited for her to continue.

Kate added, "I'm not sure Simon's vision directly connects to either John's death or the older death of Kurt. I don't know if any church is nearby either crime scene, especially with a fertility clinic beside it. I'll ask Reese to get on that. So, I'll focus more on a local church close by each deceased's apartment. We'll just have to check it out." She turned to him and shrugged. "I haven't decided anything yet." And, with that, she left him standing there, staring after her.

Rodney rushed to catch up and asked her, "Are you becoming psychic yourself?" When she stared at him in horror, he laughed and continued. "You know, a lot of people think that, just by being around Simon, you're likely to end up with some of his talent brushing off on you."

"I don't know that anything can *brush off*. It's hardly contagious, like the flu or a cold."

He burst out laughing. Then he stopped and stared at her. "Are you sure?"

"Yes, I'm sure," she muttered. "God, that's the last thing I need. I can't believe you would even question me about that."

"Maybe, but that doesn't change the fact that it could very well be a thing."

"Not likely," she countered, and Rodney genuinely looked intimidated.

"I'll drive," he offered.

"Good," she replied pointedly. "I need to think."

"You do that. Close your eyes and think on things, ... including all things supernatural. Meanwhile I will get us to Kurt's sister."

Kate let it be. No point in arguing about that. It took thirty-five minutes to get through traffic to their target neighborhood. As Rodney pulled in front of the small townhouse, Kate studied it and nodded.

He frowned at her and asked, "What was the nod for?"

She blinked and asked, "What now?"

He glared at her.

She got out, not sure that she had nodded. Even if it was a nod, it didn't mean anything. The last thing she wanted was for them to start eyeing her sideways, but Rodney already was. She glared at him as they walked up to the front door, muttering, "Don't even go there."

"No, I don't have to go there," he pointed out, "because I suspect you already have." He rang the doorbell and gave her an impudent grin.

The door opened, revealing a young woman holding a toddler on her hip. When Kate and Rodney both pulled out their badges, the woman gasped at the two of them, and her face bunched up, as if she were ready to cry. The toddler, seemingly reacting to her mother's emotions alone, started to bunch up its face too.

Kate hurriedly asked, "May we come in?"

The mother blinked several times, then stepped back, nodding.

"You're Esther, aren't you? I'm Detective Kate Morgan, and this is my colleague."

Rodney nodded and said, "Just call me Rodney."

Kate asked, "Is there anything you need to do with the baby before we have a few moments to talk?"

"My husband isn't here. He's at work."

"Right. Okay." Kate began, "We don't know whether there's a connection or not, but we had another case come up that has similarities to your brother's case. So naturally we have to check it out."

"Another case?" she repeated. "Similar how? What are you talking about?"

Kate replied, "I can't give you any details. All I can tell you is that we need to at least look into your brother's case once more."

Esther stared at her in what appeared to be complete incomprehension.

Kate tried to redirect her and asked, "Is this a good time to talk?"

Esther shrugged. "There's never a good time to talk about my dead brother. I mean, how does that even work?"

"Maybe there isn't a good time, but some days can be easier or harder. Do you have any other siblings, any family around?"

"No. It was just me and my brother." They followed the mother to a small living room, where she motioned for them to sit.

"And what was he like?"

She smiled. "He was lively," she replied, taking a seat in the recliner, while Kate and Rodney sat on the couch facing her. "He loved the ladies. He loved his life. And he loved being single. He loved everything."

"Did he have a girlfriend?"

"He did and he didn't." At Kate's raised eyebrows, Esther explained further, "He made a practice of not getting too involved. He would have a girlfriend up until she got really focused on the whole *settling down* thing, and he became single very, very quickly. It's not as if he never told them that, since he made it very clear right from the beginning that he would not settle down, at least not anytime soon."

Esther sighed. "Yet the women always seemed to think that they could change him. So they dismissed what he said and entered the relationship." She bounced the baby, who seemed a bit distressed. Maybe over the topic or maybe over the undercurrents in the room.

Kate smiled at Esther and the baby, then asked, "How old is he?"

"She," she corrected, "is eleven months."

Kate studied the baby again, trying to figure out how anybody knew what the sex was before they opened their mouth and got it wrong. In this case, blonde curls, bright blue eyes, and slightly hard features made Kate assume, incorrectly, that it was a boy.

She smiled at the baby, who reacted as if Kate's mannerism had the opposite effect. So, Kate softened her smile and faced the mother. "Do you know who Kurt's girlfriend was at the time of his death?"

"He actually was engaged back then but ended the engagement when he found out his fiancée had lied to him," she replied. "He was pretty torn up about it. So he wanted a break for a while."

Kate nodded. "I get that. Not everybody is set on settling down."

Esther asked her, "Are you married?"

"Nope, I'm not," she replied, "but I'm in a long-term relationship. I just don't feel the need to get married right now."

Esther's gaze lit up. "I thought that was every woman's purpose in life," she said half-jokingly.

Kate frowned at her, and even Rodney seemed taken aback.

Esther shrugged and added, "That's just the way some religions teach it."

"Maybe," Kate conceded, "but it's never been an issue for me. I'm very busy with my work."

"I work too," Esther replied, as if Kate had crossed a line.

Kate smiled and asked, "Was Kurt living alone at the time? Was his fiancée living with him? Did he have an apartment close by? What was his life like? Where did he work?"

By the time she got the answers, which she already had in the file, the awkward moment with Esther seemed to be forgotten, as her answers came more readily. Kate was all about getting to know the victim as much as she could before things went south.

When the front door opened, Esther looked up. Kate detected fear in Esther's gaze for a moment but couldn't be sure. A man walked into the living room. He frowned as he saw the two strangers in his home, then glanced at Esther. This was presumably the husband.

Esther bounced to her feet and walked over to him, holding up the baby. The baby launched into her father's arms. He smiled as he held her close, then turned to Kate and asked, "Who are you, and what are you doing here?" His manner was brusque.

She stood up, held out her badge, and stated, "I had a few questions for your wife about her brother's death."

His eyebrows shot up, and he turned to Esther, then addressed Kate, "Seriously, after all this time, you're finally getting around to it? That's not fair."

Kate replied, "Obviously the original detectives did what they could on Kurt's case. However, at this point, I also needed to ask a few more questions. We're done for now." She turned to Rodney and asked, "Unless, Rodney, you have anything else?"

He smiled and shook his head. "Nope, we can leave you two in peace now." With that, he walked toward the front door, Kate following behind.

Esther followed them to the door and saw them out. "Thank you. He really doesn't like the police," she whispered in an apologetic manner.

Kate nodded. "Not a problem."

When they stepped outside, she glanced at Rodney, who was frowning. As he glanced back, they got into their vehicle. Instead of pulling away, Rodney just sat here in the driver's seat. "Was something off about that?"

"Definitely something was off," Kate agreed, as she made notes, "but I'm not sure anything was criminally off, just lifestyle off."

"Maybe," he muttered.

She shrugged and shared, "It's hard for me to connect to someone who thinks her only purpose in life is to get married and have babies. I'm not sure that was even necessarily her viewpoint."

"No, but her husband wasn't terribly impressed that we were talking to her."

She pondered that and agreed. "That could be true. It's really hard to know sometimes. We weren't really there long enough to get an idea of what his attitude toward all this really was."

Rodney smiled. "I suspect, if we were to come back, Esther will have been told *not* to talk to us again, at least not without him present."

"Yeah. I'm not betting you on that one because I suspect

you're right." Kate nodded.

"Now where?" he asked, turning to look at her.

"Let's swing by Kurt's old apartment. I don't need to see inside it, but let's scour a couple blocks nearby for a church, even a fertility clinic. Bonus points if you find both, side by side."

Rodney laughed and took off to the next address, then circled the apartment building while Kate searched for churches and fertility clinics.

"Nothing. Take the next block or two." But they found no church even three blocks away from Kurt's old apartment, much less a fertility clinic.

With a sigh, Kate said, "I want to go to Kurt's workplace, where he used to work."

He eyed her in surprise. "Do you think you'll find anything there?"

"No, I'm absolutely positive I won't find anything," she snapped, "but that doesn't mean I can't go check it out again because definitely I sense a need to. Yet, for the life of me, I can't see how or in what way."

"Only one way to find out," Rodney said, as he drove off toward the highway.

"It's about a twenty-minute drive from here, which I guess is a pretty normal commute, isn't it?"

"Absolutely. Look at us. Often we're way longer than that. Of course, for *some* of us," he noted, with an eye roll, "those who landed on lucky street, they either get driven to work or have a fancy driver who drops them off."

She glanced at him, realized he was hassling her, and she told him in a mild tone, "Lay off, Rodney."

He dropped it and shrugged. "I don't think you could really do the *lady of the manor* thing anyway."

"Nope. I sure couldn't," she confirmed, and then she gave him an evil grin. "However, anytime you want me to try it out, I could."

"No, no, no, no," he muttered, followed by a snort. "I'm already sure you could do the evil witch of the west just fine."

"I think I do that fine right now," she stated. "I don't even have to practice."

He burst out laughing. "You could be right."

Joking back and forth, amiable once again, they continued the drive, pulling up to the address. "*Huh.* This company's name is nebulous as to what it actually does. Didn't Esther say Kurt was an insurance adjuster?" She checked the online file. She froze when she realized John was one too, now sharing that with Rodney.

Rodney frowned. "That is a coincidence."

"One too many," she replied.

"You really think so?"

"Both in the same field, both with red ribbons tied around them, both with a *Believe* note left behind, both of them playboys?"

"I thought John's ribbon was tied around a particular part of his anatomy."

"Yes," she agreed, "but I'm not sure that Kurt's ribbon wasn't some awkward attempt at that too." He glanced at her, frowning. She shrugged. "I'm holding back on any and all judgments for the moment."

He snorted. "Why? You're usually so good at making snap judgments. We don't want you to be wrong even once. That would be terrible."

"Jesus, Rodney, you're really sounding like a walking pity party."

"Not trying to," he grumbled. "Sometimes it feels that way."

"Not because of me," she declared. "That's all on you." He glanced at her again. She shrugged. "I'm not doing anything to make you feel that way. So, if that's how you feel, it's coming from your own perspective of what's happening. I am not here to make you feel bad," she repeated. "And I'm not here to make you look as if you're not doing anything. We're a team. If one of us succeeds, we all succeed. And anytime you want to take over these cases and make a proud showing of how you can handle it all without anybody's help, please do."

"God no, that's not what I meant." Then he groaned and added, "But you're right. I mean, if one of us succeeds, we all succeed. So, I don't know why … I'm just having a shitty day."

"It doesn't help that our original team of five is now down to just the two of us. At least that's temporary until Lilliana gets well. Plus the damn budget cuts are affecting our work and the forensics guys and maybe even Smidge. Plus everybody looks at me to get Simon on board, *since we can't possibly solve a case on our own.*"

"Can we?" He started to laugh and then added, "I can see how that would bite too."

"It does bite," she declared, "because, in the end, good detective work solves our cases."

"I will admit that occasionally it's really helpful to have Simon provide some information, but to not have his involvement sometimes would also be very helpful." Still grinning, he parked at the office building where Kurt had worked.

As they entered the main lobby, they were passed by several people talking in loud voices. As they walked into the main office, the loud voices continued. She looked over at the receptionist, who was trying to muster up a smile of welcome.

Kate held out her badge, and immediately the receptionist froze and started bawling. Surprised at that reaction, and wondering what was behind it, Kate looked around to see what was going on.

Another gentleman walked over quickly. He excused the woman from the front desk, and she got up and hurried away. He stood here with a sad smile on his face, looked over at her, and introduced himself. "I'm Barry Quinn, the manager. Can we help you?"

When she held out her badge, he nodded. "Ah, I guess we should have expected you sooner or later."

Surprised, she asked, "Do you want to clarify that?"

"I mean, he died this morning. So, of course you're here." He groaned. "We haven't even had a chance to figure out what happened and whether it'll affect any of us or not, other than emotionally." He took a deep breath. "It's just so sad."

"Okay," Kate began. "Maybe you could start at the beginning. Tell us who died, what you know about it, when it happened, what his position was here, how well he was known and loved, et cetera."

He frowned at her. "I'm sure you've already got it in the files." Then he corrected himself, "Maybe you haven't got the files yet. Robert Blake was found dead …"

"This morning?" she asked, an edge in her tone.

"Yes, in his bed. He'd been working for the company for a good ten years. He was well-loved, especially by many of the women, less so by many of the men. He was a bit of a womanizer, if you ask me. God help us. Even still, he is somebody who will be very much missed," he shared. "I don't know what else to tell you. The detective that I saw at his apartment seemed to be of the opinion that it might've been some sort of, … BDSM gone wrong, but what do I know? It just didn't seem right to me."

"And why do you think that?"

He stared at her, then shrugged. "Because he was covered in festive Christmas paraphernalia," he said, lowering his voice. "You know, wreaths and ribbons and things."

She studied him, her Spidey senses on full alert. "I see," she replied. "Do you have the name of the detective you saw this morning?"

"He gave me a card," he muttered, rubbing his forehead, "but, honest to God, I don't know where it is."

"And how did you come to be at Robert's apartment?"

He flushed and shared, "We live in the same complex." He gave her his address and his contact number.

"Was he particularly close to any of the women here at work?"

He grimaced and nodded. "Yeah, a couple of them. He broke that rule about, you know, don't fish in your own pond. So, a bunch of women will be quite upset, and some aren't really aware that others will be very upset too."

"Right," Kate noted. "So, in other words, he played the field a lot."

He nodded. "Yes, he did. And sometimes it was fine. But then other times, well, not everybody plays the game the same way. Take, for example, Lanny here, our receptionist, she was pretty sweet on him, but she's the girl you take home to your mother. She's not somebody you play around with for a few weeks then drop because you found something that tastes better." He added, his tone apologetic, "I don't mean to be crude, but you get my meaning."

"I got your meaning just fine," Kate said. "And I gathered this Robert Blake was exactly that way."

"He was. And, for that reason, the whole playboy thing earned him warnings about office romances. He would stop for a time. Then staff would change—where we hired somebody new, young, friendly, beautiful—and we had the same issues all over again. It got to be old. The hiring managers got pretty crafty in the sense that they knew to hire people who were not his … type, so to speak."

"The trouble is, his type was anything younger than what … forty?" she asked sarcastically.

"Pretty much any woman who looked *decent,*" Barry clarified, with a groan. "It was just a headache. I'm so sorry about what happened to him, but, from my perspective, it saves me from having to fire him."

"And were you that close to firing him?"

"Yeah, I was getting there," he confirmed, his voice lowered. "We had another incident with a staff member. And, you know, when things go from bad to worse, the staff are the ones who get caught up in it. It was time to put a stop to it."

"Of course," Kate agreed. "I'm sorry for your loss, since obviously, despite his faults, he was a friend."

"He was a friend, but he couldn't keep his damn pants zipped," he said, frowning. "Yet I loved him like a brother."

"What will you do now?"

"I figured when the first detective mentioned a sex game gone wrong or something, I just assumed—maybe incorrectly—that a jealous boyfriend did this, or they just made it look that way."

"Jealous boyfriend?" Rodney asked.

"Robert had more than a few. A couple of them came to the office when they were highly pissed off and upset because their girlfriends had broken up with them or when the boyfriends had caught their girlfriends cheating. Robert also left some women in less-than-delightful circumstances, shall we say."

"Do you know if he has any children?"

Barry snorted. "I don't know how he couldn't at the rate he was playing the field, even if he was being careful," he replied. "But then again, I seem to recall mention of ... I think he told me something about a vasectomy, just for that reason alone. He *didn't want to get caught*, as he put it."

The manager frowned. "I remember a discussion with a group of us at dinner one night. He shared that, if he ever needed to, he could reverse it. Some people were telling him that it had to happen within a certain time frame, and he just didn't care. As far as he was concerned, it was worth the price to confirm he didn't ... *get caught*."

"Understood." Kate turned to Rodney.

Rodney began with his questions, "Do you know anything about his family? Where they live? I need his address. Was he currently having an ongoing relationship with anybody here?"

"It's been hard to keep up," the manager grumbled, clearly uncomfortable.

Rodney asked, "Do you know if he was currently dating anyone?"

"The cops got his phone, and it was connected to a lot of apps," he shared, with a wince, "so anybody he was seeing, they would probably be listed in his Contacts or within those dating apps."

"So, you don't think Robert was *dating* at all?"

He shook his head. "I don't want to say that, but my assumption would be that it would *not* be a date. It would be more of a hookup. He was handling things at that level these days."

There was no judgment in the man's tone, just sadness that it came to this. "It's so frustrating," he shared. "I mean, he was a good man, a good person otherwise. But he was really … he just didn't want to settle down. And all these women fell for him constantly."

"Seems he was a real charmer type," Rodney suggested, with a frown.

"It was the darndest thing. I mean, he could get them to do absolutely anything. They just didn't seem to care. They would cheat or even walk away from their relationships, happy to sign up for whatever with him, based on whatever method of persuasion he had over them. He never spent a night alone unless he chose to, and, let me tell you, that bragging doesn't go over well either."

"Did he go around bragging about his conquests?" she asked.

"Not so much to me. I'm happily married and made it clear that I would not want that lifestyle. Yet somehow he frequently let little hints drop one way or another." Barry sighed. "All I can say is he angered enough people that, when I heard he had been found dead and that it was murder—God, this sounds awful but—I can't say I was surprised."

She asked Barry if she could speak to several of the other office staff. He agreed and hung around through each interview. However, Kate found the others to not be quite as open and honest as the manager had been. Still, it was basically the same story at every turn.

When she got around to Lanny, the receptionist who had burst into tears upon seeing her badge, Lanny was sobbing again, yet confirmed that she'd had a relationship with Robert early on but didn't understand what had gone wrong. However, they had parted peacefully.

"But it still hurt to constantly see him with other women." She disappeared once again, bawling her eyes out.

With that, Kate decided it was definitely time to leave, and, leaving their cards behind with Barry, asking the manager to let her know whether anybody had any idea who Robert might have been seeing or of any disgruntled husbands they could put names to—or boyfriends for that matter.

Barry nodded, accepted their cards, stated he would keep it in mind.

Back outside in the parking lot, Kate looked over at Rodney. "It's sad, you know?"

"What is?" he asked, as he got in the car.

"I mean, these three men—John, Kurt, now Robert—can apparently have everything, yet all they want is something short-term. I don't understand it."

Surprised at the comment, he faced her and shook his head. "Why is it that you don't want to get married?"

"Hadn't considered it," she replied. "It's never even been on my radar."

"And now? Even with Simon in your life?"

"Still not on my radar," she stated, with a shrug. "In our case, it would just bring up more issues to deal with. I don't see the point of changing the status quo. God, can you imagine? Everybody would say I married him for his money," she complained, with a shudder taking over. "Yeah, nope. ... That's not happening, ... at least not anytime soon."

He chuckled. "Maybe marriage is not necessarily for everyone, but, for a lot of people, it's where they're happy."

She belatedly remembered that Rodney was divorced and supposedly had been a very happily married man. And right now, it was all she could do to squash her curiosity.

He asked her, "Where to?"

She frowned and said, "We need to contact the detective handling this case."

"You think they're connected?" he asked, as he pulled up to a stop sign and turned to her.

"How can it not be? Insurance industry, decorations on the body, come on."

"So, do they have work-related meetings to find each other, as in customer and adjuster? Or is it about adjusters from within the industry who know each other?"

"Maybe," she muttered, "but that's …"

"It's far fetched, isn't it?"

"All of this is at the moment." She shook her head. "We'll call the detective when we get back to the office and see if we can get a copy of his report on Robert's death."

"He might be quite pissed off that you were here, already talking to people."

"Maybe," she conceded, "but it's not as if we were there for that reason."

"Yeah, we didn't exactly get answers on the other death, did we?"

A horrified expression took over her face. "No, we didn't, did we? Damn it!" She picked up her phone and contacted Barry Quinn.

When he answered, his voice was tired.

"I'm sorry to interrupt you again, but one of the reasons we stopped in there in the first place was to ask you about another employee."

"Oh?"

"Kurt Conner."

He gasped. "Oh yes. He died some time ago. I don't recall just how long it's been."

Kate noted, "That's two men from the same office."

"Not the same office," Barry hurriedly clarified.

"It's not the same office?"

"No, Kurt worked in a different department, different area," Barry explained, "not here at all. Thank heavens, that would be too much to deal with right now."

She pondered that as she asked him a few more questions. "Would you say they had a similar personality?"

"Oh, no, not at all. I mean, Kurt was very playful and really a good guy, engaged even, I think," he shared. "However, I didn't know him quite as well as I knew Robert. And, of course, I also live close to Robert. So, that proximity at home and at work had me getting to know Robert better, but Kurt was just an all-around friendly guy."

She asked a couple more questions, but nothing else seemed to shake loose. When she ended the call, she looked back over at Rodney and asked, "Is it really all that common for guys to just hook up?"

Rodney nodded. "It is common, but I don't think there's anything wrong with it. You just get men at that certain stage of life. It's not until later in some cases that they want to settle down. In other cases, they want to settle down and have babies right off the bat."

"But not always."

"The women don't always either."

"Right," she noted, "particularly if they've got a career. Once a woman steps back out of her career, it can be hard to get back in the running again."

"True," he agreed, with a nod. "Again, not something everybody has to consider."

"I'm a career cop," she confirmed, "so it's definitely something I have to consider."

He chuckled. "I don't think Simon would in any way want you to give up your job."

"Are you kidding?" She snorted. "I think he would be overjoyed if I quit my job. As far as he's concerned, I just keep ending up in trouble."

"After the last woo-woo case," Rodney stated, as he rubbed his still very sore ribs, "it appears you are the one always saving us, not exactly getting yourself into trouble."

She smiled as she looked over at him. "There is that, isn't there?"

"Yeah," he grumbled, glancing back at her. "As much as I hate to admit it, there's absolutely that point."

"As long as you're not holding it against me."

"I'm not," he said, "but I am certainly aware of it. Just because I might want things to look different doesn't mean they are."

SIMON GROANED. KATE wouldn't leave his mind—or this other woman he had seen briefly in his vision. Yet every time he thought about Kate, the other woman's features—that he could barely see—superimposed over hers. It was very frustrating for him. Finally he called Kate. When she answered, he asked, "Are you having a bad day?"

She snorted. "Let me just say it's not a great day."

"Okay. I just can't seem to let go of thinking about you."

"Maybe that's a good thing," she replied, with a smile in her tone. "I am not sure what you're expecting from me though."

"Nothing," he told her.

She laughed. "When most people say, *Nothing*, they're expecting something."

"Of course they are. Yet most people aren't us."

"So, don't you forget that."

He could see her frowning, and it just blew him away sometimes. "You don't need to frown."

She sighed. "I'm fine, by the way."

He groaned. "I'm really that obvious, *huh*?"

"Sometimes. Yeah." She groaned lightly. "We, *uh*, we may have two other related cases though."

Simon froze. He was in the act of going up the stairs in one of his almost-complete rehabs. He stopped, looked down at his phone, and asked, "Seriously?"

"Yeah. I'm as unimpressed as I imagine you would be."

He laughed. "It's a hell of a way to start the new year. I think you were looking for a couple easy cases, weren't you?"

"Right. Easy cases. Does anybody know what that means anymore?" she asked. "We went to an insurance office today because somebody from that office, well, a similar branch within the company, had died about two years ago. No autopsy done though."

"And that was the second case you caught."

"Right, at least I thought so. However, as we walked in, the place was in complete shambles because one of the men who worked there had been found dead this morning."

"Surely not in similar circumstances," Simon replied in shock.

"Wrong. He had been wrapped up with some Christmas-theme wrapping paper or something. I don't know. … We're heading back to my office. I'm trying to find the detective on the crime scene this morning. The manager from the office happened to live in the same building as our victim, and so he found out about it first thing this morning. The rest of the office had just found out when we arrived, so it was quite the mess and not in a good way."

"Is there a good way?" he asked.

"No, probably not, but you know what I mean."

"I do, but I can't imagine."

"At first I thought it was some sex-game gone wrong," she muttered, frowning.

He shook his head. "You frown too much."

She groaned. "I don't know how you always know when I'm frowning *on the phone*, but you can just knock it off."

"Yeah." He chuckled. "If I thought your words would help with that, I would stop it. However, your words nor mine ever seem to make any difference. Sorry about that."

She added cheerfully, "Obviously you're not sorry, but I'm fine anyway. I don't know what's going on, but I will get to the bottom of it. How are you doing?"

"I'm doing pretty well, but either your face or that other woman's face is constantly in my mind."

"You got a face?" she interrupted.

"No, I did not get a face." After a pause, he sighed. "I'm just saying that the whole vision with the praying woman keeps popping back up in my brain. And, no, I have no more information at all. So, forget about that."

She smiled.

He could almost see it. "Damn it."

"Now what?" she asked in frustration.

"You just smiled, and I can see it. I can see you right

here, … beside me."

She didn't say anything for a moment, then sighed. "As much as that is really creepy, it's also cute."

"I know," he agreed, "so I'm not upset about it, yet—"

"*Yet*," she repeated, now completing his train of thought, "you're upset about it."

"No, it's just very distracting. If it were just you, it would be fine. But, as I told you, this other woman just superimposes over your features."

"I'm not sure what that would mean."

"Let me just say that the features don't fit." He waited, knowing that she'd pretty well stopped, stock-still.

"What?"

He sighed. "Think of somebody trying to fit a *traditional wife* persona on top of you and how it won't fit, but they keep trying."

"Good God."

Then he heard somebody calling out to her in the background.

"That's Colby. I've got to go." And she ended the call.

He stared down at the phone, nodding. Was somebody trying to fit Kate into a mold? An old-fashioned mold in his mind that she never would fit into because that's not who she was. But, whatever *this* was—and he had no idea—it was all about being a traditional wife, whatever the hell that meant these days. Simon couldn't imagine anybody less interested in that role than Kate.

Traditional wives still existed obviously, but that wasn't for Kate. And anybody trying to force her into that role? She would knock them to the floor in a heartbeat, even at the suggestion that she should be a traditional wife. He imagined some church minister admonishing her but getting nowhere.

Not that Kate would punch a man of the cloth. Did the churches still demand that women stay at home, tend to the children, regardless of the hopes and wishes of each individual?

Simon shook his head. He couldn't see it. And yet he couldn't unsee the other woman's image. Was it more about their differences? Simon sighed. He needed more information, which probably meant more visions with this other woman, trying to find out more about her. Was she a spirit or was she alive and well on planet Earth? Either way maybe Simon could help her.

CHAPTER 6

B ACK IN THE office, Kate set up a whiteboard and put up all three *known* cases. She couldn't be sure that they were all 100 percent connected yet, so she left a question mark up there in the right-hand corner—until she had a chance to connect with the detective on the Robert Blake case. She and her team also needed to make contact with somebody who worked on Kurt Conner's death some two years earlier.

Rodney was working on both right now. He walked in a few minutes later, a frown on his face.

She looked over at him and asked, "What's the matter?"

"They don't really have very much for us on Blake," he began. "When I say, *not very much*, it's pretty-much nothing."

"*Of course*," she replied in frustration, "because they just found him."

Rodney muttered, "I presume so. Yet I have two things on the John Smith case. One, there are no working cameras around that whole block. Seems an outage took them all out. and none have been fixed." Kate groaned at that. "And the super's background check was clean, except for one speeding ticket like nine years ago."

"What about the older case?" she asked him.

"Kurt Conner? We've got a little bit on that one. They

seem to find the *connection* very doubtful, and I'm putting it nicely. So, that's one thing."

"But we don't really have a whole lot to date, except for the specific details, which are starting to gather momentum," she noted. She continued to write on the whiteboard and then heard Colby behind her. He asked what points she felt were indicative of this potentially being the same killer. She pointed out the couple things she had so far.

Colby frowned, then scratched his slowly growing beard and nodded. "Those are definitely red flags."

"I hate to even think that somebody could be out there doing this. We have two years between them," she pointed out.

"Only now we have an escalation if it's the same killer," Rodney pointed out, "because we're dealing with the one from a few days ago, John Smith, and now we've just got the newest one, Robert Blake."

"True," Kate agreed. "So I've asked Reese to dig a little deeper in her search, broaden it a little wider, just to see if we have more."

"More?" Colby shook his head.

"Particularly around the holidays. … That's one of the common things. Kurt Conner's death was two years ago, and we now have two more dead guys within days of each other. Did we miss somebody who died the Christmas in between? So I'm not sure if it's the same person killing all three." She hesitated, then faced Colby, before adding, "Or the same group."

At that wording, Colby's eyebrows shot up. He dropped a hip onto the corner of the desk nearby where she stood and said, "Okay, I'll need a little more information when you drop a line like that."

She shrugged. "I don't have anything to go on yet."

"Except your gut," he pointed out shrewdly.

She winced. "Yes, my gut."

"Which is starting to sound a whole lot like a *psychic*," Rodney supplied.

"No," she snapped, glaring at him. "God, Rodney, let's not be thinking that, much less speaking of it," she muttered, as she turned her back to them. However, she could hear the two men talking behind her for a moment, before Colby returned his attention to her.

"Speaking of psychics, have you heard anything from Simon?" he asked.

"I've heard a couple things from Simon," she replied. "Nothing connected to this yet."

"But you're saying *yet*."

"Yes, I am," she grumbled, turning to glare at him, "because there isn't much."

"You want to tell me what he has heard or seen or found that's new?"

She gave him the little bit she had, and he stared at her in surprise. "And, from that, your instincts are telling you it's a church group?"

"No," she corrected. "I never said that." His frown flashed again, and she raised both hands in frustration. "Let's forget about Simon and focus on good police work."

Colby's lips twitched. "I never expected us to *not* focus on that," he clarified. "Yet we're also very aware that Simon has an impact, a helpful one, on many of these cases. So, if he's got something to say, it would be a good idea to consider it."

"I am not against considering anything he says," she murmured. "I am against anybody thinking it'll be better than what we can do. If he can tell me a direction to move, fine. … However, up until now, he doesn't have that."

"Interesting," Colby replied.

She shifted to eye him shrewdly. "What's interesting about it?"

He chuckled. "Just the fact that he connects to so many cases."

"Or doesn't connect to," she pointed out. "Sometimes they aren't even our cases. Look at the building he bought and what happened there."

Colby shook his head at that. "That one still blows me away. I mean, those corpses had been hiding there for decades, their poor families having no idea where they were for all these years. Then Simon looks at a property and *bam!* Next thing you know, we've got more cases to open up."

"Yeah," she muttered, "that's the story of my life with him. More cases to open up."

He burst out laughing. "Yeah, good point. Okay, everybody just keep working away on what we have so far, and we'll see where this goes."

He headed toward his office but looked back and added, "I understand that somebody named it the *Believe It or Not* case, and I thought that was a ridiculous name—thinking something about a seasonal killer might be better. But now I see it's not such a bad name for it." With that, he exited the bullpen.

"Outside of the fact that they all were gift-wrapped in Christmas decorations," she noted, "I find their position at work to be a bigger common denominator."

Colby stepped back into the room, his brows knit. "The insurance industry, you mentioned."

"Yes," she confirmed. "Not necessarily the same company, but these three dead guys were all insurance adjusters."

He frowned, studied her, and asked, "Are you thinking payback or anger over adjustments? Because, honest to God, I'm surprised we don't have more insurance adjustors getting killed, considering they make such important and personal decisions for people. Sometimes there's just not enough money to handle everything destroyed in an insurance claim. Denied insurance claims can have disastrous impacts on people and frequently do."

Kate nodded. "Tell me about it. I'm still going through that with my apartment right now."

Both Colby and Rodney faced her, their eyebrows raised.

She shrugged. "They don't seem to think the repairs should be covered because I'm a police officer. They contend that I had a greater chance of this happening, and apparently I didn't let them know of this looming event."

They both stared at her in shock.

Rodney snapped, "That's absurd. You are held responsible for somehow knowing that somebody would come and shoot up your apartment because of your line of work?"

"Yeah, and that's where the problem comes in," she explained. "Being in this line of work, they think I should have work insurance that would cover it, so they aren't liable." She stared at him, chalk in hand, and shrugged. "So, I can understand killing off some insurance adjusters, but I'm not sure the work that these men did was their cause of death."

"I don't think it was either," Rodney agreed. "They had clients, but I don't think they were dealing with the end user of policies already in force."

"Right," she agreed, "that would be my take on it too."

"So, who do you think it is?" Colby asked her expectantly.

She shrugged. "The easy answer is a very unhappy lover who found out each of our victims were playing the field, apparently openly, yet informing all the women in their lives," she shared. "So, that's definitely something consistent with all three cases."

"Right, they were all considered playboys in a way, weren't they?" Colby pointed out, nodding.

"Yes, but Kurt less so," she stated. "When his engagement ended, even he was not thinking of settling down. We need to find out if any of them were ever married before they were killed. That could be the reason they didn't want to settle down because they had already given it a try."

Rodney picked up the stack of papers he had brought in. "This is what I've got for case files for the other two. At least what we have at the moment. No mention of prior marriages in here though."

"Good enough," she replied. "Put them on my desk. I'll take a look in a few minutes. I just want to ponder this for a bit."

At the doorway, Colby stopped again, then turned ninety degrees and looked at her. "You want to *ponder* it?"

Startled, she pointed to the murder board she was working on, then back at him. "Yeah, why?"

His grin widened. "You sound a little more like Simon every damn day."

She glared at him. "You do know those are fighting words, right?"

He burst out laughing and headed back to his office.

Still, it all had her a little on edge. The last thing she wanted was anybody thinking that what she did, or would potentially do in the future, had anything to do with some psychic ability—hers or his.

She was all about doing a good job for the right reasons, in all the right ways, and that had nothing to do with any of the woo-woo stuff that Simon kept coming up with. Yet it was hard to get it out of her mind now that both Colby and Rodney kept bringing it up. Once that started, she couldn't let it go.

She sent Simon a text, asking if he was okay.

Instead of texting back, he phoned her. "Normally you're not concerned with my day-to-day. What's going on?"

She frowned down at the phone, hating that he was as perceptive as he was.

When she didn't answer right away, he asked, "The guys are on your case again?"

She sighed. "How is it you know *that* shit, but not the other shit that I really need to know?"

He burst out laughing. "One of the wonders of the universe, isn't it? But, if I had all the answers you needed, you wouldn't have a job."

"I would," she declared, "because these people would still need to be picked up and processed, and statements of all concerned would still need to be taken. So, actually, it would be great if you had all those answers."

"I don't," he stated.

"Oddly enough, apparently most of my crew, including Colby, seem to think that you do."

"Ooh, ouch," he muttered. "Sorry. I can try and stay out of your cases for a while."

"Sure, that's *great*," she muttered. "Now if all the woo-woo elements going on in your space would also give us that consideration, it would be great." She took a deep breath. "In the meantime, you and I both know that, for whatever reason, you seem to have a susceptibility, shall we say, to things connected to my cases—even though I would just as soon you had nothing to do with them."

"That kind of a day, *huh*?"

"It shouldn't be," she stated, "except that other case I mentioned earlier can't be ruled out."

He went silent, then asked, "How is that even a thing?"

"I don't know," she grumbled. "I'm still working on that. I'm a little concerned."

"A little?" he repeated. "Concerned that there could be a lot more?"

"A lot? No," she declared, "but I am concerned that there could be a couple more. We have three deaths over two Christmases, but what about the Christmas in between?"

Simon whistled, coming through loud and clear to her.

She sat down, slumping onto the edge of the nearby desk, the same spot Colby had recently vacated. "Yeah, that's where I'm at."

"Not the easiest place to be," he agreed. "I'm sorry, Kate."

"As long as it's a good day on your end, I'll take that as a win."

"I've barely even started," he noted, "so I have no idea. I will soon see what problems I've got for the day."

"But if they haven't called you already, maybe that's a good sign." She left it at that, feeling mildly better after the call. Simon always seemed to understand where she was coming from, and that helped. It always made her feel small to even think she wouldn't want his help on something like this.

On the flip side, it just made her angry to think that other people would consider his help better than doing good, solid police work. It's not that woo-woo was better, but it was obviously difficult for everybody if she had access to some source of information that allowed her to do her job better than everybody else. All too frequently it appeared that, after laboring with limited results, Simon would suddenly pop in with something bizarre, yet clearly connected. Then everybody would jump on it, making her feel as if, had she only done something earlier, they could have gotten further along and much sooner.

It was a no-win situation in her case, and it was very frustrating. As she finished off the three cases on her whiteboard and headed back to her desk, she sat down and quickly went through the files that Rodney had left, wondering where she was supposed to go from here. *Smidge*, she thought. She should visit the coroner and find out if he had any ideas about what was going on.

If he was the coroner on all three of these cases, it would help. She checked the jurisdictions, then found out he wasn't the coroner on the case that had just come in today. Still, with the details of that branch, she pulled the autopsy reports on the previous case and headed down to see him. When she walked into the morgue, nobody was there, which meant everybody was most likely out in the main surgical area, working on the tables.

She donned the blue scrubs, pushed open the big door, only to have somebody yell at her to gown up. "I already did," she replied, immediately annoyed.

Of course Smidge had yelled at her. When he saw it was her, his shoulders slumped, and he announced, "If you're looking for answers, I don't have them yet."

"I know," she replied, "and I'm not trying to add more work to your plate."

At that, he turned to glare at her. "But ..."

"But … we may have found two other victims, potentially connected to this case." His eyes widened in shock, and a bank of fury lit his expression and filled his gaze. He reached out a hand.

She handed him a copy of the Kurt Conner file from a couple years ago. "The other one just happened this morning, but it's not in your jurisdiction. I literally walked into their business offices to question them about the death of another employee within the same company but a different location from two years ago. This one," she noted, tapping the papers she had shared with Smidge, "and now somebody else had been murdered overnight. They are over in the Coquitlam jurisdiction. I can get you a case number, and I would appreciate it if you would look at all three reports."

He stared at her. "I don't understand why."

"I don't either. I also don't understand the how. So, this third one will have its own issues."

He snorted. "They all have their issues," he declared. "And the other one?"

"This third one was two years ago, around this time of year, … so it happened around Christmastime. He was wrapped up … in tinsel and whatnot that time."

His eyes widened, and he stared at her.

Kate continued. "Also the three dead men were all in the insurance industry."

Smidge didn't say anything, just stared at her.

She sighed. "I know. We're already dealing with the suggestions about somebody's claim being denied or something along that line."

"What do you know so far?"

"All three men were lotharios. All three played the field and had very active female traffic in and out of their lives, and we don't know if that is connected."

"Yet how can it *not* be connected in some way?" he muttered, as he looked at the file in his hand. "They're all dead. I don't have time to go through this right now," he shared, tossing the Kurt Conner file on a ledge behind him and returning to the corpse on the table. "However, I'll take a look later."

"That's all I can ask," she said.

"Why is it always you?"

She turned and frowned. "Why is *what* always me?"

"Why is it always you who comes in here?"

"Nobody else will. They're scared of you," she stated cheerfully.

He frowned at her, and then an evil grin overlaid his expression with delight. "Perfect, that's just the way I like it. ... How come you're not? Afraid of me, I mean."

She looked at him and shrugged. "Because my bark's as bad as yours, I guess," she suggested. "I recognize another sheep in wolf's clothing."

His eyes widened in horror, and then he started to laugh and laugh. "Oh my God," he muttered, still in fits. "If anybody else ever told me that ..." And he left it at that.

"I know," she agreed, with a grin. "I would feel exactly the same way."

He nodded. "Besides, it's just as well that they don't come in here," he noted. "They're disruptive, and I don't like that."

"Nope, neither do I. None of us want our work ... interrupted," she shared. "So, I'm here just for a short time, to see if you've got any updates, and to hand you that third file in the hopes that you'll take a look at all three of the reports, when you get them on your desk. Then I'll expect to hear from you."

"It won't be today, you know?"

"No, of course, it won't be," she muttered, with a sigh.

"Unfortunately, it is what it is. I can contact the morgue on the newest one and see who's handling it and tell them that we might have something similar, which would be pretty damn ugly all around. However, I'm not sure what else to do," he admitted, as he stared down at the body on his table. "A very healthy, physically fit male in his prime and yet look at him. Cut down for what?"

"I don't know," she admitted. "It's that *for what* part that we're still working on, hoping we can figure it out soon."

He nodded. "You got your work cut out for you on this one."

"Don't I always. It's not as if we have any immediate insights. It always ends up a whole lot different than what we think it'll be."

He didn't say anything for a long moment, then pivoted, taking a long moment before he spoke. "This one feels …"

She nodded with a sad smile. "I know. The minute I start to say *feels* in the office, you can bet everybody started in on me about picking up psychic flashes or something. I fucking hate that."

He started to laugh, but just enough horror filled her expression that Smidge grew serious. "I don't envy you there. I can't imagine having all my good work tossed away as being something that some psychic told me."

"Oh, don't worry," she piped up. "It's definitely a challenge for me too. It just totally pisses me off."

He nodded, then, as she walked away, he called out, "Has Simon connected with you? Has he mentioned anything about this one?"

"We're not sure," she replied, turning back to him.

"He's connected to something in a vision, but we're not sure it's criminal, so there is that."

"I never even thought about that." Smidge gave her a head tilt. "He connects to a lot of things that have nothing to do with crimes."

"He does, and that's a lot of it, but now?"

His eyebrows lifted.

"Unfortunately, since he's met me, the bulk of what he connects to are crimes," she shared. "I mean, even when buying real estate, right?"

"Tell me about it," Smidge muttered. "I'm still dealing with those bodies."

"You got no help?"

"We did bring in an anthropologist, and that has helped somewhat. It's fascinating to see the deterioration of the bones in that dry and dusty setting. The bodies were almost falling to pieces."

"I'm glad it's interesting for you," she noted, with a calm smile. "Can't say I share that enthusiasm. Makes my job a hell of a lot more difficult."

"You're not on that case anymore, are you?"

"We know who did it, and we know why," she confirmed. "So, in that sense, no, but, once you're into something like that, it's not something you can exactly walk away from. Where are you at with it?"

"We're still trying to ID all the bodies that were found, and we don't have any matches for quite a few of those. In the previous property owner's letter, a couple names were mentioned, but nothing we could use to make specific conclusions at this point. So, everybody's looking for next of kin and potential DNA matches." She talked with him for a little bit longer, and he grew annoyed. "What did you find on the other victim, the third one in this file you gave me?" he asked.

"I'm still trying to figure out a cause of death."

"You and me both," he muttered. When she just stared at him, he shared, "I'm not seeing anything here for our John Smith."

"I hate those cases," she cried out.

He laughed. "Yeah, but we'll find it, even if it takes whatever it takes. Now I'll just have to wait until the tox screen comes back."

She asked, "Anything else you would do?"

"I don't see anything suggestive in the stomach, and I'm not seeing any needle marks—which, considering that he's both fit and active, would make some sense. Unfortunately not enough sense that we can get anything done here fast enough to confirm COD in a hurry, but we will run what we need to run."

She stayed and watched as he worked, both amazed and saddened that such a fit, healthy young man ended up dead at this relatively young age. She was still pondering that as she walked back outside and took several deep breaths of fresh air. Something about a morgue always made her want to stand outside and feel the goodness of being out in nature again.

She got back into her vehicle and headed to her office. She was pondering what she could do next without a cause of death. Thinking about the other two victims, the one who had no autopsy done—Kurt Conner—came to mind. She found it questionable, so she pulled over and called the sister again.

When Esther answered and realized who it was, she sighed. "I really don't want to be hashing all this up again.

My husband is very unhappy about it as it is."

That seemed to be an odd thing for her to say. Kate quipped, "I'm sorry to disturb your husband, but this is about your brother's murder, and presumably you want to know what happened to him."

"Yes, of course I do," she snapped. "Look. I'm not trying to be difficult, but my husband is not a big fan of the police, and just you calling here or visiting me can cause me trouble."

"I get it," she replied, "and I'm not calling to cause you trouble, but can you tell me why there was no autopsy done on Kurt?"

"Yes," she began, "because I figured there was no reason to cut up my brother when it seemed he died of a drug overdose."

"What do you mean?"

"I knew that he was using, that he had done drugs in the past, and there was no visible sign of trauma. The police thought it was suspicious, and they mentioned something about it on the phone, but I never questioned it," she explained. "They told me that it was foul play and that they were concerned about *not* doing an autopsy. I fought them on it, mostly because I knew my husband was very against it."

"Good Lord," Kate muttered. "Why were you against that? I mean, how do you expect the police to solve your brother's death if you don't have a cause of death?"

"There were needle marks on his arms," she pointed out. "That should have been reported somewhere in the file."

"Yes, but I'm really surprised that an autopsy wasn't done."

Silence came from the other end. Then Esther stated,

"That would be because my husband went off on it quite heavily, saying it was against our religion, and a few other choice words at the time." She took a breath, stifling a sob. "He complained that we wouldn't have a proper burial if it were about drugs, and, if Kurt overdosed, it would bring shame to the family." She sighed. "I don't remember everything. It was just a very sad time. The police told me that, if I had a strong reason to suspect it was a self-administered overdose, then they might let it go, but, if it was classed as a homicide, they would have no option but to proceed with an autopsy."

"And you signed off on that?" Kate asked.

"I did. I knew what Walter thought about it, and I tried to fight the police at first, but my husband stepped in and made quite a scene about Kurt and his problems with drug abuse, especially since he had the needle marks. I think they ran some drug testing, and it came back positive, and that was the end of it."

Kate looked down at her file copy and did find notes to that effect. "Interesting."

"Why?"

"Because that's not usually something we skip," she told Esther. "Drugs can be administered by someone else, so it could have been murder."

"That fact won't solve anything though, will it? He's dead. Kurt is gone, and no amount of anything will bring him back," Esther declared. "I wanted him back so badly at the time, and just the thought of everybody cutting into him and doing things to his body upset me horribly. Then Walter just basically threw a fit and did everything he could to stop it."

"What religion are you?"

"We're not terribly religious, but he was at one time. At least for a while, and then he walked away from it. So, at the end of the day, I don't know what he was," she muttered.

Kate found the notation as she went through the file. It wasn't even in the autopsy notes, where they would document observations and everything they did do, even if it wasn't a full autopsy. "They put it down as a drug overdose. I'm just telling you that, because we have another case that's very similar, it may impact that ruling."

An audible gasp came from the other end.

"Was any life insurance involved?" Kate asked her.

"No, not that I know of," she muttered. "Walter would have dealt with that."

"That may be," Kate replied, "but, from an observer's point of view, it looks very much like you and your husband were doing everything you could to hide something by not allowing justice to run its due course. And that," she stated, "now that I'm looking into this case file, makes me extremely suspicious."

"Of what?" she asked, with an audible shriek. "We had zero contact with him."

"You say zero contact, so what does that mean? No visits, no calls? In how long?"

"It means almost no contact. I hadn't seen him in a long time prior to his death. We used to be quite friendly, but then I got married, and he was doing drugs, and my husband would not tolerate that and didn't want me around Kurt. So, it became very difficult to even see him. ... I had to stop, and Kurt seemed to be happy with that. We would text every once in a while. I knew he was living life large, and he was doing lots of drinking, and he was ... just being Kurt," she muttered. "It's not the lifestyle that we wanted for ourselves, and, with the prospect of kids coming, it's definitely not anything we wanted around them."

"And when you say *living life large*, what do you mean?"

"When he was in high school and in college, he was always involved in whatever the latest craze was. He didn't miss a party." She took a deep breath. "He was always the popular guy, but that involved a lot of drugs and alcohol. I assumed a big part of him was seriously unhappy, and he was just trying to hide it. I don't know. He was pretty broken up about his engagement ending."

"How so?"

"For him, it was really serious, but they broke up, which had a really negative effect on Kurt. He went off the wall, but, for him, that meant he just partied more and more," she shared. "We couldn't understand that. I mean, if you're trying to clean up so you're in a better position to get married, why would you turn around and go off the wall like that?"

"Rejection can hit people in different ways," Kate noted, "so maybe that was just his way of dealing with it."

"He fell back into his same old bad habits, and I didn't see any reason to put up with that or to deal with anybody being difficult about it."

"Did he have any insurance?"

"There was no life insurance as far as I know. My husband handled it all. I already mentioned that."

"Money?"

Esther gave a dry laugh. "There was no money for anybody," she stated, "but we made sure he was buried properly. There wasn't anything else I could do except mourn him. Walter took care of everything. Honestly, I would like to park this conversation and never have you bring it up again."

"That's one way to never remember your brother," Kate replied. "I hope you find some way to honor the life that he had and to try to understand that, even though he wasn't necessarily the happiest of people, it doesn't mean that he was less than anybody else."

"I didn't mean it that way," she protested, but then she fell silent. "I don't know," she added, sobbing now. "Maybe I did. I don't know. It's been a very difficult time for me because we used to be quite close. But growing up and getting married, everything changes."

"It's supposed to change, and I get that."

"Yeah, it does, but not necessarily in the way I expected or understood. So pardon me if I don't come across as the grieving sister. It hit me very hard at the time. My husband did whatever he could to minimize the damage and to keep me sane because it wasn't that easy."

"I get that too."

"You lose somebody important in your life, and it's easy to lose perspective," she noted. "Now, if there's nothing else, I have to deal with the baby." With that, Esther ended the call.

Kate didn't have a chance to ask her about anything else.

SIMON STOOD AT the top of the building on a bare girder. He had his safety line on as he just stood here, taking in his surroundings.

Joe, his foreman on this project, stared at him anxiously.

Smiling, Simon pointed out, "You know that I come out here all the time."

"I know it, but I hate it. If anything happens to you, we're all up a creek."

Simon burst out laughing. "I don't think inspecting my property is quite that extreme."

"Oh, it's that extreme all right," Joe muttered, then waited until his boss was safely back on solid flooring before he continued. "Look, boss. I understand why you feel the need to go out there, but it's not safe."

"Oh, come on. Let it go, Joe." Simon sighed. Joe had been with Simon for years now and knew what made him tick. "Sometimes I want to do it because it's beautiful up there. Plus, it's a skyline I'm changing. It's an emotional response to the work I'm doing because it's important in so many different areas," he explained. "That is why I stand here and watch and confirm that it's all okay."

He reclaimed his coffee and enjoyed it from a safer location, now on the second floor, wondering to himself what the attraction was when he scaled to the top of his bare buildings in progress and just stared out at the skyline around him. He knew what it was to some degree and had been honest when he had explained it to his foreman, yet so much more was involved in it.

Simon filled a need within when seeing the vastness of space around him, knowing that he had a hand in the building of it, the creation of it. While he acknowledged just how massive the sight line was from any of his buildings, he also knew how absolutely insignificant his efforts and accomplishments were in comparison to the huge, huge world around him.

When he'd finished his coffee, he asked Joe, "Anything else or can I move on?"

"You can move on."

Simon nodded, as he continued to take in his surroundings. "Any problems with any of the staff?"

"Nope, everybody is doing great at the moment," Joe noted. "Yet I hate it when you even ask those questions because, as soon as you do, we'll turn around and find issues."

Simon laughed. "I think that's pretty standard for all of us these days. However, as long as you're not dealing with anything troublesome, it's all good." He stepped away, and a vision slammed into him, bending him over. Joe rushed to him, as Simon's vision blurred.

"Boss, whoa, whoa, whoa, whoa."

Simon was slipping in and out of the vision while trying hard to stay in the present. He gasped. "Help me sit," he whispered, and that was the last thing he did before he was laid out flat on the floor, his foreman barking orders for everybody to stay away, keeping watch so nobody came close, yet keeping an eye on Simon.

He sensed Joe standing there, hovering like a mother hen, and Simon kept wishing this would all just go away. Still, he knew his vision wouldn't leave until he delved into the actual details of what was going on there. Yet he didn't find anything in particular. It was just this space, a weird space. Then he heard that soft, ever-so-gentle voice.

Believe, child. It's all right. Just believe. He's here for you.

Then suddenly he was back in the present, alert again. He slowly got up, his foreman glaring at him.

"That's why," Joe grumbled through gritted teeth, tears swelling in his eyes, "that's the fucking reason why I don't want you out there on the end of those girders. … What if *it* happens out there?" Joe took a moment to calm down. "You would have been a goner for sure," he whispered.

Simon nodded. "Let's hope it doesn't because, when this happens, I don't have much control."

Joe's anger spilled over again. "I know, damn it. That's why I don't want you going out there in the first place."

Simon understood Joe's anger was really fear. Fear that something would happen to him, fear that everything they had built together would implode. Simon didn't want to consider that either. However hard it was to deal with the uncertainty of his visions, Simon really did understand where Joe was coming from. After all, *shit happens*. He really just hoped these events would pick their times a little bit better.

He made his way slowly down to the first floor, Joe walking carefully behind him to confirm that he was okay. By the time Simon reached ground level, he felt a certain sense of relief, but nothing compared to the obvious relief on his foreman's face. He punched him lightly in the shoulder. "I'm heading home for a while."

"Yeah, you do that," Joe muttered, "and maybe get an assistant to come here and there and everywhere instead of you. You need to take better care of yourself, boss. We can't lose you."

"Meaning that anybody else is more expendable?" Simon quipped.

"To a certain extent, yeah," Joe stated, "but anybody else is also not likely to be doing the things you do, probably wouldn't be out on the girders. You? … That's a whole different story."

With a raised hand Simon acknowledged his foreman's fears and took off to walk toward the downtown core. The walk would do him good. It would help him to re-establish contact with the world around him, even if it still felt unsteady, trying to clear the residual fog in his brain.

He walked a couple more blocks, heading almost instinctively to a coffee vendor outside a little park where he could sit. ... Simon just needed to spend a few minutes collecting his thoughts. Yet, if so, he should have done it right then and there. Not understanding exactly what the draw was, he headed into the coffee shop, grabbed a coffee and a breakfast sandwich, and took them outside to sit in the sun. As he settled here, he felt a weird sense of déjà vu coming over him.

He still felt the influx of energy from his recent vision in his building, yet something was odd about the energy currently around him. He wouldn't forget this vision for a while, and Joe would likely never forget. As Simon sat here, munching, he searched the energy, the source of the uncertainty, that weird sense of something going on. Yet nothing was clear-cut about it. He just noted a weird off-putting energy slipping around him, and he couldn't quite get at it.

His grandmother would undoubtedly say that he was the one who was resisting, that he should just get out of his own way. Then it would all fall into place. With that in mind, he closed his eyes and let his thoughts just drift.

He was alone in the park, yet people were walking past, more than likely oblivious to the strange man sitting on a park bench. Even so he wasn't getting anything. He finished his coffee, taking the last bite of his sandwich, and just sat here, contemplating the changes in his life, positive and negative. How very inconvenient these visions were when he was on a mission and had things to do and places to be. These issues came together in a way that made his life even more complicated.

As he went to get up, his legs collapsed out from under him, and he sat back down, hard. Suddenly he was not in the park anymore. No foot traffic passed in front of him. No movement, no sound, just ... silence. Then he heard it again, that same soft sobbing, that painful heartbreaking anguish of some grief, longing, something.

He had no idea what this vision was about, and it wasn't interactive. He couldn't reach out and talk to her. He was simply seeing this pale ghostly image of somebody, their grief spilling all over.

Grief should be private. It should be something that people had a chance to just let loose and to let go, knowing they were safe and secure from prying eyes. Yet here Simon was, a voyeur in someone else's world.

He didn't want to be a witness, but he had no other choice for the moment. Or was it his inability to step back out of it? Maybe there was an etiquette to this.

As he sat here—with no idea of who and what was going on around him, yet knowing that something was happening—he watched and waited until she calmed down. Meanwhile Simon mentally sent her healing energy, energy of love, energy of peace, energy that *This too shall pass*, all in the hopes that it would help.

By the time she finally stopped crying, he was shifted from that vision to another. He tried to stop it, to pull back out, but his whole body had been bent forward with the force of a firm hand behind his neck. Meanwhile somebody else said, *Look. You can't ignore this. … Just look!*

Then suddenly that force was gone, and he was back in the park, staring around in confusion.

CHAPTER 7

KATE SLAMMED HER pen on her desk and glared at the whiteboard in front of her.

Rodney raised his eyebrows, and she just shrugged. He noted, "Something's not making you happy."

She snapped, "I just can't see any particular reason for any of this. I mean, outside of everything superficial that connects these guys, I don't see anything. No one person worked with all three victims, which I thought was a shoo-in as to why these victims were picked."

"We have a whole bunch of nothing," Rodney muttered.

"Yeah, we do. We don't even have a list of girlfriends."

"I am still going through the phone records," Rodney noted, turning to her, "and they're taking a bit of time, but I'm not seeing anything crossover on dating or anything of that nature."

"Oh snap," she said. "That would have been a really good thought, but it didn't even occur to me."

He laughed. "That's why we're a team."

She nodded. "I was focused on a completely different angle, the workplace, but that dating angle's good too. Yeah, keep following that trail, focusing on the details for that."

"This case seems to be bothering you a lot," he noted, as he studied her.

"It's not that it's bothering me so much," she began,

"but … I saw that poor man on the autopsy table. John was young, strong, in his physical prime. He had a good job with so much ahead of him, and yet he's dead. Why? Then there's our victim Kurt, with the sister allowing a drug overdose to stand in for her brother's cause of death without an autopsy, caving to the pressure from her jerk husband. She actively participated in that and went along with a quick burial to put *the shame of it* all behind her."

Kate tried to shake off her frustration, not sure she could. "It adds to the whole distressing scenario, and I'm left to wonder whether anybody even cared about these victims, or were these guys all so isolated that they seemed to be easy targets?"

"Oh, now that's an interesting point," Rodney stated. "I hadn't really considered that they might be looked at as targets."

She shrugged. "Despite all the women they each saw, these guys remained isolated, … all of them. We're still waiting to hear more on John Smith, the first one, which hasn't been helpful to date. Then Kurt, who died two years ago, had family who didn't seem to have his best interests at heart. Now Robert Blake, the new one from today, we don't know anything about his next of kin yet. However, so far, it looks as if nobody was truly close to him either," she shared.

"So, let's bounce around some ideas," Rodney suggested.

"Okay." Kate began, "I think they are all connected, but, rather than one killer, we have multiple killers because these two on top of each other kind of rules out that one person could do it."

As Colby walked into the bullpen, he noted, "That's an awful lot for just one person to pull off that fast."

"Unless they weren't alone," Kate added.

Colby nodded.

Kate pointed out, "If it were more than one person, that would be more feasible. ... Yet I get what you're saying. It's not terribly likely to be the same killer, is it?"

"No," Colby stated. "It's not terribly likely, but we aren't that far into the investigation yet. Keep an open mind. You need to—"

"I know," she mumbled, standing up. "I'll go canvass the neighborhood regarding John, our first victim, while we wait for the reports coming in from Robert's death, just found this morning, yet may have happened the previous night."

Colby gave her a wave and a nod and took off for his office.

Kate frowned, then sighed, now turning to Rodney. "We may need to talk to Kurt's neighbors, about our victim from two years ago. We already have similarities," she confirmed, "but we don't have the right information to connect these, outside of the fact that a pretty specific MO is involved, which makes it very weird." With that, she added, "I'm heading over to John's apartment and will talk to anybody and everybody who's around."

"At our initial visit," Rodney reminded her, "all those women told us how John was a really good person."

"Yeah, I hear you. And we did speak to a lot of John's neighbors on that floor. Maybe first I'll hit the coffee shops around the corner, and the gym that he went to," she added, then faced Rodney. "You don't have to come. None of these will be anything particularly inspiring."

"Right," Rodney agreed. "In that case, I'll stay here and keep working on these phone lists."

"That would be great because, if we could come up with anybody who's connected to both of the recent deaths—"

"Or all three," Rodney interrupted, "that would be huge."

"Yes," she confirmed. "You work on that, and I'll be back in a bit. I'm just too frustrated to sit here and twiddle my thumbs while I try to figure out another angle. Better I'm out in the field doing something. At least then I'll feel as if I'm getting somewhere." With that, she took off but stopped at the doorway and called out, "And since it's already three o'clock …"

"Right." Rodney chuckled. "I'll see you tomorrow."

She nodded as she headed to her vehicle. She drove to where they had already spoken to both the property manager and John's neighbors to get her bearings. From there, she found the neighborhood gym and the closest coffee shop.

As she walked into the coffee shop, she looked around and smiled. It was neat and clean, probably doing a decent business during the day. Yet right now it was definitely more on the dead side. She crossed to the front counter and ordered coffee. She held up a picture of John Smith. "Do you recognize this guy?"

The woman looked at it, smiled, and nodded. "Absolutely. He's a regular here." She laughed. "He's great fun to be around, always has a laugh and a joke for everyone. Why are you looking for him?" When Kate held up her badge, the woman shook her head. "Oh no."

Kate nodded. "Yeah." She paused to let the woman settle with that news, then asked, "And your name?"

"Minnie," she whispered. "He's one of those really good guys. The kind you want to come in every day because he's a breath of fresh air, always has a nice word to say. He doesn't bitch and complain. He always makes you feel special," she shared, followed by a heavy sigh. "What happened to him?"

Kate paused, then replied, "He was murdered."

At that word, Minnie's face went pale, her eyes went round, and she gasped in horror. "Seriously?"

Kate nodded. "I'm sorry. He was found dead in his apartment."

Tears flooded Minnie's face, and she muttered, "That's unbelievable." She stared off in the distance, trying to hold back more tears, and shook her head. "He will be sorely missed."

"That's good to hear," Kate replied. "Nobody should go to their death with people completely forgetting them."

"That won't happen here," Minnie stated. "He was always really friendly and kind. The women here loved him."

"You too?"

She nodded. "Yeah," she confirmed, more tears spilling. "I loved him. He was a hell of a good person to have around."

"How many of the women working here right now or even among your customers would know him?"

Minnie glanced around, suddenly more uncomfortable than she had been at the beginning.

Kate explained, "I am just trying to get a feel for his personality, what he was like with people." She leaned in closer and lowered her voice. "I understand from his office and his neighbors that he was a bit of a ladies' man."

Minnie laughed. "That he was, but it was always respectful, you know? He never got in your face, and he never tried to touch or grab. He wasn't that way at all. He was always just—" And the tears once again came to her eyes. She brushed them away and shook her head. "God, this is so hard. Can you excuse me for a moment?" She quickly dashed into the back, and it was a few long moments before she came back.

Kate had taken a seat and was just sitting here, waiting to see if Minnie would return or if maybe she needed to go home. If so, Kate would contact her at another time. Minnie did eventually come back, with a box of tissues, her eyes red-rimmed, and with a man who had a truly sorrowful expression on his face.

"Is it true, … about John's death?" he asked.

Kate nodded. "Yes, it is. I'm sorry. And you are?"

"Max, the manager here." He shook his head. "Wow, I mean, that is not what I expected."

"What do you mean?" Kate asked.

Max sighed. "John was one of those bigger-than-life guys. He worked out all the time, was watching what he ate. He never seemed sad. If ever somebody should live forever, it would be him."

"Can you share the details?" Minnie asked Kate. "About how he died?"

"Not right now. My investigation is still underway."

Max grimaced. "Yeah, it figures. You know the saying, *the good die young*," he suggested. "Whenever you meet or hear about somebody you really admire and who always has a smile for everybody? *That*, … that was John."

"And was his smile bigger for the women?" Kate asked Max.

"Oh, absolutely." Max chuckled. "He was very much a ladies' man, and, as long as he didn't bother the ladies, it was okay with everybody."

"So he never became a problem, did he?" Kate asked.

Max turned to Minnie, still dabbing her eyes, and she shook her head. "No. He set more than a few hearts aflutter. If he had asked out half a dozen of the women here, I think probably all of them would have said yes. He was just that kind of a guy," she shared.

Max nodded. "I have to agree with that," he added, with a wry look. "He definitely had the ladies eating out of his hand, but he was a good tipper, he was respectful, and I never had any problems with anybody here. So, there didn't seem to be any issue with John, no need to reprimand him or to even ask him to ease up on the flirtations," he told Kate.

"He was always very respectful," Minnie stated, "for lack of a better word."

"That word works," Kate replied. "Just because you're a ladies' man doesn't mean you have to make it difficult for everybody."

"Right," Max confirmed, "and that would not have been him. Damn." He looked at her and asked, "How did he die?"

Kate shrugged. "We're looking into it, but he was found dead in his bed."

Max snorted. "I almost want to laugh at that." Kate's eyebrows shot up at the manager. "Not the fact that he's dead," Max clarified quickly, "but because he was such a ladies' man that being found dead in his bed kind of suits him." He looked over at Minnie and asked her, "Doesn't it? I mean, that's where he always wanted to be—with somebody in bed. Maybe it sounds harsh and superficial, and I don't mean it that way, but, if you had asked him how he wanted to go, he probably would have suggested something about a heart attack in bed, while enjoying himself with somebody half his age." He sighed.

"There are definitely worse ways to go," Minnie added, with a smile.

Max nodded energetically. "Oh my gosh, there absolutely ly are worse ways to go, and, for John, that would have been one of the better ways. So I'm not upset about that part," Max explained. "Yet I can see how this will affect everybody here." He turned to Minnie beside him. "Maybe it's a guy thing to die in bed, and I don't mean it in a bad way. It's just, … I think that's how John would have looked at it himself."

"I've met guys like that," Kate replied. "They don't have anybody serious. They're all about fun and games, until something happens, and it's no longer fun and games."

"Exactly," Max agreed in relief. "And I'm really not trying to be disrespectful or anything."

"I get it," Kate noted. "I'm not taking what you're saying in that way."

"Thank God for that."

"How often did John come in?" she asked them.

Max turned to Minnie, and she shrugged. "Not every day but probably at least two to three times a week." She sniffled again.

When the bell rang as somebody entered the coffee shop, the manager chose to go see to their order.

Kate turned to Minnie and asked, "Did you ever date him?"

She seemed surprised, glanced back around at her manager, then shook her head. "I didn't, no, but I know one of the girls here did."

"Do you know who it was?"

"Yes," she whispered. "Will you talk to her?"

"Yes, I need to," Kate whispered back. "We're still trying to get an idea of what happened, who saw him last, what he was doing, that kind of thing. Did you know who his current girlfriend was? He was dating someone long-term for a while."

She shook her head. "No, I don't. I think, in Mary's case, they broke up a while back. She was pretty bummed about it. She was really hoping it was the real thing. She's getting a little older," Minnie added, "and I know she was really looking for the whole marriage thing."

"Which I understand he was very much against."

"Yes, and he made no bones about it. We all warned her, but, when you fall hard, it doesn't matter what anybody says. You're always positive you can change their mind."

Kate didn't say anything, but she kept hearing that line over and over again. It wasn't exactly something she understood because the guys had the right to decide. It was their decision to make. Just like it was the women's right to want marriage. In her world, those kinds of decisions rarely changed, but she didn't have a ton of experience with relationships in the first place.

She got the name and contact information of the barista Mary, who wasn't on duty that day at all. Kate thanked Minnie for her time, waved to Max, and left to sit in her car, deciding it might be easiest to just go to Mary's apartment and take a chance that she might be there.

Plus, Kate was better able to gauge reactions if she was in person versus over the phone anyway. She keyed in Mary's address and noted it wasn't all that far away. Most people tended to find work close by, so this would only be a ten-minute drive. Traffic wasn't too bad, and she got there just before four o'clock. She walked up, knocked on the woman's door, not calling first, and, when the front door opened, a guy stood there, just staring at her.

Kate smiled, held up her ID, and asked to see Mary. He frowned, looked back, and called out, "Mary, the cops are here for you."

Mary gasped and came running, and Kate realized that she was probably thinking something was wrong. "I just need to ask you a few questions."

"Sure," she agreed, "but I don't know about what or who." Then she looked at Kate's card closer and gasped. "You're a homicide cop."

"I am," she confirmed.

"Who's dead?" she asked, her voice deepening anxiously. "Is it my family?"

"No, not at all," Kate replied. "I'm not here for a death notification but for questions about somebody who has recently passed on."

"Oh, right, of course," Mary muttered. "It's such a shock to have the police come to the door. … I'm just a little unnerved."

"That's fine," Kate replied. "The questions are about John."

"John Smith?" Mary asked, staring at Kate, and then all the color fled from her face. She whispered, "Are you saying John's dead?"

"Yes," Kate confirmed. "He was found dead in his bed a couple nights ago."

She just shook her head and whispered, "Oh my God, oh my God."

The man beside her asked, "Who's John?"

Flushed and flustered, Mary turned to Kate.

Kate offered an answer, saying, "John's an old friend of hers, a customer from the coffee shop."

The man beside her glared at Mary. "Surely you didn't know him well enough that you're completely distraught over this."

Kate addressed him. "You don't need to be here while I

question Mary. If you want to leave ..."

He stiffened and glared at her, then at Mary. "Is there any reason Mary can't talk with me here?" he asked, his tone aggressive.

Kate studied his features. "No. However, there's also no reason for you to get difficult about this. I have a few questions to ask Mary. So either you leave us alone to do that or perhaps you stay quiet. Dealer's choice."

His glare upped in wattage. He obviously did not appreciate being reprimanded.

Kate didn't really care. She had a few questions to ask, and asking them would make her investigation a little bit easier. She looked over at Mary and added, "Unless you prefer for me to ask them in private."

She sighed. "It won't matter. He'll still get upset."

"And why is it I will get upset?" he asked, still aggressive.

Mary turned to face him straight-on. "Because he was before your time, and you don't like hearing about previous boyfriends."

"You went out with this guy?"

"Yes," she snapped, staring at him. "I did. I had a life before I met you, and you need to remember that. But," she took a deep breath and added, "it was only for a few months."

He relaxed at that. "Is it that big womanizing dude?"

"Yes, that's him," Mary confirmed, as she turned to Kate. "Go ahead. What is it you need to know?"

Kate was very happy to see Mary standing up to her volatile boyfriend with his self-confidence issues. It allayed some of Kate's fears for Mary if she stayed in this possibly abusive relationship. "When did you last see John?"

"Oh my." She closed her eyes as she thought about it. "I

didn't work yesterday. I'm on my two days off. I did work the day before, but I don't think I saw him then, so maybe Thursday, maybe Friday?" she offered, with a frown. "It was a couple days ago anyway."

"Did he act any differently? Did he mention anything was wrong in his world?"

Mary considered her questions. "It's not that he was acting differently," she began, "but he definitely wasn't his usual happy, joyous self. I did make a comment to him, asking if he was having a bad day, and he shrugged it off and mentioned something about *maybe a bad life*, which I thought was a really odd thing for him to say."

Kate wrote down a couple notes about John's odd reaction and then asked, "Did he elaborate as to what was wrong?"

"No, not at all," she said. "He just made a joke about *knowing how to pick them*. I didn't know what that meant, but he was looking at me at the time. So I wasn't exactly sure what I might have done that would have been wrong," she admitted, with a roll of her eyes.

"Did you two often disagree or argue when you dated John?"

"Not really. Only one issue was between us, but it was a big one. I was looking to settle down, and he was not," she shared. "So, he was playing the field and yet chose somebody who didn't want that. Did he warn me about this issue? Yes, he did, and I guess I didn't really believe him."

"You thought you could change him," Kate offered.

Mary winced. "I know it sounds trite, but I guess that's exactly what I thought," she conceded. "I'm definitely older and wiser now," she claimed, with a hurried glance at her easily upset boyfriend. "I'm not looking for that permanent relationship anymore because I realize it's just not what most men want." She shrugged. "So, I've just shelved all that for the moment."

"Right," Kate replied. "Understood." And she did. In other words, Mary still hoped for that married relationship, but this current boyfriend would potentially not go in that direction, nor would she go in that direction with him. Either way, Mary would be better off to leave this jerk beside her than to stick around, especially if her heart wasn't in it.

After a couple more questions, Kate thanked Mary and explained, if need be, she might get back to Mary later, as they were just starting this investigation. More questions might come up.

"I only went out with him for a couple months," Mary shared. "He was a great deal of fun, but nothing was serious or long-term with him. I think that was the biggest surprise when I did go out with him. He just …" She frowned and thought about how to put it. "It's as if everything was a bit of a joke. He was deliberately never serious, and that got to be pretty wearing after a while. It just seemed as if life was always this big joke with him. After the breakup, I remained friendly with him at the coffee shop of course. I never wanted my job to be impacted, but I guess I had a new awareness that maybe he just wasn't as happy-go-lucky as he seemed. Or maybe it could have all been a front," she added, "like maybe he wasn't all that happy ever."

Kate nodded. "Thanks for the insights. It'll help as we go forward." And, with that, she smiled and stepped back.

The boyfriend slammed the door right in her face, but she heard Mary protesting his actions from the inside. And he had absolutely no reason to do that, except to initiate more power and control over something that he was very uncomfortable with. But then that was Mary's problem, not Kate's, and she just hoped that whatever decision Mary ended up making about her jerk boyfriend, she would go about it a little carefully because he didn't seem to be the kind to take a rebuff very easily.

Back in her vehicle, Kate jotted down a couple more notes about the entire scenario involving this interview and then turned her vehicle toward home. If nothing else, she could get in early, get some sleep, and start fresh in the morning. At least that's what she hoped for now. As she made the short drive to Simon's place, she started to get this really weird feeling that something was off. She pulled off to the side, knowing instinctively it was Simon, and she phoned him.

Even as she called him, she was cursing herself because calling him wouldn't help. If he were already in some vision, he couldn't answer the phone. With that, she pulled back into traffic and headed home at a slightly faster rate than was good for her. By the time she pulled in, she was incredibly worried. She raced inside, seeing Edgar at the front desk, and asked, "Is he home?"

He nodded, but his face was somber as he shared, "He doesn't look great."

"No, I haven't had a good feeling about him over the last hour," she muttered, as she raced forward.

"You want me to tell him you're coming?"

"No. It might be better this time if he doesn't get a warning."

He nodded in understanding and added, "Good luck."

She smiled. "It's not so much about good luck as let's just hope he's okay," she muttered to herself, as she went up the elevator. As soon as the door opened to Simon's penthouse suite, she walked in, finding him sprawled on the couch, staring out at nothing. Yet he didn't appear to be in a coma or any meditative state. She walked over, dropped down beside him, and asked, "How are you?"

He turned to her for a moment, silent, as if having trouble focusing. "I'm fine, but obviously you aren't."

She shrugged. "Just got a weird feeling about you on the way home—and not in a good way."

He smiled, reached out a hand, and just held hers. He didn't say anything, just holding her hand as if it were the most precious thing in the world. She stared down at their linked fingers and waited. He would tell her or not. Either way, she would have to be happy with the choice he made because he often couldn't even put these visions into words when they happened.

She settled back and just gave him time to verbalize whatever was bothering him.

<hr>

SIMON OPENED HIS mouth, intending on telling Kate nothing, only to have the words come flying out. She listened carefully, and, when he finally fell silent, he watched as she looked down at their hands. She now held his hand, stroking it as if that alone could calm him. And the foolish thing was, it was calming him, but in a way that he wasn't expecting.

"I keep finding these lost people, and I don't know what this particular woman's problem is. I don't know what her pain is," he added, "and, because I don't know, I can't help. I kept sending her all this healing energy, all this love, letting her know she's not alone in the world."

"But you don't feel as if she got it?"

He frowned at Kate. "I don't know if she got any of it. I prefer to think she did, but, of course, there's always that very big possibility that she didn't."

"But wouldn't that little bit getting through even be something?" she asked.

"That would be … I don't even know how to explain it."

"But it made you sad."

"Very sad," he stated. "Yet we have leftovers for food, so *you* don't have to be totally sad. At least there is something for you to eat."

She snorted at that. "Isn't that too funny? Glad you have a sense of humor at least."

"Sometimes," he muttered, "it feels as if that sense of humor is all that's keeping me going."

She nodded. "I get that too. Sometimes it seems as if we have no options, and this is just who we are. And I'm not sure that's necessarily true, but I can understand the message coming from your psyche when telling you that."

"It's just so sad. I don't know what it is that she's trying to do, or what's happened to her, but it feels very much as if she's at the end of a road, and she doesn't have—"

"Time? Like she's out of time?" Kate asked.

"No, that's … Well, maybe that is it. She's out of time, and I don't know what that time is or what it's supposed to look like or why a time frame is even attached," he explained. Then his eyes fogged up but soon cleared. "Maybe she's out of time, and she's a little desperate, and both of those are important factors."

"But that doesn't necessarily mean that you can help her."

"Not only that," he added, "I'm not sure she's even open

to be helped."

"So, tell me this," Kate began, as she let go of his hand and stood up. "Is this woman alive, or is this woman dead?"

He frowned at her, and a bark of laughter escaped. "I didn't even consider that." He stared at her in wonder. "I literally did not even question it, so I have no idea. How is that even a thing?"

She smiled, reached out, pulled him to his feet, and replied, "Because we know that a lot of times what we think is happening isn't really happening. So, it's important that somebody find some semblance of control in all this and make some sense. So, when and if you get a chance to see her again—you're not talking to her, right?"

"No, I'm not. Visions only. I'm just a fly on the wall."

"Then, the next time you see her again, maybe figure out if she's alive, if she's dead, if she's haunting something or someone, or if she just wants to … wallow."

He stared at her. "Do you think people want to *wallow*?"

She shrugged. "I think, when you get desperate enough or lost enough, wallowing is about the only thing that feels good. Do they want to wallow? I think if they were shown another choice, they wouldn't want to. However, when you're in such a state, I'm not sure you can see any other option is even available."

CHAPTER 8

K ATE WOKE IN the middle of the night to someone groaning, speaking gibberish, and then heard a heavy groan again. She turned to Simon and realized the sounds were coming from him. She sat up in bed and leaned closer, wondering what was going on. It was not so much praying but maybe someone fervently trying to convince themselves of something. She listened harder, trying to see if this had anything to do with the woman he kept seeing, the woman who kept destroying his peace of mind because he couldn't seem to help her.

These people in his visions seemed to come and go of their own volition, and it's not as if he had a choice apparently, which drove them both batty. Just as she did with her cases, he would dive into these vision issues, do something about it, then get back out again. Yet they didn't seem to have that option here. She listened a little longer, and his voice rose and fell in volume.

She noted a feminine quality to his tone, but she couldn't tell if it was because he was channeling someone or speaking to someone. She also couldn't believe the term *channeling* was a part of her thought process now. Kate struggled with the whole concept of channeling, but it did seem to fit here because she certainly wasn't hearing Simon's voice. When the feminine-sounding voice rose almost to a shriek, Kate lost her temper and snapped, "Knock it off. If you need help, ask. Otherwise just leave him alone."

The place went silent.

She flopped back down onto the bed and stared up at the ceiling. She waited the better part of half an hour before Simon's calm but amused voice kicked in.

"That's one way of breaking up a session."

She groaned, then rolled over to see him, those magical eyes looking at her with amusement, and muttered, "I'm sorry, but I just couldn't stand her caterwauling anymore."

He blinked several times. "Her?"

She frowned and nodded. "Let's just say it sounded like a *her*."

He nodded. "I got female all the way on it myself, but when you said *sounded*, I—"

"Yeah," she interrupted. "Sounded, as in you were her."

He frowned at that, rolled over on his back, and stared up at the ceiling.

Kate added, "And I get that probably doesn't make you happy."

He didn't say anything, but it was obvious her choice of words wasn't necessarily the best in that moment. She explained, "Look. I didn't know quite what to do about it. Her voice just kept getting louder and louder. I should probably … record it next time, so you have an idea of what you sounded like."

"How about you don't?" he muttered, quiet but firm.

"Because that would feel as if I were crossing the line, betraying a boundary of some kind?" she asked him.

He sighed. "Yes, and I know it sounds foolish."

"No, it's fine," she noted. "The only reason I would do it would be so you could hear what she's saying."

"Then I would probably be scared to go to bed at night," he shared, turning again to look at her. "Imagine if you were doing these things while you were sleeping, and somebody decided to make a point of letting you know."

She groaned. "Fine, I'll erase that thought from my brain," she muttered. "And I probably shouldn't send her away."

"Did you send her away?"

"I told her to stop her caterwauling. And basically, if she wanted your help, she should just ask for it. Otherwise she should just shut the fuck up."

He stared at her in astonishment, then burst out laughing. And kept laughing. When he could stop enough to speak again, he told her, "That's my Kate, right to the point. *Don't waste my time. Don't waste anybody's time.*"

"Right," she declared. "What's the point of doing all this if we can't help? If we can help, tell us how. And, if we can't, let us off the hook."

He started to chuckle again. "If I could figure out how to make her do all that, I wouldn't feel as if I'm wasting so much of my time on a day-to-day basis."

"Exactly," she cried out. "And just listening to you, listening to her, I know she wants help, but I don't know what we're supposed to do about it."

He didn't say anything. He just reached over a hand, clasped hers, then whispered, "If only I could figure that out ..." And he just let his voice trail away.

She nodded. "I know I shouldn't get upset. I suppose if we took a close look at what she's trying to do in that state, from God-only-knows what position she's in, we could do more to help."

Simon sighed. "I just don't know how."

"And the *doing more to help* part," she acknowledged, "sounds as if we have the ability to do something. And, of course, if you can't do something, you're just being tortured by it all for no apparent reason." His smile was bright and, as always, full of love. As he looked at her, she sighed. "I guess I screwed up again, *huh?*"

"No, not at all," he declared. "In a way, waking up to you snapping at me like that, I knew instinctively that you weren't mad at me, but your words? … They were so *Kate*. It was just you all the way. Somebody was disturbing your sleep and wouldn't get to the point."

"It's not even that she was disturbing our sleep," Kate explained, "but, yeah, maybe that's part of it because God knows we need sleep. It's more that she's been tormenting you, and you're getting all these visions, and you want to help, but you don't know how. And, if she can't give you information on how to help, what's the point of bothering you?"

He didn't say anything for a long moment.

"Did you ever talk to your grandmother about this?" Kate asked.

"Of course, but not in a way that came with clear instructions or a clear way to handle it. For the most part, as you well know, I didn't want anything to do with it back then."

"Yeah, I hear you," she muttered. "That was then, but how about now?" He snorted at that, and she grinned and rolled over. "I do have a suggestion on how to take your mind off it."

"Oh, do you now?" he murmured, his eyes alight with interest. He rolled over, tucked her into his arms, but then he yawned and snuggled right beside her.

She leaned over and gave him a kiss. "Just sleep. These visions, they always drain you."

"They do," he murmured. "Although I could be persuaded otherwise." Yet his words were already slurred, and he drifted off to sleep in her arms. She smiled and held him close, for her mind was spinning over this woman who seemed to have the ability to contact him.

When he surfaced a few minutes later, he grumbled, "Your thoughts are too loud. Shut them down."

She snorted and obediently rolled over and tried to sleep. She did sleep a little bit. She dozed off before eventually getting up and taking a shower, with the intention of going to work early, at least getting something accomplished that way. It had been a pretty rough night in the overall scheme of things.

And the last thing she wanted at this point was for anything else to go wrong. Not that anything was necessarily wrong, but it was pretty darn hard to maintain cohesiveness or whatever when everything was backed up in her brain. If she could just find a way to let her brain unwind, that, in itself, might help. She climbed into bed again, just thinking.

When she rolled over the next time, she realized, in spite of herself, she had fallen asleep again. It still wasn't necessarily time to get up, but it was certainly time to consider moving. She managed to get up again, cursing herself for not doing something constructive when she'd been awake the last time.

Now she just felt groggy and slow to get at anything mentally. By the time she had washed her face, brushed her teeth, run her fingers through her hair, and dressed for work, she smelled coffee. Following the delicious aroma, she entered the kitchen. And, of course, there Simon was, perfectly dressed, sitting at the table, shaved, clean, and ready to go.

She sighed. "How come you always end up looking as if your day is perfect and as if you haven't had a crappy night?" He chuckled, while she kept ranting on and on about it. "You look perfect, and I just end up dragging the night with me and feeling as if I'm carrying the burden of it as I head into the day."

He looked over at her. "I'm not sure what to say to that," he began, "except what years of experience tells me. If it'll be a bad day, the only thing I can do to combat that is to make it a slightly better day by being prepared and ready."

"*Right*," she grumbled. "That is such a *you* answer."

He looked at her, surprised. "You really did have a bad night, *huh?*"

She shrugged. "I should have just gone to work early that first time I got up, instead of falling back asleep, because that just made things way worse in my head."

He didn't say anything at first, studying her carefully for a moment. "Is there anything I can do to help?"

"No," she muttered, with half a smile. "I just need to shake the cobwebs from my brain and shift back over to my workday mode and get ready for whatever is ahead of me. Hopefully something new will break in this case."

"And hopefully no new victims."

She stared at him, horrified. "Don't even say that. That would be terrible."

"I can't believe you have potentially more than one in this strange Christmas-themed murder scenario as it is. It just seems completely wrong on so many levels."

"Yep. I hear you. At the same time, I'm not sure what options we've missed, if any," she admitted, with a shrug.

"It's not exactly a common MO."

"You should know by now that you haven't missed any-thing, right?"

"No," she stated, her tone bitter. "It'll just take a bit more digging to confirm nobody else is out there. Reese's working on it."

He nodded and smiled. As she headed to the elevator to leave, he added, "Another weekend is coming up. We could retreat to the *Running Mate*."

She stopped, turned to him, and frowned. "Maybe."

"*Maybe*, as in maybe if things go better than they have so far?"

"Yeah," she muttered, giving him a wry look.

"I guess that's good enough for me," he replied. "I'll have the boat ready, just in case."

Her eyes lit up at that.

He smiled. "I can see that just might be enough to turn you around."

"Oh, I'm totally happy to go out on the water, even to stay docked at the marina," she stated, "but you and I both know it depends on my caseload. If I catch anything new, who knows?" She raised both hands in frustration. "This case is already confusing enough, and I'm just not sure what else will come up as we get further into it. But, just in case, I approve of any weekend retreat. Definitely prepare the boat, and, if I can get away, that's where I would love to spend my time … with you."

"Good enough," he said, with a smile. With that, he got up, walked over, and laid a kiss on her, smiling as she stood there still struggling to regain her breath. "You really are out of it this morning."

She glared at him and announced, "It's not that I'm out of it."

"Yes, you are."

She sighed. "Let's just say that, if I had a day off coming, I could easily go back to bed and just spend it there."

"And I would be right there with you," he added, chuckling. "However, I also know that you don't have the caseload right now that would allow you to even consider taking the day off, no matter how many days you had coming. You could never make peace with that mentally."

She waved and walked out and headed to the office, still shaking the fog from her brain.

Although the traffic, crazy as it was right now, had done a lot to get her more grounded. By the time she walked into the office, she was ready for that extra coffee. The minute Lilliana saw her, she smiled and muttered, "*Uh-oh*, doesn't seem you had a great night." When Kate stopped to glare at her, Lilliana held up her hand. "Sorry."

"Yet you're right."

Lilliana nodded. "I overstepped. That's an unspoken rule, isn't it? When somebody clearly had a rough night, don't emphasize it by calling her out."

Kate groaned. "You know when you have that night and can't sleep, so you decide to just get up and at least get a jump on the day, only to fall asleep again, then wake up feeling worse than you did before?"

Lilliana snorted.

Kate continued. "Then that shitty night becomes an even bigger shitty night because your opportunity to do something proactive about it is gone."

Lilliana was laughing now and added, "There's fresh coffee. That'll help you shake it off."

"I hope so," Kate muttered. "Glad you see you're full of piss and vinegar this morning, so you must be feeling better."

She headed for the coffeepot and found Colby, who looked her over, and she knew exactly what was coming next.

"Not a great night, *huh?*" She stopped and glared. His eyebrows shot up, and he added, "Okay, I'll, *uh*, I'll just head back to my office now and maybe check in with you later." But his grin was wide as he did so.

She sighed as she grabbed some coffee and headed back to her desk. "Apparently I'll just be the joke of the office this morning."

"Until you get back to your fine old, unfettered self," Lilliana suggested, "so don't worry. We'll all be scared of you once again."

Kate turned to her and snapped, "Please tell me that's a joke."

"Sure. It's a joke, but you are quite a commanding presence when you want to be."

"Yeah, not today though," she murmured. "All I'm trying to do is solve cases.'

"And that's the thing you don't see. When you *really* get into it—into that mode—it's a very direct *get out of my way* thing. It's pretty amazing how you come across then."

"Sounds as if I come across in a really shitty way."

"No, not at all. It's a hell of a power move, and it's really effective. I always thought I was the one who was good and in control, but, at times, you absolutely put me to shame." Lilliana was still laughing as Kate settled at her desk. But then Lilliana shared, "Look, Kate. I don't mean any of that in the wrong way. You keep being you. ... That's what makes you so special. Don't ever let anybody's comments change that. You are an excellent detective with a style all your own, and the beauty of it is that it works." And, with that, Lilliana turned and ignored her.

Kate then felt a little quieter and calmer than when she had first arrived. It was such an unusual thing for anybody to really give a compliment in this department. They were, as far as she was concerned, part of a team. And, therefore, maybe that wasn't necessarily something that everybody needed to focus on.

But it was interesting to have it come up. And she was grateful for Lilliana's last words about not letting it affect her because, when Kate did get focused, she *really* got focused, and everybody should just get out of her way because, at that point, she was on a mission. And it didn't really work to have people in the way of each other.

So, she understood that part of it.

Still, it was a bit of a shock to have it called out quite so plainly. Refocusing, she pulled out the three files, wondering where and what she could move forward with today.

Colby came over, a cup of coffee in his hand, and skimmed what she was working on. "Okay, you've got two days to find some way to move this along," he told her. "Otherwise, we both know we'll be inundated in other cases."

She just nodded and didn't say anything but continued to study the files in front of her. Time limits to solve these cases were truly a fact of life here, more so when you had a busy caseload and were chronically understaffed. After all, Andy was out on an extended medical leave. Even their hopes to have a new team member hired to replace him were now useless thoughts. So, with Lilliana out sick until today, even for just a few days, it was deeply felt by the other members. Plus, Owen had been granted an extended holiday period, for whatever reason, so this team was really hurting. Their usual five members were down to three for a while now, sometimes with just Rodney and Kate showing up.

And, with somebody out sick, or others away on training or vacation or whatever, it was an ongoing issue for every department. Still, Kate was not the kind to happily let a case slide unsolved, not if she could do *something* to move it along. And, for this case, for these three, that would be a bit of a challenge.

So she sat back and, from start to finish, reread one file, then went over the second one. She barely got finished with it, when her phone rang. She glanced down to see Smidge was calling.

She lit up and reached for her desk phone. "Hey," she answered, "I'm really hoping you've got good news for me."

"Of course you are," he replied in that same cranky tone of voice, "as if I've got good news for anybody."

"Oh, you don't then, do you?" she muttered, frowning.

"No, I don't," he stated. "For Kurt Conner, killed two years ago, his death was due to drugs, and they did put it down as a drug overdose."

"Was that documented?"

"Yes, thoroughly. I did not see his body obviously, but the good coroner on this one did. I won't call anybody's skills and abilities into question on this one, but it certainly wouldn't have been wrong to have called that one as he did, particularly with the family pushing to release the body without a full autopsy. Now, I don't have anything yet on the third one, the latest one you stepped into," he added, "so you'll have to wait until we get the report in."

"What about John Smith, the first dead guy we found?"

"Ah, the case at hand. I did get the tox screen back, and his system was loaded with lots of drugs," he shared. "Now, looking at it individually, I wouldn't have been overly concerned, and it probably would have gone down as a possible suicide. However, based on the fact that we potentially have a third one, I'm not as comfortable closing it right now. Not until you get me some more information either way."

"Right. No pressure though," she quipped.

He gave a bark of laughter. "Yeah, the best thing I can do is dump it back on your plate," he said cheerfully. "So, bring me more information, and we'll go from there. In the meantime, the tox screen does say drugs were in John Smith's system, and I'm still looking for a way to see if it was self-administered."

"What are the chances of that?" she asked.

"I'm leaning for it *not* being self-administered because we didn't find any drug-related paraphernalia at the crime scene nor needle pricks on the body. However, that doesn't mean somebody didn't administer the drugs in another manner. Maybe the killer removed the drug-related implements because of a life insurance policy or whatever," he shared. "You should definitely be looking into that."

She whistled silently when she ended the call, then looked over at Lilliana, who had raised her head and was staring at her.

Lilliana shook her head. "I don't understand how you can talk to him and have a real conversation."

"Yeah, Rodney says the same thing," Kate muttered. "I don't get why you guys have such a problem with him. He's always been easy to talk to for me."

"Yeah. Something is really weird about *both* of you," she muttered. "I gather he had some information."

"More like orders for us to keep searching for more. He did say lots of drugs were in John Smith's system, but no drug paraphernalia was found at the crime scene. So, based on that, he leans toward murder, but he's not willing to rule on that at the moment because he wants to confirm nobody removed the needed paraphernalia, for instance, to get away with insurance or whatever."

"Oh, good call," Lilliana agreed, with a nod. "And then, when you complete all that …"

"Exactly, when I complete all that, Smidge will probably put it down as murder. Also a lot of fingerprints were at John's apartment, and I mean *a lot* because he had a very healthy, sexually active life," she shared, with an eye roll, "and, therefore, we'll have to sort through a lot of people on his case."

"And get fingerprints to match."

"And a lot of them we may never ID because he had so many women through his apartment who probably won't be in our police database," she pointed out. "So we'll have to figure out whether life insurance is on the table or not and work backward. I'll return to John's apartment today and check out his paperwork there and see if Rodney can track down any life insurance policies on him too."

"If Rodney doesn't come in soon," Lilliana shared, "I'm kind of at a stagnant place on my case. So, I could give you a hand with that part."

"Sure," Kate accepted, as she handed over the files. "It would help to figure out the life insurance thing and whoever was the most recent of his girlfriends. So far, we haven't found out who he spent his Friday night with. No cameras were at John's apartment."

"Possibly one of the neighbors stopped by?"

"Can't tell. No cams even in the hallways to that apart-ment building. Nothing on that line at all. He did have an affair with somebody at work, the cute young receptionist, which was frowned upon. But apparently it was broken off, and she was devastated, but he moved on, as in the same week."

"Of course he did," Lilliana muttered, followed by a groan, "but that doesn't mean *that* woman killed him."

"Good call," Kate noted. "Meanwhile I'll head over to John's apartment to search for life insurance or whatnot. Now, if you want to call Lanny, I don't want to talk to her at the office. I want to see her in private."

Lilliana nodded. "Good call. I'll let you know."

With that, Kate got up and headed out.

Rodney hadn't made it in yet, and, if he wanted to join her later, he could. Otherwise he had plenty to keep him busy for the moment, just trying to find all of John's girlfriends from his emails and texts and phone calls.

Kate just needed to get out of the office and to get something done, so she felt she was accomplishing something today. Otherwise she would just sit there and fall asleep at her desk. She drove back over to the victim's apartment and got the manager to let her in.

He took a quick look around John's apartment and winced. "The cops really don't leave it clean, do they?"

"No," she agreed. "When it comes to murder, the police and forensics teams tend to be very thorough."

"Yeah, but *thorough* means a huge mess here. Who'll clean this up?"

She smiled and replied, "You'll figure that out, while I'm still trying to figure out who was John's most-recent partner and if he had a life insurance policy." With that delineated, she closed the door firmly in his face.

She was wary of landlords after the still-unresolved issue

at her own apartment. It still pissed her off every time she thought about it. Simon had offered to get somebody to look into it. After all, he had so much experience with and dealt with insurance companies a lot.

She didn't know what the hell that meant, but, so far, there hadn't been any follow-up. She sent him a quick text, asking if he had any feedback info on it, but didn't really expect an answer.

She returned her attention to the task at hand, as she stood in the bathroom of John Smith's apartment, looking at everything he had around, wondering what she could find here. This was such a bachelor pad.

When Simon called her back, she apologized up front. "Hey, sorry, you didn't have to interrupt work for me."

"I can always interrupt work for you," he stated, a smile in his tone. "And I haven't heard back, but I will follow up," he added. "We'll definitely get it resolved."

"Oh, we'll get it resolved," she replied, with a dry laugh, "but that doesn't mean I'll get any compensation for it. At the moment, it looks as if the apartment complex is also looking for some guarantee that it won't happen again."

"We'll deal with them another time," Simon told her. "First off is the insurance."

"Right. Meanwhile I'm back at the victim's home, the first dead guy we found, ... looking for paperwork, looking for whether somebody was here at the time of his death and may have removed some drug paraphernalia, and whether he had a life insurance policy or related stuff."

"Ah, I'm sorry to hear that. It must be one of the hard parts, you know, digging into somebody's life."

"It is."

After she ended the call, she began going through the

bathroom cupboards, underneath the sink—typically utilized for an overload of toilet paper or similar items. But here, though not unexpected, were condoms by the case—which revealed a lot about his success rate attracting women—and cleansers, but not the kind she was used to.

She studied them for a minute, and then heard a strange sound in the other room. She got up and headed out to the living room, then stopped when she saw a woman standing there, looking around in confusion. Kate walked toward her, and the other woman saw her, her gaze instantly hardening.

"Who are you?" she demanded.

Kate closed the front door so the woman couldn't easily leave. "That's a really interesting question," she noted, as she pulled out her badge. "Maybe the better question is, who are you?"

The woman stared at her, saw her badge, and all the color fled from her face. She whispered, "What are you doing here?"

"No," Kate declared, "again, my questions are, who are you, and what are you doing here?"

The other woman glared at her and muttered, "I'm not playing word games with you."

"Good," Kate snapped, her tone turning sharp. "Tell me who you are, why you're here, and how you got into this apartment."

"I used to have a key, but the door was unlocked. I was hoping he was home, and we could talk."

"So, because I left it unlocked, you just walked in? That was the kind of relationship you had with him?"

She flushed. "We've been in a relationship for half of the year," she stated.

Kate mentally went back over the time frame that Norma, "his girlfriend," had been involved with John also and snorted. "I see. And who are you?"

"Angel," she snapped. "My name is Angel Delaware."

"Show me ID, please."

Angel produced her ID, while flushed with what appeared to be anger. Maybe it was something else because her lips were tightly clenched to stop her from screaming and yelling. Perhaps Angel thought Kate was in some way associated with her boyfriend or partner or whoever she thought John was to her. Or it could also be because Angel now suspected that something was truly wrong. Regardless Kate took a look at the woman's ID, took a photo of it with her phone, then handed it back. She asked Angel, "When did you last see him?"

"Is he missing?" Angel asked, staring at her.

"When did you last see him?" Kate repeated, noticing Angel's chin firming up with a surprising amount of temper, considering the question wasn't difficult. Kate had to wonder just how far Angel would go with that temper.

Angel finally relented, shaking her head. "I haven't seen him for," she frowned and said, "maybe a couple days— yeah, a couple days. The last time I was here, he refused to open his door."

"What day was that?"

She hesitated, then finally relented. "Friday," she snapped.

"And you haven't been here since then?"

"No, … we had a huge fight," she shared, raising both hands. "And it's really been bugging me. I just wanted to see if the two of us could talk it out."

"Have you had fights and talked it out before?"

"Sure," she replied. "I mean, that's what you do in long-term relationships. You fight, and then you talk it out and figure out where you're going from there."

Kate didn't know about that, but it was as good of an excuse as any. "So, you used to have a key to this apartment."

Angle flushed. "I gave my key back to him after our fight."

"And yet you just walked in today."

"Of course I just walked in," she snapped. "I mean, we literally just had the fight. It's not as if he had already picked up with somebody else." Then she glared again at Kate. "Unless you're telling me that you're his newest side piece." She gave her a snide look.

Kate coldly stared at her and remarked, "Seems your relationship is off to a really good start if that's what you're thinking he's doing in the meantime."

"He's extremely virile," she explained, while backing up. "And I don't expect him to go without for long. He would go without for a day or two, but that would be it," she noted. "So, yeah, I came to my senses, and I'm back."

"And if it wasn't you here in his apartment over the last couple days, who was here?"

Her eyes widened, and she shook her head. "Nobody. Not that way. I mean, we literally just broke up."

Kate didn't say anything about that. She continued her questions. "And you haven't seen him for a couple days?"

"No, I haven't."

"Have you talked to him?"

"I sent him a few texts, telling him that I wanted to talk and that I wanted to come over to discuss the problem that I had with what he was doing, and go from there. You know, make up," she admitted.

"Anything else you two talked about?"

"I sent him a couple spicy texts," she shared. "And I expected that he would get back to me, but he didn't. So, I came over to see if he was still really that pissed off with me."

"And yet it's a workday."

"He worked from home most days," she replied. "So that doesn't matter. I mean, he would just take the time off, but he does that anyway."

"So, in other words, you are accustomed to coming over during the day and potentially …"

Angel held up a hand and nodded. "Yes, potentially." She scrunched up her nose. "Obviously we don't do anything to get him fired. But, hey, everybody likes a nooner." Angel kept glaring, as if Kate were trying to steal her boyfriend.

Finally Kate asked, "May I see your texts to him?"

Angel stared at her, startled. "No, of course, you can't."

Kate nodded. "Okay, your verbal response is noted."

"Noted why?" she asked, her tone openly hostile.

Kate regarded Angel and explained, "Because John Smith was found dead two, no, three nights ago," she corrected herself.

Angel stared at her in shock. Then horror took its place. "What?" she stammered and sank down onto the couch, closest to where she stood. "No, that can't be."

"Why not?" Kate asked, turning to her again. "Seems he broke lots of hearts, and it's possible some of his choices came back to haunt him. I mean, why couldn't he be dead now?"

"It's just not possible. He was here just the other night."

"And yet you just told me that you didn't see him."

"No, I didn't see him," she confirmed. Then she closed her eyes and whispered, "No, this can't be."

"I need you to explain the comment you just made."

Angel looked at her and replied, "I came by to talk to him, but he wouldn't answer the damn door. But I could hear somebody in here. I wanted to talk to him, but he wouldn't answer. I got mad, and it wasn't until I realized that he really wouldn't answer that I left. Then I bombarded him with texts," she stated, hanging her head. "I wanted to know why he wouldn't talk to me, why he wouldn't answer the door."

"And this was Friday night?"

"Yes, Friday night," she snapped, staring at her, now flushing. "I thought maybe we could have a nice little weekend to ourselves."

"Right," Kate noted, studying her. "And what time was this?"

She frowned and shook her head. "About eight o'clock, I think. I don't know exactly but somewhere around that."

"Okay. And you didn't see anybody?"

"No, I didn't." Then she frowned. "Look. I thought somebody was here with him. I mean, it seemed as if somebody was here. The lights were on inside. I thought he was just being *ornery*, which is how he got sometimes. If you did something wrong, he didn't forgive easily. And he was the guy who would be like, *You had your chance, and now you're out.*"

"What about you? Were you out?" Kate asked.

"A few times," she muttered, "because we've had many arguments over the last couple months. But, for the most part, we always made up pretty soon. A couple times when we didn't, we would eventually. … It was on again, off again." She stared down at her hands, the tears just now creeping up. "You're serious, aren't you?" she asked, looking over at Kate.

Kate nodded. "Yes. What do you know about the other people in his life?"

"Nothing," she said, bewildered. "But I should, shouldn't I? I mean, we went out for quite a while. You would think that I should know something." Kate didn't say anything, just kept waiting while Angel talked. "Only now, as I'm sitting here, staring at you, knowing you'll ask all kinds of questions, realizing that I can't answer them?" She sobbed harder now. "I didn't realize just how little I knew about his life."

"And yet you were friends for years, is that right?"

"More than friends," she clarified, and then she winced. "But maybe not, maybe it was literally just …" She frowned and then whispered, "Maybe it was just sex. You're making me rethink everything right now." But the tears were still there, only they hadn't dropped.

It seemed to Kate that Angel was still hanging on for the punchline of a joke that would never end.

"I don't know," Angel whispered. "I'm, I'm just as confused as you are right now." She turned to Kate. "Definitely somebody was here Friday night. So, if not him, who was it?"

"I don't know whether it was him or not," Kate pointed out. "It depends on what the coroner comes back with as a time of death. If we have anything that's close—"

"It could just be a neighbor who came over," Angel suggested.

"It could be any number of things," Kate conceded. "Yet I need a definitive answer from you as to whether or not it was you. If I do find out that it was you and that you're lying to me," she clarified, "it won't go down well."

"No, no, it wasn't me. I, I saw him in the window," she shared. "If you go out to the car park, you can see this series of windows, and it looked as if he was here and he was home."

"So, you came in?"

"No, I contacted him," she corrected, "but obviously he didn't want to answer me. And now that just makes me feel even shittier."

"Did he do drugs at all?"

"No," she snapped a bit too forcefully. "He was against drugs because he used to do them. And he told me how it had completely messed up his life and how it took him years to get over it. So, he was very strict about his no-drugs policy."

"Policy? Would you elaborate, please?"

"He had a very strict *no drugs in the house* policy."

"Are you sure about that?"

"Yeah, he was very specific about it. One time he was trying to help somebody from his past life who had a drug problem. He did an awful lot to get them off the drugs. But, when they fell back into that lifestyle again, he declined to help anymore, saying he'd done his part, but you couldn't help some people," she whispered.

"So, you've never seen him do any drugs on his own?"

"No, not at all," she declared. "Anybody who says differently on that topic is lying."

Kate was surprised at that. "People can be different, depending on who they're with," she suggested. "While he may not have done drugs with you, he might have with somebody else."

"No way, he wouldn't have," she repeated in an incredibly forceful tone. "He was far more rigid than that. Drugs just didn't have a place in his world, and, if they had a place in yours, you needed to move along."

Kate just nodded and didn't say anything.

"How did he die?" Angel asked, turning to her.

"I can't share much in the way of details, as we're still waiting for the coroner's report," she fudged. "However, drugs were in his system."

She stared at her in shock. "No, no, you don't understand." She started pacing, and then came to stand in front of her. "John was adamant about that. I mean, early on I used to joke that we should just chill out and have some gummies every once in a while. He would get so irate at me for even mentioning it that I learned very quickly not to even joke about it or he would show me the door. So, if he has drugs in his system, somebody else must have done it."

"And do you know anybody who would have given him drugs?"

"No, God no," she muttered. "I'm not kidding. He was so against anything of the kind, so that's a hard no. No fucking way." Kate just nodded and didn't say anything, as Angel started crying again. "And now you'll tell me that I really didn't know him, won't you?"

"No, I'm not saying that at all," Kate corrected, "because I really don't know who this man is myself yet. I'm still trying to figure that out."

"He was a good man." Then she sighed and added, "He was a terrible playboy, but he was a good man."

Kate's eyebrows shot up at that. "Which is why you had such a long relationship with him, even though it was on again, off again?"

"Yes, because he was a good guy. He made good money, and he looked after his money. He didn't waste it, blowing it on sports cars or gambling. He did enjoy his booze," she admitted, "and women. If John had a vice, it was the women." Angel chuckled, tears brimming in her eyes. "That was always the problem with us. Whenever we had a problem, it was usually because I couldn't stand the fact that he always seemed to be looking for the next woman in his life," she noted, fatigue in her tone, as the tears streamed down her face. "I would take it for a while, and then I couldn't take it for a while."

Kate sighed. "Okay, so here's something I need you to be brutally honest about. Were you in a romantic relationship with John Smith? Or were you really friends with benefits?" Kate asked.

Angel stared at her. Once the sobbing started, it didn't seem to want to quit.

When she finally got a hold of herself, Kate still stood here, waiting for Angel's answer.

"W-When you put it that way," she began, "I'm very much afraid that, as far as he was concerned, it was just friends with benefits. But I really, really hope something else was there too. Or maybe there could have been later in time. I really, really cared about him," she whispered, sinking back down onto the couch.

Angel never did say she loved him, which was an interesting side note to Kate. People tended to go on and on about how much they loved someone, particularly when they found out that someone was dead. But, in this case, that was not the case at all with Angel.

She stared off in the distance and muttered, "God, I've been such a fool."

"Why is that?" Kate asked, still standing here, just waiting. It was a hell of a technique and tended to make people very uncomfortable. In an attempt to fill the awkward silence, they were compelled to talk, which seemed to be just the technique to use in this instance.

Angel shook her head. "You're right. We were just friends with benefits. He got the benefit, and I was kept on a string."

Kate asked, "And did you keep yourself on that string, or did he keep you on it?"

The tears came down even faster now. Angel eyed Kate and replied, "You really don't pull any punches, do you?"

She shrugged. "Your friend was likely murdered. This isn't personal, and I'm not trying to be difficult," she pointed out. "I'm just asking questions meant to clarify a relationship that you told me was *off and on for years*. So, you tell me. What must I do to get you to tell me the truth?"

"I am telling you the truth," Angel muttered, "but it's the truth as I saw it, which now I realize isn't necessarily the truth as he saw it. Because you're right. Now that I see it from your perspective, I probably was just there for him whenever he didn't have somebody else," she admitted, with an incredibly sad self-awareness. "I always hung on, hoping that he would be there for me, that we had something solid, and that eventually he would stop looking at all these other women, thinking that I would be enough for him. But, ... after all these years, if I wasn't enough already, it wouldn't change, would it?" Angel asked Kate.

Kate shook her head slowly. "Not likely and it's also quite likely that he continued to have all kinds of relationships on the side, particularly when he was not interested in settling down, and you probably didn't know about a lot of them."

She winced. "You're probably right." Angel stood up

stiffly, as she stared at Kate. "I really don't think I could do your job."

Kate shrugged. "Unfortunately I see an awful lot of women just like you, who think that they are the one, that they've found the one, but what they have found is that they were … only one of many." Kate sighed. "I'm sorry because obviously that's not what you want to hear. But what I do still need from you is some idea of who else he might have been involved with because somebody was here with him that Friday night."

The tears stopped but the sobs kept coming.

Kate continued. "It could have been any number of his friends stopping by for a drink, but, knowing what I've just told you about him, do you think he would have done drugs?"

"No," she snapped, "and I get that it probably seems I don't know a damn thing about him, but I'm not wrong on that. He was incredibly insistent on *no drugs*, as he used to do them, but that was a long time ago." She got up slowly. "Look. I need to go. I need to just go, just, just go," she mumbled, her voice breaking yet again.

"Maybe you need to find a place to just sit and rest for a bit. I don't want you out there driving in this condition," Kate replied.

Angel collapsed back down. She stared at Kate. "I just … I really loved him."

That was the first time *love* had been mentioned. Kate nodded. "And that's a good thing because everybody needs and deserves to be loved."

"Did he though?" Angel whispered back.

"Maybe John needed it but just didn't know how to give it, how to show it," Kate suggested. "I don't know who he was as a person, but a lot of times people are just that way because they can't handle the thought of getting old, or they can't handle the thought of not being the person in their head who they want to be. They can't handle the idea that maybe they'll grow old and end up sitting across from somebody they don't want for too many years down the road. There's no right or wrong here."

Angel nodded tearfully.

"I wouldn't blame him for being with you all those years. I wouldn't do any of that," Kate explained, "and neither should you. Your lessons were very much about the on-and-off-again part of your relationship. Somewhere along the line, when you've had a little time, you might want to ask yourself why you kept coming back, even though it was obvious that it wasn't to have a real long-term monogamous relationship. What was it about him that kept you coming back into a relationship that was going nowhere? In the meantime, you need to answer my calls, in case I have any other questions."

Angel automatically stood back up, walked to the door, then turned to ask her, "Will you tell me if, … when you find out what happened?"

"You'll hear it on the news for sure," Kate noted, "but I won't be making any direct calls. Phone the police once the case is closed, if it doesn't hit the news."

"*Right*," she muttered, "no time for personal calls. *Right*." Angel sent a bitter glance to Kate.

"I won't be making such calls because I'll already be working on the next twelve murders on my desk," Kate declared, not giving an inch, "and you can bet that their families will be screaming for me to be looking after their loved ones too and to hell with making follow-up calls."

Angel flushed. "You're right. I'm, I'm sorry," she muttered. "That didn't come across the way I intended it to."

Kate kept her mouth shut, escorting Angel to the door and locking it behind her this time. As Kate returned to the main living room, she spied one of the couch cushions up ever-so-slightly, with something peeking out. She walked over, bent down, lifted the cushion, and found a small diary inside. She smiled.

"Bingo."

SIMON SAT DOWN at the coffee shop, his morning going well, and, unlike a lot of his days recently, he had a minimal amount of problems to face. Now, if only the bank meeting in one hour would go the same way, with his longtime bank advisor, David. They would discuss some of the purchases he'd recently made and then juggle and shuffle around some money so that Simon had cash for the next set of renovation projects.

For the most part, these bank meetings were perfunctory, just a case of sorting out what was next and how to make things work. However, Simon wasn't so sure that this one would go the same way. He wanted it to, as something had been *off* about the way David spoke on their last phone call. The last thing Simon needed was a headache on that front right now. As he sat here sipping his coffee, a woman walked over, smiled, and sat down at his table.

"Hey," she greeted him. "I've seen you here quite a few times."

He smiled and nodded. "Yeah, I'm working on a construction project around the corner, so it's an easy stop on my way over."

"Ah, that makes sense."

They shared a little bit more small talk, but he just considered her being friendly. When Kate phoned a little bit later, he answered, and a look of disappointment filled the stranger's expression. So his unidentified lady visitor then got up and left.

He smiled as he shared with Kate, "Thanks for saving me once again."

Silence came on the other end for a moment. "Do I even want to know what that's about?"

"No, probably not," he agreed, with a smirk. "What are you up to?"

"I'm checking up on you," she stated.

"Ah," he noted, his smirk disappearing. "I'm having coffee before I head over to the bank for a meeting."

"Oh right. You mentioned that was today," she muttered, but now she was distracted.

"What's going on?" he asked her.

"A friend with benefits popped into the murder victim's apartment while I was there," she began. "Apparently somebody was here with our victim Friday night. She had come over to apologize after they'd had yet another argument in their long-standing strange relationship. However, when she thought somebody was here, and John wouldn't answer, she got pissed off and left. So today she came over, ready to pick a fight with him, and found me instead."

"Oh, I'm sure that went over well," he teased, laughter in his tone.

"Let's just say that she left in tears, and she got a big reality check as to just what she was doing in that relationship with John in the first place," she shared bitterly. "I hate it when people look to me for answers to the universe, particularly when it comes to relationships. I don't know the first thing," she muttered into the phone.

"I know you don't want me bringing this up," he noted, "but I would say you're doing just great in the relationship department."

"*Right*," she grumbled. "Yet you are correct. I don't want you bringing that up. Anyway"—she sighed—"I was just calling to confirm all is well."

"All is well," he acknowledged. "I'm just sitting here having coffee. Then I'll go take care of some banking business."

"*Right*," Kate noted, her tone skeptical. "Meanwhile, you haven't had any other weird visitations from that woman?"

He knew exactly who she was talking about. "Nope, and hopefully there won't be any visions right now either because I'm heading off to that meeting."

"You don't have any control over your visions? Even in case of meetings such as this?"

"Sometimes," he shared. "Sometimes I can ward it off, and other times it gets complicated, but that isn't really something I'll worry about." He deliberately did *not* tell her about the incident at the top of the construction site. He sighed. "I have enough things to worry about without bringing that one into the mix."

She chuckled. "Okay, good enough." Then she added, "This woman, … who was here today? Her name is Angel Delaware."

"Does that matter?" Simon asked.

"No, I just wondered if that name meant anything to you."

Simon noted nothing pushy about her tone but definitely a thread of curiosity. "No, I don't think so," he replied, "but if something comes to mind, I'll let you know."

"Sure, no problem," she said.

Still, he felt something else was on her mind. He hesitated, then asked, "You sure there isn't another reason for your call?"

"No," she told him. "Really just to confirm you were doing okay."

He winced at that because, of course, she worried about him. "That is not a reason I want you to call me, of course."

"Then let's just say that I was missing you."

"I'll take that one," he agreed and ended the call, a smile on his face. He glanced around and realized that the time was going a little faster than he'd anticipated. He got up and then sat right back down, as if somebody put a hand on his chest and shoved him hard to sit down again.

He swore slightly at that. This was the last damn thing he needed right now.

He looked around. The place was busy, lots of people coming and going. He had no idea what this was, doing God-only-knew what or why, but considering Kate had set off a scenario during the night about telling the woman to ask for what she needed, he wasn't sure what he was supposed to do here.

He glanced around to see if anything or anyone in particular was causing this or was showing any interest, but he couldn't see anything. Matter of fact, absolutely nothing as far as he could tell was triggering this *event*.

When he went to stand up again, once again that hand slapped him back down again. He slowly picked up his phone and sent Kate a message. **Just got slapped back into place twice and got no clue why.**

She sent him a question mark in her reply text, which,

honest to God, was a really good answer on her part because he had no freaking idea either.

He sat here and waited, studying the people around him. One woman looked downcast, sad even, and she had a scarf wrapped around her head and tucked into her jacket. He glanced outside, but, even for mid-to-late January, it wasn't that cold out. Then again, a lot of people had different concepts of what cold was. He was always on the warmer side, whereas a lot of women seemed to always feel colder than he felt. But still, it seemed a little bit much for this woman to handle.

Unless …

His gaze zipped back toward her; unless she was hiding scars of abuse.

He frowned as he watched her. She ordered coffee, waited without any movement at all, as in she just stood at the side and didn't fidget, didn't fuss, didn't look around. She kept her gaze downcast, yet staring all around her, almost daring anybody to recognize her or to say anything to her. That seemed unlikely, since everybody was ignoring everybody. The coffee shop was busy, and there was no room for people to be too bothered about anything going on right now.

He wanted to get up and try leaving again, but it would look strange if it happened a third time. Just as he was about to try again, the woman lifted her gaze and locked onto his. Her eyes widened as if she knew him from somewhere, and Simon couldn't do anything but stare back. She quickly snatched up her coffee, and, with one more final, almost scared glance in his direction, she booked it right out of the coffee shop.

Immediately the pressure in his chest eased up, and he

could now get up. He raced outside to look for her but saw no sign of her anywhere. He had to stop again, as pressure built in his chest by some invisible hand again. He muttered under his breath, "It would be really helpful if you would give me more of a warning, or at least some idea of what you want me to do about this."

But absolutely no answer came.

Of course there was no answer, and he was just talking to thin air.

But that woman, whoever she was, had a moment of recognition when seeing Simon, and he hadn't expected that because he'd never seen her before in his life. A hard mental shake had him reorienting himself back to the business at hand, and he slowly turned and walked down the street toward the bank. He had an appointment to keep and a business to run.

As he walked into the bank, that same woman was in line for the next available teller. She took one look at him, her gaze widened, almost in fear, and she turned around and escaped out the front door. He stood here, frozen, and watched her retreat.

The bank manager walked over and greeted him in a playful tone. "That's an unusual reaction when, most of the time, the women are all over you."

He turned to face David, an old friend. "It's certainly not a reaction I was expecting. I hope she's okay," he added. "Her reaction just looked off."

"Yeah, you know, that's true. It did look off." He shrugged. "Come on in. Let's go to my office."

Simon frowned, as he stared back at where she had been. "I don't know who she is, so I have no clue how to help her."

As they both settled in David's office, Simon asked, "So,

what bad news are you thinking of giving me?"

David stared at him, and then his gaze dropped to the files on his desktop. "The bank, my manager precisely, is a little concerned that you're … overextended."

Simon stared at him, something lighting up his cortex. "And are you concerned too?"

"No." There was a rueful note in his tone. "I'm not, but I don't run the bank," David explained, with a wry look, "at least not alone and most certainly not unsupervised."

"And what is it they want me to do?"

"They want you to put up more collateral."

"Why?" he asked, his tone businesslike. "I've already secured the loans. They've already approved the loans. I've been repaying those very loans."

David winced at that. "Yes," he agreed, with a nod, "you have, and they've all been approved, but upper management is concerned that you'll turn into a bad investment."

"So, what is this that we are doing here?"

"It's just a friendly warning."

"I don't think we need to go there. I have the finances secured, work is steadily coming along, everything's on schedule, so that *warning* makes no sense."

"I know," David admitted. "I'm just telling you that they don't like your current position."

"That's nice," Simon deadpanned, measuring the look on his friend's face. "Are you telling me that we'll go a legal route because you guys are causing trouble with the financing I already have?" His tone was cool. "Or is this a warning that you won't support me when I get more financing for my buildings and work orders?"

"It is not my idea, but that's where management is at," he acknowledged.

Simon studied him and asked, "And is this a position that's likely to continue?"

"What do you mean?" he asked.

"You know that we have one big job finishing within"—he stared off in the distance—"less than six months. And I don't need a last-minute curve ball thrown my way."

"Yes, we know," David replied. "And that was part of the argument I used to try and get them off your case. However, they don't like a lot of the inflation rates and real estate prices and all the rest of that right now. So, I'm just giving you a warning."

"No," Simon argued. "You brought me into your office. That is more than just giving me a warning."

"And it's also what I had to do to get them off your case," David added. "So, I brought you in, and it is a friendly warning at the moment. Yet, as far as they're concerned, you're overextended and will not be granted any more money at this time."

Simon nodded. "Good to know." He stood up because he could not really say anything to change this bank's position. David may be interested in playing games and covering his own behind, but Simon wasn't ready to kiss anybody's ass—not at this moment or ever.

"Wait, is that all you've got to say?" David asked.

"Sure, it's all I got to say because, at the end of the day, you're forgetting one thing."

"What's that?" David asked.

"You aren't the only bank around. I can pull all my money out of here today and have it all refinanced immediately somewhere else," he stated, staring at David. "So, consider me warned, but you might also want to remind your bosses that I have options too."

With that, he turned and walked out, not listening to any of the panicked cries from somebody he used to trust and no longer did.

Going through the revolving doors, he stepped into the bright sunshine, glanced around, and headed in the direction of his rehab project, where he could at least focus his energy on something doable—not banks panicked about signed paperwork and all this crap where everybody wanted to make illogical and unreasonable power plays.

Simon already had all the lines secured. The bank could try to cause trouble, and he could certainly get out of those loans and out of that bank if he needed to. But what he didn't need was the particular power play currently going on. All he could do was deal with it when it came.

And he would deal with that, and, as such, he would have to make some changes, even though he didn't want to.

But there would never be a day when somebody pulled his chain without his say-so.

CHAPTER 9

KATE WALKED BACK into the office, frustrated and fed up, only for Lilliana to call out to her.

"I got a hold of the one girlfriend who had been going out with this guy—"

"Which guy?"

"Robert Blake. Her name is Lanny, the receptionist at work. She's taking a few days off, so if you want to talk to her now, I've got the address where she's at."

Kate beamed and said, "Now, if only you had texted me that, so I could have headed there straightaway."

"I did," Lilliana replied, glancing back at her. "I didn't hear back from you."

She looked down at her phone and swore. "Yeah, you did. Okay, I had one development in that I had a woman come by John Smith's apartment who was supposedly his *long-term girlfriend*, but further discussions have revealed them to be friends with benefits in an on-and-off relationship, depending on whether either one of them had somebody else on the hook."

Lilliana just lifted her head, then shook it. "Those kinds rarely make it."

"In this case, she is pretty upset about the truth of that whole scenario. Plus, she walked in on me while I was there at John's apartment and didn't appreciate it. Also she saw somebody at John's place Friday night through the window. She thought it was him, and, when he would not answer, she got quite pissy and took off again. She then contacted him today supposedly to"—she rolled her eyes—"make up again."

"Are you thinking she had something to do with John's murder?"

"No. She was very shocked to hear what had happened to him. I don't think she could have faked that. But she's also not a very happy camper as she has finally, through some of our discussions, understood that she's really just a side piece, and that's not how she saw their relationship."

"I suspect we'll have a lot of women say that same thing," Lilliana noted.

"I'll go talk to Lanny now because I'm pretty sure that woman in particular was hanging on to a whole lot more of a crush than a lot of people really let on to. It might have been an office romance, but, for Lanny, I think it was a whole lot more than just a temporary thing."

"You go talk to her then," Lilliana said. "I'm still working on the phone calls, helping Rodney with those."

Rodney lifted a hand. "Yo, I'm here," he said. "And, yeah, these guys, all three of them, have hundreds and hundreds and hundreds of phone calls."

"So, you've checked social media and found all their hookup sites?" Kate asked.

Rodney groaned. "Lots to do here."

Lilliana concurred. "We're working on it, but again all three of these guys appeared to have been part of every possible dating site, even just hookups or meetups, that they could get their hands on," Lilliana explained. "They weren't just living a studly life. They were almost … *desperate* about it."

"Now that's interesting," Kate noted thoughtfully. "And maybe, maybe that's how they viewed it. Maybe they saw life as a short-term thing, and they had to get the best of it and the most gain out of it that they could. Either way, I will head over and talk to Lanny, one of Robert Blake's girlfriends, whom Lilliana tracked down. At least Lanny's not too far away from here," she added, as she glanced down at the address that Lilliana had texted her.

As she walked out, she wished she had seen Lilliana's text earlier. It would have saved her a trip if she had. The traffic was pretty brutal, so she was exhausted and fed up and tired by the time she got to the apartment.

When she walked up and rang to be let in, Lanny answered the buzzer. However, when she found out who it was, she started to bawl.

Kate was having trouble calming her down. "Either talk to me here or come down to the station," she finally stated, having enough and saying it forcefully when Lanny refused to respond. "And if you don't come willingly," she added, "I will send a black-and-white to come pick you up, here or at work. So, it's your choice. Either let me in now, and we'll have this conversation in privacy, or you don't let me in, and we'll have the conversation down at the station."

Lanny hit the buzzer, and Kate walked through the building to her apartment.

When Lanny opened the door, tears rolling down her face, she cried out, "How can you be so mean?"

Kate shot up one eyebrow, putting her game face on because this wouldn't go over well for Lanny. "Me?" she asked. "I'm dealing with somebody who has been murdered. What's your excuse?"

At that, Lanny stared at her in shock and then totally panicked, almost to the extent of having a panic attack but needing to be parked in the closest chair regardless. When Kate pulled up a second chair and stared at her, she asked her, "Why don't you tell me what you know about it?"

"I don't know anything," Lanny cried out in shock. "What do you mean?"

"We don't have an official cause of death yet, but drugs are a very strong possibility."

Lanny stared at her and then vehemently shook her head. "He didn't do drugs."

"And, if he didn't do drugs, then what on earth is going on?"

"I don't know," she wailed. "I mean, if you had told me it was some gym steroid things, then maybe," she shared, "that would make more sense."

Kate looked at her. "Robert was a buff gym rat?"

"Yes, yes, of course he was a big buff gym rat. That went along with his whole *I'm a big-bad-baddie* vibe he had going on," she explained, a tearful look on her face. "Look. He was a great guy, and I don't want anybody besmirching his reputation," she cried out. "He was a good man."

"I'm not trying to damage Robert's reputation," Kate snapped, "but get real. We can't confirm yet until we get the reports back but if he didn't administer the drugs to himself, then somebody else did, and I want to know who because it sounds very much as if he died from those drugs." As Lanny sat here, shaking, Kate stared at her and asked, "Did you have anything to do with his death?"

In horror, Lanny screamed, "No, no, no, of course not. I would never—"

"Would never *what*?"

"I would never do that," Lanny replied. "I can't stand drugs and won't have anything to do with them."

"Right, so what is this all about?"

"I don't know," Lanny wailed, staring at her. "You're asking me for answers, and I don't—I don't have any. I know nothing about any drugs."

Kate just sat back and stared at her. "And you obviously didn't want the office to know that you were still involved with him."

Lanny flushed. "How do you know that?" she muttered.

"Because it's obvious that you were still involved, and the fact that you took time off to be at home to deal with the loss is another good indicator."

"No, we could just be good friends," she muttered. "I'm sure a lot of women at the office are about to take some time off."

Kate studied her for a long moment. "Maybe they are. You should probably tell me exactly which ones, since odds are they're probably home doing the same thing you are."

Lanny closed her eyes, her shoulders dropping, then whispered, "There's at least one other."

Kate held out her pen and asked, "And who is that?"

"Caroline."

Kate had not met her among those seen at the office. Kate nodded and motioned for Lanny to continue.

"They weren't getting along well, and there were definitely some issues at the office. I don't know what. I haven't seen her in the last day or so, at least the day or so before I— I took a couple days off," she clarified, scrubbing her face. "I realized that, even though it might be over for me and Robert, it wasn't over for her, though I didn't even know about her for the longest time. And then he—he would just laugh and say it didn't matter and was none of my business anyway. But for me, it felt as if it absolutely was."

"Of course it did," Kate replied. "You somehow thought the two of you were exclusive, though I don't understand how you could, since apparently he wasn't exclusive with anybody. From what we've been told, he was very upfront about not being tied down and was strict about telling each woman that very thing upfront."

Tears welled up in her eyes. "For the oldest excuse ever," Lanny began, "I thought I could convince him that I was woman enough, and he would stop his catting about." She waved her hand in the air. "And yet, at times I seemed to be making inroads. Then, all of a sudden, he wouldn't be available again for a while. Then I saw him out with Caroline from the office, and he told me that I better not say anything because that meant his job and my job would be in danger."

Lanny took a deep breath. "I am not happy with myself over all this, and it is one hell of a chance to do a full reset, but, in the meantime, it's just heartbreaking. I thought—"

Kate just waited for Lanny to talk some more. After a long silence, Lanny finally looked at Kate and said, "It was such a shock when we had just found out about Robert, and then suddenly you were there." Lanny shook her head.

"I didn't know what to think. I mean, we all knew Kurt's death was likely a suicide, and that's what we had been told—a drug overdose. I don't think it was deliberate though," she noted. "That would have been a drug overdose of maybe not thinking it through carefully."

"Did you have a relationship with him too?" Kate asked.

Lanny looked at her in horror. "No, no, I didn't."

Kate just waited.

Lanny closed her eyes and muttered, "Honest, I didn't."

And then she opened her eyes and faced Kate. "But I almost did."

"And what stopped you?" Kate asked.

"I saw Kurt with Caroline too," she replied, and then she winced. "Now Caroline's lost both of them."

"Yeah, that would … appear to be true," Kate noted, staring at her. "So, just who is Caroline?"

"She's a beautiful woman," Lanny shared sadly, "like really drop-dead gorgeous, and it just made me feel as if I could never compete. After I saw them together, I realized that she had everything, and I had nothing. So it didn't matter what I said or did. Robert would never come back to me, as he was as enamored with Caroline as Kurt probably was."

"And were you …" Kate hesitated, knowing this would likely bring on a ton more tears. "Were you in a romantic relationship, or were you friends with—" Kate left it at that because she needed Lanny to make a statement, not push her into it or put words in her mouth.

Lanny stared at her, then replied, "I'm pretty sure that the phrase would be *friends with benefits*. However, in my defense, I thought we were having a relationship up until—"

"Until you saw Robert with Caroline, right?" Kate noted how Caroline had at least some relationship with both men. "And, in the case of these two men, what about Angel? Did you know Angel Delaware?"

Lanny frowned and shook her head. "Who's she?"

Kate didn't say anything.

"Who is Angel?" Lanny cried out, her voice louder.

Kate looked over at her and went back to writing her notes. "Another person who thought she was having a real relationship with someone but was not. Did you know John Smith?"

Lanny frowned again, then nodded.

"Did you date him?"

Lanny shook her head.

Kate nodded. "Angel Delaware had been in a very long-term *friends with benefits* arrangement with Mr. Smith."

"How long-term?" Lanny asked, staring at her in shock.

"Two years."

"Oh my God," she cried out. "He didn't tell her?"

"Tell who what?" Kate asked, staring at her. "Did he tell you anything?"

"No. God, no, he didn't. He didn't say anything." She sat back and sighed. "I was really a fool, wasn't I?"

And that was a direction that Kate really did not want to go. She asked Lanny, "Can you tell me about any other women who Robert or John or Kurt may have been involved with?"

"No, no, I can't. I won't."

Kate glared at her and repeated, "*Won't?*"

"Yeah, I … I knew about Caroline after I saw them together. I didn't know about anybody else. God, I didn't know," she muttered, now bawling her eyes out. "That would have been enough to stop me. I would have completely broken up with Robert."

Kate just watched her for a moment, gauging her reaction, which could be honest, but lots of anger was there too.

Lanny nodded. "I would have. I mean, I was still completely overwhelmed at finding out about Caroline," she explained. "Caroline was absolutely drop-dead gorgeous, so a part of me accepted that, of course, Robert's with her. Earlier Kurt had been with her too."

Kate asked, "What about John Smith? Did you ever see him with Caroline?"

Lanny shook her head. "Maybe John dated her too. I just didn't see it with my own eyes. Caroline's everything that I'm not," Lanny cried out. "And then I just—I just wanted to try harder. I just wanted to be with Robert and to show him how much I cared."

"And how did that go?" Kate asked.

She stared at her and sighed. "Probably the way you would expect. He took everything I had to give, telling me that he had never made any promises, but he really cared about me, and he wanted to continue to see me, but it was totally okay with him if I didn't love him enough to *not* try to change him. God, even saying that makes me sound like a complete and total idiot."

Kate sighed now. "Look. I get that you're probably going through all kinds of things right now," she began. "But I need to focus on these three men, see if somebody else was involved with them as recently as the past weekend, and, if they were, to what extent."

"I don't know," she wailed, staring at her, the tears coming again. "I didn't ... I didn't know. I didn't have very much experience with men, and I guess, ... I guess I got suckered in," she admitted. She stared off in the distance, tears now flowing onto her cheeks. "I don't know how that makes it any better, but somehow it does."

"It makes it better because you now realize that you didn't lose the man with whom you would spend the rest of your life. Instead you were separated from a toxic and harmful relationship in many ways."

She stared at her and whispered, "That's possible, but I'm not sure I can deal with that logic quite so soon."

Kate shrugged and asked, "How long have you worked there?"

"A little over two years," she replied.

"So, you didn't know much about Kurt?"

"No, Kurt died not too long after I got there, but he was flirty with me, paid some attention to me. However, I didn't really know him. He worked at a different office in the company, but we occasionally had business meetings together. But I do remember Caroline being pretty upset about his death," she shared. "And I had seen them together, knew they'd had a thing, though I don't know about the rest of the office."

"What does that mean?" Kate asked.

"I don't know about any other women from work," she muttered, staring at Kate. "It's really frowned upon, dating someone from the office. I almost lost my job because of it, and Robert agreed to be very, very quiet and keep it a secret after that. Just us, you know, *special*, just us," she repeated, a bitterness in her tone, one that indicated she was finally coming awake from the dream she had created in her head. "And I, of course, was more than happy to just be *special* with him. God, I'm such a fool," she muttered.

"No, not a fool, but you were looking for a whole lot more than you were getting," Kate pointed out. "And that's one of the sad things about these kinds of relationships. Now you have a chance to figure out what you could really use, what you would really like, and the kind of man you really want. And maybe go for somebody who is not into clandestine office relationships with a dozen women at the same time," Kate noted, as she stood up.

Lanny stared at her in horror. "Please tell me that you're joking about the dozen women."

Kate shrugged. "We don't have exact numbers at this point, but Robert's been very active, as have Kurt and John," she shared. "So, I wouldn't be at all surprised if he dated twelve women at once. Yet the number doesn't matter. He's dead, he's gone, and I need the reports back, but whether it was an accident that he took too much or was given too much, I don't know. I need to get to the bottom of it and fast."

With that, she stared at Lanny and added, "I'll leave you alone now, but, if you think of anything that could be helpful, please contact me as soon as you can."

❦

SITTING IN HIS favorite coffee shop, paperwork covering the table in front of him, Simon pored over the reports to check his options. He needed to be ready for the hammer to drop. The angry part of him wanted all his finances transferred to another bank immediately, but there were penalties in a lot of this that he really did not want to deal with—but he would if needed.

As he perused his records, his phone rang. He looked down to see it was his *ex*-banker friend. He almost smiled at that phrase because, in the business that he was in, he had absolutely no room for this BS.

Now that he understood exactly where his friend stood, Simon was now looking at other options. He ignored the ringing phone, checking to see if it went to voice mail, which it did. He listened to the recorded message, David telling him that he was trying to find other options to help him out, but, so far, he wasn't getting anywhere.

Simon moved on from the voice message. David and his manager couldn't do anything, but Simon was certainly in a position to change his own stuff if they definitely found an unfairness attached to the docs.

When Kate phoned a little bit later, she asked, "What's wrong?"

He stared down at the phone and frowned. "Who said anything was wrong?" he snapped.

She snorted. "I felt that temper from here."

In a silky voice, he quipped, "So, maybe you are becoming psychic."

"Shut your mouth," she snapped, and, for the first time today, he burst into laughter. And her response was even more hilarious, when she added, "That sounds better."

"Yeah, it sounds better," he agreed, "but it's still definitely rusty."

"It is. So, who's pissing in your pot?"

A phrase he hadn't heard but absolutely enjoyed. "The bank," he noted, his tone light. "I have been told that they don't like the amount of loans I have—already approved and signed and in force, mind you. While they didn't threaten to shut me down instantly, they more or less threatened *no more loans* and hinting at taking another look at our existing contracts."

"Can they do that?" she asked.

"No," he stated, "but you can bet that having had that position presented to me, I'm seeing my lawyer in the next hour. I'm going over the related paperwork right now."

"So does that mean we're broke?"

He stared down at the phone, and then he started to laugh and laugh and laugh. Her question was so innocent and clearly completely uninterested, but it lightened his mood. "If I were to say yes, what would you say?"

"Nothing, but, in that case, we'll need to get my apartment fixed pretty fast then," she stated. "I can afford to maintain that one. I don't know about your place though."

He smiled. "My place is 100 percent paid for, so, even if the bank wants to be a dick about this, we're not losing that."

"So you haven't used it for collateral?" she asked rudely.

He smiled and replied, "Don't you worry. I'm not even close to broke."

"If you say so," she remarked, "but is it worth the stress to continue doing what you're doing? You've bought an awful lot of properties lately."

"And I wasn't planning on buying any more for a while," he noted, "but, if the opportunity presents itself, and it's something I feel I need to do, ... then you know I'll still do it."

"Good enough," she said. "Just checking that you were okay."

"I'm glad to hear that your little Kate-Spidey-senses are in full force."

She snapped, "Don't even joke about that." And she ended the call.

But it had completely shifted his mood from anger and revenge-seeking to smiling, and he had no idea how the hell she did it, but she was damn good at it. When his phone rang again, it was his lovely banker friend again. Simon answered this one.

"Look. I know I came on a bit harsh, and I'm trying *not* to upset you."

"Too late," Simon snapped.

"I know. Believe me that I know. But still, I have talked to management. They won't do anything about the existing contracts. I'm just telling you that they aren't likely to lend you anything in the future until you clear some of the existing loans."

"*Right*," he replied. "So, I was okay, as long as I was making big, big money and paying you guys back big interest. But now that I've paid off a bunch, and I'm actually in a much better position, but not paying you guys as much, I'm looking worse—in the bank's eyes. Is that it?"

David hesitated, and that rang Simon's bells.

"I need you to be honest with me, David."

"Simon, I think somebody put a bug in their ear about you. I don't know how. I don't know why. I don't know who," he replied. "But it seems to have gotten my manager in a bit of a stew."

"Interesting," he muttered in a silky tone. "When you find out who it is, you might want to let me know. I would really love to return the favor."

"That's not what you need right now."

"Maybe, but I have a way of dealing with my enemies all on my own, so thank you for the advice, but no thank you."

"I was afraid you would say something along that line. You're pretty-damn creepy when you say that stuff."

"I'm not the least bit creepy," he corrected, "but you can bet that I don't like being threatened or treated as if I'm some criminal if I walk back into the bank looking to get more money. I have never defaulted on anything, so I'm not sure why I'm getting this treatment."

"And that's why I think somebody may have mentioned something," David repeated, lowering his voice. "And before you get on my case, I don't know who."

"Well, as I told you already, when you find out, let me know." And he ended the call.

Simon sat back, steepled his fingers under his chin, and considered that. This was not something he'd come up against before. Definitely people were out in the world who may not appreciate what he was doing, but generally it wasn't for any other reason than the fact that he did a damn-good job at it.

Occasionally he got into a bidding war over a property but rarely. Usually the ones he wanted, other people wouldn't touch with a ten-foot pole. But, for whatever reason, somebody was irate.

And that interested him far more than anything else he'd heard in a very long time. Now it was time for his appointment with his lawyer, so he needed to focus on that. As Simon walked into the offices of Allen Moore and Associates, Allen greeted him warmly, then waved him over and sat back down, an amused expression on his face.

"Ouch, somebody has pissed you off."

"Yeah, you could say that." Simon sat down and explained the series of conversations he had just had with David Sinclair. Allen, his lawyer, knew David all too well.

"Good God, Simon," he noted, "that's not like him at all."

"No, it isn't. And I don't understand where this is all coming from. But what I really don't like is that I haven't been able to stem it."

"The fact that they even thought it was a viable thing to do means something is there already."

"And David thinks it's personal."

"Did he hint at that or come right out and say it?"

"That's what he said, that he thought somebody had put a bug in his manager's ear about me. And that maybe I was, you know, going downhill, sliding financially."

"Are you?" Allen asked plainly.

"No, that's a rumor," he stated. "I've got one building completing within the next six months. I've got another one not too far behind that."

His lawyer nodded. "So, considering the potential profit coming finally on that one payday, and then the second one right behind it, you're in really good shape," he muttered. "And sure, you've got quite a few loans, and you've extended yourself, but I wouldn't have thought it was an overextension." Allen pondered that. "And is this something you want to take legal action on? It'll be hard to prove what David told you, unless he's willing to go to bat on your side, which I highly doubt David will do."

"Considering that he phoned me back this morning telling me that he thinks somebody is putting information into his manager's ears, I suspect he's trying to backtrack quickly before he ends up on the firing line."

"I wouldn't be at all surprised," Allen agreed. "David's not exactly all that flush with money himself right now. As you know, his ex-wife just started to put the squeeze on him."

"I know, which is why I was pretty surprised to hear him go this route."

"It's not a normal thing to even let you know."

"No, it's not," Simon agreed.

Allen continued. "It was a threat but an implied threat. As in, *Hey, we're not giving you any more money.*"

"Big deal. I'll just go to another bank. He stated I was already *overextended*, which, as you just pointed out, I don't appear to be. As you know, we went over the numbers in detail for each purchase, for each related loan. Even if I was overextended, I only have to make it for about six months before some liquid cash comes back in again. And I know that most people don't finance these buildings themselves, but I do. I don't want to deal with all these people telling me what I can and cannot do."

"Which, with the larger cash flow …"

Simon nodded. "Once I have the larger cash flow, I could pay off the bulk of these loans with the bank, which is why I was also surprised that David brought that up because I have, in the last year, paid off quite a bunch of these. Funny how the bank never made any comment about those prepayments. Of course, they're making less interest now because I paid those off early."

His lawyer sat here, strumming his fingers, deep in thought. "That's interesting. Who at his branch could be causing you trouble?"

"Who knows?" Simon muttered. "And, to a certain extent, I want to say, who cares? But I have to care if somebody's playing with my finances and my reputation, and maybe it's just time to change banks."

"That would certainly put a spanner in their works," Allen stated.

"I already work with two banks on purpose, so maybe it is time," Simon concluded. "Although that would certainly draw attention to my accounts, and that's not necessarily what I want people looking at."

Allen frowned at him in surprise.

"No, not because I'm hiding something," he explained, "but it will just trigger all kinds of responses from the other banks, right? They really don't like it when you pull out money, do they?"

"Nope, they sure don't. So, how much money could you pull out on a threat like that?"

"Millions," he stated simply.

"An interesting conundrum."

"I know. Anyway, I just wanted to know what legal

stance they have."

"None," he replied immediately. "You already have signed and approved contracts, and you're making all your payments, so there isn't anything within the current arrangement that they can do to cause any damage to you. However, the fact that they are listening to somebody somewhere is concerning because somebody is trying to damage your reputation, and, in your world, that can be very problematic."

"You're not kidding," Simon muttered, "and I don't have a clue who it is, which is very irritating."

"That's the part that pisses me off," Allen shared. "I can do some digging to see who the new manager over there is, and see if that's the issue. Maybe David's job could be on the line, and they're looking to rein in some of his accounts. Maybe, from the bank's perspective, David shouldn't have secured the loans for you, but it's not as if he secures them on his own."

"But if he's being blamed for something—" Simon began.

"Then it's pretty simple. Somebody's using it to try and get rid of him, and that's a whole different story."

Simon pondered that and nodded. "So, if I pull out my money, that'll put him in an even messier situation."

"Absolutely. So, you have to consider whether that's something you really want to do. I mean, are you pissed at David, or is this something completely unrelated that you can get over?"

"I can get over it," he replied, "but—"

"I know, but you don't really want to." Allen had been handling Simon's contracts long enough to know that he wasn't the forgetting type. "I understand, and unfortunately the powers that be don't really get that, when you piss off people, it pisses them off to the point that they don't want anything to do with the games that the banks are playing."

"You could be right on that. Maybe we have some greenhorn in upper management."

"If you need more financing," Allen pointed out, "you'll go elsewhere. If they want double the collateral to secure the next loan, you'll go elsewhere."

"Absolutely," he agreed, "but the thing is, I don't need to put down more collateral. I have personally secured everything I need for the next three years. So, short of my turning around and buying another building, which is not in my plans, particularly after picking up that last building downtown—"

"I heard you got that one, and I know it was on your wish list for a long time."

"I just had no idea that opportunity would present itself now, after all this time." He smiled. "That's the thing about opportunities. You can't prepare for them. You just have to keep yourself in a position to jump when they turn up. That's the challenge. If you don't, everything goes by the wayside, and you've lost out. Other people look at you and mope and whine because you got certain things that they didn't, acting as if they're victims of some conspiracy, but they're not."

Allen nodded. "They just weren't ready for the opportunity that popped up."

"Exactly."

Allen smiled. "It's always fun talking to you."

Simon snorted. "Yeah, I can so see that. Glad I could improve your day," he muttered.

With reassurance from his attorney in hand, Simon got

up and headed back out. As he stood outside on the street corner, he picked up a coffee from a vendor, smiled at him, left a decent tip, then walked back toward one of his other rehab projects, calling Joe, his foreman there. "I'm headed your way." He stopped, looked around, and added, "I'm about a ten-minute walk away."

"Don't rush on my sake," Joe replied cheerfully.

Simon arrived at the rehab site and stopped to look at it appreciatively. It was coming along nicely. It wasn't quite as far along as the other one, but it was getting there.

They'd certainly had their fair share of labor issues, and that was a problem that one had to deal with constantly too. But he had hopes of getting through this one without too much more in the way of trouble. Labor was a big part of that original trouble, but he thought they had the bulk of it handled.

As he walked up to the office trailer, Joe came down from the second floor of the building, calling out to Simon. He detoured to where his foreman stood.

Joe said, "It's up here. Come on up. We keep finding this greenhorn's screwups. He was only here a couple days, so it's frustrating as hell to see that everything he touched he fucked up."

As Simon approached the area, he didn't need to be told what the problem was. He frowned at the metal column, then turned to his foreman. "You fired him months ago and rightly so. You don't ever need me to make that call when the work is so shoddy."

"Right," he agreed, "but we've been short on staff, and I was hoping you would take a look and give the okay."

"Jesus, look at that," Simon muttered, as he saw the welds were not only not acceptable, not up to code, but would have caused a complete shitshow if it hadn't been caught. "How much other work has this guy done?"

"He was only here for a few days, then we got sidetracked with plumbing and electrical. So I'm backtracking to see what all he touched."

"He's a liability, and you don't need somebody you have to watch that closely. Did you warn the other contractors?"

"Sure did. We watch each other's backs."

Simon nodded. "Good. I don't want this fool even stepping on-site, much less picking up another tool here or wherever again. Got it?"

"I hear you." Joe was almost dancing with joy.

"You fired him months ago, and you never have to get me to second your gut instincts, you know?" he muttered.

"And I did, but I'm still finding his shit work. It's so much better when I know for sure that you'll back me up."

Simon turned to him and asked, "Have I ever *not* backed you up?"

Joe pondered it and shrugged. "No, but getting the okay means I don't have to worry about it later."

And, with that, Simon headed back to the on-site office trailer. When he stepped inside, one of the women who worked there looked up, surprised. "Hey, good timing, we have paperwork for you."

He rolled his eyes. "When do you *not* have paperwork for me?"

"Plus we've got four containers' worth of supplies sitting at the docks," she explained, "and they're giving us a bit of trouble."

"In what way?"

She shrugged. "Some of the paperwork wasn't filled out completely, so they're giving us the, *Hey, you didn't do the paperwork song and dance*, complete with fees and fines and all the rest of it."

He stared at her and picked up the phone as he looked at the paperwork she held out, and it gave him immense satisfaction to have somebody to snap at. By the time he got off the phone, he handed the forms back to her and saw the big grin on her face.

"See? That's what I mean," she said. "When you come by, you make that call, and people listen and step up and do what they need to do," she shared. "When we try to handle things without you, it's nowhere near as effective."

"You picked a good day for it too. I was just looking for somebody to snap at, and that was exactly what I needed," he shared, truly happy to rid himself of his pent-up tension. And, with that, he tossed her a big grin and added, "I'll see you tomorrow. As always, call if you need me."

She waved him off. "Maybe you should go for a run or something. The way you were snapping at them on the phone, you've got more than this to deal with."

"Not anymore," Simon stated. "I'm actually pretty good now that I just had somebody to snap at. I'm feeling pretty decent at the moment, but I still have two more job sites to see."

She rolled her eyes. "Yeah, I'm really glad to hear you have other jobs going. This job will be done before we know it, right?"

"Your job probably won't be. It'll be at least eight or nine months yet, and then hopefully I'll have two others on target at the same time."

"I was thinking that this would be it," she admitted and eyed him with relief.

"Hey, that's not how I do things. There's always paperwork and office work that needs to be done. Even as one project wraps up, we'll be looking to the next one. So I'm not looking at laying you or anyone off. If you want to keep the job, I'm sure that won't be a problem."

She smiled, and, this time, she upped the wattage. "I'm really glad to hear that. I hadn't really considered what was coming after this project was finished, but I did hear Joe say something about another six months, and hoping it'll be less than that."

"If we can get it done in four, I would be all the happier."

"Of course," she agreed, "I mean, two months without staff would save you a bundle."

"Two months without staff on *this* job," he stated pointedly. "Everybody will move to one of my other jobs."

"Really?" she asked, ever hopeful.

"Yes. I haven't laid off anybody in probably ten years," he reported, "and, yes, that goes for office staff too. And you can be forgiven for not knowing that, as you are new."

She beamed at him.

"So, if you want to work," he stated, "there's work for you." With that, he headed out the office door, took one last look at the building that had gone up, not without issues but at least in a reasonable time frame, and he smiled as he walked away.

There was a lot of good in the work he did, but one of them was working with good people. So, when he found good people, he wanted to keep them. And when he found pieces of crap who couldn't or wouldn't do the job properly, he got rid of them as soon as he could, which is why he wouldn't hesitate to fire some greenhorn spouting to be some expert. Joe took care of that one, as did his other foremen when some newbie showed up to do construction work, professing to be some expert. Simon didn't have a problem firing people when needed. With that thought, he turned and headed toward his next rehab.

As he went to cross the street, he froze as a voice pulled his attention. The whining, crying, beseeching was in a voice he recognized as his own. He was stuck midway across the street, until a vehicle honked at him. He rushed across, trying to stop the voice pounding through his head. When he got to the other side, he sank onto a park bench, and muttered, "Knock it off."

There was silence at first, and then a voice snapped at him, a woman's voice. *Who are you?*

His eyebrows shot up, and he asked, "Who are you?"

Sarah, she whispered. *I'm Sarah.* And then she added, *Are you God?*

He couldn't help but smile, and even that took a toll on his mind. "Oh no, I am so not God," he muttered. "You won't put that on me. You know how much responsibility that would entail?" She was so confused, and he sensed her questioning his humor.

Sarah asked, *But, if you're not God, then … are you the devil?*

"No, I'm not the devil either. My name is Simon St. Laurant. Why are you talking to me?"

I'm not talking to you, she corrected. *I'm praying.*

"More like lamenting," Simon corrected in a stern voice, "because all I'm hearing is an awful lot of grief pouring out of you."

You can hear me? she whispered.

"Yes, I can hear you, but I can't hear the details."

She seemed a little mollified as she realized that he

couldn't hear all the details about what she was saying. *I've just been going through a rough time. I still don't know who you are.*

"Are you in a church?" he asked, as he got up and started walking again to the other rehab. "I don't know why I would ask that, but it seems like something you would do."

Well, … kind of.

"Kind of?" he repeated, with a headshake, glancing around. He usually avoided trying to talk to people while he was walking, in case something even more bizarre happened, but it seemed as if this was his best option right now.

She noted, *I'm just looking for help.*

"Fine," he told her, "that might be something I can do, but I need to know where you are and what kind of help you need. Is it money?"

No, no, no, she argued. *I don't need that kind of help.*

He frowned. "Do you know what year it is?"

A long silence came, and then she announced, *I think I need to go now. You might need to get some help.*

He groaned. "I'm not the one who needs help. You're the one who needs help."

I don't need help from you anymore, she stated hurriedly.

Since he'd asked her for the date, she probably thought he was a little bit cuckoo. So he explained, "Look. I know what year I'm in, but I need to know that you know what year you're in, and that it's the same."

With dead silence between them, she gasped, then everything went blank.

When Simon looked around to see where he'd walked to, he found himself standing outside a huge cathedral. The steps to go in were literally right in front of him.

Taking a hesitant step, he knew he had to be here for

some reason. He just didn't know what it was. As long as he remained outside, he would never find out.

So, he took the first step and walked up into this massive stone cathedral.

CHAPTER 10

RODNEY SUDDENLY ARRIVED at Kate's desk. "They all have Tinder accounts." His excitement was palpable.

Kate looked up at him and asked, "Did they all have matching profiles?"

"No, but they were all on the same site."

"That's something, but can you tell if they have matched up with others?"

"No, and I can't tell if anybody swiped. We probably have to get a search warrant to get Tinder to even begin to cooperate with that search."

"And I doubt we can get through that approval process very fast. So, … they all sought out dating sites. They were all looking for partners, more or less. And these sites all have iron-clad privacy clauses."

"Yes," Rodney confirmed. "I can't confirm whether this Caroline woman, who supposedly went out with Kurt and Robert, was also going out with John. We need Caroline's picture."

"We haven't talked to her yet," Kate noted, as she looked down at her notes. "That's the one we'll have to get ahold of."

"She hasn't been very responsive, has she?" Rodney asked.

"No, not at all, and she was seen dating two of our victims. What we don't know is whether she knew John or dated him too. If she did, that'll be an interesting conversation. I have her address, and she told me that she should be home today."

"Oh good, that's some progress," Rodney replied.

"So, let's go." Kate bolted to her feet, sending Rodney into a fit of laughter.

He teased, "Are you sure you don't want to get a second cup of coffee first?"

"Hell no. I want to get there before Caroline changes her mind and disappears. We can pick up coffee on the way," she added, with a smirk. "I don't understand what's going on here, and, until we figure it out, I won't be happy."

"Oh, I get it," he stated. "You're very much into locking down the entire truth as quickly as possible."

"Because people lie," she declared. "People tell us stories that they make up in their mind, and then their memories start to go quickly when they're asked very specific questions. So these people are no different. We have that one woman, Angel, who supposedly was dating one of these guys, John. Yet, upon further review, it was more of a convenience thing, friends with benefits, seeing Angel when John didn't have anybody else around. Once she understood the situation, she didn't take it very kindly."

"Yeah, I suppose not," Rodney agreed, "but come on? These guys were obviously players."

"And no promises were ever made," she added. "Even still, Angel's not feeling very generous toward John at the moment."

"Maybe that will help her get over the fact that he's dead," Rodney suggested.

"Yes, he's dead, but so is the fairy tale she's been telling herself. Therefore, she's not a very happy camper, especially after being taken in as long as she was."

"And yet was she really taken in or just allowed herself to live the fairy tale? I'm not so sure," he muttered, shaking his head and looking skeptical.

"I don't know either. And I really want to. So let's go."

Caroline's house wasn't all that far away, and they got there relatively quickly. It was a nice house, not an apartment.

"Well," Kate shared, "seems Caroline is doing okay for herself." Rodney nodded. They walked up to the front door, and it opened in front of them before she could knock.

The woman looked at the two of them and introduced herself. "I'm Caroline Lippa. You must be the detective I spoke to on the phone." She looked at Kate.

Kate pulled out her ID badge and showed it to her and introduced herself and Rodney. "Yes," Kate noted. "May we come in?" Caroline held open the door. As they walked in, Kate looked around and smiled. "Fresh roses."

"Yes, I have gardens out back. I do some gardening," Caroline shared, as she led the way to a more formal-looking living room.

Kate sat where Caroline motioned them to. Kate frowned. This was definitely in the running as the most uncomfortable couch Kate had ever sat on before. But she also recognized it as the furniture people chose for that reason. So that when company came, they didn't stay. Turning to face Caroline, Kate began, "I understand that you were going out with Robert Blake up until he died."

"Yes," Caroline confirmed, "but we weren't exclusive, obviously. I know that sounds terrible, but it wasn't meant to be bad."

Kate nodded. "And were you also going out with Kurt Conner when he died two years ago?"

She frowned but then nodded. "Yes, I was. I was going out with him at the time," she stated. "But again—and this is very important—we weren't exclusive."

Kate studied Caroline for a long moment. The woman was a little older than both Kurt and Robert but elegant, aging beautifully, but maybe feeling that the first flush of her youth had passed her by. Kate asked her, "Is there a reason for that, the nonexclusive relationships?"

"Yes," she declared. "I am divorced, and I'm frankly not looking to get into another marriage that wouldn't work out. I just want to be free for a while. And, so far, at least, I haven't met anybody who has inclined me to change that position."

"I see," Kate replied. "Do you have any children?"

"No," she replied, with a frown, and her tone got frosty. "I don't know how that matters."

"I don't know that it does matter," Kate noted. "I'm just collecting information."

Caroline sagged back. "My husband and I tried, and I never seemed to get pregnant," she shared. "And it was a contributing factor to our breakup."

"I'm sorry to hear that."

She shrugged. "It was disappointing but was one of those things that hadn't really been that big of a deal to me. Then all of a sudden, as I approach forty, I had to face the reality that maybe that childbearing time was gone, slipping right through my fingers."

Kate nodded. "Kind of the classic situation where you miss something that you didn't know you really wanted because it wasn't really ever available."

"Exactly, and now that'll probably never happen. So I feel as if I should have tried harder to conceive," she muttered. "And I realize that's a convoluted way of saying that I didn't care enough at the time."

"What about now?" Rodney asked.

"Right now, Detective? … I think I do care."

Kate blinked several times at that explanation and then replied, "Got it. Now, did either of these men have—wait, let's talk about Kurt."

"What about him? He died two years ago. There is nothing to talk about."

Kate countered, "That's not entirely true."

"Okay, ask away."

"Did he show any signs of depression?"

"No."

"Did you ever do drugs with him?"

"No," she said a little too quickly. "I don't do drugs. But he was a little bit more … active than I would have liked."

Kate eyed her shrewdly and didn't speak. The other woman flushed a little, clearly uncomfortable. "We did the occasional drugs," she admitted, "but it was never that bad, and it was never serious."

Kate didn't budge, refusing to relax back and to let her off the hook.

After a long moment of silence, Caroline shrugged. "Honestly," she began, looking a bit flustered now, "I don't have a problem with a little bit of fun, but he was definitely over-the-top with—"

"So, you weren't surprised when the cause of Kurt's death was drugs."

"No," she muttered, "I was not surprised. I was upset and more emotionally involved than I realized. It was a real awakening, understanding how affected I had been and how involved we had been."

"So, you weren't surprised and didn't have any questions about it?"

"No," she stated. "Kurt was just that way. It sounds as if you think there's a link between Robert's and Kurt's deaths, but I can't see it. I mean, yes, I was involved with both of them. And they were both really good men, but they were not the kind of men who you marry," she declared.

"How so?" Kate asked.

"It was the way they lived. They weren't the kind you take home to meet your mother. Plus, your father would never let them in the door."

Kate asked, "And you knew that from the start?"

"I got that right from the beginning. And I wasn't looking to take anybody home to my parents anyway," she stated, her bitterness evident. "Been there, done that."

"And it didn't turn out to be as promised, so you didn't want to go there again," Kate suggested.

Caroline glared at her. "I just wanted to not always be alone. If I found somebody perfect, well, that might be a different story. Yet I wasn't out looking for a husband. Does that make sense?"

"It does," Kate agreed. "And that's important. We just have to confirm that there aren't any connections between these two men. And I don't really know that there is at this stage, but two men, the same company? Of course, as soon as more information comes to light, we'll have a little better understanding."

Caroline stared at her. "God, it's terrible. Robert was just so, … so full of life. He was so happy, so robust." She winced. "I know this will sound terrible, but he was so virile." And unexpectedly her tears spilled. "I feel as if I lost out on somebody who was hugely important to me. And I didn't even realize it until it was too late."

Kate tilted her head at her. Before this, Caroline had looked completely composed and calm. Now she broke down. Kate clearly felt Caroline was putting on an act. Now they had to see if she was acting before, or if *this* was the play for her. "Any chance you know John Smith?"

Caroline frowned at her. "Why?"

"Because, so far, you're the only connection we have found between Kurt and Robert, but we also have another case that could potentially be connected. Still, it's a bit of a long shot."

"Does he work for the same company as I do?"

"No," Kate replied.

"Thank God for that," Caroline muttered. "I would start looking for another job if you told me that was the case."

"Though he is in the same industry."

At that, Caroline raised both eyebrows. "Seriously? Most people in this industry with any serious level of commitment and a long-term career know each other. I mean, obviously I don't know them all, but now you're making me a little nervous."

Kate pulled out the picture of John and showed her the photo. She stared at it for a long time, then looked up at Kate and said, "I never dated him."

Kate noted a reluctance evident in her tone, so she had to ask. "But?"

"But"—her voice broke—"I did meet him. He was at a conference here in Vancouver, maybe two years back. I didn't see him again and had nothing to do with him. I certainly didn't sleep with him, if that's your next question," she declared. "And, for the record, I don't go around sleeping with dozens of people." She took a deep breath and added, "Although this situation makes me look absolutely godawful."

Kate shook her head. "It does not. You have human needs, the same as anybody else. And, if this is how you choose to find a connection with somebody, that's your choice. I'm not here to judge you."

"What are you here for, Detective?" Caroline asked her.

"I'm here to sort out if there is any connection between you and these men."

She swallowed hard. "I could swear that there wouldn't be, but now you've got me confused." Her gaze kept going to the picture that Kate still held. "I don't know what to say about that one, but I didn't sleep with him."

"Not even when you were drunk at a conference?"

Caroline frowned at her question. "God, I really have given you a hell of an impression."

"No," Kate countered, "but I have seen plenty of instances where people do things they didn't plan on doing. It's not at all unusual for someone to go to a party or a conference and have a bit too much to drink, and then plans go out the window."

She shook her head. "I didn't." Yet she winced. "I will acknowledge that, on occasion, I might get smashed. And I might have had—particularly after the divorce—a little too much to drink. But I would never have slept with somebody and not realized it or remembered it."

"Even if some *social* drugs were used?"

Caroline shook her head.

Kate nodded. "So, John Smith is not on your list of men you've slept with."

She shook her head. "No." Then she sat back and sighed. "Thank God for that. What a job you have to do to go around checking the men whom women sleep with to confirm that they aren't—" She stopped abruptly, then she swallowed.

Kate chuckled and finished her sentence. "To confirm they aren't their killer?"

"God," she muttered, "is that why you're here? Am I a suspect in Robert's death? Please check my place. I don't have any poison. Or drugs."

"I can't really look for any poison if I don't know what poison was used," Kate clarified. "So that may be something I have to do down the road."

Caroline stared at the detectives, tears filling her eyes. She whispered, "Suddenly my life doesn't look so bad when I look at yours."

Rodney's phone buzzed, and he excused himself to take the call outside.

Kate nodded at her partner, then smiled at Caroline.

Caroline continued. "Are you married, Detective?"

"No. However, I have a man whom I love and who loves me dearly. I get up and go to work, and I help to close cases where we seek justice for people who have been victimized by others," she explained. "I get that, to you, my profession and my life probably don't mean much. However, to me, both mean everything. So, no need to feel sorry for me. I'm perfectly content with where I'm at."

"Yeah?" Caroline snapped, her tone ready to kill someone. "What about when you get married? What about when you turn around and that asshole, who you absolutely loved, the one you spent the last ten years doing everything for—including sending him back to school at your expense, and taking a second job when he couldn't possibly find one and the bills were piling up—only to have him find some younger, better-looking version of you in their new law firm? Someone who would be a much better partner in his new upwardly mobile life that he's expecting to lead. How the hell will you feel then?"

Kate nodded. "Believe me. That sounds absolutely shitty, but that's a story I have heard time and time again. Unfortunately, there seems to be no way to stop shitty."

Caroline gave a broken laugh. "You're right about that," she agreed, "and he was shitty and so stupid. I worked so hard trying to support us both, getting all the accoutrements of an attorney whom I elevated to my own position. So now I'm making way more money and doing a whole lot better. Although maybe not," she added, as she stared at the picture in front of her, "because emotionally I just feel dead."

Kate didn't even want to go into that conversation, having no clue how she kept getting into these discussions. She should have Rodney take more of an upfront role in these info-gathering discussions. *That* was something she planned to change the minute they got back in their car. Women absolutely loved Rodney, and that would hopefully help Kate to avoid dealing with any of these deeply personal, intense conversations. What the hell?

She soon concluded her interview and thanked Caroline for her time.

Kate stepped outside, motioned for Rodney to join her, and headed to their vehicle. When he neared her, she asked him, "Where did you go? You'll start taking more of a role in talking to these women."

"Why?" he asked, distracted. "They seem to be spilling their guts to you. So, what do you need me for? I figured you had it handled, so I stepped out to take a call."

"No, no more taking calls because, Rodney, I'm telling you, … these women are nuts. Bat-shit crazy. And, for some reason, they seem to think I have some counselor badge on my forehead. They just want to tell me all these godforsaken tales of woe. I can't deal with it. I can't."

Rodney boomed with laughter.

"I won't. … I just can't take it," she declared.

"Easy now, calm down. Just calm down."

"New rule," she ordered. "You're always coming with me when interrogating *any* woman. You may not leave, and we'll have a signal. So, when I've reached my limit, you need to step in. I'm not dealing with all these women anymore who seem to think they must tell me all the gory details of their love lives—or the love lives they've imagined. I don't need to hear about all the heartbreaks and the secrets of their lives. I just don't want to know. Unless it's part of the case of course," she clarified, correcting herself.

Still chuckling, Rodney's tone was curious when he said, "I gather the interview got more interesting after I stepped out."

"She slept with the first two guys, doesn't know any-thing about the one from a few days ago, yet was horrified though because she recognized him."

"Oh really," he noted, perking up. "Recognized how?"

"Thankfully not in a biblical sense."

He burst out laughing at that. "Oh, you two must have had a grand old time."

"No, no, no," she spat. "I don't think those words exist together when it comes to this shit," she muttered, "Clearly you, my loyal and beloved partner, seem to be enjoying this scenario. But me? No, not at all. I'm really not into all this crap. Somehow these otherwise intelligent women apparently go brain-dead when it comes to men. Nope, no more!"

"That's just part of the job," Rodney muttered.

"Part of *your* job, which you do so very well," she stated, her tone sarcastic. "And I don't know why or how anybody would even begin to think to share this with me."

"I don't know either," he admitted, "but now I want to put a little camera on your jacket collar to see how you interact with them. You do realize that, for them to feel comfortable enough to spill their guts to you and to tell you what they're feeling, they must feel a hint of empathy coming from you. That's something you should share a little bit."

"Very funny. Let's go. … I've had my fill of this day. Let's head back, and remember that I'm not interviewing any of these women again, not unless you are with me and you are leading the questions. Don't even think of trying that *taking a call* BS exit line again either. … You can't bail on me for some stupid phone call." With that, she slammed the car door, as Rodney's laughter filled the air. Even just hearing that made her feel a little better, but, by the time she grumped her way back home, she was still rattled and seething on the inside.

When Simon saw her, his eyebrows shot up. "So, not a good day?"

She stared at him and then asked, "Do I seem to be the empathetic kind?" He frowned. "Don't answer that," she said. "Would you choose me to just bleed all over emotionally? Do I look like the kind of person who would be right there for you, consoling you and doling out life and relationship advice?" He frowned, opened his mouth, and she snapped, "Don't answer that."

He snapped it shut again. His eyebrows shooting up again, he noted, "Not a good day then."

She glared at him. "*Not a good day then.*"

"Okay," he replied, "so you've got an hour or two free?"

"I have an hour or two free," she confirmed. "I might just have longer than that since I'm getting absolutely nowhere with my case." She glared at him.

"Okay." Then he held up a big picnic basket.

She frowned at it. "It's way too cold to go for a picnic. What are you up to?" She got half a growl, half a grunt from him.

Then his lips twitched, and he shared, "I was thinking about the *Running Mate.*"

Her eyes lit up in a complete one-hundred-eighty-degree twist of emotions. "Perfect." She spun around, grabbed her coat that she had just flung onto the couch beside her. "Let's go."

"Are you sure you don't want to take a moment to—"

"No," she snapped, glaring at him again. "*Now.*"

"Okay." Then he hopped forward, trying to keep his grin in check.

She snorted at him and shook her head. "You should knock off that grin, or I'll knock it off for you."

He burst out laughing, getting the beginnings of a reluctant grin from her. "I am so sorry you had one of those days."

"I've *never* had *one of those days,*" she snapped, with another glare, "and what on earth would make anybody think I'm a sympathetic ear?"

He bit back something but still spoke. "You'll take this entirely the wrong way, but I love you enough to tell you anyway."

She gave him a narrowed gaze.

Simon began, "A lot of people think you're a really good listener, and you're really empathetic and great with people." The shock on her face had him absolutely bending over with laughter.

She continued to glare at him, now pointing a finger at him. "You have *got* to be joking."

Still laughing, he tugged her into the elevator she had just come up on.

As soon as Edgar saw them, he waved a hand. "That's perfect. The *Running Mate*, is it?"

"Absolutely," Simon said, with a smile. "Kate needs a break."

Edgar suggested, "Kate needs a holiday."

As she marched past the doorman, Kate muttered to Simon, "Edgar is not good at keeping it all locked up either."

Edgar smiled and added, "But, short of a vacation, the *Running Mate* will have to do. For spur of the moment getaways, it's just what you need."

"Yeah," she muttered, turning to him. "You got that right." She glared back at Simon and whispered, "And *you* have a lot to explain."

He was still chortling when they finally got to the *Running Mate*, the boat that Simon bought from one of his acquaintances, Baxter. Simon led the way down into its warm underbelly. She stopped inside happily, as she took off her coat and collapsed onto the big couch.

She looked around the place and sighed. The cabin was cozy and felt warm enough for her to shed her coat. "I know it makes no sense. I mean, I know that. I know that outside is probably no different than in here." She waved her hands around the space. "And that, if we were to take the same moment and go right back to the apartment, it would be theoretically the same."

His smile widened, as if understanding what was coming.

"But it doesn't feel the same when I'm here."

"That's what *escape* is all about," he noted. "It's having a space, not connected to work, not connected to home, not connected to drama, not connected to all that other stuff that just permeates our souls. And, for all the days that we have problems, everybody should have a getaway place to just escape to."

She smiled because Simon really understood what she felt.

He handed her a glass of wine before pouring himself one. Then he clinked glasses with hers as he sat beside her. "And that is exactly how we'll treat this. Just a step out of time, a moment in time not filled with drama, not filled with death, murder, and lies, not filled with subterfuge, betrayal, or anything else." He looked at her sideways. "What do you say?"

She leaned forward, put her glass on the table, and kissed him gently. "I say yes."

"Let's just park it," he muttered, kissing her back. "For the moment until we are a little bit more settled," he whispered in her ear, "just let go of it all and find something nice to talk about."

She looked over at him and frowned. "You got something nice you want to talk about?"

"Nope, I don't." Her eyebrows shot up, and then he asked her, "You got anything nice you can talk about?"

She stared at him and just mutely shook her head.

He suggested, "In that case, why don't we just enjoy

something called silence?"

Kate chuckled, picked up her glass of wine, and took a sip. "Why don't we?"

SIMON ROLLED OVER in the night, feeling the cool air.

Kate had somehow stolen all the covers—something she rarely did unless she was stressed. When he checked her, he found her arms and legs tucked up tightly, almost in a fetal position. He realized that, whatever had gone on in her world earlier today, had stressed her out more than he had expected.

It had been the right thing to get her out of the apartment and onto the *Running Mate*. They'd even decided to spend the night here and then head off to work in the morning because it offered such soul-enlivening peace for them. For the most part, every time they spent any time here, it was just … a slice of heaven, for both of them.

He got up, went to the bathroom, then snuggled back under the covers, trying to recapture some of the blankets so that he didn't freeze, making a mental note that he needed to bring more blankets on the boat. It wasn't a big expense by any means. It was just one more thing that he must remember to do. It seemed as if there were a lot of those lately.

Whether that was a good thing or a bad thing was up for debate. However, definitely some challenges had presented themselves in both of their worlds right now. He couldn't figure out just what was going on in terms of his banking mess and whether it was something big or whether it was literally just nonsense. He wanted to believe it was nonsense, but he wasn't a fool.

And he wouldn't necessarily have the right answers all

the time for everybody. If the bank manager was just worried about checks and balances, that was fine. However, if it was more than that, it was far from fine.

Simon really had no clue what started it—or who—but Simon mentioning pulling all his business from the bank where David worked had certainly caused David a bit of a heart attack. Of course Simon would only move the cash, as he was locked into the debts, unless he paid penalties on all of them.

David had texted back how that was not necessary. He shared how he'd had a long talk with his superiors about it, explaining that Simon's system was potentially unorthodox but had never been an issue.

You've never defaulted on anything was exactly what David texted. And he shared about not understanding the sudden change from management. He then further elaborated in another text how an investigation into the bank's checks and balances was underway, after another US bank had fallen.

David followed up with another text. **Of course, we don't have the same system, and everything we have is backed up by the government, but it's all made them a little edgy. So they're just doing an audit. It should be just fine.**

Simon texted back **Should?**

David replied, **Let the process do its thing. Don't worry about it. I'm here. I've got your back. That's all you need to know for now.**

Simon wasn't so sure, but he was willing to let it slide for the moment. He didn't know whether investors were getting into his quiet little corner or something else was brewing here. He didn't take kindly to something else brewing in his world as that was never a good thing. When he didn't hear anything more from David for the rest of the day, Simon had more or less forgotten about it. His life had gone a little bit sideways at one of the renovation sites.

Now he and Kate had to get up soon. It was six already. They had to go back to his place and each get ready to start their day.

He rolled over and found Kate curled up beside him and had thoughts of anything but heading back. He decided that life out there could wait for at least ten minutes.

She opened her eyes, squinting them at the rising sun.

"If only we had the time," he muttered, smiling at her sleepy face. "How fast can you get dressed?"

Her eyes opened with alarm. "Oh my God, are we that late?"

"Nope. It's only six."

She sank back and smiled. "That's not late at all."

"I know," he muttered, as he nuzzled her cheek. "So, I highly suggest we take advantage of the fact that, for the first time in a long time, we're awake together."

She wrapped her arms around him, smiling as she pulled him close. "Only if we have time." And they did, indeed, take complete advantage of the time they had.

Two hours later, as they walked out of his apartment, Kate called Rodney, saying that she was on her way into work but could be a few minutes late, then promptly ended the call.

Simon looked at her and asked, "Will you really be late?"

She shrugged. "I don't really know, but I won't push it," she replied. "He's having an okay time at the moment, but he's not the same after … the beating he took. It wasn't exactly the easiest on his ego."

Simon shrugged. "My ego is just fine, by the way," he added, with a chuckle. "But, hey, thanks for asking." Startled, she turned to him. He added, "I'm just kidding. I'm fine."

She narrowed her gaze, trying to see right through him.

God, if his grandmother were alive, she would be absolutely delighted with Kate because she was such a no-nonsense, no-frills, live-life-to-the-fullest woman, and she did it just right. He leaned over, grabbed her chin, and gave her a kiss right there in front of everybody on the busy Vancouver sidewalks.

"Honest, I'm fine. Now get to work. Meanwhile, I'm heading off to check on all my projects, as usual. However, a couple months ago Joe had to fire a wannabe welder, who ruins everything he touches, and Joe has seen him back on our site again."

"Problems?" she asked.

Simon groaned. "He didn't take being fired very well, so apparently he came back early today to cause trouble." She studied him for a minute, and he shook his head. "Obviously everything'll be aboveboard and legal."

She stared at him and asked, "But is *he* aboveboard and legal?"

"If not, I know who to call."

She rolled her eyes. "Don't bother." But then she stopped and added, "Unless you kill him." Then, with a laugh, she got into her car and took off, leaving him standing there.

He smiled, wondering how he got so lucky with Kate, when she was such a dynamo and such a contrast in so many different ways. And yet every way was just so perfect for him. With a headshake, he hopped onto the little ferry and made his way to the closest jobsite.

There he checked in with his foreman, Kevin, who smiled and pointed out, "Everything's okay on this site. I hear you got a staffing problem at another site. Joe warned me in case the guy came over here for a job."

"It won't last very long."

"Even if it did," Kevin noted, "I don't take kindly to anybody trying to cause trouble."

"Right, and causing trouble is definitely something we can't have more of." Simon shook his head and added, "We've got enough problems."

"No problems here. We don't have problems because I won't allow there to be problems. Troublemakers don't work on my sites," Kevin declared coldly. "I've made that abundantly clear to any number of potential dissidents."

Simon laughed. "Glad to hear it."

He checked out a few things while he was here. Got a couple measurements that he needed. Picked up some photos needed for the upcoming marketing campaign. Then he took his leave and headed over to another jobsite.

As he walked inside the building, Joe called out, "He's gone already."

"Damn good thing," Simon replied, his tone mild, but he knew his gaze was anything but friendly.

Joe nodded. "I warned him what would happen if he was on-site when you got here."

"And I hope the other construction groups around here understand what he's up to."

"They should. I forewarned the lot of them." Joe confirmed. "Even had one of them show up over here to talk to me about it a month earlier. This poser is apparently building himself a bit of a reputation for being a troublemaker."

"*Great,*" Simon muttered. "Why is it we are short on skilled people, but we always have too many of the lying shits?"

Joe laughed. "Not all of them are shitty. Some of them are really good."

"Sure, but those skilled workers we've already hired," Simon pointed out. "I keep them employed even if I don't have work for them."

"In this industry, it's hard to keep the good workers around unless you keep paying them. Still, you have enough projects for the most part, so it works out."

"That's the reason I do it that way, so we can keep as much quality staff as we do," Simon shared. "What I don't need is some jerk thinking he'll mess up years and years of work because he's entitled to it."

"He took off pretty fast this morning," Joe stated. "So, I don't think he'll be around here, looking for you."

"If he is, let him find me," Simon ordered, with that same hard smile that had gotten him through so much before. "Text me his name and his other details though, will you?"

"Will do," Joe confirmed. "It's Allen something. I already let accounting know too, right after I fired him, which is my standard practice, just in case he somehow pops up on any of our jobsites. Plus, I told the rest of your foremen that he's not to be hired. They are flagged in the office."

"Good," Simon stated, his tone light.

"Not a problem."

"You still taking that holiday soon?" Simon asked Joe.

"Yep, sure am. The wife, you know how she feels about it."

"I do know how she feels about it," he replied, with a laugh. "Let's hope that nothing goes wrong that could stop it from happening."

Joe eyed him in alarm. "You know that's not the thing to say, right?"

"I know," he quipped, with an evil grin. "It's one of the reasons why I said it."

"Oh, don't be doing that to me now. Come on, man. If she had even the slightest inkling that this trip could get cancelled, you have no idea how difficult my life would get."

Simon burst out laughing. "If need be, I could always be here on a day-to-day basis until you get back."

Joe stared at him in consternation, then shook his head. "We both know better. You don't have time for that."

"Won't matter though, will it?" Simon asked. Then he added, "Don't worry about it. We'll figure it out."

Joe shook his head. "I don't want to be worrying while I'm gone. And that *don't worry* line don't cut it anymore."

Simon smiled. "It'll be fine. I promise. Hey, I can handle it."

"Yeah, I know you can handle it," Joe acknowledged, "but that doesn't mean the guys will be happy. They always get nervous when you're around."

"Not all of them," Simon noted.

"The new guys do. They hear so much from the other ones that just catching sight of you makes them nervous."

"They should get used to that," Simon suggested. "If the older guys are making them mess up, have a talk with them."

"Yeah, that won't work. You and I both know that."

"I do know that," he agreed, with a smile. "It'll be fine, and I promise you can go on that holiday. I wouldn't want to face your wife over that."

"You will have to tell her if anything happens," Joe declared, as he took the hat off his head and wiped his brow. "I ain't taking that on."

Simon was still laughing as he crossed the road and picked up his coffee from one of the vendors. As he sat down on the bench on the far side, he looked around but all he got was just a nice peaceful nudge from the morning, as if everything was going well in the city. Yet he knew, somewhere in the city, somebody wasn't having a good day. For the most part, his morning was calm, peaceful, and sent off the right vibes for having a nice calm cup of coffee.

As he enjoyed his morning cup of java, he thought about Kate and everything going on in her world—as well as the unknown woman from the bank, plus the always praying Sarah in his visions. Which reminded him of his push to visit that church—and he found himself turning to look in that direction.

He'd not entered the church that day. He'd stopped right outside, his phone buzzing. However, that church hadn't left him alone, and, even now, he got up, his feet walking him to the same damn spot. As he reached the church doors, he opened them and stepped inside, wondering what on earth was driving him here.

The place was empty, but he knew he could probably find someone in the back. He sat here on one of the pews for a long moment, but, when he got up and started to walk out, a man appeared at the podium and greeted him kindly. Simon smiled, lifted a hand, and turned away.

The priest asked, "Can I help you with anything, son?"

Simon turned and smiled. "I don't think so, Father." His tone was mild. "It was an impulse. I just came to see what the church was like."

"I hope the experience was good for you. Absolutely no pressure to leave if you want to stay longer."

"Ah, that could be true," Simon noted, "but I'm a working man." And, with that, he smiled and left the church.

He stood on the front step for quite a while, staring at the street, at the sidewalks, as he watched the world pass by, yet he was not rushing. He sensed that same calm from earlier. It was a unique feeling in a way but still an interesting venture. Yet nothing here triggered the vision of Sarah, the always praying woman. He didn't have a picture of her. He had never seen her face in his visions. He had her first name, *Sarah*, but was that enough to even ask the good Catholic Father about? Simon was here today, but she wasn't. No woman was inside the church. And Sarah only appeared in his visions. Still, he had been pulled to this church for a reason. He should have gone inside the other day.

He knew he should have. That's just one of those things that he couldn't do anything about now because the time had come and gone. At least that's how he thought about it.

And yet here he was, considering all the other messes and the police cases that had come around to him throughout the years, still wondering if he had missed an opportunity to help this woman. The door opened behind him, and the priest stepped out, smiling at him. "You're welcome to come back in."

Simon smiled. "No, I meant it, Father. I do need to get to work."

"Another time then. You are always welcome here."

"Yeah, perhaps," he replied comfortably. As he glanced around, he asked, "It's such a beautiful morning. Are you expecting people all day?"

"We have classes. We have prayer. We have a special

Bible study group that comes in about an hour," he shared. "It's a pretty full-on program here."

Simon nodded. "And how are you supported?"

He smiled at him. "To a certain extent by the generosity of the people we serve. ... The rest comes from our diocese, covering some of the expenses that we can't cover ourselves. For the most part, it's a pretty even balance, cash in, cash out, which has been good."

"And so it should be," Simon stated. "I'm sure a lot of people have benefited from this church being here over the years."

"I would very much like to think so," he replied, "bene-fitting people such as yourself perhaps."

Simon shrugged. "It's been a long time since I actively participated in a church," he noted, taking in the architecture before him. "It is an absolutely beautiful building, and it has a certain ... energy about it." Daring to take a chance, he added, without mentioning any visions, "I saw a woman, and she seemed to be, I don't want to say *unhappy* but maybe a little too fervent in her prayers."

"Lots of women come here, ... for many different reasons," he replied. "Sometimes because they are hoping for children. Sometimes hoping for husbands. Sometimes hoping for the health of a loved one. They come here to pray, to ask for help, and sometimes to ask for ... forgiveness."

Simon winced at that. "Yeah, I can see that one."

The priest smiled. "We are all sinners. There is no blame. We are only here to come closer to God and to be relieved of our sins," he explained. "If that is something I can help you with, son, ... don't think on it so much before addressing it. You can come anytime you want."

Simon studied him, a faint smile on his lips. "No, Father, I fear that will not be an answer for me, at least not today." And, with that, he nodded and headed down the front steps.

"It's never too late," the priest called back. "Anytime you want to come, you are welcome."

Simon lifted a hand in acknowledgement and headed out. He didn't have the heart to tell the priest that the things that went on in his woo-woo world were not exactly conducive to staying in church, especially when talking about the afterlife and all the tortured souls he had met, while dealing with the crises that came from death.

Not that any of them were bad or that he was their judge and jury. Just some topics would not be accepted well in church, and he really didn't need other people to tell him that. With a whistle, he headed to deal with another job, one that was not fully set up and organized yet, but he was meeting with the architect.

It wasn't nearly time yet, but he couldn't wait to get started on her. This was the next building they would rehab. The architect was already working on it, and they were about to start signing contracts for structural engineers and building contractors, but Simon's foreman on each project handled all that. Simon had found over the years that handling certain aspects in-house just went better. So he no longer trusted other companies to do it the way he wanted things done.

He was constantly being asked by those other companies if he wanted a hand, but his answer was always no. He kept a very close eye on all aspects of his various building projects, and his foremen—including Steven, Joe, and Kevin—were much more general contractors than anything. They had experience regarding the big buildings, and that experience was worth so much. As Simon walked to his newest jobsite, he couldn't help but feel a weird sensation of somebody, something, following him.

He slipped down an alleyway at the end of one of the blocks, stepped into an alcove, then stopped to see if anybody would close in and follow him. Sure enough, somebody came around the corner, looking almost a little too intently to see if Simon had gone this way. He didn't recognize the man, but Simon waited to see what the guy would do.

Simon was no slouch in the self-defense or fitness department, but he had to admit that, after the beating he'd taken not too long ago, he could still feel some of his ribs complaining at the idea of a full-on fight. As he watched the other man come deeper into the shadows, Simon called out, "Go ahead. Say whatever you want to say to me. I'm just waiting for you."

The other man froze.

Simon called out again, "Yeah, you better rethink things. It'll be a cold day in hell before I let some punk stop me from doing this."

"Stop you from what?" he asked, his tone fearful.

"Stop me while I'm out here doing my job," he replied. Simon heard a very soft swear word, then suddenly the man picked up and took off. Simon gave him one final message. "Another time maybe."

Simon slowly stepped out of the shadows, not sure who had decided that somebody needed to give him a dark visit like this. Considering the banking mess, he wouldn't be at all surprised if somebody out there didn't want Simon to continue having the same successes going forward that he had experienced in the past. The trouble was, Simon really didn't have a clue who could hate him that much.

For the most part, he stayed away from people, kept his nose clean, bought buildings, sold buildings, made money, and kept the process going. But right now, for whatever reason, some asshole seemed to think that Simon should not be allowed to continue this path.

One thing that Simon knew he was *no good at* was letting other people dictate the actions of his life.

CHAPTER 11

K ATE SAT ACROSS from Rodney. "Did you source out who that phone number was?"

He shook his head. "No. All I can tell you is, it's not local."

"But all three of the men had that same number in their phone records?"

"Yes, but that doesn't mean it's not a spam call or somebody upset at the insurance payout."

She frowned, while nodding her head. "That's an interesting proposition too."

He asked, "What?"

"The insurance payout part," she noted, "although this seems particularly personal."

"Oh, I would say it's personal," he confirmed, turning to her. "I'm not sure if it's just sexual though."

"I'm not either," she noted, pondering it, "but it does have that intimate feel. I mean, wrapping them up as if a gift for somebody else? I don't know about you, but, if I was pissed off at somebody because he was having an affair with somebody else, I might leave them a gift too."

He glanced at her, then added, "I hadn't considered that, but you're right. Thinking about these men and their lifestyles, the murderer could very well have been a jealous lover."

"It could be," she agreed, "and the idea of poison is getting to me. I don't want to say it's always a woman's method of killing, but, as we well know, it's the most popular method of killing that women resort to."

Rodney nodded. "It's also easy—easy to administer, easy to get, right off the shelves at the garden store or grocery store or wherever. The internet's got all kinds of them. You just pour it into a drink."

"All these men drink too," she noted, pointing her finger at him.

"But more men drink than don't drink," he stated.

"Sure, but would all those drinking men give women access to their drinks, unless they were shagging them?"

Rodney's lips kicked up, and he chuckled at the term. "Where did you pick that up?"

"From some British guy." She laughed and added, "I mean, there're a lot of ways to put it, but, if these three guys were screwing around or having affairs with all these women, maybe somebody decided it was time for them to stop, but they wouldn't. However, none of that fits the *believe* thing."

"Maybe the *believe* thing is nothing, a distraction," he suggested. "Maybe she offered to take him on a holiday. Maybe he tells her it'll never happen because she couldn't get the money or whatever. Maybe she was like, *believe*, as in manifesting it or whatever."

"Or praying, some church thing." She pondered that for a moment. "I don't know. I don't know how that one could fit," she muttered, "and it pisses me off because everything needs to fit."

"Of course it does," Rodney confirmed. laughing, "especially with you. You're all about the whys."

She frowned at him and asked, "Do you think I focus

too much on it?"

"Nope," he replied. "It's just your way of working through things. So, if somebody has done this *believe* thing, then you'll be a whole lot more geared to sort out why they would do it."

She nodded. "I think *the why* has to be the domineering point," she noted. "I mean, if there's no why, then you just have a random killing, and that is not what this is. A *why* could just be because the people in front of him were in his way, and he was having a pissy day. I mean, ... there's always a why, whether we think it's a big-enough reason to kill somebody or not."

"The trouble is, when you get that why, it still doesn't always make sense."

She nodded at that. "Yep, you're right. It doesn't always make sense to us, but it does to them. So, what possible motive would anybody have for killing these three guys? And how long were those phone calls?"

"Short."

"And how close to the days that they died were the calls made?"

He looked at her in surprise. "That I haven't checked." He immediately picked up the paperwork that he had printed off and grimaced. "Shit, they were the same day."

She smiled. "Bingo. We need to know whose number that is."

"It's not registered anywhere, so it's probably a burner phone."

"And that would imply motivation," she muttered, "pre-planning, and somebody who was really pissed off over something."

"So, what do you think the calls were about?"

"Maybe to see what they were up to."

He looked up at her and smiled. "Yeah, confirming they were home so they could get the job done or just checking in to see if he was busy with a side piece."

"It could be anything and everything," Kate noted. "I mean, it could even be a phone call to ask to see them that night. It might be totally innocent. And it could even be somebody who's not even connected to the murders who is being asked to make that phone call."

He nodded. "You could be right about that. ... That won't make it any easier to sort this out."

"No, but I want to know. ... I'll call Caroline back, and I'll talk to the woman I spoke to at the office as well."

"Mary? Lanny? Which one?"

"Probably both of them, and I want to see if they belong to any women's groups," she added.

"What's the connection to the women's groups?"

She didn't reply, and Rodney didn't press his question either. Kate was wondering about Simon's connection in all this too.

So Rodney asked another question. "Do you think these women will be honest with you?"

"If they aren't, and we find out afterward, it'll be another nail in their coffin."

"And why women's groups?" he asked again.

She turned to him and began, "I know this probably sounds far-fetched."

He snorted. "With you, it always sounds far-fetched."

"I'm just thinking about the whole *traditional wife* thing, settling down, having kids."

"But I think we're way past the traditional wife in these cases," Lilliana interjected, walking over to join the conversation. "I think the traditional wife thing is literally staying home, producing the kids, looking after the house, not working, no higher education or training, and certainly not scrolling social media online dating sites. So, I'm not sure how that fits."

Kate clarified, "I'm not sure that *traditional wife* is the phrase I want to attach to this anyway. I'm just considering a whole group of people who want to have a family, but our three guys very specifically did not want that. So where does the whole *believe* thing enter this mess?" She turned to Rodney, who just raised both hands.

"I don't know."

She glanced at Lilliana, and she did the same.

Kate admitted, "I think we are looking in the wrong direction. ...Yet I don't know what the right direction is. That's the challenge." She frowned. "Did forensics find any feminine item of any kind which identified who could have been in John's apartment that night?"

"No," Lilliana replied, "but we have John's diary, courtesy of you, not forensics. However, it's more of a planner that he started to keep, then gave up. No recent entries were in it, so not very helpful. Also we have his phone records, with tons of call to various women."

Rodney nodded. "Plus, we have Robert's physical address book, and we have his huge Contacts list from his phone. Again tied to women."

Kate nodded. "Good. Let's start contacting these women in those two guys' records. Let's start with phone calls. However, if you get a hit off anybody as being difficult or avoiding your questions, not particularly happy to talk to you, let's lean in on them and see if we can get some more information on them and their chats with these Romeos."

"And just what is it that I'm looking for, when making these calls?" Rodney asked, turning to her.

"Maybe ask each one if they know any of our three dead guys. If so, ask them what each guy's mood was like, whether anybody was pressuring any of them to get married," she replied, "or to settle down or to change their lifestyle, those kinds of things."

"And would they know?" Rodney asked. "These guys were playboys, with no long-term plans in the dating world."

"A regular side piece might," Kate noted, with a snort. "Somebody in a *friends with benefits* deal with these guys would know that the men didn't want to make any changes. And, if so, ask each woman if they know somebody who might object? Maybe our three guys complained about somebody causing them trouble or putting on the pressure?"

"Okay, I'll get at it," Rodney said.

Lilliana added, "I'll help for as long as I can. What will you do, Kate?"

"I'll ruffle some feathers."

"How so?" Lilliana asked, amusement in her tone.

"I'll contact the detective handling the case out of Coquitlam, see if we can get a copy of Kurt's phone records, and do the same thing with his. Somewhere, somebody has to be showing up consistently in these calls. For John's death, somebody must have had access to his place, must have known when he was home, so it's likely that one person made calls to all three men accordingly."

Rodney turned to her. "Are you thinking it's the same killer?"

"I'm just covering all the bases until we know more. I don't know anything at this point," she conceded. "It's possible, but that's an awful lot of kills, particularly when there's a good chance these were all done by a woman."

"Or by a jealous boyfriend," Lilliana added.

"*Or by a jealous boyfriend,*" Kate repeated, nodding. "In a way that makes more sense, but I don't think we can cross anybody off right now."

And, with that, they each got to work. When she reached out to the detective from the older case, she introduced herself. He gave her his name, Nick Forbes. Thankfully he was willing to share info as long as she returned the favor. With that agreement in place, she waited for the list to come through and then printed it off. She shook her head as she saw the pages and pages of phone numbers on this one guy's Contact list.

Rodney looked up when he heard the printer, then whistled at the number of pages being spit out. "These guys are incredibly active."

Kate quipped, "Nothing else for them to do, I guess."

Rodney chuckled.

Kate continued. "A part of me wishes these guys could be happy for ten minutes. That they cared about the mind that went along with the body of these women."

Rodney turned to her, raising one eyebrow.

She shrugged. "It always sounds great until you're in it. Then it's just hollow."

"For some people, absolutely. They're built for that but not for all of us," Rodney clarified.

"And yet a lot of people, once they get it, they don't want it anymore," she murmured.

"What about you?" Rodney asked.

"I'm happy. I didn't go looking, and Simon just … fell into my lap," she admitted, "but I'm not stupid." She faced him. "I truly *realize* the wonderful relationship I have, but I still have days where I think it'll never work," she muttered, "especially the days when we have his woo-woo stuff going on. That's often a complete killer in a relationship, but I'm still hanging in there."

"I think he needs you for that too," Rodney suggested, staring at her. "He needs that acceptance."

"Yes, he does," she agreed, "and I'm at a place where I'm fully accepting. Yet we definitely have times when I wake up and just shake my head, wondering what the hell I've gotten myself into."

He laughed. "I think Simon would probably say the same thing about you."

She grinned and nodded. "You could be right." With that, she dialed the number at the top of her list and went on down the line.

Her questions didn't take very long to bring these women to tears, some crying out in shock, others not very forthcoming at all. Some asked what it had to do with them. All in all, Kate was gathering quite a mix of reactions. When she got to the next woman, *Sherry*, Kate went through her initial spiel, asking Sherry if she knew Kurt Conner, John Smith, or Robert Blake. As soon as Sherry heard the name *Robert Blake*, she broke up.

"Excuse me. I'm—I'll have to call you back."

Kate heard the dial tone as Sherry hung up on her.

About twenty minutes later, in between other phone calls, Sherry called back. "Sorry, my husband was at home."

"Ah," Kate replied. "I totally get that. It's definitely awkward." After a long silence, Kate began again. "Look. I'm not here to preach to other people about how to live their lives. They can do what they want, and that works for me, until someone dies. I just need some information."

Sherry replied stiffly, "Good, then we're in agreement. You don't tell anyone what I'm telling you, and we'll get along just fine."

"What can you tell me about your relationship with Robert Blake?"

"Friends, … with benefits."

Kate wasn't expecting her to be so upfront. "Okay. And when did you last see him?"

"*Um*"—she pondered that—"last Friday night. My husband didn't want to go anywhere. He just wanted to stay home, gaming with his friends. So, I told him that I was going out. I checked in with Robert, and he'd had a cancellation. So I popped over to spend some time with him."

"And when did you leave?"

"It was still early."

"How long were you there?"

"Probably about an hour and a half."

"Would he have, … I know this sounds a little crude, but would he have had somebody else in after you?"

After a moment of silence, Sherry snorted. "Honest to God, I have no idea. He might have. Don't get me wrong. I thoroughly enjoyed every moment we spent together, but it was literally a physical release with somebody whose company I enjoyed and whose body I adored. He kept himself in really great shape. He was a hottie, and I don't have any shame in saying that."

"I'm not here to call you out for anything," Kate reminded her. "I am concerned as to the nature of his relationships and whether anybody may have had something to do with his death."

"Are you telling me that he was murdered?" Sherry asked. Shock filled her tone, yet maybe not as much as Kate would have expected.

"I haven't heard from the coroner yet," Kate explained. "Plus, I have another case with certain similarities. However, that case is in a different department than mine."

"Similarities?" Sherry repeated. "Like, … what similarities?"

"I can't divulge any details of an active investigation," Kate told her. "These are ongoing cases, so obviously we have to keep the details private."

"*Right.*" She snorted again. "So I can tell you that he was fit, extremely physical, with a high need for sex. I'm not sure that it would be a *normal* amount, but I think it was him just being him."

"And when you say, *not normal?*"

"I just mean that I knew I was one of many, and I didn't care. He was not one of many in my world. Robert knew, and he understood the role he played, and we didn't argue or have any problems with it."

"How long had you been seeing him?"

"Years," Sherry replied. "My husband is not … *physical.* He has a very low libido, and he doesn't know that I have an outside relationship."

"Would he be upset?"

"I don't know that he would be," she admitted. "He's often told me that, if he can't satisfy me, then I should look elsewhere. I've just never brought it up and told him that I had gone ahead and done it. And I really don't want to have to bring it up … at all."

"So, it works for you?"

"So far, the status quo holds, and it's worked for us," she shared, followed by a dry laugh. "I don't know what I'll do now," she muttered. "Robert was special. You don't just replace that easily. And I'm starting to realize that maybe I was a little more emotionally involved in that relationship than I thought. He was a good man. So, if somebody did kill him, it's not anything he deserved."

"You say that, but don't you think that some upset husbands were out there who didn't agree with that?"

More silence came. "Yeah, probably a lot of them. Robert didn't care whether you were married or not. Even though he religiously used condoms, he still wanted someone clean—meaning you kept yourself free of STDs and got checked on a regular basis. Plus, you had to be up front about what you were doing and where you were going with this. Then it was all fun and games, … until it wasn't."

Kate sighed. "Right, … until it wasn't."

"*Right*," Sherry repeated, her sadness permeating her tone. "*Until it wasn't.* And that is where the challenge comes in because Robert really was the guy who was not after anything except sex. And I know a lot of guys are out there who are probably very similar, and I have met many of them. However, at the end of the day, while most of them wanted strictly sex, they were still looking for that perfect relationship. Robert wasn't, not at all, and he didn't have any intention of ever having a perfect relationship."

"And he really didn't care how you felt about it?"

"We talked about it, and, to him, it was just another hookup. As long as you understood what the game was, he was willing to have fun. And it was fun," she confirmed. "We were enjoying our time together, without hurting anybody else."

Until maybe your husband found out. Kate shook her head and talked further with this woman, getting an even better understanding of what Sherry's relationship with

Robert had been like. Then Kate finally asked her, "Do you know any other people with whom he was in a relationship?"

Sherry hesitated.

Kate sighed. "Look. I know you probably don't want to tell on somebody else. However, we have a massive amount of phone numbers to go through here," she shared. "So, if you could ease up some of that calling we need to do to solve Robert's murder, it would help a lot. Particularly if you think anybody may have had something against him. Do you know of any breakups that were difficult or violent or anything along that line?"

"I don't know about any breakups. However, he told me something," she began, "and I think it was probably on that same Friday night, but he didn't mention a name. He told me how he appreciated our relationship because it was drama-free. I laughed and said, *But that's the only way we do this.* And he agreed, but he said not everybody does it that way. He shared something about believing he did everything right, but somebody believed very differently."

Kate's eyebrows shot up at the word *believe.* So she asked, "And do you have any idea who this was about?"

"No, I don't have a clue. He gave me the impression that it was somebody he decided to have a relationship with and then regretted it."

"Interesting," Kate muttered. "Now, changing the subject, you never told me if you knew either of the other two guys." Then she repeated the names for her.

"That John Smith name is common, and I did see one man with that name. It wasn't for very long. And I don't know any Kurt in that context either. Why? Are they involved?"

"I just wondered if your relationships or friendships,"

she clarified, "included these people."

"No, not at all or not for long, but again there are a lot of John Smiths out there," she stated. "So I probably don't know these guys."

Kate frowned at that, since Sherry's phone number was found in Kurt's record of phone calls made. "And where do you work?" Kate asked.

"Do you really need to know that?" Sherry sighed and added, "Sorry, I'm a bit worried."

"Yes, we do need to know, but I'm not planning on going to your job and telling everybody about your past relationship."

"Right. And it is a past relationship now," Sherry muttered, and the tears almost instantly turned back on again.

Kate hurriedly moved through her remaining set of questions and then added, "Look. If you can think of anybody who may have been problematic or wanted more than Robert could give or didn't accept goodbye when he told her that it was time to be done, please let me know."

"I will," Sherry replied, "but I can't have you calling me at this number again."

"Then stay in touch," Kate declared, "because we will call you if we need to."

"*Great*. Are you telling me that I should confess all this to my husband?"

"I don't know," Kate replied instantly. "That's entirely up to you. What I can tell you is that, until these three deaths are solved, the killing won't quit. We are going through hundreds—and I mean, hundreds of phone numbers. If we find somebody who's a connection to all three men, that would be perfect. But if we find others connected to you that you didn't tell us about, things will get a little more formal."

"*Great.* Look. I'll spend some time and think about it. I've known Robert for many years. So, we've had many conversations over that time."

"Right, it must be a lot. But think about why he's doing what he's doing, how he's doing what he's doing, the reasons for the keeping the women mostly out of his life, and anything else as to *why*." Kate heard something shuffling in the background of this call.

"Okay. I understand what you're saying. I've got to go. My husband's coming. I'll call you." And, with that, Sherry disconnected.

Kate sat here for a long moment, then turned to Rodney, who had also just gotten off a call. Kate asked him, "How many of them are married?" She pointed to her phone. "I just got off with one, *Sherry*, who asked me to please not contact—wait for it—her husband."

"Yeah, I'm getting that too," Rodney confirmed. "I just talked to one who is also married but has been in a relationship with Kurt, the Coquitlam dude, for years, according to her. It was always no commitments, only if everybody was free and clear."

"So, that's almost the same thing I was told." Kate added, "According to Sherry, Robert stipulated that everything had to be drama-free."

"Honest to God, that's a smart move on his part," Rodney stated.

She frowned at him. "It really is, isn't it? Plus, if he's dealing with a lot of different partners, how does he keep them all straight?"

"Beats me. Must be hard to call them the right name. I've still got a lot of phone numbers to go through, but that doesn't mean that they all stayed current. It could have been one-night stands too. I've had several who don't know how or why their phone numbers were in some strangers' address book or Contact list at all."

"Where did these guys get these numbers then?" Kate asked. "That's what we have to figure out."

"When I check a lot of these numbers," Rodney shared, "it's basically dialed once or twice and then nothing in the last six months."

"Those are low priority," she noted. "I started a chart, and we'll rate those as low priority. And then we'll move to anybody in the last six months for all of them and see if we can come up with anybody who called all three men. That only helps if," she clarified, "we're sticking with the concept that just one person is the killer of all three men."

"And why don't you like that?" Rodney asked, curious.

"I don't know, but, at the moment, I'm open to anything and nothing," she muttered. Just then her phone rang. She looked down at the Caller ID and smiled. "And here's Simon." She answered and asked, "Hey, how's your day going?"

"It's going," he said. "How are you doing?"

But Kate noted an oddness to his tone. "Simon, are you okay?"

"Yeah. Yeah. I'm okay. Just a little … unsettled, I guess."

"Is it something I can help with?"

He gave a short laugh. "No, but I know that's—"

"You're scaring me."

"Oh no, no," he told her, then sighed. "No need for alarm, as I'm totally fine. It's got nothing to do with me or anything else on a woo-woo level."

"Okay," she muttered, relaxing back. But even Rodney

and Lilliana stared at her, puzzled. "You've got us all a bit worried right now."

"I've just realized that somebody is trying to sabotage me financially. I'm still struggling with that."

"Why would they do that?"

"I'm not sure at all, but I will figure it out and will deal with it."

"I'm here if you need me."

"I'm just checking in to let you know that I will likely be late tonight. I'll be with my accountant, dealing with something that popped up."

"Interesting, *not*," she replied, then chuckled. Everyone's shoulders eased. "If you need accounting help …"

He laughed. "I know. I also know that, if I needed you to bury a body, you would be right there."

She burst out laughing, then said, "Dear God, I hope you're … joking."

He replied, "Absolutely. Anyway, I won't be home anytime soon."

She glanced at her watch and added, "Okay, let me know when you're coming home."

"Will do." And, with that, he ended the call.

Yet she stared at her phone, frowning.

"That's not a good look on you," Rodney stated.

"No, it's not a good look, and it's not a good call from him either," she replied, pondering what he said again, her fingers tapping the top of her desk.

Rodney asked her, "Is it something you need to deal with?"

She paused. "I'm not thinking it is, but I'm also not too sure at the moment. I'll let him handle it for now, and, if I need to run, I will." She turned to Rodney and added, "In the meantime, we have a lot more phone numbers to call."

Just then Reese entered the bullpen. "First, Kate, I haven't forgotten your earlier request. I found fertility places around Vancouver but none near a church and near where our two dead guys lived. You know, some people can't afford that kind of help. Just saying. Now here's why I'm really here. I was running names between the three victims and their Contacts data that we have so far, plus all their websites visited," she began, "and I came up with three women who have dated all three guys."

"Three women," Kate repeated, staring at her. "Good God."

Reese nodded. "But I have bad news too. I found contact information for two of them. However, one is dying of cancer and is in the hospital in a medically induced coma. And I don't have any contact info for the third match. However, as we know on these dating sites, these people don't always use their real names. So, … I'm still working on it." Then she handed over a piece of paper to Kate.

Kate frowned at the numbers. "This is the woman I just talked to. And she told me that she didn't know any Kurt at all but that she dated a guy for a short while with the very common name of John Smith."

Reese shrugged, then suggested, "Maybe the men used different names. I noticed one of them with a different name on a third dating site, but he had used his own on Tinder and Romance Me."

"Oh *great*," Kate muttered, "that muddies the water. Go ahead and give me what you have so far on that third woman, and I'll see if I can get any more out of this Sherry gal, whom I just spoke to." Reese turned and left, just as Kate sent Sherry a text to call her.

When Sherry phoned, some twenty minutes later, she bypassed any greeting and said, "The text is better, but, damn, I really want you to lose my number permanently."

"Did you know Hector?" Kate asked.

Sherry paused, then asked, "Hector who?"

"Hector from Tinder."

"Oh Jesus," she muttered. "That was an awful long time ago."

"Yeah?" Kate asked, yet doubtful.

"Yeah, it was a brief … fling."

"One of our three dead men used that name. So, it appears that you may have had the honor of being one of the few women who are connected to all three of those men."

"But, … good God. Seriously?"

"Yes. Seriously."

"No, I only knew the one for sure."

"Yes. And you told me that you weren't sleeping with anybody other than Robert."

"Right. That John Smith guy who I saw was a short-lived meetup. And I met Hector on Tinder a very long time ago. I wasn't even counting those as relationships."

"I'm counting them as relationships," Kate declared.

"You need to take another look at what you consider a *relationship*," Sherry quipped. "Look," she began, then hesitated. "I explained to you that these aren't relationships but hookups."

"I hear you, but, when I find out that the same woman has slept with the dead guy in three different cases of mine, I need more details."

"Christ," she muttered. "Look. How about I come to the station tomorrow morning? We can talk in person then."

"Fine," Kate muttered. "I want you here at 9:00 a.m. sharp."

"*Great.*" Sherry ended the call, her tone pissed off.

Kate looked over at Rodney and nodded. "That's one of the three women who met up with all three dead guys. Let's see if we can get ahold of another one."

"I'm working on it," Lilliana shared.

Kate looked over at Rodney and shared, "As much as I asked Sherry to come in, I don't see her as being our killer. She sounded … more lost than angry or hurt."

Surprised, he turned to her and asked, "Why do you think that is?"

"Because she's married. She's happily married, legitimately happy."

"And yet she's—" Rodney shook his head.

"Her husband, … he apparently has a very low libido. So, from her perspective, she's taking care of business." Kate gave a wave of her hand. "She's getting the attention she feels she needs in order to keep her marriage going in a positive direction."

"Christ," he muttered, "but it seems wrong—"

"We aren't marriage counselors, and enough people have asked me about that shit lately that I'm more than a little afraid more of that crap is coming my way. Do I look like a social worker for the lovelorn all of a sudden?" As she glared at him, his lips twitched.

He replied, "No, I can't really see you as a marriage counselor. You would probably pull out your weapon and tell them to make life easier for everybody by at least talking to each other."

"Communication is the number one killer of all relationships. Yet everybody says, *Oh, we get along great. We can talk about anything,* but then they don't," Kate snapped, glaring at him. "How many times have you heard our suspects or witnesses say the same thing? And then you turn around, and they're here on our suspect list. And they're so convinced that they can communicate really well, but somehow they choose not to. It kills the whole meaning of communication. Doesn't it?"

Rodney smiled and offered, "I'll call the second one."

"You do that. And, if there's any suspicion, just bring her in tomorrow too."

He nodded and then suggested, "You should probably go chase down Simon." She stared at him and frowned. He nodded. "Call him."

Kate shook her head. "I don't know that it was a call for help, but it was definitely a call for, *Hey, I'm out of my element. So, it might be nice to have you around.*"

Lilliana looked over at her and put her hand to her heart. "I would definitely call him. Hell, I would already be hunting him down, … especially if I had someone call me and say that."

"I would have done the same." Rodney seconded Lilliana's response.

Kate stared at them, surprised. "He's usually very self-sufficient."

"Yeah, until they need you but don't want to ask for help," Rodney shared.

Lilliana agreed. "*Usually* but not right now though. The *usual* Simon deals with some woo-woo stuff that he's never had to deal with. You can't help him with that. None of us can. But this time it's not that he needs help, but he might just want some support, even just a little more *you* time."

"What about our murder suspects?" Kate asked, attempting to change the topic.

"You tell me," Rodney suggested, "so we have something

else that we can work on tonight."

She frowned, just about to say no, when her phone rang. She looked down and announced, "It's Smidge."

Rodney immediately turned around. "I'm not even here."

"Yeah, of course you're not," she muttered. She answered, "Hey, Smidge. How's it going?"

"Shitty," he snapped, direct and to the point and as prickly as always. "But I can confirm that there is a good likelihood that all three men were either killed by the same person ... or—"

"Or," she repeated, "maybe by the same group of people, following the same MO?"

Dead silence followed. Then Smidge exploded. "So, why the hell do you even need me? If you'll come up with all this shit on your own, why am I wasting my time?"

She snorted. "I still need you to tell me that I'm not crazy when I do come up with this crap on my own. It's really the only thing that makes sense, except for the fact that we do appear to have three women who slept with all three of our victims."

He whistled at that. "How does that happen?"

"I don't know. You have any clue?" she asked. "I would have voted for dating apps."

"Oh Christ," he muttered. "That makes a horrible kind of sense."

"Yeah. It is a horrible sense, and that's what worries me. I have one of the women coming in to talk to me tomorrow. I already had a long talk with her, but she doesn't want her husband to find out."

He snorted. "Of course she doesn't," he muttered. "That could be an *inconvenience* for her."

"Exactly. She also seems to feel as if her husband wouldn't be terribly bothered, but I also cannot rule out any husbands in this instance."

"No, you can't rule them out," Smidge agreed thoughtfully, "but considering poison and drugs—"

"We don't have the tox results on the third one yet, Robert Blake, do we?"

"Oh, we absolutely do. And it was drugs."

"Shit."

"So, maybe we have two connected, the *don't do drugs* victims, and one isn't, or you have three connected, and somebody just decided that it was a hell of a lot easier to take a druggie out by just giving him more of his poison of choice. Anyway, over to you now." And his tone was positively cheerful. Then he laughed and added, "Don't bring me anymore." With that, he quickly ended the call.

Rodney was staring at her, as if she had sprouted wings. "Did he just laugh with you?"

She nodded. "Yeah, we often laugh."

He frowned at her, then looked behind her.

She turned to see Lilliana staring at her with a similar expression.

Finally Lilliana spoke. "Kate, you're the only person who can get that man to even smile. The thought of him laughing is preposterous."

Shaking his head, Rodney added, "It's absolutely dumbfounding."

Kate clarified, "In this case, he was laughing because everything associated with these three cases are now dumped back on my desk and then warned me to not bring him anymore." She gave them a smirk. "So, yeah, he's laughing because I'm not."

At that, the others nodded.

Rodney nodded. "Okay, that makes a little more sense."

And they all returned their attention to the cases at hand.

<hr>

SIMON WAS WALKING through a jobsite, checking on the plumbing, the building scheduled to be completed in the next six months. Yet supply chains messed with that. There was always a problem getting in enough product when you needed it.

Bathtubs, sinks, faucets, … it was endless. Trucks upon trucks upon trucks. Some of them were stuck at the loading docks in Vancouver, which was never good.

That was money just sitting there, but, when there were shipping problems, they affected more than just him. He tried his best to close his eyes on all that—the things he could do absolutely nothing about—and just keep track of issues within his control.

Then his accountant called him, getting Simon out of his head. "Hey, Quinn, how you doing?"

"I'm doing fine. Look. … Can you talk?"

"Yeah, just give me a minute. I'm walking out of one of the buildings here," he replied. "I'll be just a couple minutes getting back to the ground floor."

"Good enough," he replied.

"Problems?" Simon asked.

"No, maybe some clarification but I'm really not sure."

"Oh, that sounds critical."

"Not critical. The important word here is that it's *not* critical. I'm just not sure how to handle it from here. It's about David."

"Okay, and what about David?" he asked, as he stepped out into the sunshine, waving at his foreman, pointing at his phone, and walking away.

"I talked with him today, and he's in a tight spot."

"Moneywise? He can always come to me. He's good for money, and the way he is taking care of things, you are authorized to make transactions on my behalf."

"That's not what I'm talking about. Somebody's been getting some intel from someone at your company who supposedly knows that you're overextended and running into all kinds of financial issues, which is giving the whole crew the heebie-jeebies."

Simon froze in place. "Somebody here is telling people that?" he asked in shock. "Nobody even knows my finances here. I deliberately keep it that way for a reason."

"That was my thinking. I wasn't sure what the scenario was, or if you were having issues with any of your foremen, but I wanted to get it out into the open."

"Nope, not one person on these jobs knows how I handle my finances. They don't know," he declared. "I mean, the office staff would have a little bit to do with it, but nobody knows the overall picture, except you and me."

"That was my assumption," he noted, "and David's hoping you can find where the leak is."

"Why didn't he tell me that himself?"

"Because you were in his office, and he's worried some illegal activity may be happening in the bank and didn't want anyone overhearing what he wanted to tell you. He feels that could put him in grave danger."

"He could have called me at home anytime."

"I know, so I'm thinking that calling me maybe was his way of trying not to get his ass in trouble legally, and, yet at the same time, trying to help you."

Simon pondered that. "I'll have to think about that one. For Christ's sake, what's next?"

"I know you are already worried and pissed, so I absolutely understand." Quinn continued. "The bottom line is, you've got somebody somewhere causing trouble, right? So, what do you need?"

"That is something I can handle. It would help, though, if I had a name."

"David didn't have a name, but he thought it was potentially family of somebody within the bank system."

"That's clear as mud."

"Yes, I know," he muttered. "I've started a search to see who might be related to someone involved in your renos because obviously we have to nip this in the bud."

"If you can get the names of the honchos in David's bank or of the bank management in general, then maybe we can do a run to see if any sisters, sons, or whoever may work for me. Not that anybody will know anything about my finances, but obviously they don't have to know the facts to cause trouble."

"Exactly. If he's just intent on causing trouble, he's making up lies."

"Yeah. That's called defamation."

His accountant laughed. "You have lawyers on tap for that. If you want to do something about it, we'll have to find out who it is first, and then we'll go from there."

Feeling better and yet having absolutely no idea how that worked, plus realizing that he probably no longer needed to see his billing accountant tonight, he texted him to double-check and got an all-clear. So, he headed back home, hoping that maybe Kate would get home early. He sent her a text message. **Evening plans are canceled. You coming home?** Immediately he got her reply.

Yes, providing …

The three dots dragged after her proviso. He knew that meant *providing nothing helpful came through on her case or one of them.*

He pondered that because it was so much harder for her to find information sometimes, and, if he could do anything to help, he would be happy to. He just had no clue what that would even look like. And how did anybody find a possible killer in this scenario? It made no sense to him. And yet it made a lot of sense in some ways to Kate, as usual.

As he walked, he pondered the issue only to realize that he was right back at the same Catholic church. He frowned as he walked up the front steps and entered the building, finding the same priest here.

The priest looked up and smiled. "Come in, my friend."

Simon sighed as he walked in. "I really don't know why I'm here."

The priest laughed and shared, "You would be surprised at the number of people who say that to me on a regular basis."

Simon nodded. "I'm not really surprised about that," he clarified, "but I'm not exactly here for myself."

The priest focused on him and nodded. "If you need to talk about something, I'm here to help you if I can."

"Yeah, but you don't work with the police, do you?"

"The police?" he asked, his eyebrows shooting up. "No, not generally, but, of course, we've had some instances where the police had to be involved. However, we do our best to help our congregation and our neighborhood without bringing them in. Are you in trouble with the police?"

The question was simple enough, and concern filled the priest's gaze. Simon laughed. And it was such a carefree, joyous laugh that even the man of the cloth had to smile. Simon shook his head. "No, I'm not in any trouble."

"That is good news, indeed."

"I'm fine, Father. I have some of the usual ailments that plague a lot of people. For example, somebody is trying to tell my bank and others that I'm in a desperate financial position, which isn't true, yet it is still causing me problems. It's always so *great* when you have that level of betrayal in your world."

The priest nodded. "Lost souls, right?"

"And what about the souls that are even more lost? I understand that if somebody's in a confessional, you can't tell the police what they say, but how does …" He pondered it for a moment. "I shouldn't even be talking to you."

"And yet anything you say to me," the priest explained, "I can certainly try to keep as a confidence if you have done something wrong."

"No, no, no. I have not done anything wrong. You don't need to be worried about that."

The priest still watched him closely, waiting for the other shoe to drop.

"My partner is a homicide detective," he began. "A couple cases right now are driving both of us a little bit wacky. And I know it's not my problem, but, if I could do something to help her, I would absolutely do so," he explained, trying to keep his own involvement minimized.

"What's the problem?"

"The problem is, in each case, this card was left behind, with a weird message saying, *Believe*."

He frowned at him. "As in, *believe* in God? Believe in

justice? Believe in love? What exactly is the insinuation here? I mean, that's a fairly open-ended message."

"That's the problem," Simon agreed, smiling at him with appreciation. "All those instances could fit, but we have, ... *she*," he corrected, "has three cases open that could have been foul play. One of the cases is possibly an overdose. The other two appear to be murder," he shared. "Yet the third case is too similar for it to be ignored, since it followed the same pattern."

The priest asked him, "You're not talking about Detective Kate Morgan, are you?"

"Yes, I absolutely am," he stated, with a nod. "Are you familiar with her?"

He nodded. "She is a woman driven to help, but the pathway she has taken in this life is extremely difficult," he replied. "I worry for her psyche."

"I had no idea you even knew her. Like you, I also worry for her, and I care very much for her."

The priest eyed him shrewdly and noted, "And yet you haven't made an honest woman of her."

Simon chuckled. "I haven't even brought it up. She is very much a free spirit, and I have been trying to avoid upsetting the apple cart and changing the status quo. As long as she knows I care about her, I am not worried about putting a ring on her finger, though I'm not against it either."

The priest nodded. "That seems to be the way of so many these days, doesn't it?" he noted.

"I'm not here to discuss our marital life."

"But you are interested because you think I have knowledge of this," he pointed out, focusing on him.

"But you do have your ways."

"If you're asking if anybody has confessed to murder recently," he offered, "I can absolutely tell you no."

"That's a good thing," Simon said. "I guess part of what's got me wondering is, do you see a return of women to being traditional housewives?"

"I don't know if there's a *return*," the priest clarified. "I think women who absolutely want to stay home and raise children have always been in the background. However, I also see more women seem to want the independence and the ability to have a career and to not focus solely on the children—or doing both even. So there has always been that group of women too. I guess I'm really not sure what you're asking."

"No, I'm not either," Simon admitted. "I guess I'm wondering if this killer could be somebody who wants the men to believe in monogamy."

The priest stared at him, and his lips quirked. "My son, that is probably something you would have a much better idea about than me."

It took Simon a moment, and then he burst out into a big chuckle.

The priest was grinning from ear to ear as well. "I am glad I have made your day that much easier."

"Father, you have, indeed," Simon declared, with a bright smile. "I don't have the answers I want, but you are entirely correct in that you have certainly given me a much lighter heart," he shared. "And, for that, I'm grateful."

"And you are most welcome. I have no idea how to help you with your quest for her, but you can certainly tell her to come back and visit. She is always welcome here, as are you, anytime."

"Thank you," Simon muttered, "though I'm not entirely

sure she would appreciate it."

He chuckled. "No, maybe not. However, she too has a place in this world and a place in all our hearts. She does a job that is incredibly difficult, and she should be honored for that and for the sacrifices she makes along the way."

"What's your name, Father?"

"Call me Father McCain."

"It was nice to have someone to talk to, … without being judged."

As Simon turned to walk away, Father McCain called out, "Just remember, my son, that you don't live forever. So, if something is important to you, experience it now."

"Meaning?"

"Meaning that life can take unexpected turns, and what you think you have a long time for, you actually don't."

"Words to live by," he muttered to himself as he stepped back out of the church and then glanced around to get his bearings, now heading back home.

CHAPTER 12

K ATE WALKED IN, Edgar wincing when he saw her. She glared at him. "Don't bother."

He chuckled. "I'm sure the other guy looks way worse," he teased, "so that always gives me hope. But, boy, when you get yourself into trouble, you get into real trouble."

"Even worse," she muttered, "I asked for this one."

When he frowned at her, she laughed. "I was at my dojo, brushing up what my master called some of my *dated and a little-too-predictable skills.*" She lifted her chin, not a tad bit ashamed of the bruise that had already started to show there. "So, the beating I took is apparently something that I most likely deserved." When his eyes widened in horror, she laughed and waved her hand. "It's all good, but I'll have a puffy eye later too."

"Uh, too late, you already do. Better get some ice on that."

"That's the plan." As she headed toward the elevator, she asked, "Is he home?"

"He got in just ahead of you."

"Oh, good," she replied. "Maybe we can grab something and head to the boat tonight."

"If you need food, just let me know."

"I'll need food," she declared, "but I have no idea if anything's upstairs. You would think I would know, but I have more things to keep track of than whether we have food to eat or not."

He smiled. "You know who to call."

She nodded and headed up to the penthouse. As she walked in, Simon was there, sorting through the mail.

He glanced over and smiled. "There you are."

"Yeah, go figure. We're both early." She hesitated only a moment, then asked, "Any chance we can grab dinner and run out to the boat?"

His eyes lit up, and he turned to face her. "Wanna get changed into something a whole lot more comfortable for boat wear? Then we'll head out and pick up something to eat."

"I wondered if we had any food. Edgar asked if we needed to order anything, and I had absolutely no idea," she muttered, chuckling.

He finally took a good look at her and stared, all the joy in his face falling away, as he attempted to control whatever he was thinking and was about to say.

She reached up, kissed him, and whispered, "Happened at the dojo." His eyebrows shot up, and she added, "Yeah, apparently I've gotten a little too … *predictable* in my self-defense."

He frowned. "If that's the case …"

"I know. I know," she said, "that means I deserve it."

"I won't say you *deserve* it," he protested.

"No, I get it," she replied. "Believe me that I know. You don't need to say it."

He clamped down on the words threatening to bust loose.

Meanwhile she walked into the bedroom, changed out of her work clothes, and put on warmer but much more casual choices for the boat. She grabbed a sweater too. "We probably should just keep everything we need at the boat."

"I thought we had enough," he noted. "We've got quite a bit there now."

"It's really just the food that we need."

"I've already ordered it, so we'll pick it up on the way."

"Perfect." As she walked out of the bedroom to rejoin him in the kitchen, she asked, "And your day?"

"It was fine," he said, with a headshake. "I don't want to talk about it. What about yours?"

"It was fine. And I don't want to talk about it either."

He gave her a big grin and nodded. "Good thing we can communicate."

She nodded, followed by a snort. "Good thing."

And, with that, they headed out the door. As they stopped for food, he paid, and she gathered it up, carrying the food, as Simon had blankets and other stuff with him from the penthouse.

They walked outside and headed to the boat. He asked, "You want me to help with that?"

"Nope." She chuckled. "At least if I hang on to the food, I know I'll get some."

"I have never once starved you, not a single time."

"Not yet," she teased, with a laugh. "I know. However, that *yet* always keeps me on my toes," she shared, grinning.

Soon they were at the boat and settled in the small kitchen in the cabin, eating pasta from Mama's. Kate stared at it and muttered, "We'll have to carry just as much food back out again."

"It's okay," Simon noted. "At least this way, if nothing else, you'll have breakfast."

"Pasta for breakfast always works," she declared, with a big smirk.

"Most people eat eggs or a piece of toast," he commented.

"Yeah, well, *most people* don't have the potential level of physical activity in their day as I do," she snapped. Yet it was an easy camaraderie instead of actual temper. When she finally put down her fork, she looked over at him and muttered, "I don't know about you and your problem, but this case of mine is driving me crazy."

"Yep, I'm definitely there with you," he shared. "I stopped in and talked to the priest today."

She froze, staring at him, her gaze serious. "Any particular reason why?"

He looked over at her, startled, and then smiled. "For the last couple days, I found myself sitting on the front steps of that bloody place three different times."

"So, you went inside?"

"I went in a couple days ago, but I found myself right back there again today. So, I walked in, and the same priest was there. I spoke with him more today, and he remembered you. It was Father McCain."

She winced. "Probably not a great memory."

"He did say that you were welcome to come in and visit."

"I'm sure he is quite sincere. If there was ever a lost soul, in his eyes, it would undoubtedly be me."

"He remembered you and had a lot of good to say, including that you were doing a very difficult job and that your soul and spirit needed to be kept. Something about *somebody needs to look after you.*"

"What else did he say?"

"Well, he also asked me about the *living in sin* thing." She stared at him, her eyes wide, her jaw dropping, and he nodded. "Yeah, I know. I thought that was pretty cheeky of him too."

She started to laugh. "Oh my." She shook her head in wonder. "You really did have a conversation with him. And why the devil did you go in? Like, what's going on that you stopped there? Is this a crisis of the soul?"

"No, but it could very well be a connection to your case."

She froze in the act of reaching for a piece of garlic bread. She put down the bread, leaned back, and asked, "How do you figure?"

"I don't know that I *figure* as much as I was trying to ask him something. I was doing a very muddled-up job of it. And when I mentioned something about *believe*, he asked, *Believe in what?* Believe in love, believe in marriage, believe in …" And Simon listed off the other things that had been mentioned.

Kate nodded. "My team touched on those too. I'm just not sure that we've come to a conclusion about any of it. And, no, I'm not sure that this, in particular, will give us any answers."

Simon sighed. "I just ended up there—three times as I mentioned. So, you know me, if it feels as if I should walk that path, I do."

"Of course," she agreed, "and I would too, especially with any sense of needing to. It is very interesting that you ended up there though."

"I have to admit that a part of me wondered whether he was coaching women who were about to get married or maybe somebody who had lost a child or I don't know what," he shared. "It's way too open-ended."

"We're going through *a lot* of John's relationships."

"Which one's John?"

She explained that he was the one she was called in on first. "Then we found that similar death of a guy from two years ago, *Kurt*. It's a bit harder to get info on Kurt's cause of death because no autopsy was performed. It was assumed to be a drug overdose, yet ruled accidental. Nobody put it down to suicide, just that these things happen when you play with crap in your body." She shook her head at that. "So, the details aren't available. Thus I spoke to the Coquitlam detective on that case and asked for Kurt's phone list. He shared that with me, and we're working on it too."

"What are you looking for?"

"Trying to find the same lover for all three dead men," she replied. "Also looking for the same groups. I am looking for the same … everything."

He nodded. "That would, in some ways, make sense."

"That's what I thought," she muttered. "We did get a hit of three women who dated all three dead guys. However, we haven't really gotten anywhere on that angle yet. And I need to get somewhere because the clock is ticking, and nothing is more unkind than old Father Time. Especially in my industry, where the fun just never ends," she quipped. "Still, your questions about Father McCain's group efforts could be an interesting line of questions," she noted, staring off in the distance. "I wonder if he is teaching and/or runs something like matrimony classes. Is that a thing?"

Simon nodded. "It certainly was a trend at one time. I don't know if it still happens. Maybe only in smaller centers, where they would have classes before you got married—on what marriage is, how it's meant to go, all that stuff," he guessed, with a helpless-looking shrug.

He continued. "Are men required to attend these classes?

I don't know how that works in the Catholic church, if it's a requirement even for the women. For all I know, it's potentially *Hey, this is in your best interests, so we want you to show up and to do this.* I'm not sure how that works," he conceded. "I suspect you can't force it, but, in close-knit communities, it's quite possible that it becomes, if not mandatory, at least something that's highly recommended, shall I say."

She stared at him. "It sounds so … archaic."

"Just another belief system," he noted.

"Right. Well, … it's not mine."

"No, but what if it's accepted as mandatory by somebody involved in your case? What if she, or even he, believes very highly in monogamy? What if they believe in marriage and forever after? And what if their wife has other lovers? You've already found the one woman, Sherry, to be heavily involved in outside relationships, and supposedly her husband doesn't mind?"

"Yeah, I don't know about that *her husband doesn't mind* thing," she clarified. "I haven't got to the point where I need to speak with her husband, but I might have to if Sherry moves any higher up on my suspect list."

"Why is she on there in the first place?"

"Because she had affairs with two of three guys. Maybe possibly hooked up with the third. The only reason I question that is her argument how she dated one John Smith, noting there are many others of the same name."

He stared at her and nodded. "That's a good reason."

"But not if I can connect her to the third one."

"Unless you can connect one of her friends to the third one."

"Right, and that would be the next issue," she noted.

"But how does any of that hit the *believe* part?"

"Maybe that's got nothing to do with it," Simon suggested. She turned to him, and he frowned. "What's that look about?" he asked her.

Kate declared, "Because that whole *believe* thing is also something I feel is coming from you."

He stared at her for a moment. "I'm not saying it is. I'm not saying it isn't. I don't have a feeling either way. What I can say is, *believe* doesn't really fit. So, maybe it's just an anomaly."

"Maybe," she muttered skeptically.

Simon shrugged. "Maybe *she*—if we are dealing with a female killer—left the message on the one guy and then it blew up from there."

"But why start with *believe*? Believe what? Believe in matrimony? Believe in marriage? Believe in one woman, not a dozen?"

"I don't know." Simon smiled at her. "Now we're into the whole psychology of people, and that's a whole different story."

"It's the psychology of one person hopefully," she clarified. "And, more so, the psychology of a potential killer."

"I think you have to decide whether your killer is male or female."

"I can't do that. Not yet. Not enough info."

"Then you may have to ..." He left it hanging.

"Don't even say it," she grumbled, glaring at Simon. "I've been waiting for somebody to tell me how I need to talk to the staff shrink to see if he has any idea about what's going on. So far I have managed to avoid anybody even bringing it up—until now."

Simon winced. "And yet you know—"

She held up a hand and glared at him.

He sighed. "You know his insights could be helpful. You need more information, more input, other eyes on this."

"Maybe," she muttered. "Yet, if it's coming from him, I don't know if I can trust it."

He grimaced, then added, "I'm sure that would upset him to no end."

"Possibly," she replied cheerfully and gave Simon an evil grin. "Can't say I particularly care, though I suppose I should."

"Why don't you send Rodney over?"

"I should," she agreed, with a bright smile. Then she frowned and added, "Then I would have to explain why I didn't go."

Simon burst out laughing. "You can't win for losing, can you?"

"No," she muttered. "I don't know why everybody is so gung-ho about my talking to him anyway."

"Because he has insights, and, if it moves your case forward, you should be all over it, trying to get his take."

She shot him a look. "That's a low blow."

He chuckled. "Yet it's not. I would have expected you to completely chomp down and decide that, if nothing else, you would figure out what he had to say and discard it if it didn't feel right."

She frowned, then nodded. "I probably should. I've blocked out that he's even there, to be honest."

"I'm sure that makes him feel wonderful."

"Probably not," she noted with glee, "but I'm *not* in the business of making him feel great."

Simon had to laugh at that. "True, but you are trying to solve this, and, if he has anything to offer ..."

She just stared at him.

"What?" he asked. "I hear you, but I don't know what you want from me."

"I don't want anything from you," she replied. "If you had anything to give me, even woo-woo stuff, you would have shared it already. I want an angle to pursue, but it can't just be any old angle that I pull out of my ass."

He burst out laughing. "Yeah, well, particularly not when your ass took such a beating." She glared at him, but he smiled back. "You're right. I shouldn't have brought it up."

She groaned. "Doesn't matter. I'll contact the shrink tomorrow and see if he has anything valid to offer."

Simon knew about her aversion to shrinks, after that fiasco of a case where she trusted a shrink, who was a pedophile and a murderer. It had been brutal.

He added, "If you wanted to be really proactive about it, you would make that appointment tonight."

CHAPTER 13

KATE WALKED INTO the shrink's office early the next morning. Dr. Dudley had accommodated her request by seeing her before his regular work hours. After all, Sherry was reporting in at 9:00 a.m. for her interview with Kate. Other than that pre-hours appointment, the shrink was pretty swamped. However, if case-related, he would make the time.

Dr. Dudley studied her as she walked in and noted, "That looks painful."

She shrugged. "Not even from a case." His eyebrows popped up, and he gave her a shocked look. She shrugged. "I wasn't paying attention in my karate class."

His lips twitched, but she had to give him credit. He didn't burst into laughter outright, which most of her team had. She had her own sense of humor about it because it was her own fault. She never asked for special treatment and never expected it. She was just trying to save her life most of the time. And, if getting beat up at the dojo was what it took, then that's what she did.

He just smiled and asked, "What can I do for you? You got my attention when you told me that it was urgent."

She frowned. "If you don't have time, that's fine."

His eyebrows shot up again, and he shook his head. "Stop being so prickly. What is it you need help with?"

When she glared at him, he just waited.

Finally she spoke. "We have an odd case."

He nodded. "I figured as much. Otherwise you wouldn't be here," he pointed out. "What's so odd about it?"

She went through the two deaths that were poisonings and then the possible third case linking to the other two, but it was deemed a drug overdose. Maybe self-inflicted. Still, she couldn't rule it out.

He stared at her at the mention of the third death. "To do it once is bad enough."

"Exactly," she replied. "And then you consider how it's potentially three times? That's worse. So, one of my questions to you is, *What on earth would be a motivation for this MO?* Is it even feasible?" Then she hesitated and added, "I'm leaning toward a woman, but I don't have any clue as to why, … outside of rejection."

"Do you have any evidence supporting that?"

"No solid reason, just my gut instincts."

"It could also be the boyfriend of one of these women, who has decided that these playboys are the reason he can't get serious or can't get anybody to go that step further into what he really wants, which could be a marriage commitment."

She nodded. "That is also a concern, though we don't really have anything to go on in that regard."

"I don't have to tell you that poisoning tends to be a woman's preferred method to kill someone."

"Right," she agreed, "though, if I were a man, trying to make the murder look like a woman had done this, then using that method would throw the suspicion off of me."

He nodded. "Yet there are other ways and means, and how would somebody get access to the three victims' apartments?" he asked curiously.

"The killer was let in, as far as we can tell," she shared, and he nodded. "Nobody has cameras on their front doors, and nobody had security at that level. In one case, it's been so long that, even if they did have security video, it would have long since been copied over. That was the death deemed to be a drug overdose from two years ago, so no autopsy, no criminal investigation at the time." She took a deep breath. "All I can tell you is that these men were very careful but very dedicated playboys."

The doc shuffled his papers for a few minutes, thinking about it. "So, you tell me. What are you thinking?" he asked, looking up at her curiously.

"I'm thinking mid-thirties, female, somewhat desperate."

He stared at her with a questioning look. "Interesting, why mid-thirties?"

"My take is that somebody wants more than what these men can give, but they are the type of men whom she attracts, for whatever reason. While she can be a bedmate, she's not finding any men interested in long-term relationships. Over time, either she has realized something's wrong with this ecosystem or something's wrong with the men that she's seeing."

"Or the easiest solution but the most painful revelation is how something's wrong with her."

"Exactly." Kate gave him a sharp look. "These men want casual sex, just flings, nothing permanent. ... I don't know whether it's a matter of refusing to have a long-term relationship or just not wanting monogamy. None of them apparently ever expected anything out of their partners, except the freedom to be consenting adults. No force was used here. There is no regret on the men's part. From a couple women I've spoken to recently, they had no regret on their part either, except they have thought about being exclusive at one time or another."

"And how do they feel about it now?" the shrink asked.

"It's interesting, but the same two women who I spoke to, though they describe their relationships as friends with benefits, now have realized just how much they cared about this person and hadn't really understood that until they were gone."

"So, are you thinking that a lot of them were hoping secretly that maybe a real relationship or a more long-term relationship could be there?"

"I'm not sure I can say that," she hedged. "One is bitterly divorced. The other is married but has a husband who doesn't particularly have a sex drive, so this is her way of keeping her marriage safe."

"Right. Although I disagree that affairs keep anyone's marriage *safe*, still the lack of sexual compatibility is not an uncommon complaint. In fact, that's one of the biggest reasons why a lot of men start wandering as well."

She agreed. "But that doesn't have any pertinence to these cases. That one married woman did, however, say that, upon hearing of his death, she felt emotions that she didn't expect. She was surprised to be so affected by this loss. She was thinking that she would be cool and casual and calm with my questions, right up until she found out he was dead."

"So, she had a very strong emotional response?"

Kate nodded.

"Which is not that far off, given that she's also been quite free with her body with him—and for some time, if I understood you correctly."

"Exactly," Kate noted, curious as to what he was getting at. "So, I'm not necessarily surprised at seeing that emotional reaction from her, but, in a way, I am surprised. However, I don't feel she is the one killing these men."

"And you're saying these guys are very fit, very buff, right?"

Kate nodded. "They're physically in their prime. They're the male predator, … at their prime. And somebody has been cutting them down, cutting them to size."

"Do you think so?" he asked curiously.

She pondered that and then added, "I don't know enough about these cases, but I do know this. … A lot of emotional baggage is involved. The killer wrapped up their victims in decorations, in gift cards even, and that's the part I don't understand."

"And that's the part that makes me think that it's a man."

She stared at him but shook her head. "I could not, in any way, imagine a man wrapping up another man, as if wrapping a gift. That makes no sense to me."

"No, maybe not." He smiled. "I was thinking more along the line of, you know, a gift *for* someone, or maybe a gift *to* someone. It's easy to default to believe the killer is female, especially when poison is used to kill, because, if these victims are physically fit, no way for the average woman to take them down easily. So, poison would definitely be a woman's trick here."

Kate nodded. "It would be, except for the jealousy factor. I could see an insecure man, a weakling if you will, poisoning these three men—or overdosing the third with a cocktail of drugs. I could see how many men would question their manhood when compared to these three males. So such a man—not buff, not confident, not strong, not dating much, perhaps not even dating a small fraction of the number of women these three buff playboys have snared—could feel compelled to erase some of this competition. That's quite possibly what's happening here."

She sighed and added, "Plus, leaving behind a note that says *Believe* in these latest two murders." Dr. Dudley just frowned at her. "I know, right? Nebulous. Maybe related to church beliefs, advising monogamy? Maybe to the role of the traditional wife, staying home, having babies? I have no idea on that note and how it figures into murder, three of them even."

He smiled at her. "You seem to have made up your mind, Detective. Remind me, what did you come to me for?"

She smiled sweetly. "I was hoping for a profile."

He shook his head. "I don't have enough information, but you're pretty close on what you're thinking. I'm just not sure you're quite there yet."

"No, I'm not there yet. And the trouble is, I don't want another man to die because I'm a little slow on the mark." She got up and paced around in frustration.

"Obviously that won't be on you," the shrink pointed out, "but I can see that, as much as you care about your work, you will take that personally."

She snorted. "Yeah, … ya think?" Then she frowned and muttered, "I wonder how many men are like this?"

Confused, he asked, "What? Buff men or insecure men?"

"The insecure ones." She shrugged, pacing slower now. "I would love it if there was a club, a club where these insecure men hung out, and I could find out if there would be another victim. That's the part that really bothers me, even while I'm trying to untangle all this. Is another man about to die and has no idea that he's now one of many? And, of course, with the city as big as it is, no way for us to know that."

He pondered that for a moment, and suddenly a glint filled his eye.

She didn't miss the change. "What are you thinking?"

"You are looking for a motive, right?"

"Yes."

"What about the women who had been active with the men now deceased? Did they replace him? And, if they replaced him, with whom?"

Startled, she pondered that. "That could be a worthy pursuit, although I'm not sure that the women in question will be open to those kinds of discussions."

"Make it official," he suggested. "Tap phones, get a hold of their phone records, and see who else is checking their dating apps."

"That'll mean subpoenas and warrants," she muttered. "Lots of them."

"Yeah, I know, … but, if you are thinking we potentially have another incident about to happen, we need to do everything we can to keep the next intended victim alive."

She walked back to her office, deep in thought.

Rodney looked up as she came into the bullpen. "Penny for your thoughts?"

"A penny? It'll take at least one silver dollar," she grumbled, with a shrug. She sat down, then turned to face Rodney. "So, the shrink gave me some other angles, but nothing clicks with me yet. And I've got Sherry coming in at nine for her interview, so help me out here with questions to ask her. Let's start with, you're male …"

His eyebrows shot up, and he chortled with laughter. "Yeah, I am. Thanks for noticing."

She blinked, then snorted. "How would anybody find these particular victims?"

He frowned at her. "I don't understand. You mean, to kill them?"

"Not necessarily to kill them." She rolled her eyes. "Obviously that's been the end result, but I'm not sure our killer is starting there. I guess the biggest issue is that, if our killer is a woman, has she found her fourth victim, or is she still looking?"

"Oh God, don't even say that," Rodney whispered, staring at her in shock.

"Where would be the best place for anybody who has now lost their casual sex partners in this dating venture to find a new one?"

"That would be the dating apps," Rodney stated. "All kinds of them are online. They're mostly just straight hookups with time, place, meet, have sex, and leave."

"That sounds so hollow and empty," she noted, staring off in the distance.

"But that appears to be exactly what we're looking at, … hollow and empty," he pointed out.

She nodded. Rodney was right. "So, all those phone numbers were handed over to Reese. She's compiling a spreadsheet or entering into some database or whatever. Therefore, she could run that mess of phone numbers on these three cases through a program to cross-reference *everything*, which is way more efficient than what I was doing."

"Okay," Rodney replied. "So are you thinking we also need to find which dating app was most commonly used by our three vics? And what was the length of their association with each app?"

Kate frowned. "Do you think that makes a difference?"

"I would think, at this point in time, our three playboys had a really good idea of what works for them—and maybe a good idea of what doesn't. So the rejected apps might be useful."

Kate slowly shook her head, pacing the bullpen now. "Maybe we're looking at this all wrong," she began. "Maybe it's not somebody who wants these men to settle down and to stop their sinful ways, but maybe it's somebody who wanted to get to first base and can't."

"That could be thousands of women—and men," he noted.

"I know. And that's why I'm beyond frustrated at the moment." She groaned. "Way-too-many avenues."

She sat down at her desk, her mind running through all kinds of scenarios, yet knowing that the unknown was likely to be the correct one more than what she could try to force the data to create. When her phone rang, she glanced down and saw it was Simon. "Hey," she greeted him.

"How did it go this morning with the shrink?"

"It was okay," she muttered, "not that we're any further along because we still don't have enough information to really get a profile. He's leaning toward a male. I'm leaning toward a female. Or two working together. However, we also have to consider that anybody who can't get all these women could see our buff lover boys as an object of great envy and, if their competition were out of the picture, the women would be more available. In which case the dating apps would be a huge source of disgruntled males, as would many of the online social media groups. So, we're looking into all that."

"Not necessarily a fast process though," Simon noted. "Those three men probably looked at all the same dating apps and used all of them."

"At the end of the day, maybe not this particular killer though," she declared. "We will still find whoever is doing this. Because of the role of social media in our fact gathering, it's taking quite a bit more time and manpower. And I've got my nine o'clock coming soon."

They talked some more, and, when she got off the phone, she walked over to see Reese. "Can we do a run of all the victims' social media accounts, private DMs, anything that you can get a hold of, and see if we have anything consistent between them?"

Reese raised her eyebrows. "I've asked for social media usage by Kurt, the case in Coquitlam. I can call them and see if they have done it yet," she offered. "However, Kurt Conner's online accounts from two years ago have been canceled by now."

Kate swore about that. "I'll contact his sister again and see if I can come up with anything else. First, I've got an interview to deal with."

She questioned Sherry, touching on all the various suggestions made by Dudley and Rodney, but eventually confirmed that Sherry was not their killer.

As she got back to her desk, she sat down and phoned Esther.

Kurt's sister just groaned and started to bitch. "I really want this all to go away."

Kate snapped, "I know you do. So do I, but I want it to go away *after* we know exactly what happened."

"And yet, as far as we're concerned, it was an accidental drug overdose."

"Yes, but can you tell me if he was plagued by anybody on social media or on any of his dating sites? Were there threats or anything weird? Anything at all along those lines?"

The sister swore. "He did get a bunch of threats a couple years ago, maybe three."

"So one year before he died? Or right before he died?" Kate asked.

"I don't know. I'm really not sure on the timeline."

"Any idea what the threats were about?"

"Something about the way he was acting." Then she added, her voice rising, "Something about stealing girlfriends."

"Did he ever send you any DMs or anything to show these threats to you? Did he ever report these?"

"I think he may have contacted somebody from the police force, but I don't think he got very far. They could do nothing at that stage but, if it got worse, to let them know."

"Interesting," Kate murmured, and she wrote down a bunch of notes.

"Do you really think something happened to Kurt? Like he was murdered?"

"The thing is, we have no clue," she replied. "But I can tell you that, because I do have two other similar cases, we must take a serious look at Kurt's case."

"Oh my God," she murmured. "All this time I've just been blaming him for being an out-of-control druggie, and now you're saying—"

"I'm saying there's a possibility. Yes. Could you please search your phone? If you happen to find any of those messages, could you screenshot them and send them to me?" Kate quickly gave Esther her email and added, "If you remember anything else, call me."

"Right," she muttered. "I know you told me that before, but I put it out of my mind because I thought this was all just a waste of time and police money. And now I don't know what to believe."

"Neither do we. So please," Kate pleaded, "take the time to go through everything you have in terms of communication from your brother and let me know if anything shows up."

With that done, she headed back over to Reese and gave her the update. "See if you can find a case file under Kurt's name regarding a harassment report."

"I don't know if they even open one for those complaints," Reese remarked, turning to her. "It could have been an informal conversation."

"Okay, but just see if anything's there. If you find something, let me know so I can talk to the officer directly. You could also give them a call."

"I have a lot of data running, and I have a lot of phone calls pending, particularly into the Coquitlam office. I'm not really getting very far on that one."

Kate looked over at her and nodded. "I'll call them." And, with that, she returned to her desk and called the Coquitlam detective on Kurt's death.

He replied, "You guys keep asking for stuff, and we just haven't gotten there yet."

"We're trying to help you guys along, and you keep turning us down, but I get it," Kate responded. "You're swamped, we're swamped, and everybody's dealing with their own stuff. But there's a damn good chance that I have connected your case to my two cases. Yet these won't solve themselves if I can't get that information on Kurt."

"I just can't believe that you think there's a connection

between this case and your two who died just a few days ago. That's too many, too fast, … and your MO is poison."

"I understand," she said, "and, being poison, you would think it's a woman, but it could also be some skinny scrawny male with a self-confidence issue, who's using poison because these vics are prime specimens of men in a physical sense. So don't go down that pathway of thinking you know all the answers."

A huffy silence followed, then a grunt. "*Fine*. Give me a little bit, and I'll try to get you some more information as to what we've collected. It's not even been put into the reports yet."

"I understand that," she shared, "but let's not have another body show up because we couldn't get our paperwork sorted out." And, with that, she ended the call.

Rodney looked over at her and raised one eyebrow. "They say honey and sweetness go a long way."

She glared at him. "Yeah, that's me. All honey and sweetness. Then there's all that BS about who'll get the credit when we solve their case," she pointed out, "but I do not care one damn bit."

He laughed. "You might not care, but that's because you've already got a hell of a roll going on here in our department—but they might care. And your successful closing rate on some of these cases may be something the Coquitlam detective is already well aware of, so he's being very defensive, very protective."

"And that would be the stupidest thing I've ever heard," she snapped, looking at him. "This isn't about us. This isn't about some percentage written down somewhere. It's about the victims."

He smiled, looking over her shoulder to Lilliana, who now chortled with laughter.

"I'm really glad to hear that," Lilliana interjected, sharing a good laugh with Rodney. "Please don't ever change, Kate. But don't be so naïve as to think the rest of the world will go along with that. In case you hadn't seen the news lately, greed is rampant, and egos are completely out of control."

SIMON'S MORNING HAD him standing in the rain in front of the next building to rehab on his list. This one was on Howe Street, tucked back a little bit, definitely commercial, and would need to be a moneymaker at the end of the day. This wouldn't be a rehab.

This would be one of those few that he did to earn some cash. So it needed to come together fast and efficiently, but it would still be years later. That's just how these jobs went. He looked over at the architect, Dean Thomas, who stared at him intently.

"Second thoughts?" he asked Simon.

"Oh no, not at all. This one is purely business, so my heart isn't in it. It's not the soul project that I really enjoy," he shared, "but it is a moneymaker that I can't walk away from."

Dean turned to the building and shook his head. "You have a very different idea of what a moneymaker is."

Simon laughed. "I might have a different idea than a lot of people," he noted, "but just because it's different doesn't mean it's wrong."

"No, I've worked with you too long to make that call," Dean stated. "It's impossible to miss the fact that you have a unique ability to make money on projects others won't even look at."

"Yet somebody is," he grumbled.

"What's that?" Dean asked.

"Somebody seems to want to trash my business by telling tales at the bank."

"What?" Dean stared at him in confusion. Simon explained, and Dean was shocked. "But that's complete BS. There's a process, a really well-defined process for all this stuff. That's got to be somebody at the higher end, pulling rank or something. And, if they're doing that, they sure as hell better have a good reason for it. That is not a normal way of conducting business."

"Right. I know that, and, because it's not a normal way of doing business, I'm thinking it's got to be family or something personal somehow. I've asked Quinn to pull the names of all the family members of the current management team at that bank to see if there's any connection."

"You won't go after them though, will you?" Dean asked in alarm.

He snorted. "No, that's not my style. But that doesn't mean this doesn't involve somebody whom I've had to fire or in some way remove from a job or something like that. And, if that's the case, I've got lawyers on tap for that stuff."

"Right. And that would be totally within your rights," he agreed, shaking his head. "But, man, who needs that legal headache?"

"Oh, I hear you. The legal headache that may come is a match for the lack of sleep I'm getting now, while trying to figure out who is out there hating me and acting on it."

"Yeah, that's just life apparently," Dean muttered. "So, since you've already approved these plans, what am I doing here?"

"You know that I like to do a once-over again before we

go ahead, which is why we're here," he shared, with a smile. "I've still got to get all these plans approved through the city, and I need to know that there won't be any headaches in that department."

"Right, and you have a lot of buildings on the go right now," he acknowledged.

"Yeah, I do, but that's okay. I've got a couple extras I just picked up. Not so much because I wanted to but because there was a need in the moment—like for that one with all the bodies."

Dean winced at that and grimaced. "God, I still can't believe that even happened. But if anybody can handle that one, it's you."

"That one will have to be dropped. It's become a hazard, and, once we get it cleaned up, I'll have you come in and take a look," he explained. "And, of course, I bought that other one."

Dean stared at him and nodded. "Now *that one* has to be a labor of love."

"It absolutely is. I've had that building on my list for a very long time," Simon admitted. "So, when it came up at a good price, it was pretty hard to ignore."

Dean shook his head. "You just tell me when and where, and I'll get to work on it."

"Keep her in mind, as she'll be next. Once we get it down to the studs, you can get started."

"Okay."

"If I can get that part taken care of, then we'll have a fairly clean slate to start with."

"A clean slate would be nice for a change," Dean said, with a laugh. "You do challenge my skills at times, but there is definitely a certain amount of joy to start with something at least partially fresh and clean."

"It'll probably be the only one you get in a while," Simon warned him. "This one that we'll be working on first isn't quite a clean slate, since you'll have to work within the footprint of the building," he pointed out. "However, that's the only limitation."

"Yeah, that's way better than a lot of them."

"Yeah, you're not kidding," Simon agreed, staring at the space before them.

Dean asked, "What's the date for this one?"

"It'll be in the next six months, hopefully four," he replied. "I've got the city planners on it, but they haven't got back to me yet."

"Is there any reason for that to be an issue?"

"Not as far as I know, but then I wasn't expecting the bank to give me any headaches either," he pointed out. "Somebody out there is trying to cause me trouble. I just don't know who."

"There always is someone ready to take you down. The minute you become successful, somebody out there will try to pull the rug out from under your feet just because they're jealous."

"If it were just jealousy, I wouldn't mind, but this has a little uglier feel about it."

They spoke for a little bit longer, and, when they parted, Simon headed to his favorite coffee shop, noting that there was too much rain today to sit outside. He took a spot in the very back. Hearing a noise, he looked up. David walked toward him, and Simon raised an eyebrow.

David sat down and began, "Look. Some really ugly stuff is happening at work."

Simon nodded and didn't say anything.

"And I think I probably caused it, but I have this list for you."

"And what's this?" Simon asked.

David glanced around and whispered, "Quinn asked for it."

Simon smiled, accepted it, and asked, "This data is all public record, right?"

"Yes, it is. It just feels, because I'm the one delivering it, that I'm in the worst spot here."

"You're not in trouble for sharing this with me because it's public information. So, there's absolutely no reason for this data-sharing to be an issue."

"*Yeah*. You say that but …"

Simon smiled and nodded. "The only thing I can think of is that somebody within the company is listening to somebody else, and that's never a good thing."

"No, it's really not. And I was thinking about that," David noted, with a head tilt. "The only one we've got that's recent enough to matter is the chairman's nephew, Stanley, who has just come on board."

"What kind of a guy is he?"

"The little weaselly kind," David replied. "I wouldn't be at all surprised if that isn't part of your problem."

"That would be assuming I know this Stanley guy and that he would have some reason for causing me trouble."

"I don't think that matters here. It seems to me that the nephew is just trying to make a mark. I don't think he's too bothered about knowing the people he's trying to crush. He's already gotten two people fired from the office."

David glanced around again. "I'm looking for a new job myself. I've been there for a very long time, but, once this kind of shit starts, that is not good news for anybody." And, with that, he got up, smiled, and added, "Anyway, I'll keep you posted." Then he turned and walked out.

As he left, a man in the corner turned to watch David. Then the man faced Simon.

Simon didn't recognize him, but it was obvious that the young man had something going on. Simon texted David and sent him a picture of the man.

David sent a text right back. **That's the nephew, Stanley.** Another text came right after that. **Watch your back.**

Simon sent a reply. **You better watch yours because he saw you talking to me.** And, sure enough, he got a text two hours later while he was walking out of one of his rehab projects from David, saying that he'd just been fired.

Eyebrows shooting up, Simon stared down at his phone and then sent the picture he'd taken of Stanley to Quinn and then off to Allen, Simon's lawyer, to see what they could rustle up. Allen called him back a couple hours later. Simon was working from one of the trailers at one of his worksites and took the call.

Allen jumped right in. "So it's an interesting tactic this young man is using."

"What's that?"

"Apparently Stanley worked for your company, using his middle name, *Allen* oddly enough. I got his information, and your accountant ran it through your company. He worked for you, and you fired him."

"Great. What for?"

"He stated he was a welder but, in your terms, was grossly incompetent."

"Oh crap," Simon muttered, pulling out the photo again. "I didn't even recognize him. Because of the suit, I suppose," he noted. "Yeah, he was a mess, and Joe didn't waste any time sending him on his way, which I was totally on board for when I saw his shoddy work. So, who is he?"

"He's Leonard's nephew. As in Leonard, the chairman of the board."

"*Oh great.* So, who else is on that board of directors?"

As soon as he got the names of the people currently on the board of directors, he told Allen, "Before they meet again, set me up a meeting with … George maybe. You know George Hammond, right?"

"Yeah, I do know him—quite well actually."

"We could have a one-on-one, ahead of the next board meeting."

"That could end up being quite the shitshow. Apparently the nephew is Leonard's favorite among a whole list of family members."

"That could be, but I'll be speaking with George. He's always in my corner, and he has solid sway over the board."

"You think it's a good idea to ruffle feathers like that?"

"Probably not, but I just don't have the time or the stomach for this BS. I want to know what the nephew is up to and the best way to find out is to get it all out in the open. So, confirm you have whatever paperwork we need in order to make this happen."

"Listen," Allen began, his tone sharp. "I don't think you need to start a war here. Plenty of people are around who aren't that happy with the way you run things."

"But here's the thing, … they aren't happy, but they are making money with me and *the way I run things.* So, it shouldn't matter to them."

"Still, I would advise caution."

Simon thought about it and realized Allen was probably right. It wasn't the first time Simon had been in hot water over finances, and it wouldn't be the last. "Why don't you meet with Hammond then?" he suggested. "Then I can meet with him afterward. That way you could get a feel for things. You think it would be better that way?"

"Oh yeah. You've got to give him a chance. Particularly if you have, … if it's been a decent relationship," he pointed out. "Then in the second meeting we'll find out what the nephew's saying and who he's saying it to."

"Yeah, that'll be fun."

"I'll get a subpoena for phone records."

"And you'll also need to subpoena Leonard's records too."

"Subpoena the phone records of the chairman of the board of the bank you've been using for your business loans? You really like to make waves, don't you? It's not that simple to get something like that approved, and that will take a lot of pull to get them to comply."

"Defamation is not a minor charge," Simon declared, "particularly in my industry. And I haven't heard from the city on one of the projects that I'm about to start on. If the nephew has gotten to the point of causing me trouble on that level, there will be a much higher payout required for them to not end up in jail at the end of this."

"That's only if you can prove it," Allen stated, his tone forceful. "Remember that defamation is still one of the hardest things to prove."

"It might be the hardest to prove, but something rotten is going on there. David got fired this morning, and that was after the nephew saw us together at the coffee shop," he shared. "There is that to consider too."

"Crap. David is your bank, um, your investment advisor, isn't he?"

"Yes, he was. He had called me in to warn me that there was an issue with some of my loans that shouldn't have been an issue. And it took a bit for him to get around to it, but he did admit that it looked as if some sabotage was going on, but he just didn't know who or why or how. Then he told me today about this nephew who had moved into a power position with his uncle on the board for the bank. Then we happened to see the nephew at the coffee shop today. David was fired within a few minutes of getting back to his office."

"Wonderful. Do you happen to have a copy of that, or can you get the video from that coffee house?"

"Of course I don't have it," he replied, "but, if you need to get it, you can file a complaint officially and get a copy yourself. I do have a picture of the nephew. I sent it to David when I noticed this guy staring at David as he left the coffee shop."

"Send it to me."

Simon pulled it up and fired it off, then took another look. Honest to God, it was a great photo because it was obviously the coffee shop, complete with their signature logo with coffee cans in the back. And he's staring directly at David's back as he leaves. His lawyer waited for it to come through.

"Yeah, this'll be a good start," he said, a smile in his tone. "But we'll need a hell of a lot more to win a defamation lawsuit in court."

"You know how to make that work."

"And, if you need any help, what about Kate? Is she likely to help you?"

"I don't want her help," he stated sharply. "This is something I want to keep completely separate from her."

As soon as he went to get up from his office chair, he got

slammed back down with such force that it knocked the breath out of him. He could hardly even breathe. Thankfully he was alone in the onsite office, the staff having already left, and he'd been hoping to leave himself now. He was about to contact Kate and see if she was close to the end of her day.

When this happened though, he sat here, trying to control his breathing, feeling everything inside him clenching tighter and tighter and tighter.

When he was almost to the point of pounding the table in agony, it eased up ever-so-slightly. Then he cried out, "What the hell do you want?" The reply he got was crying again, just crying. And he realized the pressure he'd been feeling in his chest was not his. It was hers, her pain.

He took several minutes to get control and to ease back the pain. Not sure how to help her, he now knew that, whatever this was, it was absolutely killing her. He whispered, "I'm here. You're not alone, you know?"

And she gasped again.

"And all that stress you have? I'm feeling it in my body as well, and it's agonizing."

She gave a harsh, brutal laugh and whispered in his mind, *Yeah, so how do you know what I'm feeling?*

"You need to tell me something about this, tell me what is going on, so maybe I can help."

Nobody can help, she whispered, the sobs once again racking through her system. *I don't know that anybody can help.*

"I work with a lot of people who can help with various issues."

She just kept sobbing.

"But you'll have to open up and tell me something."

Is this where you ask me what year it is again?

"I do need to know that because I don't know if you're a ghost of this century or if you're alive and well and sitting at a coffee shop around the corner."

Coffee shops, she murmured. *That seems to be a distant memory.*

He frowned, not sure what a distant memory would mean in this case.

Then she replied, *I have to do something. I can't keep living like this.*

"Whoa, whoa, whoa," he interjected. "What do you mean by *do something?*"

She gave that same sobbing, half crying reply, *I just … I can't keep living like this.*

"Yeah, I hear you, but I don't know what *living like this* means."

Then you aren't really feeling what I'm feeling then, are you?

Her bitterness came with the instant flip of a switch. Her moods were mercurial enough that he wasn't sure from one minute to the next how she was doing. "Look. I don't know what I can do to help, but you could start with where you are or even what city you live in, so I at least know something about you."

Vancouver, she muttered.

He closed his eyes and nodded. "Okay. So, I'm in Vancouver too."

Are you? Well, … of course you are. Otherwise, how would you feel what I'm feeling?

He frowned at that because it made no sense. But this conversation in his head wasn't making any sense either. "Whereabouts in Vancouver do you live?"

She didn't say anything.

"Particularly if you're looking for help—"

I'm not looking for help, she stated bitterly. *There is no help for somebody like me.*

"What does that mean?"

She cried, and then cried some more.

Finally he began again. "Look. I need a little more information. Why is there no help for you? Are you dying from some disease? Are you incapacitated in some way?"

All he could think about were all the possible scenarios. But her voice, when she finally whispered her answer, shocked him. Then she suddenly disappeared. He stared down at the business paperwork in front of him, knowing that he needed to get up and move, but his mind was completely flummoxed by her words.

She was infertile.

And that's why she was deemed completely useless and why her life wasn't worth living. He frowned as he stared at the table, his gaze lifting to look around in an almost blind haze. He knew how some women were incredibly overwhelmed at the idea of not being able to have a child.

But did this have something to do with Kate's cases?

Or was this something completely separate?

And was this—he didn't mean it the way it sounded—but was this just a woman suffering? Or was this a woman who had taken her suffering to a whole new level?

CHAPTER 14

K ATE WAS STILL at work, running through paperwork and the numbers.

When Reese came in and sat down across from her, she had a single sheet of paper in her hand. Kate looked up with a hopeful expression. "Have you got something?"

"Well, … I've got *something*," she emphasized. "Honest to God, I'm not exactly sure what it is."

Kate snorted. "Welcome to the club. What did you find?"

"One of the numbers that we ran? … It contacted Robert, one of your current cases."

She frowned. "Not Kurt, the Coquitlam one?"

"We're still waiting for that. I ran this number through because she contacted a bunch of places, then told Robert in a text that **It was positive**."

Kate sat back and stared at her. "As in a pregnancy test?"

"I don't know. There's no context."

"And he's dead, so we can't ask him. Yet his boss and next-door neighbor told me that Robert had a vasectomy to avoid that issue."

"Really?" Reese replied. "That changes everything then."

Kate nodded. "Exactly. Could be some woman thought she could catch Robert. I wonder if any of his women know about this vasectomy? Might be interesting to see who mentions it—or not. What about the woman's telephone number?"

"No longer in use."

"Of course. If she thought she could snare Robert with that ruse, I'm sure he dropped her in a nanosecond. Now the woman caller, if truly pregnant, would be in a kerfuffle, trying to figure out the father of her child."

"Maybe this happened with all three men? Did you ever get back to Kurt's sister?" Reese asked.

"I did, yes. Of course this subject didn't come up. You?"

"I've got another call in to Esther, but she hasn't yet gotten back to me. I need to try her again, maybe talk to her about this angle. But, with these guys, if they got somebody pregnant, does that change anything though?"

Kate shrugged. "It's not that it changes anything, but it could definitely have an impact somewhere along the line as to the motivation for these guys' deaths. I mean, what if a husband found out that his wife's pregnant, but the baby's not his?"

Reese winced. "Unfortunately that happens way more often than we even want to think about, doesn't it? You don't even want to think about it happening at all, but people being people—"

"I know," Kate interrupted, with a smile. "People being people."

With that, Reese got up. "I'll keep digging. And, whenever I speak to Esther again, I'll run that pregnancy angle by her."

Kate stared at the phone number for a long time and then decided to call Caroline again. This time Caroline answered quickly.

"You do know I have to work, right? It's bad enough

that people even know about this."

"And what about the other woman, Lanny, the receptionist at the company right now, who had an affair with Robert too?"

"How should I know? Why don't you talk to her instead of calling me?"

"Why don't *you* talk to her? You've both been through the same thing, so that's common ground for the two of you."

"I can't because she's already turned in her notice and quit. I guess there was just a little too much commentary about her involvement in Robert's life," Caroline noted. "I'm not sure that I'll escape that either. Now, what is it you're calling about this time?"

"*This time*," Kate stated, "I have a question. Did Robert ever talk to you about anybody who may have gotten pregnant?"

Caroline was startled for a moment, as a stunned silence fell.

Kate asked, "You there?"

"Pregnant?" she repeated. "That was against his rules."

"Yeah. We have a text message to that effect to Robert from somebody, but her phone number is no longer active."

"Oh my God. He would have been absolutely livid. He was almost to the point of making everybody sign some contract, regarding *no strings, no whatever*," she explained. "Gosh, I can't even imagine how that would have gone over."

"So, he didn't mention it to you?"

"No, he didn't. But I do remember a couple times when maybe he wanted to say something but didn't, and, well, ... the sex was really hard and furious after that. So I figured, whatever the problem was, he just needed to wear it off."

"What would he have done if it were you, for example?"

"Oh, I wouldn't have carried it to term," she declared, finality in her tone. "I'm divorced, remember? With nothing but bitterness in my memory of it. Even if some married gal got pregnant with Robert's child, I would think it must be a nonnegotiable issue because of the husband. Plus, don't some of the married women who play around have kids already? I don't see a married woman taking her fuck buddy's child home to raise. Sorry, … that's just the way I see it. Hell, if I get pregnant from any of the men I'm sleeping with now, no way in hell I'm keeping it. After my divorce, I don't want a man except for sex, and I sure as hell won't raise his little rug rat on my own, while he's out bopping half the country."

Kate didn't say anything in response to Caroline's tirade.

"Now you probably think I'm some heartless bitch for saying that too."

"I don't have an opinion on any of this unless it has to do with the case," Kate stated. "I'm not looking to judge anybody. I'm just trying to figure out who that might have been."

"Well," Caroline began, her tone very perky now, "we had somebody who worked here." She pondered it and added, "I think her name was Betty, and she may have had an affair with Robert."

"And why does she stick out to you? I mean, we have Mary, Lanny, obviously you, yet Betty stuck out to you. Why?"

"Because things got really ugly in the office, and then suddenly she was gone. I'm not even sure how much of a notice was given before she left. She took some holidays, then, *boom*, she was out."

"So, do you know what her name was? Full name? Contact information?"

"I don't have contact information, but her first name was definitely Betty. Let me think about her last name. It started with a *B*, I think. Berkeley, I'm pretty sure."

"How long ago was that?"

"Gosh, that was a while ago. At least … maybe six, eight months ago."

Kate didn't say anything.

"And before you ask again, no, I don't know anybody else. I didn't even think about Betty until you mentioned a pregnancy."

"Did you think at any point in time that Betty was pregnant, or was that just the gossip in the office?"

"It was office gossip. You know how it is. Nothing is crueler than office gossip, particularly when the person is gone," she noted. "I'm guessing your office isn't any different."

"I don't have any illusions about gossip." Kate felt Rodney staring at her. She glanced over, and he had one eyebrow raised. Kate continued her phone inquiry. "So, do you think anybody else in that office dated Robert? And would that person, some two years back, have had anything to do with Kurt in his different location, yet working for the same company?"

"Oh, I don't think so. Yet maybe plenty other women were involved with Kurt, John, and Robert, just within the office staff at both locations."

"Very true," Kate acknowledged, "but I will call you back if I have any other questions. However, right now, I want to get ahold of Betty, which is the only lead I have."

"Call HR. They should know how to contact her," Caroline snapped and ended the call.

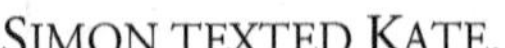

SIMON TEXTED KATE.

When she called him back, she began, "When you text, asking if I've got a minute, presumably you're asking for business reasons?"

"Not necessarily," he clarified, "but, at this very moment, I am definitely checking to see if you're okay."

"I'm okay, but … What happened?"

He frowned, staring down at the phone. "You're way too perceptive these days."

"What happened, Simon?" she repeated, her voice rising ever-so-slightly, with an edge of impatience, as if he were lying to her, and she wouldn't tolerate it.

He sighed. "So, I communicated with that … woman again."

"Right," she replied. "What about her?"

"She lives in Vancouver—or lived in Vancouver anyway."

"Good God. We don't even know if she's in this time frame, do we?"

"Nope, we sure don't," he noted, with a smirk, knowing that she couldn't see it. Still, her response was so typical that it just made him smile to even think about her dealing with all this woo-woo stuff. She was so black-and-white, so cut-and-dried, and he kept pushing her limits of believability on a daily basis.

"And what did she say?" Kate asked.

He filled out the conversation for her, and she went silent for a moment. "Fertility, really?"

Such a thoughtfulness came with her question that he wondered if she had picked up on something he hadn't. "Is that important?" he asked cautiously.

"I don't know," she admitted. "With these three cases, there is definitely an element of sex, and with sex comes pregnancy, fertility, and all the rest."

"Exactly," he agreed.

"I just found out about a possible pregnancy, but I'm still waiting to get the number to confirm with the woman in question. This may have been yet another office romance with Robert Blake, the latest one to pass away. Yet here's the wrinkle. He supposedly had a vasectomy."

He pondered that and asked, "So, you still think it's connected?"

"No, I don't know if it's connected at all," she grumbled. "I haven't even had a chance to talk to this woman. For all I know, she was using it as an excuse to pressure him into a relationship or trying to scam him into child support or—"

"Maybe it was somebody else's kid," he suggested.

"Yes, all of the above. I still don't know. All I have is a bunch of bits and pieces, and none of it is coming together. The whole thing is driving me wacky."

He smiled. "I get that. I just thought I would fill you in on that little bit of information."

"Good enough," she replied, but then she did a double take.

He could almost see her frown forming.

"Is anything else going on?"

"No," he stated, his tone forceful, and he chastised himself for taking that one with her. "Everything's fine. Why?" She went silent for a very long moment. He thought he even picked up on her pain too, her reaction to his tone, his lie.

He winced. "Okay, fine. I just may have found a problem that I'll sue somebody over."

"Oh, that's *great*," she commiserated.

Yet she lost interest as soon as she sensed it was business. He had to laugh. "I know. Absolutely nothing to do with you or your cases."

"Sorry, it's not that I'm trying to separate things to that extent, but, if it won't hurt you, kill you, or do anything else along that line, it's really just more day-to-day BS. And you can handle the day-to-day shit all too well on your own." And, with that, she ended the call.

He had to howl with laughter because, in her world, that's exactly what it was. It was just more day-to-day BS. And in a way, that meant *just don't bother her with it.* Someone else might have thought of her attitude as insulting, but he knew she meant it when she stated that he was fully capable of handling his business. She knew that and believed it completely.

He made a happy sound as he picked up a coffee and headed out, walking over to another one of his project sites. Along the way, he walked past another building he'd bought to rehab in the future. He stopped, smiled at her, and promised, "Your time will come, girl." He had loved that building since forever, and he couldn't wait to get started.

But he also had to confirm that he did her justice. And doing her justice could look very different, depending on a lot of factors right now. One of them was the lovely mess that somebody had decided to add to his plate, creating an unnecessary nightmare for him.

When Allen called him back a little later, he filled him in on the information they had picked up so far. Allen was cheery, perky even, as he announced, "I have a bit of good news. George Hammond will speak with you."

"He will?'

"It was a really good idea for me to talk with him first. So, at least now he has some idea of what's going on and why you might want to meet with him."

"Yeah, you're not kidding. Where's the meeting?"

"He suggested a place downtown and as early as possible."

Simon pondered that for a moment. "Let's do it. I'm downtown right now. So, he can make the trip if he wants, and we can talk over coffee."

Allen laughed. "You really want to take a chance of his showing up and you not having a recorder on you?"

"Oh, I have a recorder," Simon declared. "Don't you worry about that."

"You think it's that bad?" Allen asked.

"I don't know what to think at the moment," Simon admitted, "but get him down here, and I'll gladly talk to him. Maybe he can ward this off before it gets too far."

Allen suggested, "Or maybe he's looking at something completely different."

Simon hadn't been off the phone for very long before George called him.

"Simon," he greeted him, "seems we need to talk."

And that was George. Crisp, clear, and, as usual, no bullshit. "Yeah, it seems we do. I'm downtown," he replied, with the same crisp, clear, no-bullshit manner. "If you want to join me—"

After a moment of hesitation, he asked, "Whereabouts are you?"

Once Simon provided the location, got the okay from George, Simon sat back and waited.

Sure enough, a limousine pulled up not long afterward. George got out, telling his driver to head around the block and to find a place to park. Then he walked over to Simon. The two shook hands. George looked around and noted, "You do prefer to be outside, don't you?"

"Yeah, I do."

George winced as he slowly sat down on the bench beside Simon.

Simon pointed to a vendor. "We can have a coffee if you want."

George turned to it and laughed. "It's been a long time since I did that."

Simon smiled as he hopped up, walked over, and got two coffees from the vendor. When he returned and sat down, handing George his coffee, George nodded, staring at the to-go cup.

"Something is so very unconventional about it, and that is always a pleasure," George noted.

"It always was a pleasure doing business with the bank and with David," Simon began, "until all this bullshit started happening."

George grimaced. "Yeah, I wondered if you'd heard about it. When I got the phone calls from your attorney, I knew you had some idea."

"That's when you realized that I'd fired Leonard's nephew Stanley, right?" Simon asked. "Only he used his middle name, Allen, on my construction site."

George frowned at him. "I did not know that."

"He had applied to be a welder, and, when we gave him a simple welding test, he failed terribly. However, the welding test wasn't given immediately on his first day because he had been so confident and because we really needed a welder. So, they put him right to work. He cost me a lot of money, fixing the foundation work that he butchered. I showed him what he was supposed to be doing, but he couldn't even begin to put out the same weld," Simon shared.

"So, this Stanley guy, some supposed experienced professional, can't even begin to weld better than me? He's obviously never done this work in a production capacity. So, needless to say, he was fired on the spot. I don't know what on earth made him think that he could pass muster as a welder—except for his sheer ego thinking that he was somehow something special. However, as you know, I don't deal in special. I deal in competent."

Geroge sighed. "Well, now he apparently hates you. What am I supposed to do about that?"

"Yes, he has a lot of hate directed at me, but believe me that it's not good for you or the board or the bank either. A defamation lawsuit is hanging over all your heads."

George eyed him, pondered it all, his face a mask of nothingness. "I guess if what you're saying is true, you could have a chance at making a case," he admitted, still looking at him sideways. "Do you have any witnesses?"

"You bet I do. Including the people who were there while Leonard's nephew supposedly showed us *how it should be done*," Simon added. "Don't know if I have that on video, but it would be fun finding that out, wouldn't it? I'll have to check and see."

"If you have that on video, I can put a stop to it. My board, however, is of the opinion that you've been running amok for way too long, and the bank is not willing to extend any more credit."

"I don't care if they extend more credit or not," he announced, "but you don't go around threatening to pull credit that's already been approved."

"There are lots of ups and downs in the business world. It's standard procedure, and, if there's a problem, we have to take a closer look." George glanced at him, a small smirk on his face.

"Oh, yeah, that's well within your purview, but then you turned around and fired David."

"I didn't. … David has been let go for not picking up his slack."

"That's bullshit. He was fired after he had coffee with me, oddly enough when Leonard's nephew Stanley was in the same coffee shop, watching David the whole time he was here." He quickly pulled up his phone and handed it over.

George's face darkened. "I see." He stared off in the distance.

"Yeah, and you lost somebody who was extremely good at his job."

"I hear what you're saying," he said. "Of course we're looking at it from a different perspective."

"I'm sure you are, but you should also consider your clientele. If you're trying to tell me that David did anything wrong, then you need to explain that to me. And please remember that I came to you guys because I had a good relationship with David, not because of your banking model."

George flushed but didn't say anything.

"Also remember that I can go to any bank and can get the exact same credit," Simon pointed out, with some added emphasis, "but I was working with David because I liked working with David. So, let's just confirm we are absolutely clear. I've worked with David for a long time. And, depending on where he ends up next, I may very well end up right there with him."

George sighed, then groaned. "This whole family drama thing is such a pain in the ass."

"Maybe *family* shouldn't be allowed to interfere with business. Nepotism is usually not part of banking. However, if the bank chooses to hire family, confirm that they've proven themselves. And I don't mean with a paternity test. You know, like the welding test I gave Leonard's nephew." Simon gave George a casual look, then took a sip of his coffee that was turning cold.

Simon sighed. "Not trying to tell you how to run your business, but, if this is how the bank and the board want to do it, you're likely to run it into the ground."

"Are you threatening me?"

"Absolutely not. Stating my opinion. However, do consider this a full warning that I will protect my business reputation from Stanley's interference, no matter whose nephew he is. So, if this goes to a defamation lawsuit, your company will be dragged through the mud."

"It will, and you too," George pointed out, his tone turning silky.

"You forget that you're not the only bank I deal with. I have a lot of money in a lot of places, and plenty of bankers and investment firms have absolutely no issue with me. They know perfectly well what defamation can do to a reputation."

George stood up, tossed the half-full cup of coffee into the nearby garbage can, and adjusted his coat. "Point taken. I'll get back to you … soon." And, with that, he turned and slowly walked away.

To the casual observer, someone might have thought

George saw absolutely no indication of an issue.

To Simon though, he knew differently. George had fisted one hand and punched it into his pocket. Simon smiled and muttered out loud, "Yeah, you do that, George."

As he got up to walk away and head back to one of his rehab jobs, he found himself standing at the base of the same damn church. He looked up and swore.

Somebody walked by and laughed at him, adding, "The building isn't to blame, you know?" And the man kept right on walking.

Simon turned to him, surprised, then took note of the church building itself. He nodded and tried to walk past, but absolutely no way he could. He groaned. "I don't know who this is, but it needs to stop."

And then she spoke; it was Sarah again.

I don't know what has to stop, she replied in irritation, *but you're becoming a pain in the butt. Can you go away, please?*

"I would love to," he replied, "but you're the one who has me standing in front of that damn church again."

She gasped. *I don't go to church anymore. Those places are terrible.*

His eyebrows shot up at that, and he said, "I would not say that."

That's because you are part of the problem, aren't you? she cried out. *How dare you interfere in my life like this?*

Surprised and confused, he said, "I don't have a clue what you're talking about, lady." And his part of this discussion was said out loud, just now realizing that other people nearby might think he was losing his marbles.

Embarrassed, he shook his head. *Really not cool, Simon. Get a grip.* Then he turned back to the church's steps. This time, he vowed, "I'm not going inside." He turned and walked away. But the farther away he got, a ringing sound started in his head, an alarm bell ringing, an alarm bell that was hard to miss. Swearing, he turned and headed back up to the church at a quick pace.

In more of a fit of temper than anything, he walked into the church and sat down inside near the door because finally he could breathe again. As soon as the pain in his chest eased, he looked up and froze. He saw a foot angled into the aisle, with the rest of the body out of sight. He bounded to his feet and drew closer.

He found the priest to whom he had spoken several times crumpled on the floor, seemingly dead.

CHAPTER 15

K ATE STARED DOWN at the phone in shock as Simon's panicked voice pounded in her ears. "Father McCain, the priest at the church, is dead," he cried out. "The same church I've walked into several times this week."

She bolted to her feet. "Stay there. I'm on my way. Did you call 9-1-1?" She raced out the door. Rodney, having heard part of it, picked up his jacket and ran behind her.

"I have," he replied, "but I can confirm that he's not alive."

"And how do you know that?"

"He's not breathing. He's bloody all over."

"Christ," she muttered, and she bolted out to the parking lot.

Rodney grabbed her arm and offered, "I'll drive."

"Let me know when the medics get there," she told Simon, her tone rushed. "We're on the way now."

"Good," he whispered.

"Was anybody else in the building with you?" she asked him.

"Not that I could see," he noted, his tone calming down.

Yet Kate knew that the scenario had unnerved him. "And you didn't see anybody when you got in there?"

"No," he stated forcefully. "Honest to God, now I feel like shit because I refused to walk in earlier. If only I had come in then—" He stopped, and she waited so that he could collect his thoughts. "Look. I don't know how to explain it, but I didn't want to be forced into the church. ... So I refused to go up the steps and to come inside."

"So why did you now?"

"I turned around and left, but I got warning bells in my head. So, I raced back. I didn't know why I was running, but I was. And when I came in, I sat down in a pew and looked around, still pissed off and fed up. Then I saw a foot sticking out into the aisle, and I bolted forward. It's the priest I spoke to—Father McCain." He groaned. "He's dead."

"It's okay. I'm on my way."

"Like, ... dear God, he's dead."

"Are you afraid you are somehow responsible?"

"No, I'm not responsible. Yet I do feel like. ... If I had just listened to the first prompt to check inside the church, if I had not fought over coming into this damn place, I might've either been able to stop it or to see the killer."

She didn't say anything to that because that was an awful lot of *what ifs*. "We'll deal with what we have to deal with. You did not kill the priest, and that's what I care about. I want you to step back so that you're not putting your DNA all over the place any more than you have to. And take another look around and confirm that you can't see anybody there."

She was already searching their surroundings to see where they were. Her heart raced at the thought of Simon being the next victim. "And Simon ..."

"Yeah?"

"For God's sake, be careful." She ended the call, looked over at Rodney, who was driving as fast as possible, sirens blaring.

Rodney nodded. "That'll be a tough one for him to get over."

"I know, and its BS because it's not his fault."

"But you can't ignore the possibility that if he had listened—"

"I don't want to hear about any possibilities here. We don't know that," she snapped. "That's like saying, if you hadn't done something, you could have walked away from God-only-knows what kind of mess."

"I know. I know. I feel bad for Simon. He walks into a church, and there's a dead man."

She groaned. "A dead man he has spoken to a couple times recently … about our cases."

Rodney shot her a horrified look.

She nodded. "So, now Simon's really afraid that he had something to do with this."

"Oh, good God, that's even worse."

"It's worse from his perspective. Yet I don't know," she muttered, looking out the windshield. "Something's just been completely off about all this. I feel as if we've been running around in circles, and we've never known quite what we're doing."

Rodney snorted. "This has been very much that kind of a case. I don't know myself from one moment to the next what's going on. So, it's a case that isn't like a lot of them. It's not clear. We keep waiting for something else to happen."

"Well, something else has happened," she declared, "and this needs to be the last thing."

"You really think it's connected?"

"Yes, I absolutely think it's connected. Matter of fact, I'm sure of it. What I don't know is which of my suspects had something to do with it."

He shot her another startled look. "What suspects?" he asked. "I didn't think we even had suspects yet. You want to fill me in?"

"I'll see what today brings," she explained, "and then I can absolutely try to fill you in. But, if you're looking for the whys and the wherefores, I don't have it. All I've had so far is bloody instincts."

His lips twitched.

"And that's got absolutely nothing to do with psychic ability."

He laughed. "You can say that until you're blue in the face, but that doesn't mean anybody else will believe you."

"Maybe not, but we have plenty of other issues to deal with right now," she pointed out. "So, let's just keep that one closed."

Rodney pointed when they pulled up to the church and found that the 9-1-1 responders were already here. The police and the fire department were coordinating, and the place was being cordoned off.

She looked over at him and noted, "We got here pretty damn fast, and yet we're still behind."

"I know it," he said. "I'll start a perimeter search first, and the cops inside should do a complete sweep of the church."

She nodded. "You handle that. I want to confirm that nobody's outside watching everything."

She walked over to one of the cops, who was holding the gathering crowd back. She pulled him aside and suggested, "We need to confirm that somebody here doesn't have a particular interest in keeping an eye on things."

He nodded.

"So, start taking photos, will you? I want a snapshot of every person who's gathered here to see what's happening."

He didn't say anything but immediately pulled out his phone.

She smiled at that and headed inside. As soon as she got in, she was surprised to find Smidge here and not in his regular coroner's outfit.

He turned and glared at her, his hands on his hips. "Is there no end to the carnage you bring me?" His tone was unpleasant.

She shook her head. "Apparently not." She glanced at his outfit. "I gather you weren't at work."

"No, I wasn't. I *was* at work," he clarified. "I was trying to go home until you brought me this lovely BS."

"Yeah. Lovely BS is right."

"Who kills priests?"

She looked at him and shrugged. "Unfortunately, there could be a lot of people."

He snorted. "It was a rhetorical question. You didn't need to give me an answer."

"Yeah. And it was a rhetorical answer," she replied. "You don't need to give me a lecture."

He froze, stared at her, and started to laugh. "Good God, don't ever change."

"Wasn't planning on it," she quipped cheerfully.

Several of the cops looked at her in shock, as if understanding that she had some sort of a relationship with the brusque coroner.

She smiled at them and waved them off. "Anybody checked the entire building?" she asked the uniforms. "I want it checked out top to bottom. Confirm that there are no places where anybody can hide, and I want the outside camera feeds like now."

Smidge gave her a narrowed gaze, and she nodded at the poor victim. Smidge asked, "How are you here this early when the 9-1-1 call was made—"

"Simon found him." She didn't want him to put out feelers and to reel Simon in. Better tell him, so that his name stayed out of the way.

His eyebrows shot up, and he nodded. "Well, hell."

"Yeah. Well, hell is right. He feels bad that he didn't get here in time."

Smidge looked down at the body. "I don't know how quickly Simon got here, but the priest's been dead … maybe two hours."

She turned to him. "I'll say that's good news for Simon because he didn't want to come into the church today."

"Why?"

"That's not for me to say, but, as he tried to walk past it," she lowered her voice and added, "his *system* wouldn't let him."

Smidge shook his head. "I'm really glad I don't have his *system*. I deal with this shit all the time. Yet I can't imagine going to places that I'm not even called to and getting caught up in something like this," he muttered. "Where is he?"

"He'll be sitting around here somewhere."

Just then a voice called out from the far side, "I'm here." He came closer. "I just figured you guys could, you know, do your little hellos before anybody dealt with me."

Smidge walked over to him and asked, "What did you see?"

"I saw nothing except feet," he replied, as he stared at the dead man. "I came in, not sure what was upsetting me. I sat in that pew over there." He pointed it out. "As soon as I sat down, I saw one foot. I bounced up again, came over immediately." He stopped for a moment, then added, "I've talked to this priest several times over the last few days." He shrugged and turned to Kate. "I mean ..."

"I know," she replied.

"What do you know?" Smidge asked, facing her.

"It's heartbreaking." She shrugged. "That's what he would say. It's heartbreaking."

Smidge looked at Simon. "Is that what you will say?"

"Yeah, it is." He frowned at her. "Stop reading my mind."

She retorted, "Stop being such an open book, making it so easy to read your mind."

Smidge snorted. "The two of you are a class act. Now the trick is to coordinate enough so this shit doesn't happen," he snapped, growling at the two of them.

"Agreed." Simon nodded. "I would absolutely love for that to happen." He looked down at the priest and then turned back to Kate. "Kate ..."

"I know. I've got people all over the place on this one," she told him.

"It has to be the last one," he whispered, facing her. "It has to be." And then, obviously upset, he walked over to the far side, where he sat down alone and just closed his eyes.

Smidge stared at him, then at her. "The last one?"

She frowned, glanced down at the priest. "When you look at this case," she suggested, "look at it from the perspective of it being connected to my other three."

He stared at her, shook his head, and muttered, "Oh, hell no."

She nodded. "Oh, hell yes."

⌘

SIMON SAT SEVERAL pews back, where he could watch the goings-on in front of him. Nobody asked him to leave, which was either because of who he was and his relationship to Kate or the fact that he was the one who found Father McCain. Neither option was something he particularly wanted to be here for.

He closed his eyes and tried to recenter himself. His emotions were all over the place, with anger, frustration, and guilt overwhelming him. He'd had the instinct to come in here, yet he had ignored it.

He didn't want to go inside the church and deal with whatever was going on, but it never occurred to him that somebody was dying inside the damn door. To even think that would have changed the scenario here and that the poor priest would still be alive if Simon had made that move earlier, was enough to send his emotions spiraling again.

As Smidge walked past, he stopped and told Simon, "You couldn't have stopped it." With that, he turned and kept on going.

Simon twisted to watch as the older man walked out without turning back again. When he turned around to the front of the church, he saw Kate standing there, her hands fisted into her pockets as she stared at him steadily.

"He's been dead for a couple hours," she told him. "You couldn't have stopped it."

Simon sank back, closed his eyes, and then gave a quick nod. "Thank you for that."

She sat down beside him and added, "We need to find out just what you know though."

"Sure," he agreed. "And what I know is absolutely nothing." He gave a broken laugh, shook his head, and asked, "What the hell's going on, Kate?"

"I don't know," she said, as she glanced around, "but believe me that this one is hurting all of us now."

"And you really think it's connected?"

She turned to him and asked, "Don't you?"

He swallowed. "Yes, but I don't know why."

"This was rage," she noted. "This was not a carefully thought-out plan. It was rage—sheer unadulterated rage."

He blinked. "So then?"

"So, we think it's still connected. We can't guarantee it's the same killer. Obviously the MO is completely different, and that would make it very hard, short of confession or some forensic evidence, to prove that connection. That in itself will be a challenge."

He looked at her and shook his head. "It's all a challenge right now, isn't it?"

"It absolutely is," she murmured. "And I don't know any way to make this any easier on you. I'll get Rodney to interview you, and I'll listen in. But, just in case it ends up causing trouble, I want to confirm that I am clear and outside of it."

His shoulders sank again. "It's quite a challenge having me around, isn't it?"

"No," she argued. "I don't know who else would have seen this before you. I'm grateful that you saved some poor woman or some young person from coming in here for solace, only to find something beyond unimaginable horror." She gave a light chuckle. "And, no, I'm not happy that you found him because I know what you already go through," she added.

Simon nodded. "So, there isn't a good-case scenario. There is, however, a certain amount of respect. And I feel as if you do have that for him."

She nodded. "I absolutely do."

"And I don't know in any way that I could have changed anything. I don't know what that initial impulse was, to come inside. Then I walked away. And I was determined to leave, but I wasn't given that option," he muttered, turning to look at her. "And I get that now."

"Do you think," she began but paused, as she sat here, watching forensics doing their thing. "Do you think that was because you were meant to find the body? Or do you think that was because the killer was here in some way?"

"I have no way of knowing that," he replied.

"Okay, when you have these feelings," she began, then remarshaled her thought. "Is there an emotion attached? Is there anything attached that you can separate out? Not necessarily a *why* but maybe a *who*?"

"Even if there were," he said, frowning at her intently, "I couldn't give you a specific who."

"Right. I understand," she replied, as she stared around the church. "It's such a beautiful place."

"It is," he agreed, "but it apparently is also deadly. We've had way too many deaths in church lately. And he remembered you."

She smiled and nodded. "I have spoken to him a couple times. He was a good man, and it's such a sad thing and a terrible loss. He helped a lot of people."

"I think he would have been happy to have breathed his last breath in this room. It was his home. It was his … solace."

"And his work is now done," she stated, "and it's up to us to carry on."

"I don't know what happens within the church itself, you know? How long before they find somebody to replace him?" he asked.

"I don't know. Those things are not included in my job description. However, I do know that he will be missed. He had heart and soul," she shared. "And I don't say that about all that many people."

He looked at her. "He said he would call you."

She turned to him. "When did he say that?"

"I think it was the day before yesterday," he shared, with a frown, "but I may be getting it confused. I was asking him about religious classes and marriage counseling and all that stuff. Just wondering if anything or anyone who came to mind. He didn't mention anybody, but he was really clear when he told me that he hadn't heard anything in the confessional that was a crime. You know, to put my mind at ease that nobody had admitted to killing anybody. He shared how he was held to a greater standard for confidentiality, but that he could put my mind at ease on that."

"Good to know," Kate said, studying him. "That's a great question to have asked him."

"It doesn't clear anybody, but it does help to more succinctly understand what the church's involvement in this might be, which really isn't anything," he pointed out. "Except that this occurred in the church."

"Oh, it was more direct than that," Kate noted. "That stabbing of Father McCain was very much an outpouring of emotions. We don't have the weapon yet, but we are all looking for it. What I don't know is whether the killer's outpouring of emotions were deliberately against the priest or he just happened to be ..." She frowned as she searched for the word again. "Let me just call it an unlucky victim at the moment."

"Is that even possible?"

"Sure," she said, with a shrug. "People become angry and lash out, not necessarily at their victim, but because of him," she replied. "And that's what I don't know in this instance. I'm really hoping forensics will have something."

"What about all the apartments of your three dead men?" he asked her. "Any evidence there?"

She nodded. "Yeah, lots and lots of forensic evidence. Unfortunately way too much."

"Right. I remember you telling me how a lot of people passed through John's apartment."

"Yes. Through all their apartments. We're still cross-checking to see about a common denominator, which would be a lovely indication that something was there. So anybody who has killed once and will potentially do it again or was part of a group involved in multiple killings isn't necessarily stupid enough to *not* wear gloves."

She sighed. "So it makes sense that a killer who plans a murder would wear gloves, in theory. However, in a more highly charged passionate killing, like this one—"

"Right." Simon nodded. "No preparation. No plan. No gloves."

"So that's what we're hoping for," she shared, turning to him. "This was sheer rage. He has an incredible number of stab wounds."

"I only saw the blood … everywhere," he whispered, turning to face her.

She nodded. "A quick discussion with Smidge has given us a different take on that," she shared, "and he's bumped this case up to a priority. He was on his way home when this call came in, but, because of who it is and the potential for a connection to our other cases, Smidge's headed back right now to work on it. He's not convinced about the connection theory, but he's willing to move into this with an open mind in order to help us sort that out."

"Good," Simon muttered, shaking his head. "He must love you."

"Nope. When it comes to this shit, I'm at the bottom of the barrel when it comes to his friend list. And yet," she added, "I think we understand each other quite well."

"Whether that means what we would like it to mean or not?"

"I don't know," she admitted. "Obviously we'll never be the kind of people who go have a drink together after work. But, if we were at a party together, I don't think we would avoid each other."

"That's good to know," Simon whispered.

Kate added, "Can't say he's exactly on very many people's friend list. Most of my colleagues seem to be half-scared of him. Or let's just say he's not well-loved. And I'm not even sure we could say he's well-liked. However, that's an entirely different issue, and it doesn't matter because he's damn good at his job."

She sat here with Simon for a long time, until Rodney came over and whispered in her ear, "Will you ask him for a statement?"

"You'll take his statement, if you don't mind," she replied. "And I'll just listen in."

He nodded, then sat down and proceeded to ask Simon exactly what had happened.

Simon provided the facts, and then added in the instinctive pull he had felt to come back and his inability to ignore it.

At that, Rodney winced and put a note off to the side of his page. "Yeah, we'll, *uh*, we'll put that down, you know, somewhat obscurely."

Simon didn't say anything.

Of course they couldn't quite put down everything he said because it just wouldn't give any validity to the case.

"One day," Rodney said, "you'll say exactly what you need to say."

Simon nodded.

Rodney continued. "And, when that day comes, we'll be very happy that you have that freedom," he noted. "Right now, it's enough that all of us know that you were called here. And obviously there was a valid reason for that. I'm sorry that you are involved again."

Simon looked at him, then snorted.

Rodney added, "But you know what you're *not* sorry about?"

"What's that?" Simon asked.

Rodney smiled at him. "That you weren't involved."

"Yeah, you're not kidding," Simon agreed, with a nod. "You would think I would be numb to all this. Instead it just never, ever seems to end."

"It will end, or at least this one will," Kate declared, still at his side. "But there will be another one soon enough. I think that's one of the reasons I do what I do. Just as soon as you think that you're free and clear to rest between cases, something else happens."

Simon frowned. "Sounds very … negative."

"No, not negative, just fatalistic." She smiled and stood up. "I'll walk over to the forensics team and see if they found anything interesting. You guys finish this up, and then I'll take Simon home," she told Rodney.

"And do what?" Simon asked. "Drop me off?"

"Yes," she stated, turning to him. "You don't need to be sitting here."

"I would like to stay," he told her, "if for no other reason than to spend time …" He frowned. "I want to say good-bye." His voice caught on an odd note.

She gave him a quick hug and then headed to the forensic team that was all over the church.

Simon glanced at Rodney and saw the smirk on his face. "She'll be here all day and likely all night, won't she?" Simon asked, his tone light.

"Here, … outside, … all around."

"Figures."

"She's already ordered any available camera footage from outside. And, before she starts snapping at me, I've got to start looking for witnesses, other than you."

Simon nodded. "Street cameras are at the junction and in the left parking lot."

"We've called for all those. There's any number of things we'll be working on tonight," he noted, "because it's still fresh. And, if you have anything to offer, feel free. Although I know that she doesn't particularly want you to feel obligated to help."

"If I had anything to offer," he began, "you guys would be the first to know. Has she told you about that woman who keeps talking to me?"

Rodney turned to him and asked, "No, what woman?" He gave him the shortened version of it. And Rodney frowned. "But what do you do with that, when they are just visions mostly?"

"I don't know," he admitted. "That's the thing. That's probably why Kate hasn't mentioned anything to you guys about it because we don't really know what we're supposed to do with it."

"Good God," he muttered. "So, this woman is upset and

lamenting the loss because she's infertile? She's living in Vancouver, but we don't know what the time frame is?"

"Yeah, … something like that, "Simon muttered, with a smile. "After all those bodies were found in that one building …"

Rodney immediately closed his eyes and then shivered. "Yeah, don't remind me about that. This was pretty horrific too."

"So, for this woman, I can't really say that she's dead or alive, at least not yet. And I don't know if she has any connection to this case."

"With just your visions to go on, I can't imagine that she would, but you're right. We can't take that chance." Rodney wrote down a couple notes about Simon's ongoing visions with this one woman. "I'll, *um*, I'll see if anything pops up."

"Are you expecting something?" Simon asked.

"As a matter of fact, I am."

"Why?"

"Partly because of the motivation behind this current case, and I'm not talking about the priest. But that whole *believe* theme, not to mention that the use of gift wrap and decorations is pretty specific."

"Yet it was also seasonal," Simon noted. "So somebody with a snarky sense of humor may have thought that was an appropriate ending for somebody."

"Two of them were wrapped up, and," Rodney explained, "the one was not. … Two were about poison. The one was not."

"And you guys have no idea."

"We have no forensic evidence, *way too many* phone numbers, not to mention dating apps, which we have to cross-reference, and we're not finding anything, other than three women who dated all of the dead men, or at least two of the men for sure. We've spoken to several of the women who had recently dated our three guys, but no leads so far. There's no payment system involved, and there is an abundance of fake names and fake profiles. And maybe the fake part got them into all this."

"Did you consider that?" Simon asked.

"I think we've been questioning everything, but, if you've got any insights to offer, we're always ready to listen."

Simon laughed. "Whether you want to or not."

"Yeah. Whether we want to or not," Rodney agreed, with half a smile. "There are just some things we would prefer not to have to consider, but that's not an option. So, if you've got anything coming and going—"

"Why would you even think about fake profiles?" Simon cut off his train of thought.

"People catfish all the time on these online platforms. And I don't necessarily mean any of our vics were out there prowling for new dates because, in a way, I think each one was probably as upfront and as clear as he could be about these sex-only relationships. Still, that doesn't mean the women were. The insurance office gossip was that Robert got somebody pregnant."

"Ah."

"So, he may have been upfront and clear about his intentions, but that didn't mean that the women were really on board for the same thing, even if they supposedly agreed to his terms. I know it sounds pretty harsh, cruel, and maybe even unbelievable, but some women get pregnant and then don't want to deal with the baby's daddy. Though that doesn't mean that they won't return at another point and file for child support—even though the man has no idea, which may be why these men have been so strict with their upfront rules."

Simon shook his head. "Wow. With these guys, they should have all had vasectomies. Robert supposedly did. Is that something you could check on? Is that a normal part of an autopsy on dead men?"

"No clue. And believe me that I won't be the one asking Smidge about it."

Simon chuckled at him. "Still don't get along with him, *huh?*"

"I don't understand how anybody gets along with him," Rodney admitted. "I mean, just the job he does is enough to freak me out. And I know it's necessary, and he's really good at it. Yet even the fact that he's good at it seems creepy."

Simon laughed. "And yet—"

"I know." Rodney held up one hand. "We're very grateful that he's good at it. We are also incredibly grateful for someone in the department who seems to have special powers when it comes to him. And I don't want to say he bends over backward for Kate, but it almost seems like it. That in itself seems somehow miraculous because he's just not *that* guy."

Simon instinctively looked over at Kate, who was standing still, staring at the stained-glass windows.

"So, all in all, it's a good thing," Rodney noted, "because if you have somebody who can make things happen and can, better still, make things happen a little faster than normal, it helps a lot."

"It does, indeed." Simon then turned to him. "Outside of this, are you doing okay? Are you all recovered from the beating you took?"

"Yeah, pretty much. It took a little longer than I wanted," he shared, "and of course the office has been good about making sure I get back into fitness and self-defense training. So that's taken it out of me too right now."

"Yeah, and I bet that's why Kate was back at the dojo and got her ass kicked. Sounds like her instructor was pretty unimpressed that she had let so much slide," Simon said, with a smile. Just then came a commotion at the front.

Rodney stood up and called out to Kate, who immediately lifted a hand and waved at him. "You stay in here, and I'll go see what's up."

As Rodney headed toward the front, Simon watched carefully, trying to figure out just what was going on. That same little voice in the back of his head whispered, *Go ahead and watch, but it's too late.*

"What's too late?" he asked.

He's dead.

"I know he's dead," he snapped at Sarah. "I'm the one that found him."

You might've found him, but I'm the one who killed him.

CHAPTER 16

KATE STUDIED THE small footprint in the blood close to the side door of the church. She crouched to get a closer look at it. It was too hard to identify the brand of the shoe, but it appeared to be a sneaker. She looked over at the forensics tech taking a bunch of photos of it and said, "I would say a female."

He immediately nodded. "Yeah, about a size seven. We'll have more when we get this back. We'll take a mold of it and find out exactly what sneaker it is."

"Perfect." She stood up and took a look back. "So, a couple of the footprints are here, but this is the most distinct one."

"Yes, and it goes straight out that door," he noted.

"No weapon found yet?" she asked him. He shook his head.

She stepped over to the door, which was open, and found blood on the handle. "Why would blood be on the handle if the killer used gloves?" she muttered to herself, but of course that wasn't the same thing as somebody coming prepared. None of the evidence so far in this case was about somebody coming prepared. This was sheer fury, for whatever reason.

She stepped outside, careful to leave no trace herself as the little bit of blood trailed out to the parking lot. From where she stood, she noted a commercial lot across from her and a small parking lot around behind the church. So, this person could have come from either spot, could also have potentially just walked from around the block or from another area.

As she walked past the hedge and headed up the block to see what was around, she then crossed the road and came back down the other side. Only as she stood here, her hands on her hips, staring at the door she had come out of, did she catch a twinkle ever-so-slightly in the light. Focused on that, she walked across the street, nearly getting hit by a vehicle, now honking at her.

She raised a hand in apology, found the object again, and came straight for it. She bent down and smiled. She immediately pulled out her phone and called Rodney. "Got a weapon here. I need forensics outside in the left-side parking lot across the road."

"On my way."

With that, she ended the call, pocketed her phone, and stared at the item.

This would imply that whoever the killer was, a woman had walked on this side of the sidewalk in order to toss the knife into the hedge.

Rodney joined her a few minutes later, took one look, and the forensic tech immediately took a bunch of photos, then reached down with gloved hands and pulled it out. He looked at it and nodded. "This could be it. Seems to be more of a ceremonial dagger though."

"I don't know why a ceremonial dagger would be in a Catholic church, but I guess it's possible."

He didn't say anything.

"She also could have brought it with her and then tossed it."

As he held it up, he turned it over. "There's blood on it."

Kate frowned and asked, "What are the chances that she cut herself in all this rage?"

He looked at her in surprise and nodded. "Pretty good really," he replied, as he studied it. "It's pretty sharp at the base, and she might have nicked her hand. That would explain the blood on the knob as well."

"See if you can get any prints off anything," she muttered. "And, if she was walking this way," she thought out loud, as she saw it in her mind, "she would have come down the steps, bolted around the corner of the hedge to hide from anybody at the church. She would have walked down here, what, twenty, twenty-five feet?" she guessed, turning to judge the distance to where the sidewalk met the short walkway up to the steps. "Then tossed it, as if in a panic to get rid of it.

"And then what?" she muttered to herself, as she turned and glanced around. "She would have just kept going." And, with that, she headed toward the end of the block, Rodney with her. "Are any cameras in this area?"

"It's a side street, so not likely." Rodney told her.

She nodded and then noted a series of residential houses, unless she kept going around the corner to the right, which was another entrance into the parking lot. She stopped at the entrance to the parking lot and pointed. "She could have just gone this way. Then came around here, headed to the parking lot, and got in her vehicle." She looked down and pointed out, "Is that blood?"

Rodney took a closer look and then called over one of the forensic techs. They looked carefully and immediately picked up what was likely a very faint blood trail that led around the block and to the parking lot.

Kate nodded. "So, her vehicle was parked here. Now my

questions are, *Were any other vehicles here? Who else was here this morning? Are there any cameras for the parking lot itself?*"

Rodney nodded. "I'll find out and hopefully fast." He took off at a lope.

Kate remained here with the forensic techs as they photographed the area, then picked up the rocks that had a little bit of blood spatter. Following the bloody trail back, it stopped right behind the church.

She looked around. "Obviously she's got a small injury, probably from the knife itself. There weren't any defensive wounds that I saw on the priest," she murmured to herself. "And I didn't see anything broken." She turned to look at the two forensic techs, now standing in front of her.

She asked them, "Did you find any broken glass or anything else sharp that she could have cut herself on?" They shook their heads. "Then it's got to be that knife."

As she turned to go back inside, she saw Simon standing at the bottom of the front steps to the church. "Hey," she said, with a smile, and then she froze in reaction to the look on his face. She raced toward him and grabbed his hand. He was cold as a block of ice. "What's the matter?"

He glanced at the two men behind her, but they walked on by, busy in their own conversation about their tasks at hand.

"She just told me that she killed him," he whispered, his voice heavy.

Her eyebrows shot up. "Who?"

He glanced around and whispered, "Sarah, that woman in my head."

"Oh crap," she muttered, as she scrubbed her face. "Why is it that they never just say the truth? *My name is Sarah. At 10:00 a.m. I killed the priest.*"

He turned to her, and a gleam of amusement flickered for a brief moment before disappearing. "Wouldn't that be nice?" he muttered. "That would be absolutely fabulous if somebody would be so kind, but it won't necessarily be the answer that you're looking for."

She asked him as many questions as she could, but he didn't really have much in the way of answers. He had plenty of questions too, but she was the one who would have to find the answers, ... for both of them.

CHAPTER 17

WITH RODNEY AT her side, Kate set about canvassing the houses in the area. And it seemed as if nobody saw anything.

Most had been at work. Now they were just curious, wondering what was going on at the church. She refrained from giving too many details.

If they hadn't seen anything, didn't see any vehicles at the church, either didn't attend the church or weren't active in the church at all, then she just kept moving. She wondered if anybody had seen anything at this point. Even Rodney was starting to give her side looks.

Rodney noted, "It's amazing that nobody ever sees anything."

"I know," she muttered. "Where are the older men and older ladies who used to just sit by the window, being nosy neighbors?" Kate sighed. "It seems as if everybody's buried in their TVs or their smartphones or something."

"Or something," Rodney replied, "as in our deceased studs."

"I know," she muttered, "but it's really not great when it comes to getting information about them."

She came to one of the houses right at the corner. She knocked, and a woman, mid-forties maybe, opened the door and stared at her. Kate quickly identified themselves of them and held up her badge.

The other woman frowned with instant concern. "Oh my, I hope everything's okay."

But her gaze was bright and inquisitive, and it gave Kate hope. "We're looking into any disturbance around the church today. The parking lot, any vehicles racing past, anything at all that looked suspicious."

"When you say *suspicious*," she began, "I don't know about that. I mean, I live here obviously, and I'm home all day, but I can't see very much from here. The church is around the corner."

"Yes, but the back entrance to the parking lot is right here."

"Yes, yes, of course it is," she confirmed. "And I do sometimes see vehicles coming and going, but it's not a regular occurrence."

Kate nodded. "So, you haven't seen anything that caught your attention today?"

The woman shook her head. "Nothing comes to mind." Then she clued in and her eyes widened. "Oh my gosh, please tell me nothing bad happened at the church."

Kate grimaced. "I can't say that because unfortunately there's been a murder."

"At the church?" The woman stared, the color fading from her face, as she whispered, "Please, not Father McCain."

Kate's eyebrows shot up, and she slowly nodded. "I'm sorry, but it was Father McCain."

"No, no, no, no," she cried out in horror. "He's such a good man. He's been so good to this community."

Kate nodded. "And I'm sorry. I know it's not news any of us wants to hear, which is why I'm out here right now, asking if you saw anything today."

"No, no," she replied. "I haven't seen anything along that line in a very long time. I don't even know what I'm saying. I haven't seen anything period. I mean, that's just awful," she muttered.

"And when you said, *in a long time?*"

"It's just ..." She shook her head. "I don't want to get anybody in trouble."

Kate agreed. "I hear you, but just no time to be worrying about that right now. We have to act fast to get any information we can. May I ask you some questions?"

"Sure, ask away, and I'll tell you anything I can."

"Did you know Father McCain?"

"Yes. I used to clean the church, and I used to volunteer to help on some of the Sunday school events and stuff, until my husband got very sick. Since then I've just been home more than out lately." She glanced out the door and around her front yard. She opened the door wider and let them in. "My husband was sick for a long time, but there were also some other good reasons why I just didn't feel quite the same about the church anymore. And I know that's probably confusing."

"So, there was some incident at the church?" Rodney asked, redirecting her.

"Oh, there absolutely was something. It was maybe a year or two or so ago now. It was difficult for a lot of people around here. Father McCain was quite perturbed by the way some of the women acted. He didn't understand it, and I'm not sure I did either," she shared.

"Maybe you could go back to the beginning and give us a little more detail," Rodney suggested.

She looked at him and smiled brighter, maybe noticing

the hunk of a detective, but then she frowned and looked uncomfortable.

"It's fine," Kate told her. "I know you don't want to get anybody in trouble, but we really do need to know what that incident was, just so we can understand it, so it isn't impacting every conversation we have as we interview folks in the neighborhood."

"Oh, yes, I see what you mean," she noted. "Yes, that would make sense."

"Okay, so could you tell us a little more, please?"

"Father McCain used to have these counseling sessions for women before they went through their marriage ceremony."

"What kind of counseling?"

"You know, the relevant scriptures, respect for the husband, and all that good stuff," she said. "I think to a certain extent they still do them, although I don't think he does them quite the same way anymore. I know he was a little perturbed by how it ended up back then."

"How what ended up?" Rodney asked.

She stared at him and continued. "So, a few women were in the group, and one of the women knew the fiancé of another one. And the woman in question was infertile and had known about it for a while, I guess, but she hadn't told her fiancé." She sighed, shaking her head.

"So, the one woman who knew the fiancé claimed that he deserved to be told, that the infertile woman was damaged goods. I think that is how she put it. The prospective husband didn't have any idea, but he really wanted a family, and it wasn't fair of her to marry him without giving him the opportunity to know what he was getting into. Anyway, that didn't go over well, as I'm sure you can imagine."

Kate and Rodney remained silent, all in an effort to keep her talking.

"It didn't go over well with a lot of the women who were against what was going on. But the argument between the two women, who both knew the fiancé in question, just got more heated. One told the other that it's none of her business, and she was jumping the gun. The other one said that she was just being a liar and trying to get a husband by hook or crook."

"So, there was a physical fight?" Kate asked.

"Oh, not at first. Initially it was a war of words, and it very quickly went downhill."

"I can imagine," Rodney noted, drawing a look from Kate. He just shrugged and added, "You get into a catfight like that, it can get pretty ugly."

"Exactly," the woman confirmed, with a heavy sigh. "So, it ended up getting physical, and this upset a lot of the ladies in the counseling session that day. I know that one got quite concerned over all the drama. It got so bad," she added, "that the police were called."

Kate stared at her. "I don't think I've seen any report in relation to that."

"No, and I'm pretty sure that Father McCain would have done everything he could to keep it off the record, if possible," the lady shared. "Again, I'm not trying to ruffle any feathers, but his pants were on fire for a while there."

"Sure," Kate replied impatiently. "Go on."

"So the one woman who knew the fiancé told him."

Beside her, Rodney whispered, "Crap."

"Exactly, and that caused him to, well, … understandably he was upset, and he broke up with her. But she had also been working with Father McCain quite a bit over the years to get her infertility … rectified. The church does believe in miracles, and they believe in all kinds of things being fixed without medical intervention."

Kate glanced at Rodney and saw her confusion reflected in his expression.

The woman continued. "I know that Father McCain was of the opinion that, if she would relax about it all and just not get so worked up, it would possibly fix itself. Anyway he always said that, *If you just believed strong enough, hard enough, everything would be fine.*"

"Good God," Kate whispered.

Rodney shot Kate a sharp look at the word *believe.*

"So, what happened after that?" Kate asked.

"I'm not exactly sure what happened after all of it," she said. "I heard the fiancé broke it off and went on a bender, ended up dying from an accidental overdose. His addiction was really bad by the end of it all."

Kate was in complete shock. She sat back and stared at her. "Was that man Kurt Conner by any chance?"

Her eyebrows shot up, and she squealed, "Yes, that's exactly who it was." She smiled and added, "He didn't live all that close to here, but he knew the two women from our church. I don't know at what level," she noted. "I don't know how close they were. So, that was part of the accusations coming from the poor infertile woman who got jilted because she felt that her relationship had been intentionally sabotaged by the other woman. That led to the idea that maybe there was more to it than just meddling, which made it all uglier still."

She sighed, then added, "Now, I don't believe that there was necessarily anything hostile toward Father McCain, but things were very rocky for quite a while. Naturally people took sides, so the whole church experience had a bad taste for a while, let's put it that way."

She looked out the window, checking the neighborhood, and then her gaze landed back on Kate. "I don't think he particularly saw it as a happy ending, but, when things calmed down, I'm sure he felt things were at least good enough and better now that everybody would be over it all.

"So the one woman who exposed it all ended up with a partner, a long-term relationship, but the other one, the one jilted, never really let up about how that woman's involvement had deliberately ruined the infertile woman's engagement. Yet she didn't seem to have a problem getting in the middle of the other woman's relationship." She sighed. "I don't know all the details at this point. You'll have to contact the parties in question if you think it's really important. I understood that there was potentially some other affair and that man recently died too."

Kate sat up, ever alert. "I need the names of these two women, please. And, if you have any contact information, that would be helpful."

"You could certainly get it from the church." Then she winced. "Or maybe not."

"Right," Kate agreed. "*Maybe not* is quite true. I don't know how much they'll be willing to hand out at this point, but I do need the contact information for both women. And when you shared how another man died recently, how do you know this?"

"I have been running in theses circles for a while. I do get up and about at times, and someone from church told me."

"Do you know where he worked?"

"No, but I think he was an insurance adjuster somewhere."

Beside her, Rodney muttered, "Bingo."

The woman frowned at him. "What do you mean, *bingo*? I don't think they played bingo."

Kate stood up and looked over at Rodney. "We'll need to contact these women." She turned back to their witness and asked her, "When did you last see either of the women?"

She pondered it for a moment and frowned. "Not all that long ago. … A couple days ago maybe."

"And where did you see them?"

"Oh, they were over at the church," she replied. "I just happened to be—I may have seen one of them today. But two days ago I was out working in the garden, and I know it's way too early, even in Vancouver for fussing with gardens. However, I took advantage of the bit of a break in the weather. I have so much thatch out there and the weeds and whatnot," she explained, with an aimless view toward the front garden.

"And I did see one of their vehicles, maybe today," she announced. "I just caught it out of the corner of my eye. But I couldn't be positive," she added.

"Of course not," Kate noted.

It was so typical of people to hedge by saying they weren't positive, so they couldn't be taken to court and forced to give evidence and be proven wrong. Everybody wanted to have a whole lot more security in their answers than what they were often willing to suggest they had.

When Kate finally got the names out of this woman, the witness added, "I don't have phone numbers for them."

"That's fine. We can round them up," Kate said. "Do you know what they drive?"

"Yeah, one is—They're both driving similar vehicles. Those little cars, the ones that look to be chopped in half, the smart cars?"

Rodney pulled up a picture, and she looked at it and nodded. "Yeah, that. One's got a blue one, and the other I think is red. I haven't seen that one for a long time."

"Now, are you saying that both of their partners are now dead?"

"Yes," she confirmed. "That is my understanding."

"Interesting." Kate eyed Rodney and then spoke to their witness. "I need your contact information in case we have more questions."

"Oh, my." She seemed half-thrilled and half-horrified at the idea, yet provided the requested information.

Kate thanked her. As she walked out, she asked, "If you see either of the women coming around here over the next few days, can you call me, please?"

"Sure," the woman replied. "I don't know why they would though."

Kate asked her, "Why wouldn't they?"

"I mean, they had been really good friends up until that point in time, I think, until they both started attending the classes. Something was between them that just didn't make a whole lot of sense. I mean, I think that's what bothered Father McCain. He mentioned it to me once, about something just being off."

"Interesting. Thank you for your time."

Kate headed back outside, with Rodney rushing along behind her. She walked back to the parking lot, and Rodney repeated, "Something off?"

"Yeah," Kate agreed, "something is very off. But I think I may have just found what made it off. We need both these women in the station at the same time, please." When he looked at her in surprise, she shrugged. "This is a case that will be solved in the box, not out here on the streets."

"If you say so," he muttered.

"I do say so," she declared, "and let's really try for tonight. I need a good night's sleep."

"There'll be paperwork to file."

"But the puzzle will be solved, and that's all we need … for now."

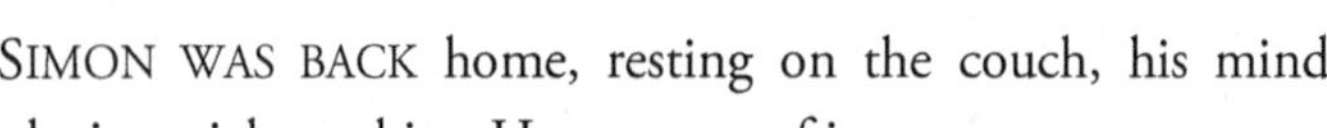

SIMON WAS BACK home, resting on the couch, his mind playing tricks on him. He was sure of it.

This woman kept bobbing in, bobbing out, crying, upset, then defiant. When the phone rang, he knew it would be Kate, and he just answered it. "I presume you're not coming home tonight."

"I'm not coming home right now," she clarified. "I'm trying to find a couple women and get them in tonight for questioning, if at all possible."

He sat upright and frowned at his phone. "Have you got something?"

"I think so," she claimed. "In a way, it's just a little too far out to believe, but I'm hoping," she added.

He heard the exhaustion in her tone, but something else was there too, a hint of excitement perhaps—as if she finally had something to bite on.

"It would be a very sad end if this is what's happening, but I don't know. I could still be barking up the wrong tree."

He smiled because Kate hated to make a statement and then be wrong. "I highly doubt you're barking up the wrong tree."

She froze and then asked, "Are you getting any information?"

"No, nothing," he said. "Wait. No, that's not true. I mean, Sarah is in my head, out of my head, in my head, out of my head."

"How does she sound?"

"She's a basket case," he declared. "She sobs. She's all upset. She's sad. Then she's really defiant. Her emotions are all over the place, mercurial even."

"Interesting," Kate noted. "I've got shit to do, and, with any luck, I might still get some sleep tonight. However, for the moment, I am all over this case, so please take care of yourself."

"Oh, I will," he told her, "but you need to look after yourself too."

"I'm working on it." With that, she ended the call.

Simon frowned. Just something about Kate's tone meant that she had obviously snapped onto something—something that mattered. But she didn't know how much or just how important it would be, so she thrummed with both excitement and dread.

He found the dread part interesting. He got up, poured himself a glass of wine, then sat back down again. Suddenly the woman in his head popped in again, and this time Sarah was bawling, that *absolutely at the end of her rope* kind of bawling.

He tried to shut her down, but she was so intense in his head that it was hard. And just as he was ready to get up and go for a jog, do anything for a distraction, his phone rang. He looked down to see it was George, from the bank board, getting back to him as promised.

George greeted Simon in a quiet tone. "So, you may have solved your problem," he began, "but you've given me one."

"I'm not sure if that's right or wrong, but I feel as if it never should have been mine in the first place."

"I agree," George replied. "It shouldn't have. For your information, the one slandering you was, indeed, Leonard's nephew, Stanley. We are now in the process of pulling him off the board. Leonard's pissed, calling for legal action, all kinds of caterwauling. However, when it was revealed exactly what his nephew had been up to, how he leaned into the defamation, Leonard has now gone very, very quiet."

"Which is probably even more dangerous."

"Exactly," George exclaimed, his tone bitter. "So, there could be some backlash and maybe even more anger directed at you, which is why I'm letting you know. Yet I'm also telling you that, as far as the bank is concerned, you're free and clear."

"Which I was anyway."

"You were," he agreed, with a note of amusement. "So, let's not push that whole defamation line. Just know that there isn't any issue as far as we're concerned as members of the board, and no issue was directly affiliated with the bank. What we'll do from here, I don't know. It depends on how expensive it'll be to get rid of Leonard and his nephew."

"Which it shouldn't be at all, if things were run properly."

"Yeah, well, the banking industry is all about trust and confidence, and we have to do whatever we can in order to make that happen. So, I very much appreciate you bringing this to our attention."

"Right, so *we thank you, but please forget about it?*" Simon chuckled.

"Yeah, something along that line," George admitted, and he ended the call.

With that, Simon lay back down, feeling a certain amount of relief. He quickly texted both his lawyer and accountant, then David.

David phoned him right away. "I've been offered my job back as of today," he shared. "I'm not sure that I want it though, given how quickly things went south because of something that wasn't even in my control."

"I hear you, but the banking investment firms are pretty rough right now too. So I suggest you just think about it. Then, if you want to go to a different one, you do that."

"Maybe, I don't know," he muttered. "I'll let you know down the road."

As he went to hang up, Simon added, "And thank you."

After a moment of silence, David replied, his tone warm, "You're welcome, and I am so sorry for the way it all came down."

"Me too, but just think, we managed to make something good happen out of it. Leonard has been booted off the board, along with his nephew. I haven't decided on the defamation lawsuit yet. George is really hoping I'll just put this all off to the side."

"Which, as you well know, if and when you need financing, and it's looking a little bit on the tight side, it would be good to have them in your corner. I don't want to say *in your pocket* because that reminds me just a little bit too much of the weasels that we're just getting rid of. However, it's never a bad thing to have somebody like George on your side in the future."

"I *was* thinking about that," Simon replied, "and lawsuits are bloody expensive, even when you have lawyers on retainer. Maybe especially then. I swear to God, they're more expensive because of it," he declared, with a laugh. They spoke for another few minutes, and then he ended the call and stretched back out again to try and sleep, at least for a little bit.

He could go to bed later, but right now he just wanted to remove some of the stress that had been ramped up in his system over the last few days. As he lay here, a smile on his face, Sarah came shrieking back into his psyche, screaming at him.

Get her away! Get her away! Don't you understand? Get her away from me!

He bolted to his feet, glanced around, hating that instinctual reaction to turn and fight the danger, and yet he wasn't even in the same damn room as the shrieking woman. As soon as Sarah shrieked one more time, he asked, "Get who away? I can't help you if I don't know who you're trying to chase away."

Sarah kept screaming at him, *She's yours. Get her away, or I'll kill her too.*

And, with that warning, his brain went completely quiet. Simon had no doubt who Sarah planned on killing next.

He immediately grabbed his phone.

CHAPTER 18

KATE WALKED UP to the address in question.

She had several other black-and-whites on their way, but, when she got to the address, she decided she would take a quick look around and see if she could get a feel for what was happening. As soon as she got into the apartment building, she glanced around. This was a pretty standard building, not necessarily low-income but definitely not a high-income location.

Maybe a good family area, but she wasn't hearing any kids. As she knocked on the apartment door, a deathly silence came from inside. She pounded on the door again. "Open up, police."

Absolutely nothing came in response, but another neighbor opened her door and poked their head out. Kate raised her badge. The woman winced and went back inside and closed her door.

Kate knocked on the door again. She needed to speak to this woman.

Rodney, having driven his own vehicle, just now arrived. He walked toward her, and Kate called out at the apartment, "Police, open the door."

Suddenly the door opened, and there stood a woman, a scarf tied over her head, tears in her eyes, probably crying steadily for some time. She stared at Kate, and venom filled her tone when she cried out, "What do you want?"

"To talk to you," Kate replied, facing her, noting how, aside from the anger, this woman was probably once really pretty. Was the scarf to hide that beauty? Then Kate's wandering gaze noted a lot of poinsettias in view behind the screaming shrew—a dozen or more. Kate frowned. "So you really like poinsettias, I gather."

"They die after Christmas," the woman screamed. "I don't have anything to say to you. I don't have anything to say to you at all ever. You're his, and he's not here."

Kate raised one eyebrow. "I'm whose?"

"You're his," she spat. "That man, … who's following me."

Not sure exactly what or who she was talking about, Kate nodded. "I see." The woman kept staring at her. "I don't know anybody who has been following you."

"Yes, yes, you do," she snapped. "He's making me crazy."

So this must be Simon's Sarah. Privately Kate thought that it was already too late for anybody to make this woman crazy. To Kate, it seemed this woman was either heavily under the influence of drugs, was having a psychotic break, or perhaps was off some medication that she badly needed. She studied the other woman and asked, "Are you Sarah Carroll?"

Sarah snorted. "You already know that. He told you all about it."

She stared at her and added, "We want to bring you down to the station to ask you some questions."

Sarah shook her head. "That won't happen."

"Really?" Kate asked. "And why is that?"

"Because he's the one who's in trouble for letting you get

to me."

"You're not making any sense," Kate muttered under her breath.

Rodney then stepped forward a bit and introduced himself. "Hey, I'm Rodney. I work with Kate here. We have some questions to ask you about a couple murders."

"Murders?" she repeated, turning to him. "They weren't murders. Who's calling it murder?"

"Can you tell me what it was?" Rodney asked.

"They were justice."

Kate stiffened, stared at her, and repeated, "Justice?"

"Yes, justice," Sarah snapped. "But then you don't understand anything about it. And, if it wasn't for that bitch, you wouldn't even be here right now."

Kate frowned at Sarah, then eyed Rodney, who looked equally confused. "Okay, you just lost me there."

Sarah shrugged. "That's not hard to do, is it?"

Kate wasn't sure where this was going, but Rodney motioned to the uniformed officers who had just arrived. They put Sarah in cuffs and then led her out to the black-and-white car. Sarah screamed the entire time.

Kate turned to the neighbor who had opened her door again, as soon as things had calmed somewhat. "Hey, can I ask you a couple questions about Sarah? Your neighbor?"

"Yeah, sure," she replied. "She's kind of, you know, loopy."

"Okay, and has she been that way a long time?"

"As far as I know, yes," she replied. "She's got this thing about men and what justice is supposed to be. But I don't understand what she goes on about. She's a bit insane, but she's harmless most of the time. She needs help."

"I get that," Kate replied. "And do you know anything

about her? What she does? Where she works?"

"She used to work at an insurance company, as far as I know," she replied. "I haven't seen her leaving much at all here lately. But then I work from home, so, I can't really keep track of any of it, and I don't want to. I mostly try to fly under the radar."

"Does Sarah ever have any friends over?"

"Just this one woman, and they usually end up in a fight every time. Anytime I've heard yelling and seen anybody leave, it's been that same woman. No one else comes around anymore."

"Any idea who that woman is?"

"Nope, sorry. I don't know if the cameras outside work or not, but maybe they've cached something and could tell you. I don't think she lives in this building, but I don't get the sense that she lives very far away. I think she walks here."

"Why do you think that?"

"I've not seen a car, and she never carries anything. Not even a coat. Just like when you slip out to pop in and see somebody? It's like that. But last time was pretty wild. They were yelling at each other, almost threatening. I was about to call the cops when they finally just shut up. I've never wanted to get involved," she added, with a shrug.

Kate nodded and asked, "Has Sarah lived here long? Do you know anything about it?"

"No, I don't have a clue," she stated.

"Any idea when you first started seeing this other woman?"

"No."

"Do you think they had a romantic relationship?"

"Oh, I don't think so," she muttered, with a loopy smile, "but I guess I've never really thought of that. But, if they are in a relationship, they really shouldn't be … because, I'm not kidding, it can get pretty wild between them."

"Understood. Okay, so we'll be in touch if I have any other questions," she said, with a nod.

As she headed outside with Rodney, he asked her, "Do you have a clue what's going on here?"

"Yeah, unfortunately."

He stared at her in surprise. "Goddammit, how is it that we get the same bits and pieces of information, and it makes sense to you, but it does not to me? I swear to God, I'm not a complete dumbass, and nobody else in the office puts these pieces together the same way you do either."

"Well," she muttered, "maybe I've just seen too much of the world."

"You haven't been a detective half as long as I have," he muttered. "Sometimes I feel as if I'm a complete loser in this department."

She turned to him. "No way. I will admit that my brain seems to work differently and has adapted to this job fairly quickly," she admitted, "but you should never feel you aren't good enough because you're doing exactly what you should be doing, and you're doing a damn good job of it."

"Says you," he muttered.

"Rodney, do you know that your timing and instincts in these interviews is perfect? I go too far, push too hard, and they clam up, and just as I'm wondering what the hell to do, you make a subtle move, ease your way into the conversa-tion, then suddenly they are talking again. It's brilliant."

He shook his head. "I don't know about that, yet I shouldn't whine. I don't know exactly what's going on these days, but I've got to tell you, it's been a hell of a time."

"It has, indeed," she agreed, with a laugh. "Now, let's go

back to the station. I have one other person I want brought in."

"Yeah, but I don't know who that other person is."

"You might not right now," she noted, "but I suspect you'll understand when you see her."

When they walked into the station a little later, he stood in the observation room to see who was in the second interview room. He looked back at her and shook his head vehemently. "No way. You're wrong, or I still don't have a fucking clue."

She smiled. "You'll see it soon enough."

And, with that, she headed to the first interview room where she stepped in, checked on Sarah—who took one look at her and started hissing. Kate sighed. "That'll make it a little more difficult to talk to you."

"I'm not talking to you ever."

"Okay," Kate replied, then she turned and walked back out. As she went to close the door, she added, "I'll just leave you here to think about that for a while."

Then she headed into the second interview room, Rodney at her side. As they entered, the woman looked up, fear in her eyes. Kate nodded. "Hi, Caroline. I figured it was time we had a more formal talk."

SIMON COULDN'T SETTLE. He paced around the apartment, then finally switched into casual clothes, put on his sneakers, and headed down to the lobby.

As he walked to the front door, Edgar stopped him and asked, "Hey, are you heading to the boat?"

"Maybe," he said, turning to him, shoving his hands deep into his pockets. "To be honest, I'm a little out of sorts.

Things are happening for Kate right now, so she won't be home anytime soon. As much as I want to go to the station, I don't want to mess up whatever is happening in their world."

"Understood," Edgar noted. "That gal works too hard."

"She does, indeed, but right now I think she's caught a break in the case, and she's on it," he shared, with a shrug. "But, for me, it just feels, I don't know, *off* somehow. It's been a weird day."

"Understood." Edgar suggested, "Maybe a trip to the *Running Mate* would be a good thing."

"I was thinking about it, but maybe just getting out and getting some walking in will help." He shook his head. "Something to wear down some of the excess energy I've got."

"Good enough, just remember good things aren't always out there."

"Right, and I'm not looking for good things," he replied. "I just want to chase away some of the ghosts once in a while."

As he walked toward the front door, pulling it open, Edgar raced to grab it first. "You could at least let me do my job."

"I could," Simon conceded, "but I'm also perfectly capable of opening a door."

"Hey, Simon," a voice called out from the dusky light outside the door. He turned as Edgar was pushing the door open for him.

"Who are you?" Simon asked the stranger. He stepped into the light, and Simon recognized the young wannabe welder. That was no good. "Look at that," Simon noted, his voice calm, even as his brain locked onto the fact that a handgun was pointed at him—and right behind him was

Edgar, who may or may not have seen it. "You brought an accessory. So nice of you to show up with presents, Stanley—or should I call you Allen?"

Simon also noticed his hands were firmly on the handgun. "You're the kid who tried to tell us how you were an experienced welder, but you didn't even know how to hold the damn stick properly," he declared, shaking his head. "The gall of youth completely overcame you, and you wound up looking stupid. But then again, you're looking pretty stupid now too, aren't you?"

"Hell no. My uncle believes in me."

"Leonard might believe *in* you, but that doesn't mean he'll believe you. And you can bet that this stunt won't go over very well either."

"You're the one who's going down," Stanley vowed. "We don't need shits like you in this world," he snapped, as he pointed the handgun at Simon and took a step closer. That step closer was his mistake because Simon just smiled and kept him talking.

"I'm afraid your uncle's getting a rude awakening right now too." Without warning, Simon lashed out, kicking out his long leg and hitting the handgun, sending it flying into the sky. "So, I would not in any way"—he followed up with a hard right punch to the kid's jaw—"be talking like that."

But the kid was no longer talking at all. He had dropped to the ground, completely out cold.

Edgar raced over to Simon, swearing a blue streak. "Oh my God!" he cried out. He checked on the kid who was breathing but obviously not going anywhere.

Simon walked over to the weapon, kicked it up toward Edgar.

"*Uh*, yeah, I've already got the cops coming. But, Jesus

Christ, man, that was a hell of a kick."

He nodded. "Remember how I got caught in a fight on one of Kate's latest cases? And just as she is brushing up her skills, I decided it was time to brush up on mine," he shared, turning to him. "So, yeah, good thing I did, *huh*?"

Edgar stared at him and shook his head. "You know, if that kid had any experience—"

"He would have shot first instead of shooting off his mouth."

"Do you know why he's angry at you?"

"Yeah, he's been shooting his mouth off for a whole lot of reasons and none of them good or true," he murmured. "And he was taking a big fall at my hands. I'd already fired him from my company because he applied as a welder, but he didn't know the first thing about the craft. Then his uncle hired him at the same investment banking firm where I have a bunch of business loans. Stanley, our gunman here, apparently recognized my name and started bad-mouthing me to his uncle, who happened to be chairman of the board for the bank, so all kinds of shit started to happen there.

"When I found out who was giving me a hard time, I contacted somebody else on the board—somebody with a whole lot more smarts. So now the kid has been fired from that job too. His uncle is still protesting, saying that his nephew is a good kid and innocent of any wrongdoing, but this should put an end to all that nonsense," Simon declared, with a nod.

"Sometimes families just don't want to believe what their relatives have been doing," Edgar noted.

It took a few more minutes for the cops to arrive. When they did, they took statements from both Simon and Edgar, then quickly picked up the slowly awakening punk, handcuffed him, and took him down to the station.

As they left, one of the officers asked, "Are you okay? Do we need to get you any medical treatment?"

Simon shook his head. "No, I'm fine, but I might come down to the station after all."

He frowned at him. "No need. We can handle it from here."

"Oh no, that's okay. That's not what I meant. My partner is Kate, … Detective Kate Morgan," he explained. "I know she's caught up in a case right now, and I just want to check in with her and be there."

He stared at him, and one of them even whistled. "Wow." Then he shrugged. "She's good people."

And, with that, they left, but there was no doubt that Kate's reputation as being a hard-ass would have earned a smile, maybe a chuckle.

Simon turned to Edgar, who nodded and added, "Glad to know she's getting the respect she deserves."

Simon shared, "She is good people though."

Edgar snorted. "She's still a hard-ass. And you know something? You just had a really close call," he pointed out. "So, if you want to go down to the station and sit at her desk until she's got a few minutes to spend with you, don't even second-guess that shit. Go on. You don't know when you'll face a gun again. And, in this case," he added, "that kid, he could have shot both of us."

"I know," Simon agreed, looking over at him. "You need hazard pay."

Edgar snorted. "And you know as well as I do that they'll blame you."

"It wasn't me," Simon argued, with a smile, "but I can see how they might want to blame me." He shrugged. "We could always move to another building. Sometimes I think about doing that."

"Don't do it on my account," Edgar said. "Ain't nothing here to chase me away. I'm happy."

"If you're happy, we'll just keep it all quiet then."

He laughed. "You can't keep it too quiet. The police will be around, and, hell, management will probably throw a fit."

"You're right. I guess we can't keep it quiet at all. On the other hand, we also don't have to make a big deal out of it," he suggested. "So, I'll head down and see where Kate is at by now." He stopped and frowned. "I don't even know that she has her wheels. I think I dropped her off this morning, but I can't remember." He yawned. "I'll drive and, *uh*, we'll let you know if I'm coming back tonight."

"Okay, sounds good. The question is whether you'll need food." Edgar laughed, then corrected himself. "What am I saying? Kate will need food. That gal can eat, and she needs it. She's burning through a ton of calories, so you might want to pick up some sustenance and take it with you."

He nodded, considering Edgar's suggestion. "Do you mind putting in an order at the sandwich shop? Some of those hot rolls they have that are all stuffed with meat and veggies and whatnot?" he asked, "I could go for a couple of those myself. I'll pick them up on my way."

"How many do you want me to order?"

He thought about it, shrugged, and decided, "A full crew is probably at the station tonight. So, maybe three or four dozen?"

Edgar laughed. "Good enough. You can always bring home the leftovers."

And, with that, Simon headed to his car, made a side

stop, then had to wait a few minutes for the order to be ready. Once he collected it, he drove to the station. He'd spent more time here since he had hooked up with Kate, more than he'd ever spent at a police station in his life.

Maybe that was a good thing. He didn't know. It just seemed as if so many things in his life had changed. And this was just another example.

As he walked into the station, Lilliana appeared ready to leave. She took one look at him, sniffed the air, then turned around and came back. "What's the occasion?"

"I just faced another gunman," he shared, "so I figured maybe I would come see Kate."

She looked at him, surprised, then walked over and gave him a quick hug. "That's really sweet. She probably hasn't really had a moment for you, has she?"

"That's okay," he replied. "I figured that the smell would get her here eventually."

Lilliana burst out laughing and grinned. "You're right about that." Then she sniffed the bag and asked, "What are these?"

"There's a sandwich shop around the corner from me, and they have all kinds of interesting hot sandwiches," he described. "I didn't know how many people would be working tonight. But I figured that, with what Kate was doing, she wanted this thing solved tonight. So, I guessed a bunch of people might be here."

She turned to eye him, incredulous. "Are you telling me that Kate's got this thing wrapped up?"

"I didn't say that," he clarified. "I just feel she might have something on the case now," he hedged, trying for some wiggle room.

She shook her head. "I don't know how the hell she does

it, but she is absolutely dynamite on these BS cases," she muttered. She looked at him and pointed to the bags. "Are you saying you brought enough to share?"

"Absolutely. That's why I brought dozens." He walked over to one of the empty desks. "Can I put stuff out here?" Then he proceeded to do so without waiting for her to answer.

Lilliana told him, "I'll go see where she's at."

"Yeah, if you can do that, it would be great. In the meantime, I'll stop in and say hi to the captain, if he's around."

"He is. Go for it." She gave a nod toward the captain's office. "I'll check in with Kate if I can, and I'll get back to you." She turned back to him and asked, "Where was the gunman?"

"He came to my apartment."

"Ah, shit," she muttered. "Was he after you, or was he after Kate?"

He gave her a ghost of a smile. "This time he was after me."

Her eyes widened in shock. "Shit. You're okay though, right?"

"I'm okay," he confirmed. "And the kid is in the custody of your finest."

"Good," she muttered, "and we all need to hear that story." She pointed toward the interview rooms. "But you just sit tight and relax for now."

And that's what he did. Grabbing a coffee from the sideboard, he opened up the bag so the aroma would hit the office. He hadn't even gotten to the captain's door when Colby stepped out, sniffing the air in confusion, then turned and saw Simon.

"Did you bring dinner?" Colby asked.

"I did," Simon replied. "It's been a bit of a rough day, so I figured maybe I wasn't the only one who could use a little sustenance."

And, with that, Colby reached out a hand to shake his. "You are always welcome here."

Simon laughed.

CHAPTER 19

CAROLINE SAT BACK, swallowing hard. "I don't know what you're talking about."

"You should know," Kate reminded her. "I mean, we know a lot. Obviously we don't know everything because I can't really get inside the mind of some people."

"Sarah's freaking crazy," Caroline cried out. "I mean, look at the damn woman. She's nuts."

Kate nodded slowly. "I suspect she will use that excuse, or her lawyer will, at least." Then she turned, stared directly at Caroline, and asked, "But what is yours?"

Caroline paled immediately. "No," she muttered, shaking her head. "I didn't have anything to do with it."

"Really? So, it was all the crazy lady?" Kate asked, with a note of irony. "Absolutely nothing to do with you? And you have no idea what I'm talking about, right?"

Caroline, her eyes wild, suddenly broke and started bawling. "I didn't want to. I didn't want anything to do with it," she cried out. "Nothing. It's all just too godawful."

"Yeah, it's godawful all right," Kate agreed. "So, what the hell is it you think you've been doing?"

"I haven't been doing anything," Caroline muttered, but she sobbed and sobbed.

Rodney looked at Kate, then over at Caroline, and the confusion and frustration on his face was evident. Finally he got up, stepped outside, and then came back with a box of Kleenex and put it on the table for her.

Caroline sobbed as she picked up the tissues and tried to dry her eyes. She looked over at Kate and asked, "How did you figure it out?"

"It wasn't easy," she began, "but the killing of Father McCain was pretty evident."

Rodney just stared at her, but she didn't look at him. She felt his gaze boring into her face.

Caroline stared at her. "Why she did that, I don't know."

"I'm not sure Sarah particularly understands it either," Kate noted, "but I'm more concerned about the other three murders right now."

At that, Caroline's face fell, and she sobbed into her tissues. When she finally went quiet, Kate just sat back and said, "Anytime you're ready."

Caroline bit her lip, then looked at Rodney, back at Kate. "I don't even know how it started."

"How about the fight in the church?"

Her eyes widened. "You heard about that?"

"Of course," Kate declared. "It's amazing how many people find out about shit and either don't want to talk or can't wait to talk. So it's a really good time for you to start with the truth. And maybe, if you're lucky and if you cooperate, things will go a little easier on you."

Caroline stared down at her tissues and slowly shredded them, as if trying to get up the guts to tell Kate what happened.

"Start with the fight," Kate suggested.

Caroline sighed. "It was stupid," Caroline began. "I mean, it was really stupid. I didn't even know what to say, but it was … Look. My husband divorced me after I paid for his college, replacing me with a younger version."

"That you have already told me, so maybe skip to the parts that I need to know, and stick to the facts, please."

Caroline winced. "Okay, okay, so we're at this church counseling thing, and I had been a good girl up until then. I don't even know how it all started, but we got into this massive fight when I found out about Sarah … and her fiancé. I used to go out with him a long time ago, and I didn't really, … I didn't really get over him."

"Go on."

"I was still really hung up on him, but I didn't want to have kids. That wasn't something I was interested in, but he really wanted a family. Yet I also knew that Sarah was infertile. It had been brought up somewhere else, and she'd been having a really bad time with it.

"We used to work at the same company but different divisions. Anyway I heard about her failure to conceive quite a few years ago. So, during this church thing, I realized who she was talking about, … who she was marrying. I was angry. God, I was angry because the reason he broke up with me was because I didn't want to have kids, and here he was now, marrying somebody who wanted kids but couldn't have any. And then I found out that she hadn't told him yet. She lied to Kurt."

"How did that come up?"

"We talked. Before all this, … we were still talking. She hadn't told him, and I was unbelievably livid, thinking how are you supposed to start a marriage if you're doing it under such false pretenses?" She turned to look at Rodney, who just nodded as if he understood perfectly.

Kate waited, her face a mask.

"Anyway, it was kind of ugly. It was bad of me. I was so pissed off, and honestly I was really hurt. It just really hurt."

"And?"

"At this point, I'm not sure what to say. What can I say?" she asked no one and then shook her head. "Anyway, I contacted him, and I told him that Sarah was infertile. We got into a big fight because he didn't believe me. Then I told him how Sarah and I were just in the same church group counseling session, where I found out that they planned to marry. I couldn't believe that he would marry somebody who couldn't even have kids. Not even someone like me, who at least he could maybe persuade to change my mind later, but this was literally a flat-out fact that Sarah cannot have kids. He called me a liar. It got pretty ugly, and I mean, it got *ugly*, ugly."

"What happened next?" Kate asked.

"I don't know what happened next, but he eventually came over to my place, and we had a bit of a row. I think he saw her afterward, and they had a bigger row. Then he went home, and, as far as I know, he ended up overdosing on drugs."

"So, that was Kurt? Kurt Conner?"

"Yes, and he did do drugs. He absolutely did do them. I just didn't think he would do them while he was with Sarah because she was a goody-two-shoes in that regard. So, as far as I was concerned, it was horrifying, and it was terrible. And it's not my fault. It was an accident."

Caroline looked to Kate, back to Rodney, who gave her a sympathetic look. Kate, on the other hand, tried hard to control her features, to not give any indication of what she felt.

"At least I assumed it was an accident." Caroline continued. "I was more than willing, wanting to believe it was an accident, and then, sure enough, Sarah ran down my boyfriend, told him about my relationship with Kurt, even though it was not new. Kurt and I had a thing, but it was years ago. She made it sound as if I was cheating on my boyfriend with Kurt now, which meant my cheating broke up Sarah's engagement."

Caroline sobbed. "I hadn't cheated on my boyfriend, but she lied and made it sound as if I had. Of course my relationship got very ugly, and we started having issues."

"What did you do about it?" Kate asked.

"I tried to fix what Sarah broke, but it was a difficult time. And, when things didn't improve at home, ... well, I have needs. So I went and met John," she admitted, closing her eyes.

"Now, Sarah didn't know about John, but it made me feel a hell of a lot better," she shared. "I know that's no excuse, but I was still smarting from an extremely difficult set of emotions because of Sarah, over what she had told my boyfriend. She had lied to Kurt, her own fiancé, and now she was lying to my boyfriend. He believed her, so much so that it just finished us, but I was seeing John at that point. And somehow Sarah found out about it."

"Did you confront her?" Kate asked.

"She followed me to his place, and we had a fight at his place, and I left. Absolutely no way I would stick around, but then he died, and apparently you guys called it murder. I knew it had to be Sarah. I called her and told her that I knew what she did and that no way in hell she would get away with it. Then she twisted everything around. She apparently told John that I was pregnant, and he was so upset afterward. John's big thing was to never get serious, no getting pregnant. That she told him about *me* being pregnant," she pointed out. "Apparently that's what she told John, which was John's big thing. He was adamantly opposed to any pregnancies. So, he ghosted me."

"How do you know that he was told all this?" Kate asked her.

"John and I had quite an argument. I ran into him downtown accidentally. He ripped into me something awful, and I told him that I wasn't pregnant."

Kate was trying to take notes and listen at the same time.

"I didn't have any clue what the hell was going on, then I found out Sarah had told him that. In the end, he didn't believe me. So, I contacted Sarah and told her to stay the hell out of my life, and that my relationship with him was none of her business. She told me that it wouldn't matter because he would be dead soon. I asked her what she was talking about, and she told me how they had just had a hell of a fight. They had a bottle of wine together at a café, and she took him home. I went over to his apartment to try to talk to him, but he was already passed out drunk, so I left."

She raised her gaze, looked at Kate in tears. "Sarah supposedly went over afterward, and apparently he was already dead."

"John was dead?"

"Yes, she left the wine there but sent me a picture with the wine bottle and then the bow. She wrapped him up with this bloody bow," she whispered. "I couldn't even breathe when I saw the picture." She pulled out her phone and held up the photo.

Kate took the phone from her, studied the picture, and asked, "What about the card? Why does it say *Believe?* What's that all about?"

Caroline sighed. "That's a Sarah thing. She always want-ed to believe that she could have children. It was Father McCain's idea really. He kept telling her that it was God's will, and, at some point in time, she would have children. She just needed to believe in the goodness of life, to believe in men, to believe in all that stuff. Of course she knew that John was a hell of a playboy. He'd had that reputation a long time ago."

"The same as she knew Kurt was a playboy?"

"Yes, I told her that this had to stop, that she had killed John. She told me that the bottle was supposed to be for me." She pulled up her phone again and showed her the text.

Kate read the text and sat back, nodding at Rodney.

Caroline continued. "Sarah told me that she had left it there for me and that I was the one who was supposed to die. That I must have given it to John, but I didn't. John had already pounded it down before I even got there."

"How did she get the poison?"

"You'll have to ask her that. He had come home, upset, pissed off, and started drinking that wine. Sarah told me that she had used a needle of some kind to get the drugs inside the bottle. I don't know," she added, sobbing again. "I mean, Sarah's bloody devious. Apparently the poisoned bottle of wine is what killed John. And it would have killed me too, if he hadn't already drank it all."

Rodney nodded, and Caroline put her hands on her face and rubbed it hard. "Sarah wrapped John up in that god-damn bow, as a gift to me. And I just haven't been the same ever since."

"And yet you didn't come to us."

"No," she confirmed, closing her eyes, "because I'd picked up the damn wine bottle, and my fingerprints were all over the thing. I didn't know if you would even believe me."

"Why not? You're sitting here with the texts."

"I know, but, short of Sarah telling the truth, I wouldn't have had any way of getting you to see my side of the story."

"That's not true. You're sitting here with the texts to prove your side of the story. However, your fear that we wouldn't believe you has nothing to do with your failure to contact the police. It has to do with the second death, … Robert Blake. You killed him, right?"

Caroline closed her eyes, and she whispered, "I'm so sorry."

"Because you're the one who killed him?" Kate asked.

She pursed her lips, and then the tears flew nonstop.

"Why did you do that?" Kate asked.

"Because Sarah had fallen in love with him," Caroline wailed, tears pouring from her eyes. "She had found somebody new, and, after what she did to John, I couldn't stand the thought that John's death would go unpunished."

Kate snorted. "So, you decided to take it upon yourself and to kill another innocent man who had nothing to do with any of this, all because of Sarah?"

"Yes," she said, "all because of her."

"Holy shit," Rodney muttered, as he pulled away, looking at her as if she were a viper. He got up. "Excuse me." And he walked out in shock.

Caroline looked up at Kate and asked, "I'm really in trouble, aren't I?"

"You tell me. … You just confessed to killing a man."

She nodded. "After I found out about John, I met Sarah outside her apartment, and she was just losing it. She was screaming at me and telling me how I had ruined her life so long ago, and she wanted me to pay the price. She just made me so angry. I asked her about her new boyfriend, and she told me how he was the best man ever, but no way he would ever talk to me."

"So, how did you manage to kill Robert Blake? You knew nothing about him."

"I snatched her phone while she was distracted, screaming mad. She was losing it. She was just not all there sometimes. So I saw his text on her phone, and I got the contact information and his address. I dumped her phone back at her doorstep. She had even told me what poison she used to kill John. Do you want to know how she told me?"

Kate kept quiet, just letting her talk.

"She was laughing like a loon about killing John, telling me the name of the poison and how it slowly kills. She told me that she even still had it in her car, so I took it, the same poison she used."

"She knew you took it?"

"Yeah, she knew. She practically gave me the bottle, but I think she was just trying to get my fingerprints on it. *What will you do? Give it to the cops?* That's what she told me. *It's not as if they'll give a shit. Your fingerprints are all over that now.* Then she laughed and laughed, calling me a killer, a crazy woman, and all kinds of shit."

Caroline kept sobbing and sobbing.

"What did you do next?"

"We were back in her apartment, and she was telling me how she would spend the night with her new man, and then she just laughed and laughed. *Not that you'll know anything about love again because I'll just keep killing them and framing you.* So I followed her, and she was walking around outside as if she had absolutely lost it, and I realized that maybe she really had.

"I mean, she just wasn't *there*. ... Then, somewhere along the line, between here and there, I lost me too," she acknowledged, shaking her head, but more dry-eyed now than she had been.

She looked at Kate and added, "I don't even know what came over me. I was just so upset over John and what Sarah had done, that I didn't even think," she noted. "I pulled up the information I had taken from her phone and did a quick check on Robert.

"He was a real man, a 240-pound muscled-up heap of a man. And he was just so much like John. Robert was just one of those men who were constantly out there. So I got an idea to show up Sarah—I would sleep with Robert. That's all I would do. I would sleep with him, and I would take a picture and show her that she couldn't get the better of me by killing John. I went to Robert's profile, and, when he swiped right, I asked if we can hook up. His reply was instant."

"So, you went over to his place?"

"I was twenty minutes away. He was all for it, and, yeah, he just let me in," she said.

"Just like that?" Kate asked and Caroline nodded. "So, you had sex?"

"No, I didn't. Robert felt too much like John all over again," she shared, "but I had brought the bottle of wine."

"Where did you get the wine?"

"I grabbed one off her shelf before I left, and I brought it to his place. He looked at it, smiled, and said that he knew somebody else who drank that, and he was good with it."

Oddly enough, the sobbing had stopped now, and right now Caroline was narrating the events—calm, calculated, even smiling—still with tears in her eyes as she remembered the little details.

"I told him that I was having cold feet about this. When he gave me an odd look, I shared how I lost somebody recently, so this was kind of the first time, and he didn't push it."

"Did he say anything?"

"He just told me that, anytime I changed my mind, he would be happy to hook up. I just left and sat in my car for a long time. Then I called him back and told him that I had changed my mind. He laughed, but his voice was slurred. I went back up, went in, and sat down beside him, and he seemed woozy, but then he went into a seizure. That's when I realized the bottle of wine I brought must have also been poisoned, and I had killed him with it," she explained.

Kate noted, "You could have called an ambulance."

"I was shocked. I had no idea that the wine was poisoned."

"So, he died while you were there?"

"Yes, and I needed it to look like it was Sarah again, and I didn't know how to make that happen. I looked around his place and saw he had a bunch of Christmas tinsel, and I just wrapped him up. I took a napkin and tried to wipe off everything I had touched, then took a picture of him and sent it to her. Honest to God, I think that probably sent her over the edge, but I'm, I'm right there with her."

She sighed. "I have fallen so far, and I don't know why. ... Everything had to do with her blowing up my world. And, yes, I know that I am to blame because I told her fiancé that she couldn't have children, but he was also a really good friend of mine at one point in time. I knew how he felt about being a family man, and no way in hell he would sign up for somebody who was infertile." Suddenly she stopped talking, turned to Kate, and said, "I only heard about Father McCain on the news." She covered her eyes. "I'm really, … *really* hoping it's not what I think it is."

"I can confirm that he is dead and that he was stabbed."

Caroline closed her eyes and nodded. "I didn't do it."

"No, I don't think you did," Kate replied, "but you might have pushed somebody else to do it."

She looked at her in shock. "Do you think Sarah killed the priest?"

"Don't you mean, you killed him?"

"No! I didn't mean to kill anyone, … no one," she cried out. "It was the wine Sarah had in her home, and I didn't know," she sobbed. "I didn't know."

Kate stared at her. "I'm not even sure what to say about this right now," she admitted. "I will speak to the DA. I mean, you went there with ill intent but not to kill."

She repeated, "Not to kill. Not to hurt anyone."

"But that was the end result. You gave Robert the wine, knowing that Sarah had already used a bottle of wine to poison somebody else, and you didn't even stop to think that there might be poison in this bottle too?"

"No," she wailed.

"But the wine was in your possession, in your car. You brought it to Robert, which makes you look like you set up both similar murders."

She stared at her and started bawling. "I didn't though. I didn't," she cried out. "You can have my phone. There's all the texts. You can see it all. Sarah set *me* up."

Kate went through Caroline's phone while she sat here before her. Kate's mind was spinning, wondering how this would all play out. Was this manslaughter? Was this murder one? It couldn't be murder one because there was no intent, but, holy Hannah, all the texts were here on Caroline's phone. All those texts between her and Sarah.

Kate shared, "I have Sarah here as well."

"She's crazy," Caroline declared. "She's an absolute lunatic."

"She for sure is now."

"What?"

"Killing the priest has pushed her right over the edge," Kate replied. "And I'm just waiting for forensics to confirm it's her blood and fingerprints on the knife that killed Father McCain. So there are no winners in this game. Kurt Conner, John Smith, Robert Blake, and Father McCain. Four innocent men who died because of this feud between the two of you. *Four that I know of.*"

"I didn't mean—I didn't mean for anybody to get hurt. In my own defense, I was trying to protect a friend of mine, and somehow it just went to shit from there. ... Including the death of Father McCain. I don't know why Sarah had to kill him. Maybe because he's the one who made her *believe.* He's the one who kept telling her to believe in good things, to believe in a future, to believe in love, to believe in children," she suggested. "Sarah finally realized that *believe* might work for other people but not her. In the end, I just don't think she could handle it."

"That's possible because, when it came down to finding out that she killed somebody and that you had killed somebody, somebody she cared for—"

"I don't even know if she knows," Caroline interrupted.

"Are you kidding? You sent her a picture. She knows," Kate stated, raising her head, staring daggers at her. "Even if she doesn't know all the details, she knows, and that you can count on." Kate got up and stated, "You'll be booked and will get one phone call afterward. I'll be waiting to hear from the DA's office on specific charges, but you will not get off scot-free. … As for Sarah, do you know how many others she may have killed?"

Caroline went ghost white.

"Kurt died two Christmases ago. Then you and she each killed a man after this most recent Christmas."

"I didn't do anything," Caroline wailed again.

"So who died the Christmas before?" Kate asked Caroline.

She shook her head, whispering, "Ask Sarah."

Kate smiled. "I'm asking you." When Caroline went silent, Kate added, "Don't worry. The DA's investigation will go broader than ours did, covering more cities. I hope you weren't involved in all that."

"I didn't do anything," Caroline kept repeating.

"You delivered the bottle of wine that you took from Sarah's house and that tainted wine killed Robert. You should have realized any wine bottles taken from Sarah's house were contaminated as Sarah had already explained to you how she poisoned the other bottle of wine for you to drink and die. Instead John drank it."

"But I didn't know that this other bottle was poisoned," she repeated, staring at her in horror. "I did not know. I would never have killed that man."

Kate stared at her. "You don't have to convince me. You should worry about convincing a jury, and, frankly, you'll have to do a whole lot better than this. As far as I'm concerned, I totally see you as guilty." And, with that, Kate walked out, closing the door very, very quietly behind her.

She leaned against it for a long moment, her eyes closed, and then hearing a sound, she opened her eyes and turned to see Simon standing here in front of her, a concerned look on his face.

He opened his arms, and she didn't even question it and walked straight into them, and they closed around her and held her tight for a long moment.

She looked up at him and asked, "Do I want to know why you're here?"

He pondered that for a moment, and then a chuckle escaped. "You won't be happy about what happened before I got here, but I'm here because I just wanted to be nearby."

She smiled. "Everything else is secondary then." He explained it to her, as they walked back to the main office, and she stopped to see every one of her team members, even Colby, sitting there, munching away.

She looked closer, and then turned back to him, surprised. "Are you kidding me? Are those hot sandwiches from the deli?"

"Yeah," he confirmed. "I couldn't settle at home after all the excitement, so I figured that maybe you guys could use a meal too."

She looked up at him and laughed. "You know that everybody here has homes to go to, families to go to, and food at home too, right?"

He shrugged. "There are two kinds of families. There's the one you have, who you married, who you love and adore; and then there's the family you work with. They're different, but they're both very important to nurture. As I have found out, it's even more important to know those you are working with," he acknowledged. "So, I didn't think you would be too upset."

She laughed and shook her head. "No, I'm not upset. Some lessons are harder to learn than others, but hopefully today we both won a round on something very ugly, and it's a win that we both needed."

He tucked her up against him, then dropped a kiss on her forehead. "You're absolutely right. It's a win we both needed, and we also both got it, so here's to us." With that, he leaned over and gave her a hard kiss in front of everyone.

With the cheers and laughter going on around her, she reached up and gave him a kiss in return, then stepped back. "But, if you think that gets me out of all the work to be done now, you are so wrong."

"I can settle for a weekend. A weekend on the *Running Mate*."

"Oh, now that would be awesome," she muttered. She looked back at the massive crew assembled here and announced, "You guys had better eat up because, man, we have got a messed-up case. One that we've got to straighten out enough to present to the DA."

"So, they did it?" Lilliana asked.

"Yeah, both of them did, but we'll have to figure out if Caroline intended on killing Robert or not. She says she didn't, yet she handed a poisoned bottle of wine over to Robert Blake, and then went back in to make it look very much as if our Sarah had killed Robert. And Sarah won't stand for trial because she's not mentally stable enough for that. Yet I'm afraid she killed at least one man, sometime after the prior Christmas. We'll see what the DA finds."

"Good Christ," Lilliana muttered, "all these deaths and for what? Why?"

Kate turned to Rodney and asked, "You got any ideas to help summarize the why on this one?"

He shook his head. "Jealousy, maybe envy. I don't know," he muttered.

"Envy," Kate stated. "I think maybe envy." She turned back to Lilliana. "It was a doozy," she muttered. "An infertile woman, Sarah, engaged to a man who wanted a family, Kurt. Another woman, Caroline, stepping in to out the secret. The engagement broken. Sarah scorned. So she killed her fiancé, and then two years later killed Caroline's boyfriend, John, as payback. Then Caroline wanted payback, supposedly by sleeping with Sarah's new love, Robert. Yet she brought poisoned wine to his house, which he drank and then died from. I fear at least one more man died around Christmastime in between our known deaths. I hope the DA has a bigger budget and, with his bigger reach, can untangle this mess."

"But you're bringing him Sarah and Caroline," Lilliana pointed out, with a big grin. "That's what counts."

"Yeah," Kate muttered. "Too damn bad it took so long to get to the bottom of it."

Lilliana rolled her eyes. "It's been less than a week, and you found the killers of four people, including one from two years ago. So, take the win while we can, and, tomorrow, it'll be back to the battle, and a whole new battle at that."

Simon agreed. "Take the win because you and I both know that tomorrow's a new day, and who knows what the hell will happen then. But, in the meantime, we are planning a weekend away, and if anybody here has a problem with that—"

"Nope."

"Nada."

"No problem here," Colby agreed, waving his sandwich.

"As long as you get out before another case hits," Lilliana warned. "Because after that …"

"Right," Simon replied, as he looked over at Colby. "So,

when she's wrapped up—"

"Yep, she can have a couple days off," Colby announced, with a nod, as he picked up a second sandwich. "Damn, these are good."

"How about a week off for Kate?" Simon asked and then laughed. He smiled down at Kate and noted, "At least I know how to make your team happy."

She sighed. "Yeah, not exactly hard to do. I mean, just bring food." She grinned at everybody, happy that this home, this family was, indeed, hers and that, for the moment, all was well.

This concludes Book 12 of Kate Morgan:
Simon Says… Believe.
Read about Kate Morgan: Simon Says… Sink, Book 13

Simon Says... Sink: Kate Morgan (Book #13)

Step into a world of suspense with a gripping dark thriller, where Detective Kate Morgan and her team are on a relentless quest to solve a chilling series of murders. Young women, transformed by extensive plastic surgery, are being tortured and discarded in the depths of the ocean. As the investigation intensifies, Kate's partner Simon uses his unique psychic ability to connect with the victims, providing crucial insights that could crack the case wide open.

Amid escalating danger, a wealthy man's daughter goes missing, entangling him in a web of deceit. Parental neglect, the pursuit of wealth, and the dark side of vanity and manipulation weave through the investigation. Despite their efforts, Kate's team struggles to prevent further murders, highlighting the challenges and frustrations of law enforcement.

Kate's courage and determination are truly tested as she uncovers the truth and faces a murderer looking for a way to escape—at all costs …

Find Book 13 here!

To find out more visit Dale Mayer's website.

https://geni.us/DMSSSSink

Sneak Peek from Simon Says... Sink

End of First Week of February

A WEEK LATER Kate walked into the office. She stifled a yawn even as Rodney came into sight, carrying a big cup of coffee. On the mug was written the words *With Her*.

She frowned at it, pointing, then asked, "What the hell does that mean?"

He glanced at his coffee mug and then howled with laughter, which led to a blush. He shared, "My new girl-friend gave it to me."

She smiled. "So your girlfriend has a sense of humor."

"She does, indeed," he replied, but he was grinning and happy.

She nodded at him. "Must be nice if it makes you smile like that."

"You should try letting your relationship make you smile more too," he suggested, "and God knows that it should, considering Simon's loaded."

"Which, once again, means absolutely nothing to me," she snapped, glaring at him.

He held up his hand. "I know," he replied. "That's why you two are perfect for each other. I don't think Simon could have found anybody else less likely to give a rat's ass about how much money he has. And the fact that you can handle his ... *abnormality* is also pretty sweet."

She sighed. "I don't think I would call it that exactly but thank you. Now, what are you grinning for?"

He just chuckled and muttered, "Nothing. I'm in a good mood. Can't a guy be in a good mood?"

"Yes, Rodney. Enjoy your good mood," she said, as he headed for his desk.

Then he turned and added, "Of course, we won't be in a good mood soon."

"Why is that?" she asked, walking up behind him, heading for her desk.

"Because Lilliana has a case. And it requires all of us."

"Yeah," Lilliana agreed, turning from her desk, "and it's hardly my case, as we'll definitely need all hands on deck."

"Good enough," Kate declared, as she opened her drawer, tossing in her keys and her wallet. She walked over to where Lilliana was putting notes up on a whiteboard. "You should get Reese to help with this," Kate suggested.

"Reese is off this week," Liliana shared. "Remember that overseas wedding she's going to?"

"Oh, right. Damn, so who's replacing her?"

Lilliana snorted. "Why do you think I'm doing this?"

"Good point," Kate acknowledged. "Okay, so what have we got?" she asked, rubbing her hands together.

Lilliana frowned at her. "Seriously?"

"Hey, it's been a quiet week."

"For you it was a quiet week but not so much here," Rodney supplied.

Lilliana muttered, "Why it is that you're the only one who appears to be absolutely thrilled to get so close to the craziness again?"

Kate shrugged. "I've been away for a week. ... Simon's world is calm right now, and everything seems to be going well for him. So, maybe this will just be a normal case," she declared cheerfully.

"Right. I don't think anything is normal about this." Then she put up a picture that made Kate's heart ache.

A beautiful young woman. That was her *before* picture.

Lilliana continued. "Now, this is the picture one of the underwater divers took."

And there the woman had a rope trussed around her, its free end floating up toward the surface. However, it didn't reach all the way up, falling maybe ten to twenty feet short.

"What's holding her down?" Kate asked.

"Lead boots."

She whispered to the woman in the photo, "Oh, dear God, what on earth happened to you?"

Lilliana nodded. "That's the thing. This woman was found by divers who were looking for pieces of a tugboat. Remember that big accident a couple weeks ago?"

"Yeah, I remember."

"They were down there to pull up some of the missing pieces. The waterway is not completely shut down," she noted. "They wanted to recover a bunch more of the debris so they weren't adding more refuse in the harbor."

"Right. That's understandable."

"While they were there, one of the divers came across this nightmare," she explained, pointing to the *after* photo.

"Wow," Kate whispered. "Unfortunately it takes a lot for somebody to do this."

"Not really," Lilliana countered. "I don't suspect it took that much at all, considering that, in reality, she's quite small. She's, let me see here," she muttered, as she checked her notes. "She's about five-five and 125 pounds."

Kate considered that and added, "Still, dead weight is hard to carry. I mean, sure, a man obviously could have picked her up and tossed her over."

"But why the lead boots?" Lilliana asked.

"Because he didn't want her found anytime soon," Kate stated.

"That's an obvious answer, but it's not an answer as to why he killed her."

"And it's always about the why," Rodney chimed in, as he came over to review the images.

"Yep, it's always about the damn why," Kate muttered. "This wasn't a random act. Somebody came prepared and obviously didn't want this beautiful woman to surface anytime soon. How long would it take in this situation for a body to decompose?"

Lilliana tilted her head. "Hard to say. The water's cold, and the temperature affects decomposition in water. Unless the body's eaten by something, I would say six months, eight months maybe. We'll have to check the tidal patterns, and we should take a closer look at the animal activity because anybody down there is a buffet."

"Oh, did you have to say that?" Rodney asked, as he frowned at the doughnut in his hand.

Kate chuckled. "If that is all it takes to throw you off a doughnut, we know things have been hitting you hard."

"She's beautiful," Rodney muttered, as he stared at her *before* picture.

Kate nodded. "Yes, she was. And somebody decided to snuff out that beauty," she muttered, turning to look at him. "The thing we have to figure out is why."

Find Book 13 here!

To find out more visit Dale Mayer's website.

https://geni.us/DMSSSSink

Author's Note

Thank you for reading Simon Says… Believe: Kate Morgan, Book 12! If you enjoyed the book, please take a moment and leave a short review.

Dear reader,

I love to hear from readers, and you can contact me at my website: www.dalemayer.com or at my Facebook author page. To be informed of new releases and special offers, sign up for my newsletter or follow me on BookBub. And if you are interested in joining Dale Mayer's Reader Group, here is the Facebook sign up page.
http://geni.us/DaleMayerFBGroup

Cheers,
Dale Mayer

About the Author

Dale Mayer is a *USA Today* best-selling author, best known for her SEALs military romances, her Psychic Visions series, and her Lovely Lethal Garden cozy series. Her contemporary romances are raw and full of passion and emotion (Broken But … Mending, Hathaway House series). Her thrillers will keep you guessing (Kate Morgan, By Death series), and her romantic comedies will keep you giggling (*It's a Dog's Life*, a stand-alone novella; and the Broken Protocols series, starring Charming Marvin, the cat).

Dale honors the stories that come to her—and some of them are crazy, break all the rules and cross multiple genres!

To go with her fiction, she also writes nonfiction in many different fields, with books available on résumé writing, companion gardening, and the US mortgage system. All her books are available in print and ebook format.

Connect with Dale Mayer Online

Dale's Website – www.dalemayer.com
Twitter – @DaleMayer
Facebook Page – geni.us/DaleMayerFBFanPage
Facebook Group – geni.us/DaleMayerFBGroup
BookBub – geni.us/DaleMayerBookbub
Instagram – geni.us/DaleMayerInstagram
Goodreads – geni.us/DaleMayerGoodreads
Newsletter – geni.us/DaleNews

www.ingramcontent.com/pod-product-compliance
Lightning Source LLC
Chambersburg PA
CBHW051540030726
47592CB00001B/69